CURIOUS INCIDENTS:

MORE IMPROBABLE ADVENTURES

CURIOUS INCIDENTS:

MORE IMPROBABLE ADVENTURES

EDITED BY A.C. THOMPSON

MOCHA MEMOIRS PRESS
GREENSBORO, NC

Curious Incidents: More Improbable Adventures Copyright © 2016
Introduction © A.C. Thompson
The Case of the Tainted Blood © Liese Sherwood-Fabre
The Case of the Burning Man © Lucy Blue
He-Who-Knows © Derrick Belanger
Shadows of Time © Thomas Olbert
Fear of the Dark © Melissa McArthur
The Culverton Mine Disaster © Katie Magnusson
Shave and a Haircut © KT Pinto
Shadows and Hounds © Jason Gilbert
Reborn © Selah Janel
Terror in the Air © Robert Perret
The Case of the Potters Bar Siren © Trenton Mabey
The Curious Case of the Tombstone Dragon © Dan Shaurette
Crippled Playthings © S.H. Roddey
The Final Solution © Alexandra Christian
The Old Woman in the Woods © C.L. McCollum

Cover by: Anne Rosario
http://annezca.daportfolio.com/

Formatting by: Susan H. Roddey
http://www.shroddey.com/

ISBN: 978-0-9840042-9-4

Published by Mocha Memoirs Press, LLC
www.mochamemoirspress.com
Greensboro, North Carolina

Printed in U.S.A

Praise for

Curious Incidents:
More Improbable Adventures

"A Marvelous Menagerie of Mysteries featuring the world's most legendary detective! Rich characters, compelling mysteries, and awesome writing makes this collection a must-own."

- John G. Hartness, author of *The Bubba the Monster Hunter Series*

CONTENTS

Acknowledgements

I don't think words could ever express how thankful I am to have such a body of inspiring and talented voices participating in this anthology. Some folks from the first anthology graced us with another story, others had to bow out, but know that if you've been a part of this duet of books that you are an extraordinary artist and it is my privilege to call you colleagues and friends.

"Shenaniganators"—you know who you are. Thanks for being there.

Once more, Anne C. Rosario, you are a visionary and a genius.

I should probably give a special shout out to the BBC. Every time a new episode of Sherlock airs, the book gets a huge bump in sales!

Finally, I have to give a very special acknowledgement to one of the most wonderful editors in the business. Melissa M. Gilbert, a freelance editor and owner of Clicking Keys, LLC, had the daunting task of editing my own contribution to Curious Incidents. Her eye for detail, her knowledge of story, and her boundless humor and intelligence helped me take a broken toy and turn it into something I can be truly proud of. You're a rock star, lady!

INTRODUCTION

HERE WE ARE AGAIN, FRIENDS. ONCE MORE INTO THE BREACH WITH THE great detective and his long-suffering companion. This time Holmes and Watson traverse boundless alternate histories and futures. There are vampires, dystopian soldiers, hard-boiled detectives, space travelers, and cyborgs. If you can think it, we've probably tried it here with the goal of pushing Holmes to the outer limits of his character without losing sight of the genius underneath.

If you'll remember, on our last journey I related a story about how I had intended to create an anthology of Holmes adventures that crossed time and space, and instead got a whole book full of cleverly crafted Victorian horror pieces. Perhaps I underestimated my authors a bit.

Won't be making that mistake again…

A.C. Thompson, January 2017

Sidenote: I thought about beginning this introduction with the slogan, "Make Holmes Great Again," but I figured it was already taken. And much like America, Holmes was already great to begin with. —A.C.T.

THE CASE OF THE TAINTED BLOOD

Liese Sherwood-Fabre

THE EPIDEMIC ARRIVED FROM THE CONTINENT IN **1889**, AND A YEAR LATER, our world had shifted on its axis, plunging survivors into a nocturnal, feral existence. Had it not been for a peculiar turn of events one spring evening in 1891, that world might have consumed both Holmes and myself.

We were both involved in the change from the beginning, although we didn't recognize it at first. As a medical doctor, I was called in to treat a number of extreme anemia cases, which all led to general organ failure and death. While I responded to medical emergencies, Holmes assisted in the investigation of a series of quite gruesome murders involving ripped throats, but a complete lack of blood in the victim or the surrounding scene.

And no one was immune from infection or attack.

I sent Mary to the country early on to avoid the illness's rapid spread. Two weeks after seeing her off, I received a chatty letter from her, giving no hint of illness, and a telegram an hour later informing me of her death from rapid-onset anemia. At the time, I considered my inability to protect her my greatest failure.

Of course, events soon overwhelmed the medical and law enforcement communities, and many fell victim to the infection themselves. When Inspector Lestrade called on us a few weeks after Mary's demise and provided a full explanation of the disease, we were forced to make a decision—survival or death. A year later, I wondered if we had made the appropriate choice.

Vampyre.

The name dredged up images of an all-consuming and soul-less thirst, but the true transformation was to society itself. At the beginning of the epidemic, an ample supply of humans existed. Over time, however, the scales tipped and alternative sources developed as the human population faded from this earth. Animals were no longer kept for their meat—only for their blood.

My friend foresaw the inevitable near-extinction of all mammals and had cleverly captured his own stock of rats to maintain his and my existence. But survival is not always living.

The night in question began as it had since our transformation: my friend checking on our stock, ensuring proper food and water, and then selecting some for their contribution to our nightly ration of blood. That night, I stared into the cup's thick, scarlet content and exhaled through tight lips. After feasting on a few of my patients and fellow physicians, I had to say rat blood was a poor substitute. One could compare it to a glass of water instead of an aged Madeira wine. Both quenched one's thirst, but true pleasure was in the second.

All the same, after raising it in a short salute and draining the glass, I forced down the urge to lick the thin layer of corpuscles still clinging to its slick inside. While the amount was enough to maintain, the lust for more never left.

Holmes pulled my attention from the little pool at the bottom of my glass when he placed his own upon the mantel of the long-cold fireplace and sighed.

"I'm not certain I'll be much longer in this world."

"I'll admit this is hardly a feast," I said, "but quite enough to sustain us."

"I'm not referring to our meal—or whatever one calls what we just consumed. I'm discussing remaining on this planet."

With a trembling hand, I set down my glass before it slipped from my fingers. I'd observed such melancholy in my friend in the past, but for some reason, his talk this time raised the small hairs on the back of my neck. I had to probe lightly to gain more insight without encouraging him.

"Are you suggesting—?" He turned to me, and I knew my answer. "Surely you're not? Holmes, really, *suicide*?"

"One could make the argument that we are already dead, and therefore beyond any moral or legal jurisdiction if we choose to end our life, or should I say existence."

"How would you—? How would it even be done?"

"I've made a short study of it. There is, of course, the most obvious—simply staying out in the daylight—but fire is also a possibility—simply an extension of sunlight, I suppose. And we have found a stake through the heart quite effective as well." He flicked his wrist and the spring-loaded stake he carried up his sleeve flew into his hand. Given the bestial nature of some of the remaining population, we felt it prudent to always be prepared to defend ourselves. Turning the piece in front of his face, he ran a finger across the point.

"Although I think that would be more difficult to achieve on one's own."

A selfish thought slipped from my lips before I had a chance to stop it. "You would leave me like that? Alone in this world?"

Mary's absence was a pain greater than I'd experienced even in my worst moments after my wounding in Maiwand. I carried her last letter with me at all times in my coat's breast pocket. But I still had Holmes. Without him, I might contemplate an end myself.

"I simply cannot continue to live without more stimulation than rat-keeping offers me. I would write a treatise on the practice, but who would publish it? Let alone read it? We have fallen, my friend, into some sort of primitive culture without any intellectual pursuits beyond the hunt for blood. There is no true crime anymore. Theft? Gone. Why steal when there are stores aplenty lying open for anything the heart desires? Treason? Eliminated along with countries and governments. Murder? We are all *dead*, Watson. Who is left to murder?"

"I'm sure there will be…Perhaps in the future…"

I let my ideas trail off. For in my own way, I understood him. My occupation as a physician had been eliminated. Vampyres didn't contract illnesses. This infection cured all other physical maladies.

As was his wont—even before our transition—my flatmate read my thoughts. His brow creased as he said, "Not all disease, Watson, has been eliminated. Unlike your wound from the Jezail bullet, my need for cocaine has not left me." He stared into the cold grate for a moment before retrieving the pouch sitting next to the empty glass. Pulling out the needle and vial, he caressed the syringe with his forefinger. "The addiction is gone, but it was never about the physical need for the drug. You know I used it to quiet the thoughts circling my brain. Now that has been denied to me. And at the same time, I am much more acute to all that surrounds us—sounds, scents, and…emotions. I cannot stop them all from swirling about in my head."

"I'm sorry," I said, a sinking feeling forming in the pit of my stomach. "I-I have no cure for you. My understanding is that the…condition bestows different gifts to all. I'm afraid yours has made you more attuned to all around you."

He turned to me. "And tonight, I sense a certain…*distress* in the population. Just as some herds communicate fear or danger to one another, I have that same kind of connection. I tell you—"

Stopping in mid-sentence, he pointed wordlessly to the street.

The sinking feeling in my stomach formed a hard knot. Someone approached our apartment. We listened to fluttering of leathery wings and then footsteps on the stairs leading to 221B. I armed myself with my service revolver and a spear I'd brought back from my time in India. Holmes checked the stakes in his sleeves, and we positioned ourselves on either side of the bay window overlooking Baker Street.

When I peered below, the sight of Wiggins waiting patiently at the door nearly collapsed my knees. I hadn't seen the leader of the Baker Street Irregulars since before the epidemic. I checked my friend for his reaction and noticed for the first time in months the hint of a spark in his flat eyes.

"Ho, Wiggins," Holmes called to the young man below. "What brings you here?"

"May I come in, sir?" he asked, glancing first up and then at the front door.

I opened my mouth to welcome him, but my flatmate held up his hand to still me. I could see the logic in his decision. Vampyres cannot enter an abode unless invited. As long as we denied entry to all, our rat supply was safe from those who would raid us.

"Why don't you tell me from there?" he said.

Wiggins glanced up and down the street before answering in a low voice. "There's been a-a murder."

"Rubbish," he said. "Not possible. Besides, I have no interest in such cases anymore."

"I knew you's were goin' a say that, but I tell you—he was *burned.*"

"A vampyre staying out in the sunlight is hardly murder."

"From the inside out."

My friend paused. "That certainly does put a different spin on things. It might be amusing to observe. Wait for us on the street. You can lead the way from there."

Once we had prepared ourselves for a variety of eventualities, we descended and joined Wiggins on a short flight across the rooftops.

When first infected, I found the ability to transform into a bat the most electrifying of all my new powers. I thrilled at the wind coursing over my wings and stinging my face as well as being able to experience the city from a vantage point only pigeons had been privy to before. This skill, however, no longer carried any allure. Nothing remained to captivate the viewer except streets empty of all life.

Gliding downward, the three of us joined a small cloud of bats spiraling toward one point. Once transformed back into human form, we pushed our way through a ring of fellow night-creatures to the center of curiosity.

As a former military physician, I'd witnessed many atrocities to the human body. From bayonet wounds to decapitations by flying shrapnel. Never, however, had I seen an injury such as the one garnering the group's attention. The man—I had to deduce that from his trousers and coat—lay sprawled on his back. Below the bulging, sightless eyes, the face had been burned away, the neck bones clearly visible through the gaping hole leading from the face to the stomach.

For a moment, I thought the man had been human. The scent of fresh blood drew me in, as it did the others around us. More than one licked his lips and bared his fangs as he stared at the corpse. What held them back, as it did me, was a taint to the scent.

Calling on the remnants of my medical training, I ignored the basic revulsion caused by whatever hovered about the victim and knelt beside the man.

My comrade did the same thing on the other side.

I raised my gaze to meet his. "Good lord, Wiggins was right. The man's been burned from the inside out. What could cause such a thing?"

"Surely, old chap, you recognize the force repelling all away?"

I stilled as I considered the sensations rippling through me. The dread, a revulsion on the most primitive level, had manifested itself to me before. When I had—

"There's something blessed by a priest near him," I said.

"Precisely," he said and pointed to a vial still in the man's grasp. "It emanates from that." I reached forward, but he blocked my arm. "I don't think you want to touch it."

He discharged one of his stakes and used the point to pry the vial clear of the man's hand. The glass cylinder rolled a bit across the bricks toward the crowd. Those in its vicinity leapt backwards to get out of its path—as if it contained the most potent of poisons.

Avoiding all touch, my friend bent over it and sniffed. His lips curled back in disgust, and he rolled back onto his heels. Once he contained his obvious distress, he turned to Wiggins. "It was murder all right. There is no way for a vampyre to have created that concoction on his own. Quite a unique approach, actually. The murderer provided one of our species with the vial, and allowed nature to take its course. Thank you for alerting me to the case." He stood and swiped his hands together. "There's no more to do here."

"Hey, now," the former Irregular said. "Are you just goin' a leave the poor sod here like this?"

"It certainly isn't my responsibility to clean this up," he said. He glanced to the east. "The sun will be up in a few hours, and it should burn up what's left of him. I would advise you all to simply leave him as he is. And whatever you do, don't touch that vial. It contains holy water."

With that, he transformed and flew off.

By the time I'd done the same and made it to 221B, he was already in his smoking jacket and pacing back and forth through a cloud of his own creation. I could only stare at him, opened mouth, letting some of the noxious fumes float into my nostrils. I'd not seen him use his pipe since the day after he'd turned. At the time, he'd noted that his heightened senses made the habit too unpleasant. Despite my own increased sensitivity to the pollution now filling the chamber, a smile crossed my lips. Within the space of an hour, he exhibited an animation I'd not seen in months.

He stopped when I closed the door behind me, pausing long enough to face me. "I believe, old friend, we have just seen the tip of a spear. Some *human* is behind this murder, and there will be more. Many more."

I stared at the man. "There are still humans living here? In London? Impossible."

"While it seems unlikely, it's the only explanation. If you wish, we can consider the evidence. We know the vial contained holy water. Who else can handle it? In addition, the blood was fresh. Did you not see how its scent drew so many towards it? We've learned that blood drawn and stored loses the appeal of fresh."

"Suppose it had been manufactured in some way…"

"How and from what? And most importantly—who?"

I sighed. "I'll give you that the blood was human, then. And fresh. But how is it that the humans have gone undetected? As you said, the scent of just that small vial of blood drew a crowd to it. A full grown human would call to all within blocks of him or her. And if we're speaking of more than one—"

"Precisely. I would propose this human has somehow blocked his or her scent, despite a vampyre's heightened sense of smell. What do we know of items that would do so?"

"Garlic, of course. There was that belief—"

"Which depleted the stores of the herb here and throughout Britain. While it certainly mucked with our olfactory organ, it didn't repel us or mask the scent completely. Whatever this scent is, it's more potent than garlic. I would suggest we spend some time at the British Museum where we may just find some additional information on our species and our aversion to certain scents."

As with other relics of our past life, the British Museum had also lost its splendor. As one of most renowned repositories of human knowledge in the world, the building brimmed with collections from all over the world. With little interest from the remaining populace, its magnificence had crumbled from neglect by those who remained. Layers of dust covered display cases, shelves, and floors. Despite its abandoned state, I still felt like a trespasser and trod lightly, our footsteps echoing through the empty halls.

In spite of the darkness, I could see footprints—single and male—passing straight through the exhibits to the Reading Room. Previously, a pass was required to access the library housed under the cylindrical dome. Now, the stacks were left unprotected and open to anyone wishing to peruse—or raid—their contents.

The room had the same layer of dust we'd found elsewhere. We stood in the center of the room, the empty reading tables reaching out around us, and gazed up at the floor upon floor of book stacks encircling us. Whoever had been here before us made no effort to hide his presence. The prints led up the stairs to a one of the upper levels.

"Our visitor seems to have an interest similar to our own," my friend said. "The references to our species are in that area there, and the prints appear to be heading in the same direction. And *human*. No vampyre need bother with the stairs."

He gave a short jump before flying up to the area. I followed, landing just a second after him. Before I could even get my bearings, Holmes cried out.

"They've taken them." He pointed to a set of empty shelves in front of us. "All of them."

"You mean the ones who poisoned the vampyre? How can you be certain? It could have occurred months ago."

"If it had, there would be the same dust as we've found elsewhere. See? Dust, yes, but not years' worth."

He approached one of the shelves and crouching to eye-level, studied the dust as if measuring its depth. "About six months, I would estimate."

Mimicking my friend, I stared across the shelf as well. As I did so, golden flecks stood out among the ordinary grey debris. "There's something…I'm not certain what…Do you see it?"

"Good eye, old chap. Something worth taking back to the flat for further analysis. Do you have an envelope on you?"

I patted my coat and pants, but I knew the answer. Mary's letter was still in my breast pocket. Hesitating a second, I finally said, "No. Sorry. No need for them anymore."

My friend eyed me for a moment, then shrugged. "No matter. I'll improvise." He pulled a volume off another shelf and ripped a page from the front. "I doubt that the head librarian, if he even still exists, will come after me for using the title page of this particular volume."

As he tossed it back onto the shelf, I noticed the spine read *Vampyres: Facts and Myths*. I picked up the slim volume and dropped it into my coat pocket, curious as to what the author had gotten right about our condition.

My friend scraped some of the dust into the paper, folded it into a sort of packet and glided from the building.

Once back in our flat, Holmes immediately moved to the corner where his microscope and chemistry set had remained to collect dust just like in the museum. Without another word, he set about analyzing what he'd found at the library. Glad to see his thoughts of suicide abated for the moment, I passed the time until almost daylight skimming the book I'd brought with me. As much as I'd wanted the author to amuse me, in the end, I had to admire how accurate a study of our species he'd done.

As dawn approached, I checked on my friend and asked a question to which I already knew the answer. "Aren't you going to rest?"

He glanced up from the beaker in which he now boiled some liquid over a candle flame and shook his head.

"I think I'll work a little longer. You know me. Once I'm on the trail, I cannot possibly sleep until I have the answer. The shutters will protect me."

Once again, I couldn't argue with the man. As the author in the treatise I'd been reading explained, vampyres didn't *have* to sleep during the day. They simply had to avoid sunlight. I shuddered as I recalled the first time I'd watched one newly turned of our kind burst into flames when the first morning rays hit him. The memory gave me pause. Had the man whose corpse we'd examined earlier experienced similar anguish? I imagined him salivating at the mere scent of the human blood in the vial. So overcome with desire, he failed to notice the horrendous addition until it burned past his lips.

The image remained with me even after I retired to my room and fell into a troubled, but deep sleep. Throughout the day, all manner of bright, flaming creatures pursued me in my dreams. I woke with a start, gasping for air as if I'd actually run the entire day. A moment later, I realized what caused me to wheeze was a pungent smoke drifting into my room.

I covered my nose and mouth with my hand and opened my bedroom door. A heavy, acrid cloud poured in, and I quickly shut it until I found a cloth to cover my lower face. My plan was to locate my friend and vacate the building, for surely the place was on fire.

To my surprise, when I called to him, Holmes answered from the center of the noxious haze. "Come here. I think I've found it."

"Found what?" I asked, stifling a cough. "A way to give vampyres asthma?"

"So glad to see your humor back," he said and sneezed. "This concoction, my dear friend, appears to blocks all odors."

"I can believe that. Any objection to my opening the shutters?"

"I suppose it won't do any harm."

"Unless there are any neighbors left within at least a mile radius."

"It is rather pungent, but that's the intent, is it not?"

After creating a cross-breeze from the front to the back of our quarters, I waited for the usual scent of the evening air. Normally, my heightened olfactory abilities allowed me to enjoy the perfume of the Thames's crisp water (now cleared of all the waste that had once plagued it) and the green pastures leading to the salt-tinged sea beyond.

Tonight, however, despite standing directly in the window, I found myself unable to detect a single aroma.

"I told you," Holmes said without glancing up from his work at the acid-scarred table. "I have re-created the formula that blocks all odors."

I stepped to the table, now littered with various boxes and bottles, a mortar and pestle, and a kerosene lamp that had been converted into service as a Bunsen burner. "That burning cloud of stink'um? It certainly destroyed mine, but surely any pile of garbage—?"

"You know as well as I do our olfactory functions have ferreted out humans from sewers, garbage heaps, and even the great piles of dead." He shook his head. "No, whoever took the books from the museum has developed a formula that masks theirs—and all—scents completely. This, I believe allows them to hide their existence. I am convinced what we observed last night was an experiment. A trial run, if you will, to determine if the mixture in the vial would attract and destroy vampyres. If we are unable to find and destroy the human behind the scheme, I believe our kind will be eliminated."

He turned and paced in front of the table. "We have two avenues to pursue. The first is the blood. Where did the victim obtain it? The second, is the dust found at the library. Based on the analysis I completed, it's not actually dust, but ash, which I attempted to recreate last night. Judging from your reaction, I think I succeeded."

"But the orange specks—"

"Precisely, there was ash, but it was mixed with this." He held up a vial containing a thin, orange thread and handed it to me. "We happened to have a bit of this left from the time you tried to make your own curry, which I dare say, rivaled my own efforts today. Check the scent."

I unstopped the vial and whiffed. For an instant, an overpowering aroma, sweet like honey and green like hay, filled my nostrils. Corking the bottle, I found, once again, I had no sense of smell.

"Good lord. I had no idea that saffron carried such a punch. And my nose had just started working. So the effect is about fifteen minutes."

My friend breathed deeply. "It depends on the mixture's saffron potency. I would venture it might last up to thirty minutes—once one is no longer in its presence. We can deduce the perpetrator has sprinkled this mixture liberally upon his person to prevent detection. Which also explains why it was found in the library. His exertions in removing the books most likely caused it to brush off."

"Saffron is not easily obtained, especially in any quantities."

"True. A pound of spice requires between 50,000 to 75,000 crocus flowers. As such, only a few places exist would have it in sufficient quantity. At the same time, detection would be difficult as well. Hence, I suggest focusing on the blood. Much easier to ferret out that scent. And where will it most likely be offered for sale?"

I met his gaze and spoke the answer we both knew. "The blood market."

As the sources of fresh blood dwindled, this once free and plentiful commodity transformed into the one remaining commercial venture. The Metropolitan Cattle Market still housed vendors who were supplied by those still possessing living animals to bleed. Vampyres would barter for the bottled substance. The price—one's own blood. When a vampyre consumed another's blood, it endowed the recipient with the victim's attributes. Holmes had never fancied sharing his superior intellectual and deductive skills with others. Hence, an additional incentive for rat-keeping.

"And the perfect place to put out the warning to be on the lookout for tainted vials," he said with a nod of agreement. "Let's pay it a visit, shall we?"

Even in the dark, we had no problem identifying the market's central clock tower, a white finger extending upward into the night. I followed my friend as he circled the area, starting at the perimeter of the open field and moving toward the center in tighter and tighter orbits. The market itself continued to be conducted in the open, although the live animals that had once occupied had disappeared more than a year ago. As with the murdered vampyre from the previous night, a large crowd marked the end of our search.

My heart squeezed tight in my chest when he pushed his way through the crowd. Those he passed hissed and bared their fangs at us. I kept pace with my friend, wishing my service revolver offered more protection. At least the bullets would slow down any beast attacking us. And I do mean beast, for they had lost all sense of humanity.

The cause was obvious: *fresh human blood.*

The scent alone pushed some of them almost beyond reason. I, myself, was not immune. Its sweet iron aroma was a narcotic in and of itself. The closer we came to the center, the greater the rush of adrenaline pumping through my veins.

Holmes and I finally broke through to the center, only to find a wizened man glaring at the crowd. The little vampyre hardly appeared capable of holding off the surrounding multitude until one spied the hulking mass behind him. The man guarding the old one must have been in the circus or one of those traveling curiosities. His height and breadth were super-human. Even at this distance, he exuded an aura of power warning of his ability to rip the head of anyone who touched his diminutive companion.

"Ah," the little man said when we stood in front of him. "Two more customers for my blood. And what do you offer? I seek a buyer with superior strength to barter. While you might think I could use it, I find that sharing it with my friend here keeps us both safe. We have, what you might call, a symbiotic relationship."

Tearing my gaze from the hulking menace behind the man to my friend, my heart formed a hard rock in my chest at the confrontation I knew was about to occur.

Holmes stood straight, a sneer on his face that was certain to offend the vendor and his guardian. "I have no interest in purchasing your vial, and neither will any of those about when I tell them what's in it. I've come to destroy it."

The man had been holding the vial in his outstretched arm, enticing the crowd with its allure. At Holmes' pronouncement, he pulled it defensively against his chest and took a step back under the protection of his oversized companion. When he exposed his teeth and growled at Holmes, the others picked up his response. We found ourselves surrounded by vampyres prepared to prevent us from eliminating the precious commodity the man offered.

"I doubt anyone will allow you to do that," the man said. "Unless I choose your barter. And I don't think I will."

Without taking his eyes from the vendor, Holmes grabbed the arm of the nearest spectator, flipped him onto his back and released a stake, pressing the point into the vampyre's chest. The victim writhed and howled under Sherlock's weapon.

All the others stepped back from us, creating a ring quite a respectable distance around the five of us.

"I am a master of the art of *baritsu*, a skill few outside of Japan possess," Holmes said, stepping back and letting the poor creature transform and take flight into the night. "Imagine your escort here with a bit of that in his repertoire. I offer that in exchange for the vial."

The man glanced at first at Holmes and then at his guard. "Goliath, collect our fee."

A smile formed across the hulking creature's face, fangs glinting in the moon light. He stepped from behind the man, but Holmes spoke before he'd taken two steps.

"First, I wish to examine what I'm purchasing." The man squinted at him and pulled back, slipping the vial under his coat. "You can hold it, if you wish, but I want to examine it by inhaling its full aroma. You say it is human, but it could be laced with some other animal blood."

The vendor hesitated, drawing in his lower lip until his fangs appeared over them. After staring at my companion a moment longer, he gestured to his guard to follow behind him. Together they moved within an arm's length. Without moving his gaze from Holmes, he slowly revealed the vial and pulled the stopper from it. Throughout this slow dance, I held my breath, pushing down the primal urge within me to leap in front of the wisp of a man and down the flask's content before he could even react.

The instant the vial was within reach, Holmes thrust his wooden stake forward and slapped the hand holding it. A bit of the crimson liquid splashed onto the vendor's hand, immediately burning the skin. The affected areas blackened and smoked. The little man screamed and dropped the vial. The glass shattered at his feet, and Holmes and I jumped backwards to avoid being splashed as well.

Goliath moved with a swiftness I'd never witnessed and far surpassing what his size would suggest. Before our feet hit the market's soft earth, he had us both by our necks. His hold was tight enough I knew transforming merely put us at more risk. We'd be bats still held in his massive hands, and it is much easier to rip off a bat's head than that of a human.

Both Holmes and I pinwheeled our legs several feet above the ground. I knew one word from the little one would end our lives, but he was too preoccupied with the dark holes now bored into his hand. Unlike other injuries, burns of this sort didn't heal. Except when…

Unable to turn my head, the most I could manage was to slide my gaze in the direction of the vendor, who whimpered and cradled his injured hand. Black spots floated in my vision, obscuring the man's face.

"Can. Help. Physician," I managed to choke out through my constricted airway.

His stare told me he was debating about trusting me after my companion's actions.

In an effort to convince him, I whispered, "Promise."

Just before spots blocked all sight completely, he spoke. "Release him. But only him." His gaze settled on me. "Goliath will end your friend's life—and yours—should you deceive me."

A moment later, I dropped to the ground, falling on my hands and knees, and gulped air between coughs. Recovering after a few breaths, I rose and checked over my shoulder at Holmes. His legs hung a few feet from the ground, but his eyes were open, and he blinked at me to let me know he was still conscious.

Only the four of us remained. The crowd originally drawn by the scent must have fled as soon as the blood spilled and the behemoth grabbed us.

I stepped to the man and held out my hand. He eyed it, but did not move.

"I have a way of treating your burns."

The man slowly extended his hand, and I examined it, turning it over to study both sides. "These aren't severe, but, as you know, they won't heal on their own."

I pulled back my coat sleeve and prepared to bite my wrist.

The man snorted. "What would your blood do that any others' wouldn't?"

"When I first turned, I'm afraid I feasted on a few of my colleagues—some quite gifted physicians. Their ability to heal has been passed on."

After piercing a vein in my wrist, I let the blood drip onto the burns. A slight *sizzle* followed as the burns closed, and the skin appeared as new.

Holding up his hand to examine it, the man flexed his fingers. Without taking his gaze from it, he said, "Release him."

Holmes dropped to his hands and knees and proceeded to inhale and cough as I had done. When he had finished, however, he remained on all fours and crept closer to the stained spot in the dirt. Using the point on his stake, he flicked at something lying in the middle. I recognized it as the cork used to stopper the flask.

Once the cork was free of the blood, he leaned closer to it and sniffed. His face contorted for moment, but then relaxed. Rising, he dusted the soil from his hand and inhaled as he turned about in a circle.

"The inside portion of the cork was treated with the same ash as we found in the library," he said. "That's why the holy water wasn't detected. The outside of the bottle was smeared with a bit of blood to further mask its poisonous content." He frowned. "The whole effort is an ingenious one. Whoever devised this scheme of reducing the vampyre population has thought it out carefully."

"And who knows how many vials have been created?" I asked. "This could lead to an epidemic of tainted blood."

Sherlock strode to the vendor who had been watching him with great interest. He now cowered under my friend's stare, and Goliath once again moved with incredible swiftness to grab the back of Sherlock's neck before he reached the little man.

Despite my companion being firmly restrained by the behemoth, the old one cringed and whimpered under Holmes' glare.

Goliath's grasp was not as tight because my friend could speak quite clearly. "How did you come by this flask of death?"

"I-I found it. Among my stores."

"Unless you want the entire population of vampyres to descend upon you and destroy you and Goliath here as only those of our species can, you'd best show us exactly. I have only to send out the information to one or two attracted here tonight and soon all will know."

The man's eyes flitted under his creased brow as he glanced first at me and then my friend. Finally, he fixed his stare on his guard. "Drop him. They can follow us."

We flew over the city to the part of London near the wharfs and landed in front of a dark, cramped storefront. The sign outside read "Fordham's Emporium," which I felt overplayed the establishment. Inside, the place was lined with bottles and cabinets of an apothecary who serviced the poor. My mouth drifted into a sneer as I considered all the quackery stored in the place. Worthless herbs and concoctions that took a poor man's money and did nothing to relieve his suffering.

The man didn't pause, but led us through to a work room in the back where various tables held large glass containers surrounded by smaller flasks similar to that broken by Holmes. My mouth watered at the various scents surrounding us. The container on the first table was labeled *Cat*. Another was marked *Mouse*. Despite my previous intake of rat's blood, the sight of this variety and cornucopia of species made my tongue involuntarily travel around my lips.

Stepping to a table with a large flask marked *Rabbit*, the man pointed to a wooden box divided into small squares, all holding full vials. Indicating the one empty hole in the box, he said, "It was in there. The moment I awoke tonight, I sensed its presence. The vial it replaced is on the table next to it."

Holmes stepped to the table and studied its surface and then dropped to his knees to examine the floor. He ran his finger across the floorboards and then the table top, making a line in the dust on the second. He rubbed his fingers together and sniffed.

Heading to a door in the back of the work room, he studied the small set of steps leading to an alleyway running behind the building. Without a word, he proceeded outside and down this back way. Pushing past the two vampyres, I caught up with him. Knowing better than to question him when he was on a trail, I merely matched his stride as he tracked something only he could identify. He halted outside a large warehouse and turned to me.

"Take a deep breath," he said.

I did so and immediately lost all traces of the lingering garbage and decay that characterized this part of the city. For a brief instance, I *had* caught the scent of saffron and then—nothing.

He nodded, noting he'd come to the same conclusion as I. "A spice warehouse, I would surmise." Dropping his voice, he asked, "Have you your service revolver with you?"

When I withdrew it from my pocket to show him, a large hand clamped over mine, and I could feel the bones in my hand turn to dust under the pressure of Goliath's grip. While the giant vampyre's attention focused on me, my companion transformed and re-transformed behind the vendor. Taking the little man by surprise, he flipped him on his back and had a spring-loaded stake on the man's thin chest faster than in his earlier demonstration.

Through clenched teeth, Holmes said, "Tell him to let my friend go." When the man whined but said nothing, Holmes pushed the point into his chest, drawing blood. "Tell him."

Twisting under the stake, the man turned his rounded gaze to Goliath and nodded. The sudden release of pressure caused the revolver to drop from my fractured grip and land with a soft *thud* on the ground.

"Now, Mr. Fordham," my friend continued, "I wish to assure you I will be faster than your guard should you signal him to attack me. This stake's point lies at the border of your heart, and I will plunge it in before he can grab me unless you do exactly as I say. Call to the human."

"I don't know how you mean."

He gave a squeal as Holmes turned the stake again. "I know you've been receiving and selling human blood from a contact inside this warehouse. There was no saffron powder inside the workroom. If he'd slipped it among your wares, there would have been. Instead, I found traces of it on your footprints coming and going from this site. Call. Him. Out. Now."

Holmes leaned on the foot holding the vampyre to the ground, and I could hear his ribs cracking from where I stood.

"Holmes, please, you're crushing his chest."

"His ribs will heal soon enough," he said, continuing to stare at the man. "Hasn't your hand? I would suggest you retrieve your revolver. We may need it."

I opened and closed my hand. The bones *had* knitted themselves. With a glance at Fordham's guard, who appeared to be immobilized with the turn of events, I scooped up my weapon and pointed it at the warehouse entrance, prepared to fire at whatever or whoever stepped through it.

"Mr. Fordham, I'm growing tired of your stubbornness," Holmes said.

He gave one more whimper, glanced at Holmes, and called out. "Professor. Can you come out? I need to speak with you."

While I couldn't smell the human, I could hear his footsteps on the warehouse floor. The door squealed open, and a man emerged carrying a large flask. He was taller than the one still writhing underneath the foot of my companion, but his slumped shoulders made him appear almost the same height. He most resembled a chimneysweep, dressed in black and covered in soot. By this time, however, I knew it was no ordinary soot and I would not detect his presence by his scent.

My focus, however, was upon his eyes—sunk deep below a high-domed forehead. Despite the darkness, they sparked with an intelligence I'd only seen matched in my friend's.

With the arrival of the human, Holmes withdrew the stake and without so much as a glance at them, allowed Fordham and his bodyguard to fly away.

The human held up the flask. "Holy water, in case you don't recognize it. Any movement toward me, and I will toss this over both of you."

"You enjoy burning vampyres, Professor Moriarty?" Holmes asked. "Yes, Professor, I've known of you. And followed the makings of your criminal network. Even the good doctor here has read your treatise *Vampyres: Facts and Myths.*"

At the mention of the name, I started and studied with greater interest the author of the book I'd removed from the Reading Room. No wonder he'd left that particular book behind. He probably had that information memorized. It also explained his ability to survive when most others had not.

Now, the professor raised one corner of his mouth—in amusement or contempt, I wasn't sure. "It all depends on perspective to call my network 'criminal.' I believe in ridding the world of your kind, Mr. Holmes—yes, I know of you as well—and have both the knowledge and network to do so."

"One vial of blood at a time."

"It's taken me over a year to set up my connections. Supplying blood to different vendors around the world. Developing their trust in my wares. Now, mixed among them all, we've begun to include something extra. Our own version of Russian roulette, if you will. Will a specific vial sustain you, or kill you? Only partaking of it will tell."

"A clever plan, Professor."

He gave a slight bow. "A high compliment coming from you."

"And what would stop me from seeking them out and destroying them? Or destroying you and ending your network?"

"Are you familiar with the starfish? When you pull an appendage from one, the piece generates a new creature. You might destroy me, or another, but the others will continue and regenerate into a new network."

"I would assume the tainted blood is but one of your schemes?"

"To be certain," he said, a slight smile upon his thin lips for a moment before they turned downward into a frown, followed by a shake of the head. "How ever did we come to this point? Two species fighting for control of the planet? Especially when you consider your species *was* our species only a few years ago. And what has yours accomplished? Stagnation and decay. Nothing has been created or achieved except the hunting of all mammals almost to extinction. And what will become of the world once extinction is achieved? What will your species do then? You may live forever, but where? And how? Revert to caves and learn to live on reptilian blood? It is the humans that created civilization. What will your species contribute?"

Holmes stared at the man for a moment. For one of the few times in our friendship, I saw him waver in his resolve. He opened his mouth, closed it, lifted his hand as if planning to make a point, but then dropped it back to his side. Finally, he turned to me. "Lower your revolver, Watson."

"But Holmes, he'll burn us with the—"

"No, he won't," he said, his voice calm and steady. No sign of the earlier hesitancy, but with a hint of…defeat. "His threat was out of self-defense. If we let him go, he'll not harm us. Correct, Professor?"

"At least for the present."

Holmes' shoulders slumped and I feared the return of his earlier depression. Would he now fulfill his threat to end his existence? "Let's go home, old chap. There's nothing more we can do here."

I lowered my arm, and the man stepped backward until he reached the warehouse entrance. He slipped inside, and I heard the bolt on the door slide into place.

I opened my mouth to suggest we could still follow Moriarty, but Holmes transformed and was gone before I could even form the words.

Only when we were once safely secured in our flat did an inkling of his true mind-set reveal itself. As soon as I closed the door, he strode straight to the kitchen and the rat cages. At first I thought he was checking on their safety. Instead, he reappeared with two glasses filled to the brim with their blood.

Offering one to me, he said, "I have, for the first time in months, a true appetite." He held up his glass in a toast. "To Professor Moriarty, a human who matches me in knowledge and skill."

"I'm still not convinced you should have let a murderer go," I mumbled before downing its contents.

"Because, my dear friend," he said, his gaze fixed on me when I lowered my glass, "The man was correct. Destroying him would accomplish nothing at this time. Instead, we now have a mission." He rubbed his hands together. "We have no time for delay. There are flasks of tainted blood for us to ferret out. The game's afoot."

THE CASE OF THE BURNING MAN

Lucy Blue

FOR WATSON, IT STARTED WITH THE GIRL.

He had just locked up the clinic for the night and was waiting for the elevator. It finally opened with an oily wheeze, and the four employees of the second floor accounting firm came out, each one giving him their own version of the stink eye as they passed. "Evening," he said, tipping his hat to the prune-faced receptionist. "Y'all have a good night." Usually he took the stairs specifically to avoid these little scenes. But tonight it was raining, and his leg was paining him, and these California crackers would just have to cope.

He was just about to step inside when the girl ran in from the street—blonde, tall, soaking wet with her little blue frock plastered to her body like a second skin. With an inward sigh, Watson stepped back to let her board the elevator without him. "I'll wait for the next one."

"There's only one, and it's slower than Christmas," she said, laughing. "Come on, don't be ridiculous." Miss Prune Face had stopped at the street door and turned all the way around to gape at them, and her mouth dropped open like a dead trout's as he stepped inside. The blonde waved to her and stuck out her tongue just as the doors heaved closed.

"What floor, miss?" Watson asked, suppressing a smile.

"Three," she said. "I work for Mr. Holmes."

Watson had never stopped on the third floor, but he'd seen the name on the directory in the lobby. "So what does a consulting detective do?" he asked. "Spy on cheating husbands, that kind of thing?"

"Nothing like that," she said. "At least not so far. To tell you the truth, all I've seen him do since he hired me a week ago is think a lot and teach me to make what he calls an almost passable cup of tea. He's English."

"Oh." Even Watson, who wasn't particularly inquisitive by nature, wondered what kind of tea brewing she meant to do at seven-thirty on a Friday night. But then, seeing the way her wet dress clung to her hips, he reckoned he could guess. "Here we are then," he said as the elevator lunged to a stop. "Third floor."

"Thanks—Dr. Watson, isn't it?" she said.

"It is." She was a pretty girl; he hoped this English Mr. Holmes deserved her. "Have a good night."

"You too." She took his dangling hand and shook it. "I'm Grace." She stepped out and started down the hall. "Good night." When the elevator closed, he was still watching her walk away.

The rain was still pounding when he stepped out on the roof. The pigeons stirred and cooed as always, sidling along their perches, jockeying for position. "Sorry, kids," he said, filling their troughs with seed. "It's too wet to fly." The old man who had left him the birds as payment of his bill had spent hours on the roof, day and night, rain or shine, talking to his pets and letting them fly for hours. But Watson didn't have that kind of time. He tried to release them to exercise for a little while every day, but he didn't keep the careful count when they came back that Mr. Rosenbaum had, and over the past month, he'd lost a few. He wouldn't have grieved much if they'd all flown away for good; keeping pigeons was not his idea of a good time, and the stairs were murder on his leg. But the old man had been his first patient when he'd come to Los Angeles. He'd never mentioned or seemed to notice the color of Watson's skin, only that he was a doctor close by who made house calls. He had trusted him, respected him, befriended him, and he had died. So Watson took care of his birds.

A crack of thunder made the building shake under his feet, and the pigeons screeched and fluttered as lightning lit the sky. But he heard something else, too—a woman's scream. "Help!" It was Grace; he was sure of it. "Somebody help!"

He sprinted down the stairs, leaping the last flight in a single clumsy bound, ignoring the pain in his leg. Her screams rose again, sharper, wordless with pain. His brain flashed on the revolver locked in his desk drawer on the ground floor then on the heavy cane he'd dropped on the roof, but he ran on.

The door to the Sherlock Holmes Consulting Detective Agency was standing ajar. As he reached for the knob, still running, it crashed open, knocking him backwards, his forehead cracking the glass. He only caught a glimpse of a male figure dressed in black, some kind of big, floppy coat and a hat pulled low on his brow, shading his face. But he smelled him, a pungent, acrid smell like burning leaves. The mystery man had disappeared into the stairwell before Watson got his bearings. He thought of going after him, but the girl was still inside.

But she wasn't screaming any more. He found her on the floor behind the desk. She had been stabbed in the chest; there was blood everywhere. But she was alive.

He fell to his knees beside her. "John." Her voice was weak but urgent. Her pretty face was deathly pale and slick with sweat. "Listen." Her dress had been ripped open, and her chest was gushing blood in spurts in rhythm with her weakening heart, too much to actually see the wound. He tore off his jacket, wadded it up, and pressed it to the blood flow. She screamed, grabbing his arm, and he felt her sternum giving way.

"Holy God." The bastard had cracked her open like a surgeon.

"Dying." Her red nails dug into his wrist. "Tell Mr. Holmes…the fox." Blood bubbled from her lips, and her eyes went blank.

"No!" He could hear footsteps coming closer, voices from below. At night, the empty building was like an echo chamber, but he thought someone was coming up the hall. "Somebody help me!" he shouted. "We need help!" But Grace was gone.

"Don't move," a man's voice commanded. "Stay exactly as you are." He heard the door creak, and looked back over his shoulder. "I said don't move!" This man was white and dressed in brown, a strange, cloak-like tweed coat and a hat Watson's grandfather would have called a deerstalker. Watson started to stand. "Please, be still one more moment." Watson froze as the man's gaze moved around the room as precisely as if he'd been pointing a camera: the dead girl on the floor; Watson bending over her, his hands now raised though the stranger hadn't pulled a gun; the broken glass in the office door; then back to the dead girl. His expression was blank except for his eyes which were alive with interest.

"Upstairs!" He heard the unmistakable voice of Mrs. Hudson, the sweet old Bolshevik crazy who owned the building, coming from below. "I heard screaming!"

"Get up," the stranger ordered. He took off his strange hat and coat as Watson stood. "Give me your shirt, quickly. We only have a few moments."

"What?" Watson knew he was in shock; he felt like he was suddenly trapped in a thick, cold fog.

"Dr. Watson, you must compose yourself," the man ordered. Crisp, English accent—Sherlock Holmes, he realized. "If the police find you in this condition before I can ascertain what actually took place here, I doubt even I will be able to assist you." Watson suddenly realized how an L.A. cop would see him at this moment, a black man covered in a dead white girl's blood. "Give me your shirt," Holmes repeated, holding out his own coat.

Watson ripped out of his bloody white shirt and tie and the undershirt underneath and took the overcoat. Holmes grabbed the blood-stained clothes and dropped them in the trash, then grabbed Watson by the arm and steered him toward the window that led to the fire escape. The Englishman was strong for his slender frame; and his grip was like iron. "I saw him," Watson said as Holmes opened the window. "The guy who did this. As he was running away, I saw him." He heard the whine of the elevator.

"We'll talk later," Holmes said. Their eyes met for a moment, and Holmes nodded. "Now go."

He climbed out the window just as a police car drove past the alley, lights flashing and siren wailing. Staying close to the wall to hide in the shadows and avoid the curtains of rain that were still falling, he crept down the fire escape as quietly as he could as Holmes shut the window behind him.

He heard the hiss and click of a safety lighter. Directly below him, he saw the yellow flash of flame and the outline of a low-brimmed fedora. "You!" he said, forgetting his throbbing leg and the police inside. "Stop!" He half-climbed, half-slid down the ladder to the alley and saw the dark man's outline in the street light as he disappeared around the corner.

There were cars on the street, but the rainy sidewalk was deserted. "Stop!" he called again as the man ducked down another alley. Watson knew that alley; it dead-ended into the blank brick wall of a four-story warehouse. Wishing once again for his gun or his stick, he rounded the corner.

The alley was dark, but he could see the shadow silhouette of the man. He was facing Watson with his back to the wall. He flicked his lighter again, and the flame illuminated a pale, pointed face under the brim of the hat. "I don't know you, boy," he said. His voice was soft with a slight German accent. "And you don't want to know me."

"You killed that girl," Watson said.

"Yeah." Except it came out close to *ja*. "So what?"

Watson took a step closer. Suddenly the lighter's tiny flame shot up and out like the stream from an M2 flamethrower, engulfing the man in fire. Watson jumped back swearing and shielding his face with his arms. The German laughed. Then suddenly he was gone.

Watson swore again, batting at himself, expecting to find himself burning. But the fire had vanished with the man, leaving nothing but a stench of sulfur behind.

He took refuge in a second floor bar and pool hall across the street from his office. He watched out the window as more cops turned up, then an ambulance. The rain had slacked off, and he'd finished his second beer when he saw them wheel out the body, strapped to a stretcher and covered with a sheet. He saw Sherlock Holmes come out just behind the stretcher, deep in conversation with a plainclothes detective with a notebook.

"What happened?" one of the pool players asked. "What's going on down in the street?"

"Bunch of police," Watson said. He had cleaned up in the men's room, but he still had no shirt. He resisted the urge to pull Holmes' overcoat closer around him. "Meat wagon, too."

"A white girl got stabbed," the bartender said. "Hey, Doc, ain't your office in that building?"

"Yeah, it is," he said. "I must have just missed it."

An hour later, he was drinking coffee and the last of the cop cars was driving away. After what he hoped was an unremarkable interval, he paid his tab and left.

The lobby of the building was deserted, but he could hear Mrs. Hudson on the phone in her first floor apartment. "Right upstairs, can you believe it? Such a pretty girl." He crept past her door and up the stairs.

The lights were on in the detective agency, and the door was standing ajar. "Hello?" He tapped the broken glass. "Mr. Holmes?"

"In here." The reception room was empty and just as he'd left it except Grace's body was gone, replaced with a chalk outline on the floor. A lamp was burning on her desk, and the door to the inner office was open. Sherlock Holmes was stretched out on his sofa with a glass of what looked like whiskey balanced on his stomach. "How's your head, Watson?"

"Not bad." He had looked over the goose egg in the mirror in the pool hall men's room, and it hadn't looked serious—there was no cut. "I saw the killer."

"So you said," Holmes said.

"No, after."

Holmes sat up, catching his drink with a street hustler's grace. "Where?"

"I chased him down the street into that blind alley about a block down." He felt like a kid in school called to recite, standing up while Holmes sat in front of him. "He spoke to me; he admitted he did it. But he disappeared somehow—some kind of magic trick." Suddenly he felt dizzy and sick. "You mind if I sit down?"

"Of course not." Holmes got up and swept a stack of newspapers from an armchair. "Do you want a drink?"

"Better not." He sank down in the chair. "I had three beers already."

'Idiot," Holmes said.

"Excuse me?"

"Skip it." He leaned back on the edge of his desk. "Tell me everything— from the beginning, please."

So he did, starting from the moment he heard Grace's scream. "You keep pigeons?" Holmes asked.

"They were a gift," Watson said. "I inherited them from the old man upstairs when he died."

"Fine," Holmes said. "Continue."

When he came to Grace's last words, the detective stopped him again. "Repeat that," he said, picking up a notebook for the first time. "What did she say exactly?"

"She said, 'Tell Mr. Holmes the fox,'" he said. "I think—the woman was dying, bleeding out. I could have misheard her."

"I doubt it." For the first time, Holmes looked troubled.

"So what is the fox?"

"I have no idea." He made another long note in his book. "So then I came in, we spoke, and you left. But you say you saw the killer again."

"In the alley, yeah. I saw him as I was going down the fire escape. He saw me and ran, so I chased him."

Holmes was barely smiling. "Are you armed, Dr. Watson?"

"No, sir."

"Africa or Europe?" Holmes said. "In the war, I mean."

"Both," Watson said. "I started out driving an ambulance in North Africa and ended up in a field hospital in Germany. The killer's German, by the way. I recognized his accent."

"So he did speak to you."

"Yeah. I had him cornered, and I said, 'You killed that girl,' and he said, 'Yeah,' like that, real German."

"So all he said was that one word?" Holmes said.

"No. He said he didn't know me and that I didn't want to know him."

"Did that frighten you?"

Watson laughed. "Mr. Holmes, I'm a black man from Valdosta, Georgia, living in Los Angeles. I've been to war on two continents. One skinny white man with a knife is not likely to scare me."

Holmes smiled. "I'll bear that in mind. So he was Caucasian with a German accent and slight in build?"

"Yeah, but tall, about as tall as you or me. Very pale with dark eyes, brown, maybe black. And a pointed face."

"Pointed?"

"Yeah, sharp—long nose, pointed chin, small features."

"Like a fox, perhaps?"

"Maybe," Watson said. "I guess you could say that, yeah."

"So how did he get away?"

Watson closed his eyes for a moment, trying to remember every detail. "Like I said, it was like some kind of magic trick. He had a lighter, and he lit it. And then all of a sudden, the flame shot up, and I thought we were both on fire. But it was just him." Holmes had gone pale himself. "He was covered in flames like a devil in hell. Then he and the fire were just gone. Vanished."

"And you didn't hear him run past you?" The detective's tone was suddenly more urgent. "Footsteps? A car?"

"No, nothing," Watson said. "I mean, he must have run past me, but I never saw or heard a thing."

"Is there anything else you can tell me about him?" Holmes said. "Any detail you've left out?"

"I don't think so…wait." He looked back through the open door to the outer office. "There was a smell. When he first ran past me before I found Grace, I smelled him. It was a burning smell, like burning sulfur. And I smelled it again in the alley after he disappeared. It must be something to do with the trick."

"That seems likely," Holmes said, standing up. "But hardly certain." He went over to a filing cabinet.

"So what will you do with all this?" Watson said. "Take it to the police?"

"Good God, no," Holmes said. "We won't speak to the police again until we've solved it." He took out a white shirt still in its wrapper from the cleaners. "You'll need a tie and jacket, too, I suppose."

"We?" Watson echoed. "Mr. Holmes, I'm a medical doctor, not a detective."

"You are observant, resourceful and brave to a fault," Holmes said. "Just the sort of person I require to assist me." He held out the shirt. "My overcoat, if you please."

"I appreciate the compliment, but I am very tired, and if you don't mind, I think I'd rather just go on home." He handed over the coat but didn't take the shirt.

"I do mind," Holmes said. "What about poor Miss Reed? Grace—the damsel who cried out to you in her moment of distress?"

"Grace was a sweet girl, and I wish like hell I could have saved her," Watson said. "But she's dead and gone. I don't expect you to understand, but I cannot be crossing up the police, even for her. Things are different for me."

"I understand better than you realize, Dr. Watson," Holmes said. "Which is why it grieves me to point out that I still have your bloody coat and shirt, and the police have no viable suspects."

Watson's heart skipped a beat. "You're blackmailing me?"

"Only if you leave me no better choice." He held out the shirt again, and this time, Watson took it. "Rest assured, Watson, I will do everything in my power to prove your innocence."

"Why don't I feel better?" Watson said as he put on the shirt. It was a little tight across the shoulders, but it would do to get him home.

"Because you've only just met me," Holmes said, opening the closet to reveal a rack of clothes. "You don't realize yet that I'm a genius."

"Is that right?"

"It is." He took out a jacket and striped tie. "We should hurry. It's nearly midnight, and even an Irish wake winds down eventually."

"Irish wake?" Watson said. "The girl just died."

"Not the girl, Watson. A woman." He handed over the coat and tie and stripped out of his own. "The wife of Senator Hayward McRaney was murdered earlier this week."

"By the same guy?" Watson said, putting on the tie. It looked old, but it felt like pure silk.

"I didn't think so," Holmes said, putting on a fresh tie and a slightly less rumpled jacket of his own. "But after what you've told me, I'm not so sure."

"One last question," Watson said, shrugging into the jacket. Again, the fit was snug but not bad. "How do you know I didn't kill her?"

"Oh Watson, really?" The detective seemed disgusted that he'd even asked. "Starting with the obvious, why would you inflict a near-death wound then neither finish her off nor leave the scene? Why would you then use your own jacket to attempt to save her?" He waited, obviously expecting an answer.

"I don't know. Maybe I started to kill her then changed my mind."

"And were struck with such remorse you waited around for me or someone else to turn up as you attempted to save her yet not so much remorse that you would confess," Holmes said. "An admirably impossible theory of the crime, Watson, and one I have no doubt the good men of the LAPD would be glad to embrace with open hearts and empty minds given the chance. But let's look at the actual evidence." Holmes was obviously enjoying himself. "The glass in the door is broken from the outside in, and you have a knot on your forehead at the precise same height and of the precise same size as the break; therefore, you were struck with the door by someone already inside as you attempted to enter."

"Maybe Grace hit me," Watson said. "Maybe I chased her in here, and she was trying to get away."

"Then she would have pulled the door closed, not pushed it open." Holmes went back out to the front office, and Watson followed. "You were covered in Grace's blood, but only on your hands and sleeves from your efforts to staunch the bleeding, not across your chest and face as you would have been if you had actually stabbed her, and from the state of her body, it was obvious you would have had no time to clean up. As a doctor, you might possess the expertise to deal the poor girl such a wound, but not with your bare hands. You had no knife on your person, nor was there any knife in evidence in the room. Therefore, the killer must have already gone and taken it with him before I arrived, leaving you here with Grace to watch her die." He looked very pleased with himself as if he'd just explained a devil of a puzzle, not the death of an innocent girl. "Precisely as you reported it to me."

"That's amazing," Watson said. "You figured all that out while the police were here?"

"My dear Watson," he said, putting on his overcoat. "I deduced most of it within the first five seconds after I entered the room."

"That's why you told me to be still."

"Precisely. Once you removed your shirt, I confirmed my original hypothesis when your torso was blood free and I saw no concealed weapon. Your lack of hesitation in undressing was most reassuring." He rummaged in his trousers pocket. "I performed the final check as you went out the window," he said, holding up Watson's own keys. He'd been carrying them in his own trousers pocket before the murder, and he hadn't missed them yet. In addition to his other talents, Mr. Holmes was apparently a pretty slick pickpocket. "By the way, I see you have your own motor."

He means car, Watson's spinning brain told him. "Yeah...yes, I do."

"Good." Holmes tossed him the keys. "You're driving."

The streets were mostly deserted, and traffic was light because of the rain. They had just made the turn through the gates of the Bel-Air neighborhood when a police cruiser pulled in behind them and flashed his lights. "Pull over," Holmes said. "Don't be nervous."

The uniformed cop swaggered up to the car like a baby with a diaper full of prizes. "I can't wait to hear this," he said as Watson rolled down his window. "Boy, what can you be thinking bringing this hunk of junk into Bel-Air at this time of night?"

"What seems to be the problem, officer?" Holmes said. Before the cop could answer, the detective handed him a white card he had taken out of his wallet.

As he looked at it, whatever snappy retort the cop had been cooking up died in his throat. "Nothing, sir," he said, handing it back. "Enjoy your evening. You drive safe, boy." He waved them off and stood watching as Watson drove away.

"That was handy," Watson said. "You want to tell me what that was about?"

Holmes put the card back into his wallet. "You weren't the only man of use during the war." He pointed to a set of high iron gates standing open to the left. "That's the one."

The long, circular drive was lined with cars a lot shinier than Watson's and led to a mansion so new he could still smell fresh paint. He shouldered his car into the last available space behind a blooming bougainvillea and followed Holmes to the front door.

The double doors were standing open, but they were guarded by a pair of white men with close-cropped red hair and dark gray suits. "Sherlock Holmes, Consulting Detective," Holmes said, presenting one of these Irish gorillas with his card. "I must see Senator McRaney at once on a matter of gravest importance."

"More important than his sainted wife's memorial?" the one without the card said. "Shove off, Professor, and call at the office next week."

"This ain't one of those," the one with the card said, giving his partner a tug back. "Wait here, please, Mr. Holmes." His eyes barely slid across Watson as he took the card inside.

After a few minutes, he was back. "The Senator says he'll come talk to you in his study when he gets a minute, if you'd like to wait," he said, handing back the card.

"Of course." Holmes started inside, but when Watson took a step to follow him, both gorillas blocked the way.

"Your man will have to wait outside," the slick one said.

"His man?" Watson echoed.

"His chauffeur, then," the rough one said with a nasty smile. "You like that better, Rochester?"

"Dr. Watson is a physician and a war veteran," Holmes said, putting a hand on Watson's arm. "He is assisting me in my investigation."

"Listen, bub, I don't care if he's the crown prince of Ooka Pooka Land, he ain't coming in here," Rough said, violence gleaming in his pale blue eyes.

Holmes turned his back on the gorillas. "McRaney can get us access to vital clues." From his grip on Watson's arm to the set of his jaw, he made it clear he wanted to sock these two almost as much as Watson did himself. "Will you wait outside, Dr. Watson, please? For Grace's sake?"

Watson made slow, unwavering eye contact with Rough over Holmes' shoulder. "Sure thing, Sherlock," he said. "I'll be right outside."

"Hey Henry," Rough called out to the young black man leaning on the car parked directly in front of the door. "Take care of *Doctor* Watson. Take him around to the kitchen and let him have a biscuit."

"Yes, sir," the young man said, standing up. He walked with a limp, heading around to the back of the house. It occurred to Watson that if what they wanted was information, this Henry was more likely to have it than these two at the door. With a last nod to Holmes, he followed.

"You can't let ol' boys like that get your goat," Henry advised as soon as they were out of earshot. "It's just asking for trouble."

"Is that how you got that limp?" They rounded the corner into a concrete paddock between what looked like the kitchen door and the garage.

"I got this limp in Italy." Half a dozen men in chauffeur's uniforms were standing around with their jackets unbuttoned and their ties untied as if they'd been there quite a while, smoking and talking. Through the screen door, he could hear a radio. "If you really are a doctor, you ought to write me up a little something for the pain."

"Where's the shrapnel?" Watson asked. "Hip or knee?" He had seen more than one black man patched up with a lick and a promise by white surgeons who thought themselves too good to work on them at all.

"Metal in the hip joint," Henry said. "Piece missing from the knee." He pulled up his pants leg to show a knee joint swollen big and round as a coconut. "Army doc says I'm supposed to be better and tells me to take an aspirin."

Watson could see at a glance how to treat him, and all his instincts told him to do it. But he was supposed to be thinking like a detective. "I can fix you up," he said. "But what can you do for me?"

Henry looked suspicious. "What do you need?"

"Information," Watson said. "Holmes says the lady of the house was murdered. What do you know about that?"

A couple of the chauffeurs had stopped talking and cocked their heads to listen. "Man, I don't know nothing," Henry said, walking away.

"Hang on," Watson said, following. "I thought you needed a script."

"Not that bad I don't," the other man said. They were behind the garage now, out of sight and hearing of the others. "How'd you end up with Sherlock Holmes, anyway?"

"You know him?" Looking back toward the house, he could see people moving behind the windows. It was well past midnight, but the place was obviously packed. Henry saw him looking and motioned for him to follow deeper into the gardens through a grove of live oak trees.

"Mrs. McRaney knew Holmes," he said. "From the war, I think. She was English, too. She used to get me to drive her to some of the most ungodly holes you ever saw to scrape him up and wring him out."

"So he's a drunk?"

"Way worse than drunk." He grimaced. "Maybe I ought to ask him where to get a painkiller."

"No need." He filed this piece of information away with a sinking heart. "Come on by my office tomorrow. I'll drain the fluid off that knee and give you something for the infection and the pain. But you've got to help me out. Give me something to go on." He thought about the fox-faced man in the alley and his magic trick. "Haven't you seen anything strange going on around here?"

Before Henry could answer, women's voices singing or chanting in unison came from the distant shadows of the grove. "What the hell is that?" Watson said.

"Nothing," Henry said. He didn't look happy, but he didn't look surprised either. "Come on; let's go back to the house."

"No, but what's going on?" Over the other man's shoulder, he now saw the flickering glow of a bonfire through the trees. "Who is that?" He started towards the light and saw dark, robed shapes passing through it. Having grown up in Georgia, he had a powerful instinct to move away from robed white people dancing around a bonfire, but from something about the way these moved, he was pretty sure they were all women. The party was inside; what were they doing out here?

"I said come on," Henry said from behind him, not coming any closer.

"Why have you summoned me?" This single voice was also female, but louder than the others. The chanting went on in a language Watson didn't recognize, but this woman was speaking plain English—English English; she had an accent. "It's too soon." Her voice seemed to waver, like someone shouting into a telephone over a bad connection.

"Who is that?" Watson said, moving closer. Henry grabbed his arm, but he shook him off.

Up ahead, he saw the women were gathered in a circle, holding hands, swaying back and forth. Their chanting grew louder, more frantic, and a column of flame shot up from the center of the circle as the Englishwoman's strange voice shouted, "No!"

"You cannot be here!" Henry said in a desperate whisper, grabbing Watson's arm again. His eyes were wide, and his face was slick with sweat.

"What is going on?" Watson asked him. "What are they doing, Henry?" The chanting was breaking up; some of the women were crying. One broke from the circle and ran away into the trees in the opposite direction from Henry and Watson.

"You stay if you want to, Dr. Watson," Henry said as he turned away. "I'm gone."

"Hang on." Watson half-ran to keep up, his own knee screaming with pain. He had at least a dozen questions, but he was pretty sure Henry would only give him one. So he tried for what seemed most important. "Who was that woman?"

The chauffeur stopped at the edge of the grove. "The late Mrs. Adaline McRaney," he said. If he'd been lying, Watson didn't think he would have looked so scared. "Is that strange enough for you, doc?"

Instead of answering, Watson turned and ran back in the direction of the grove. A few times he could have sworn he felt someone brush past him in the darkness, but the light from the distant fire was gone, and whenever he turned, he saw no one.

When he got to the clearing where he'd seen the circle, a pile of embers was smoldering at the center, but the women were gone. It was nearly pitch-black dark; the only light came from glow in the sky over Hollywood. Without it, he could have been in a forest primeval from a fairy tale.

When he made it back to the house, Henry was with the other chauffeurs, sitting on the back steps smoking a cigarette. "Come see me," Watson said, handing him his card. "I'll fix you up." Nodding to the others, he went back around the house to his own car to wait for Holmes.

He didn't have to wait long. He had barely gotten the radio tuned when he saw the detective being frog-marched up the driveway between the two gorillas from before. He got out just in time to catch him as they tossed him towards the car.

"You all right?" Watson asked as Holmes straightened up.

"Yes, of course." He got into the car, and Watson followed.

"So did the Senator tell you anything useful before he tossed you out?" he said, steering back down the drive.

"If a useful idea ever came into the Senator's mind, the loneliness would kill it," Holmes said, but he was smiling. "Let's find a bar, shall we? I could use a drink."

As they drove back to Hollywood, Watson told Holmes what he had seen and heard in the Senator's garden. "More magic tricks?" Holmes said.

"I guess so," Watson said. "Henry looked pretty spooked."

"You did give him good reason to lie," Holmes said. "He wanted to show you something remarkable enough to convince you to give him drugs."

"I would have treated him no matter what he told me," Watson said.

"Yes, but he didn't know that."

"Besides, he didn't take me around back to hear those women. He didn't even want me there. As soon as he realized what was going on, he started trying to drag me away."

"Which could have been part of the performance." Holmes rolled down the window and lit a cigarette. "It certainly suggests that Henry knew what was going on."

"He seemed to, yeah." *Did Holmes automatically doubt Henry because he was black?* Watson wondered. *Did Watson automatically trust him because he was, too?* The questions made his head ache; he hadn't slept in almost twenty-four hours now. "No, I don't think Henry was part of it, whatever it was," he decided. "I think hearing those women was a shock to him and that he really believed the voice he heard was Mrs. McRaney."

"I'm prepared to move forward based on your analysis," Holmes said. "Which makes what you witnessed less likely to have been staged at all. If you weren't the intended audience, who was?"

"What are you saying?" It was raining again, and lightning split the sky, striking a radio tower on a building up ahead. "That I really did hear the ghost of Mrs. McRaney calling out from the grave?"

"That would not be my first hypothesis," Holmes said. "I think it more likely that someone was impersonating her ghost for the benefit of the others you heard. The question then being why." He pointed with his cigarette. "Turn left at the corner."

"Henry said you and Mrs. McRaney knew one another back in England." Holmes was directing him to just the kind of ungodly hole the chauffeur had described. "He thinks y'all worked together during the war."

"We did," Holmes said. "Before her marriage to an idiot, Adaline McRaney was the best spy I ever knew." They had pulled level with a seedy-looking storefront with a broken neon sign blinking "Cocktails" in the window. "Park here."

The bar was empty except for the bartender who barely looked up from his newspaper. "Whisky neat," Holmes said. "And something for Dr. Watson."

"I'll have a cup of coffee if you've got it," Watson said, hating the bright edge of anxiety in his own voice. He had already faced down too many racist gorillas tonight. But the bartender just nodded and hauled himself up to fill their order.

Holmes sat down in a booth at the back and took a leather case from his breast pocket. "So why do you think Grace's murder and Mrs. McRaney's murder are related?" Watson asked as he joined him.

"A moment, please, Watson." The detective opened the case and took out a small vial and a syringe. He lay these on the table and shrugged out of his jacket.

"What the hell are you doing?"

Holmes rolled up his sleeve. "After a great deal of research, I have determined that a seven percent solution of cocaine administered intravenously three times daily sharpens my acuity to its best possible performance." He tied on a rubber tourniquet. "Though at this late hour, I suspect my schedule and dosage will both require adjustment."

"Mr. Holmes, cocaine is illegal in this country." He watched as the detective filled the syringe. "Stop it."

"I am well aware of the legal status of narcotics, Dr. Watson." Watson reached across the table and caught his wrist. "I do beg your pardon," he said, raising an eyebrow, just as the bartender appeared with their drinks. Watson let him go.

"Would you like cream and sugar, Dr. Watson?" the bartender said as Holmes injected the drug.

"No, thank you." Watson stood up and dropped a dollar on the table. "I'm leaving."

"Watson, for god's sake, don't be a child." Holmes might have been speaking a little faster, but otherwise, he seemed unaffected. "Sit down, please."

"No, sir, I will not." Watson loomed over him. The bartender seemed content to watch. "I don't know what your game is, and I don't care. But if you think I'm some negro coke fiend you can blackmail into driving you around and finding you a fix when you need it, you are very much mistaken."

"Watson, why would I imagine you to be a coke fiend when I am the one using cocaine?" Holmes said as he untied the tourniquet. "I would never expect you to facilitate or even condone my methods." His color was heightened, and his eyes were bright. "And if I require a driver, I am quite able to summon a taxi." He seemed to notice his whisky and the man who had brought it for the first time. "Thank you, Jones."

"My pleasure, Mr. Holmes." Jones smiled at Watson as he turned away.

"Dr. Watson, please sit down," Holmes said. "We have no time for this. Can't we agree that I am an irretrievable degenerate and get on with the case?" He took a swallow of his drink then noticed Watson still standing. "Please?"

"Who are you?" Watson said. "Who are you really?"

Their eyes met. "Sit down, and I'll tell you."

Curiosity was stronger than good sense. "All right," Watson said, sitting down. "I'm listening."

"For me, this story began a very long time ago." He took a picture from his wallet and passed it across the table. Two young white men dressed in striped coats smiled out at the world from at least two decades in the past. Their arms were flung around one another's shoulders, and both were holding beer bottles. One was a much younger Sherlock Holmes. "James Whitesell was my best friend from the time we met in school until he was murdered during the war." Holmes sipped his whiskey, no longer meeting Watson's eyes. "He was more than my friend; we were lovers. You say I am blackmailing you because I know your most dreaded secret; now you know mine." He looked up. "I see a peculiarly American homophobic panic in your eyes, Dr. Watson." The detective's own eyes were still bright from the cocaine with dilated pupils, and his crisp diction had turned as bitter as the bartender's thick, black coffee. "Let me reassure you. My relationship with Whitesell was entirely singular. I have felt no other such attraction for man or woman since, nor do I expect I ever shall."

Watson handed back the photograph. "You said he died in the war?"

"He was murdered." He put it back in his wallet. "Like me, he was working for the SIS. Adaline Kitteridge was his partner."

"Mrs. McRaney."

"Just so. They were dropped into France just before the invasion at Normandy and posed there as a married couple for the next nine months, gathering intelligence. Adaline was the genius, but Whitesell had his own talents. My own work allowed me to check in on them from time to time, and we were all…" He broke off and finished his whiskey. "Whitesell was tortured to death, burned alive by a German double agent we knew only as *Der Fuchs*."

"The Fox," Watson translated. "But when I told you Grace's last words, you said you had no idea what they meant."

Holmes smiled. "I didn't know you then, Watson. I wasn't sure I could trust you."

"So you think this guy, the Fox, killed Grace and Mrs. McRaney," Watson said. "That's the connection."

"I think that is one possibility to be explored," Holmes said. "Adaline and I hunted the Fox for the rest of the war and beyond, called in every favor, exploited every asset. We never found so much as a real name." He signaled to the bartender. "After the war was over, even his alias disappeared, and our superiors liked it that way. The official story was that he must surely have died." Jones refilled his glass. "I gave up any ambition I might have had in government service by refusing to abandon the search." He picked up the glass. "Even my own brother turned his back on me."

"Did Mrs. McRaney think he was dead?" Watson asked.

"In time, yes," Holmes answered. "She emigrated and met her husband and left her former life behind. Then when things for me in England became entirely intolerable…" He trailed off again, staring at his drink. "I owe Adaline a great deal."

"So why would the Fox come after her now?" Watson asked.

"That would be the pertinent question," Holmes said. "That's why until you told me what Grace said to you, I refused to consider the Fox as a suspect. It seemed too farfetched, a product of my own obsession. But Grace's last words and your description of the man and his magic trick…" He trailed off again and took a swallow of his drink. "And there's something else connected to the way Grace was killed. In your medical opinion, what was the intent of the attack? Why did her killer inflict those specific wounds?"

Remembering, Watson felt sick. "He was trying to cut out her heart."

"So it would seem," Holmes agreed. "I didn't see the body, so I can't be certain. But my sources tell me that whoever murdered Adaline removed her brain." He finished his drink and went to the bar. "Jones, your telephone, if you please." He took a card from his pocket as Watson followed. "I found this on McRaney's desk," he said as he dialed. "The copper investigating the murder. Detective Lestrade, please," he said. "This is Sherlock Holmes." A pause. "I am a consulting detective engaged by Senator Harold McRaney." Another pause, only now Watson and Jones could hear a voice on the other end buzzing like a hornet. "My best guess would be he considers your department entirely incompetent, and based on your progress so far, I'm inclined to agree with him." More buzzing; Jones grinned at Watson. "His exact words will not comfort you, Detective. Besides, we haven't time. There's been another murder, a young woman named Grace Reed."

"What's he going to do when the cop calls McRaney?" Watson asked Jones.

"By then, he'll have solved it," Jones said.

"So you know about Miss Reed. Then I assume you have her address. I need you to meet me at her apartment at once. Now, Lestrade. We haven't a moment to lose." He hung up before the man could answer. "Thank you, Jones," he said, handing back the phone. "Now Watson. If you wish to go home to bed and abandon this enterprise, I won't make any attempt to detain you. I'm sure Mr. Jones will be happy to call me a cab, and the items we discussed earlier this evening will be returned to you first thing tomorrow morning. I understand your eagerness to be away; I'm sure your pigeons miss you horribly. But if you'd prefer to come with me and see this through, I would certainly have no objection."

They were both looking at him, Jones with one eyebrow cocked. "Oh, to hell with it," Watson said. "Why not?"

Detective Lestrade was waiting for them on the sidewalk under a streetlight. "You Sherlock Holmes?"

"I am." Holmes' gaze flickered over the cop. "My apologies to the young lady."

"What young lady?" Lestrade said. "Grace Reed? Are you confessing?"

"Don't be absurd," Holmes said. "The young lady you were with when I called."

Lestrade's neck flushed. "I'm not married, Mr. Holmes. Not that it's any of your business."

"I'm sure your companion for the evening would be gratified to hear it," Holmes said, starting toward the door to the apartment building.

"How did you—what makes you think I was with a girl?" Lestrade said, hurrying to catch up. Watson followed, smiling in anticipation.

"Your clothes are disheveled as if you put on yesterday's suit in haste over a clean shirt," Holmes said. "Yet you are freshly shaven, less than twelve hours by the pink scrape on your neck. The smear of crimson on your earlobe can only be lipstick." He leaned closer and sniffed. "We've only just met, but I doubt Evening in Paris is your customary scent."

"All right, I get it," Lestrade said, blushing red to the roots of his hair now.

"And the blonde hair on your lapel, taken with the perfume and lipstick and your fresh shave, suggest a young lady of better than average allure," Holmes went on. "So again, apologies." He went inside.

"I know," Watson said. "He should hire out for children's parties." He offered his hand. "John Watson."

The cop took it and shook. "George Lestrade."

Holmes' voice came back to them with no thought for the sleeping neighbors. "Did I mention we're in a rush?"

Grace Reed's little apartment was so sweet and homey, Watson could have cried. "So tell me, detective," Holmes said, going through her kitchen cabinets. "When I told you the two murders were related, you didn't seem surprised."

"Yeah, I had already figured that much," Lestrade said, looking into the icebox. "Just from the tattoos."

"Tattoos?" Holmes echoed.

"Yeah, turns out Miss Reed has the same little tattoo on her hip as Mrs. McRaney," he said.

"Don't be ridiculous," Holmes said. "Adaline McRaney was not the sort of woman to have a tattoo."

"Her corpse down at the county morgue said she was," Lestrade said. "I saw it. I'm surprised you didn't know about it yourself, Mr. Holmes."

Holmes looked at Watson and raised an eyebrow. "So what is your theory of the crime, Lestrade?"

"Beautiful bored housewife. Beautiful secretary. I'm thinking love triangle." He opened the back door and found a tiny service hall leading to the back stairs. "Mrs. M. finds out about Miss R. and confronts Mr. X. X. loses his temper and offs her.

"My goodness," Holmes said. "How sordid."

"Then he finds out Mrs. M. already confronted Miss R., that little Grace knows the score. She wants more than romance to keep quiet, so he does her, too."

"Did you share this theory with Senator McRaney?" Watson said.

"Not yet," Lestrade admitted.

"Very wise," Holmes said, going to the little writing desk in the living room. "So who is your suspect? What sort of man surgically extracts his lover's brain in a fit of temper?"

"The same sort who marks his women with a tattoo," Lestrade said. "My first thought was a Cuban. You know, hot Latin blood."

"Right," Watson said as Holmes snickered.

"But to tell you the truth, Holmes, your muscling in on my investigation this way got me thinking. You knew both women, right?"

Holmes stopped riffling through Grace's letters. "I'm your suspect?"

"Well, you've got to admit, it kind of adds up," Lestrade said. "I looked up that tattoo. It's a Tudor rose, a symbol of Great Britain. You're English, aren't you?"

"Yes, I am, Lestrade; well spotted," Holmes said. "Though to be fair, so is Winston Churchill."

"Yeah, but Grace Reed wasn't his receptionist."

"Holmes couldn't have done it," Watson said.

"It's all right, Dr. Watson," Holmes interrupted before he could say why. "The detective has simply given me another incentive to find out who did. Shall we search the bedroom?"

"What are we looking for?" Watson said. All this rummaging through a dead girl's things was making him feel sick.

"We'll know it when we find it," Holmes said. "Right, Lestrade?"

"Right." The cop led the way down the hall. "Please, God, no cats. I hate it when they have cats."

The bedroom was a lot fancier than the rest of the apartment with a big, brass, four-poster bed and pink silk sheets. Tall lamps with red shades were set at each corner of the room. "Cripes," Lestrade said, making Holmes snicker again.

Holmes opened the closet door, but instead of a closet, they found a photographer's darkroom. Pictures hung on clotheslines to dry crisscrossed the room at eye level, and black strips of film hung on a rack against the wall. "I knew Grace was a photographer," Holmes said. "She mentioned it when she applied for the job in my office."

"Blackmail," Lestrade said. "She was blackmailing someone."

"Possibly," Holmes said, taking down a picture. "Watson, was this the man you saw?"

Watson took it. "Yeah." The man in the photograph had his fedora pulled low, but the long, sharp profile was unmistakable. "That's him."

"Wait a second," Lestrade said. "He's a witness? You never said you had a witness."

"Lestrade, the sum total of all you don't know would fill a library with volumes to spare," Holmes said, opening a folder full of more photographs. "Oh my word."

"What is it?" Watson and Lestrade said at once.

His word indeed. The photographs had obviously been taken in Grace's bedroom and featured a beautiful brunette Watson recognized from the movies, posing stark and stunningly naked. In the first few shots in the stack, she was alone, smiling at the camera, merely seductive. But as the series went on, another woman joined her on the bed—Grace Reed.

"Oh my giddy aunt," Lestrade said as he took the pictures from Holmes. "Would you look at that?"

"Stop it," Watson said. "It's not decent."

"He's a detective, Watson," Holmes said. "Let him detect."

"There it is," Lestrade said, holding up one of the most pornographic shots. "The same tattoo."

"So it is," Holmes said. In the picture, each woman's left hip was clearly visible, and each was marked with the same Tudor rose tattoo. "And you say Adaline had the same mark."

"In the exact same spot," Lestrade said. "And you're telling me you never saw it."

"I'm telling you I never saw it," Holmes said. "I never had occasion." He studied one of the other photographs. "If only we knew the identity of this other woman."

Lestrade looked at Watson. "He's kidding, right?"

"No," Watson said. "I don't think he is. Sherlock, that's Irina Russell. She's a big movie star."

"The tabloids would kill to get their hands on these," Lestrade said. "Not to mention the studio. That sounds like one hell of a motive to me."

"Changing your theory, then?" Watson asked.

"Don't be ridiculous, Lestrade," Holmes said.

"What's so ridiculous about it?" the cop said. "Maybe little Gracie had herself a sideline business, seducing and blackmailing rich dykes."

Watson thought from the look on his face that Holmes would punch the cop, and he braced to grab for him. Then they heard a crash from the living room. "Maybe she had a cat after all," Watson said as Holmes sprinted past him.

A woman in a red silk head scarf and full-length mink coat was running out the front door. They all three chased her, but Holmes vaulted the last flight of stairs and caught her just as she reached the sidewalk.

"Speak of the devil," Holmes said, holding her by both arms. "Miss Russell, I presume?"

"None of us would have ever hurt Grace," the woman said. "I loved her. Please, you must let me go." She looked smaller in the flesh and much younger, barely more than a kid. "There's no time." One side of her face was bandaged, and Watson saw a cut over her other eye.

"Miss Russell, who hurt you?" he asked.

"A demon." She sounded near tears, terrified. "He tried to take my eyes."

"Say, let her go!" a man's voice said. "What gives, Irina?" Watson recognized the man coming towards them. He was an actor, too, Johnny Rose. He had starred opposite Irina Russell in her last movie. Watson had seen it the week before.

"Johnny?" she said. "Johnny, help me, please!"

"This woman is under arrest," Lestrade said, blocking his way.

"Under arrest? That's crazy." He looked and sounded just like he had in the movie. "Under arrest for what?"

"She is not under arrest," Holmes said, giving Lestrade a stern look. "We simply need to ask her some questions."

"I have to go," Irina said, struggling. "It's nearly sunrise. I'll tell you whatever you want to know, but after."

"After what?" Holmes said.

"If she's not under arrest, turn her loose," Johnny said. He was even wearing the same suit he'd been wearing in the movie Watson saw. That seemed strange.

"Miss Russell is in danger," Holmes said.

"If she is, I'll look after her," Johnny said, taking Irina's arm as Holmes let her go.

"The observatory," Irina said as they started to walk away. "I have to get to the observatory."

"Don't worry, honey," Johnny said. "I'll take you just where you need to go."

That smell, Watson thought. *It's that smell.* Johnny looked like a movie star, but he smelled like brimstone and ash. "Stop him," Watson said. "That's the guy."

"What are you talking about?" Lestrade said.

Holmes grabbed for the girl, and the thing that looked like Johnny snatched her back. He pulled out a long, silver knife, and Irina screamed. Holmes lunged, pushing the girl aside as he wrenched the arm that held the knife behind Johnny's back in a single fluid motion. Watson caught Irina as she stumbled, but she didn't fall. She whirled around and whipped something from her pocket that he first thought was a gun.

"By the goddess, show yourself!" she shouted, holding up a sort of knotted cross. The thing pretending to be Johnny snarled, jerking free of Holmes' grip, still brandishing the knife. His face and clothing seemed to melt, boiling and bubbling into the shape Watson had seen in the alley—the Fox. He struck at Holmes with the knife, and the detective fell back.

"Give me the girl," the Fox said in the same thick, German accent as before. "Don't make me burn you, Sherlock."

"Get back!" Lestrade shouted, drawing his gun. The Fox turned toward him as he raised it, and suddenly the cop's sleeve burst into flames.

"No!" Holmes shouted. "Watson!"

Watson snatched off Lestrade's coat, but his shirt sleeve was burning too. Swearing a blue streak, the cop dropped to the ground and rolled.

The Fox made another grab for the girl, and her cross caught fire. She shoved it into his face just as Holmes grabbed him from behind, one hand on the nape of his neck, the other clamped on the wrist that still held the knife. The Fox snarled like an animal, baring his teeth as he struggled...

Then suddenly, he was gone.

"He called you Sherlock," Irina said. "You're Sherlock Holmes."

"Lestrade needs medical attention," Watson said. The fire on Lestrade's sleeve and Irina's cross had disappeared with the Fox, but the cop was still badly burned.

"Just help me up," Lestrade said. "Get me to my radio."

"Where did he go?" Holmes said. "What in hell--?"

"Yes, exactly," Irina cut him off. "Please, Mr. Holmes, you have to help me. We have to reach Griffith Park before the sun rises. It's the only way to destroy him."

"Sorry, miss, but you're going to the city lock-up until we get this straightened out," Lestrade said. He was on his feet, and he pushed Watson away. "Holmes, take my cuffs."

"Mr. Holmes, please," Irina said. "Adaline said it could be centuries before we have another chance. She formed the coven for just this purpose. If we don't complete the ritual, she and Grace will have died for nothing."

"Holmes, what is she talking about?" Lestrade said.

"I don't know," Holmes said. He was still holding Irina by the arm, but he was steering her towards Watson's car, not Lestrade's. "But I intend to find out." He opened the car door, and she ducked inside. "Watson, your keys, if you please."

"Oh hell no," Watson said. "I'm driving."

"As you wish," Holmes said, climbing in back.

"The Fox isn't just a man," Irina said as they drove away. Watson saw Lestrade in his rearview mirror doing a little dance of rage. "He is the vessel of a demon."

"Preposterous," Holmes said, lighting a cigarette.

"Adaline knew you'd never believe it," the girl went on. "That's why she never told you. But in her research, she found accounts of him all the way back to the Middle Ages. She traced him all the way back to a German alchemist named Josef von Fuchs who was said to have sold his soul to the devil."

"Didn't somebody say that about every alchemist in the Middle Ages?" Watson said.

"Only the smart ones," Holmes said. "I know about Von Fuchs, Miss Russell. He was burned at the stake in 1421."

"Burned but not destroyed," Irina said. "And how do you explain the account of that same Von Fuchs causing the combustion of a castle in 1122? Or the destruction of a village in 1735?"

"The same way I explain this entire fantasy," Holmes said. "Superstitious hysteria."

"I don't know, Holmes," Watson said. "I've got nothing against a black cat, and I don't mind walking under a ladder. But I've seen this bastard disappear into thin air twice."

"You have seen him appear to disappear," Holmes said. "Just because we haven't discovered a practical explanation does not mean none exists."

Irina laughed. "Adaline knew you'd say that. She did a pretty good impression of you, you know."

"So why are we going to Griffith Park?" Watson said.

"To vanquish the demon," Irina said. Holmes made a rude noise, but she kept going. "Adaline figured out that the way to defeat him wasn't to attack his body. That can always regenerate. You have to destroy the demon inside."

"I'd be curious, Miss Russell," Holmes said. "You said the Fox attacked you. How did you escape?"

"Easy," she said. "I shot him six times point blank in the face."

"That would do it, I reckon," Watson said.

"Except it didn't," she said. "By the time I got to the door, he was already getting up. The only way to stop him is to banish the demon inside him back to hell."

"Hell is the fantasy of frightened monkeys living in a cave!" Holmes said. Up to then, he had sounded amused; now he sounded furious.

"Adaline found the astral date of the demon's original fall," Irina went on. "This morning at dawn will be the millennial anniversary."

"Oh for God's sake," Holmes said.

"Is He a fantasy, too?" Watson said. The black sky was showing streaks of lavender in the east.

"Shut up, Watson."

"Just asking."

"If our circle can conjure the Fox and hold him at just the right moment, we can vanquish the demon and capture the vessel," Irina said. "With both Adaline and Grace gone, I don't know how we'll do it, but we have to try."

"You say we," Watson said as they drove around the gates of Griffith Park. "Who is we?"

They rounded a bend, and he had his answer. The hillside opposite the observatory as covered with people dressed in hooded white robes, hundreds of them forming concentric circles and singing. "Holy Moses," Watson said. "Who are all these people?"

"You'd be amazed," Irina said, smiling. "Adaline has been preparing for years, recruiting people with the proper energy."

"She was the brain, I take it," Holmes said. "And Grace Reed was the heart."

"Exactly," Irina said. "And I'm the seer. I inherited second sight from my grandmother. I'm the one who first saw when the ritual would be possible."

"Of course you are," Holmes said.

"Mr. Holmes, you must promise not to interfere," she said. "Stop the car; I'll walk from here."

"And we'll walk with you," Holmes said. He pulled a pistol from a hidden pocket in his jacket. "We won't interfere unless it's absolutely necessary."

"Mr. Holmes, please," she said.

"We can always go to the police station instead," Watson pointed out.

"Fine." She obviously wasn't happy, but she looked resigned. "Let's go. We're almost out of time."

"Hang on." Watson opened the compartment his grandpapa had installed under the seat in 1929 and pulled out the loaded shotgun. "Now I'm ready."

"Watson, you are a man of rare resources," Holmes said as they started up the hill.

"Are you really believing all this hogwash about vanquishing demons?" Watson asked.

"Not for a moment," Holmes replied. They had entered the chanting, circling crowd, and Irina, walking ahead of them, made no sign she had heard.

"I think it much more likely that Miss Russell is the Fox's willing accomplice, that she is orchestrating this farce to cover up Adaline's murder."

"But what about the cuts on her face?" Watson said. "She's an actress; her face is her fortune."

"I met women in Germany who had strangled their children on his orders," Holmes said. "The Fox can be very persuasive."

Inside the central circle, they found nine women waiting. "Irina!" one of them said, rushing forward to hug her. "Thank the goddess!"

"There's no time," Irina said. "Take your positions."

"But who are they?" another woman asked, a girl with Asian features who couldn't have been any older than sixteen. The faces were all colors, all races, including two women who were black.

"They're friends of Adaline's, here for our protection," Irina said. "Now begin."

The women linked hands to form a final circle with Holmes and Watson standing just outside. Two women away from Irina on either side, the women held a twisted branch between them, forming two blank spaces in what should have been a circle of twelve. "First we must call back the spirits of our sisters," Irina said, her face glowing with the inner light that had made her a star. "Only with their help will we succeed."

The chanting grew louder and faster and the weird, swaying dance more frenzied. The wands in the blank spots began to glow orange as if they were burning from within. Wisps of golden mist rose and curled around them, undulating in the dance.

"Nifty trick, eh, Watson?" Holmes said in his ear. Watson tightened his grip on the shotgun.

"Now we must conjure the demon," Irina said. "Call him up! Compel him to appear!" The chanting changed again, and Watson could have sworn he heard two extra voices and saw the golden clouds of mist take on the vague shapes of two women.

"On your guard," Holmes muttered. "Here it comes."

A column of green fire burst out of the ground at the center of the circle, filling the air with the stench of burning sulfur. Crouched at the center of the flames like an animal at bay was the man Watson had seen in the alley—The Fox.

"Mindless cattle," he snarled, turning his ugly sneer on each witch in the circle in turn. "Paper dollies, dancing too close to the fire. I will destroy you!" He pointed toward Irina, and green flames shot from his fingertips. Someone in the crowd behind them screamed, but the chanting grew louder, and the spurt of fire was blocked as if by a wall of glass inches from Irina's face.

"Notice his choice of victim," Holmes said, sounding amused. "Very clever."

"Your powers are useless here, demon!" Irina shouted. "Your evil is nothing against our circle of light."

"Is that so?" The Fox sounded as amused as Holmes. "But your circle is broken." He shot more flames at one of the clouds of mist, and it shuddered. Watson could have sworn he heard Grace Reed cry out in pain. "Sorry, dearest Adaline," the Fox went on, turning again. "Once again, your plans will fail." He fired more flames at the second cloud of mist.

But this one didn't shudder. "Arrogant to the last, Von Fuchs," a woman's voice spoke from it, the same voice he had heard at the McRaney mansion. "How inspiring." The mist resolved into the shape of a woman and seemed to grow more solid as the Fox's flames tried and failed to touch it.

"Is that Adaline?" Watson asked.

"Of course not," Holmes said, though his face had gone pale. "But we're meant to believe it is."

"You think I fear you and your little bovines, woman?" the Fox said. "Do you think you are the first coven who has sought to vanquish me?" He turned again and shot more flames at the other cloud of mist. This time they penetrated the shield, and an unmistakable scream of agony tore through the fading night. As the sun edged over the horizon, the women holding the rod began to shudder, and their voices as they chanted trembled as if they were in pain. The mist faded, and the rod caught fire.

Adaline's voice rang out again. "Sherlock!" The detective had raised his pistol and aimed it at the fiery specter. "Help us!" Adaline's spirit cried. "Join us, Sherlock, please! Help me!"

Sherlock's face twisted in grief and rage as he tossed the pistol away. "Don't lose him, Watson!" he shouted. He grabbed the hands of the women holding the rod just as it crumbled into ash, keeping the circle complete.

"Now!" Adaline and Irina cried out in unison. All the members of the circle raised their hands as the sun burst over the hilltop. The rays of sunlight seemed to flood into the golden mist of Adaline's spirit and pour around the circle. The Fox screamed and fell to his knees as the light flooded over him, extinguishing his flames. A huge, dark shadow like a monstrous dog rose up and blotted out the pink and purple sunrise sky. Then it dissolved like smoke in wind and disappeared, leaving a small, trembling man crouched at the center of the circle.

Adaline's spirit was fading. "All clear, Sherlock," she said, her voice weakening and echoing around them. "The coast is clear." Then she disappeared, dissolving into the light.

Holmes broke the circle and snatched up his pistol. "No!" Irina cried as he pointed it at the crouching figure of the Fox.

"Do it." The weird, commanding quality was gone from his voice; he looked and sounded broken. "I am exhausted, little man." He looked up at the pistol Holmes had pointed at his face. "You cannot imagine how little I care what happens to me now."

"Sherlock, remember what Adaline said," Watson said. He kept his own shotgun aimed at the Fox just in case. "It's all right now. The coast is clear."

In the distance, they could hear sirens coming closer—lots of them, from the sound. The white-robed witches were starting to flee, running for their cars at the foot of the hill.

Sherlock lowered his gun.

Lestrade got his man. He arrested Josef von Fuchs, a/k/a, the Fox, on two counts of murder and one count of aggravated assault for his attack on Irina Russell. The cop didn't seem the slightest bit bothered by or interested in any supernatural or otherwise unexplained details of the case. "Hinky stuff happens all the time, Dr. Watson," he said as the German was led away in handcuffs, docile as a lamb. "You can't let it bother you."

Watson got his bloody shirt and jacket back. As their last task before calling it a very long day, he and Holmes burned them in a barrel on the roof of Mrs. Hudson's building. "Nice pigeons, Watson," Holmes said as the birds wheeled overhead.

"Thanks." He hadn't felt so tired since the war, and he still wasn't sure exactly what he'd seen. But he felt an unfamiliar sense of satisfaction he thought he could learn to like. Whatever had happened, they had helped take an evil out of the world that had been there before, and that was something.

"Where do you live?" Holmes asked.

"In my office, same as you," Watson said. "Why?"

"It's damned inconvenient, isn't it?" The detective lit a cigarette. For a moment, Watson thought he recognized the lighter and panicked. Then Holmes turned his hand and the shadow moved, and he saw it was an ordinary lighter. "Mrs. Hudson can't find a tenant for the top floor apartment."

"Mr. Rosenbaum's place."

"That's the one. She wants too much money for a flat in this neighborhood."

"Yeah, she does. And Grace's getting murdered in your office won't do her any favors."

"Indeed." He smoked as the barrel fire burned. "Of course, with two of us throwing in together, we could probably swing it."

For a moment, Watson thought he was kidding, that this was some weird, insulting white man's joke. But from his face he seemed serious. "We probably could at that."

"There are two bedrooms, plenty of room," Holmes went on. "We should be able to stay out of one another's way easily enough."

"We should," Watson agreed. He was sick to death of sleeping on the cot in his examining room.

"And with business likely to pick up, I will need someone reliable nearby to assist me," Holmes said. "With cases, of course."

"Of course." He doubted Sherlock Holmes would ever be an easy roommate, but he'd never be boring. "We could try it and see how it goes."

Holmes smiled. "We could indeed."

HE-WHO-KNOWS

Derrick Belanger

EAGLE EYE CURSED HIMSELF FOR MAKING A FOOL'S ERROR. WHILE TREKKING his arduous journey from his tribal home, the careful and observant warrior tripped over a rock jutting from the ground. He twisted in the fall, stumbled down a rocky hill, and slammed the right side of his torso into a boulder. His body was now bruised, his right shoulder slashed and bleeding. Wincing, Eagle Eye cursed his fortune, for now He-Who-Knows would not see a careful and observant fighter but a bumbling fool asking the great one for advice. He-Who-Knows, the man who solved the impossible riddle of Wolf Rider's tomb, the man who showed Eagle Eye's tribe the way of storing the harvest through the cold months; the man who legend claimed had been birthed by Father Sky and that is why he was all-knowing and all-seeing.

Blood still oozed from the deep gash in Eagle Eye's right shoulder, and if He-Who-Knows refused to see him or dismissed him out of boredom as the man of knowledge was wont to do, then his journey would be for naught and his tribe would be at war with the Shadow Walkers. Still, he knew he could not fail, that he must complete his mission, for if he did fail, he would still be a dead man, cast out from his tribe and forced to be a solitary hunter. He envisioned this grim scenario and saw himself living off the meager twigs and berries of the forest, hunting the four-legged ones on his own, destined to die a slow death through starvation or disease. Perhaps his own tribe would perish as well at the hands of the Wild Men of the woods. Eagle Eye brushed aside his fears as he climbed the seventeen stone steps up to the chiseled granite rooms of He-Who-Knows.

At the top of the steps was a door of thick pelts. As per the ritual for calling the gatekeeper, Eagle Eye took a loose rock beside the entryway and banged upon the exterior cave wall three times and waited. Soon the pelts moved aside and a hooded figure emerged. A white-haired woman with a turned up nose eyed Eagle Eye carefully. She said nothing to the man, her mouth a thin line, her green eyes looking into the man's soul. Eagle Eye finally said, "I am here to parley with He-Who-Knows."

"Young man," the woman answered. "With your wounds, it is not He-Who-Knows you should seek but Healing Hand. Come, they both await." Eagle Eye held himself as tall as possible and steadied his breathing, trying his best to compose himself and not reveal his pain and exhaustion. Once he calmed and steadied himself, he stoutheartedly entered the cave of He-Who-Knows only to lose his composure when the skins and furs were pulled back revealing a chamber unlike any the brave had ever seen. Eagle Eye had expected to find a somewhat barren cave with furs on the ground for sleeping, some painted figures on the walls, and perhaps a pit for fire. The dwelling had some of these features, but at an intricate level which Eagle Eye never knew existed.

Surrounding the walls of the cave were stumps and slabs covered in plants, herbs, and soot. The center of the room did have a single fur, that of a grizzly bear which lay between several odd seats. One was a long chair cut into a massive log, wide enough to hold two people. The seat and backing were cushioned with tall grasses tied and twined together. Two stone chairs faced each other on opposite sides of the head and arms of the bearskin rug, before the hearth of the cave. A small fire was burning in the pit and Eagle Eye noted that a slab had been removed from the cavern's ceiling, revealing a hole through the roof to the open air, so the smoke could escape into the sky. A man sat in each of the stone chairs, both smoking long clay pipes. One man was strongly built, with skin as brown as a nut, dressed in thick pelts, a dense and billowing moustache above his lips. The other man was striking. He had piercing silver eyes, jet-black hair and a pale, gaunt face. His nose looked much like the beak of a buzzard and his lips were as thin as his frame. He wore a loose cloak, and when he spoke, it was in a high-pitched airy voice almost as if the wind which whistled through his cave had merged with the man and they spoke as one.

"You have traveled a great distance Eagle Eye, son of Thunder-Over-Plains, leader of the Valley Walkers. Ah, surprised that I know your identity, eh, but who but the Valley Walkers adorn their necklaces with the beaks of crows, and who, but perhaps your brother wears a vest of elk hide instead of bison, a symbol of your lineage. Yes, I know all about you Eagle Eye, from your odd amber eyes almost scarlet in their hue, and I know for one such as you to consult me, the matter must be most urgent."

"Ev- ev-everything you speak is true," stuttered Eagle Eye. "Your wisdom is proof that you are a master of sorcery."

"Not sorcery, though I am well versed in the, shall we say, abstract arts. But everything which I have said comes from simple observation, from not just looking but seeing with intent. You are noted for your incredible vision, but you need to use both your eyes and your-" here He-Who-Knows extended his long arm and pointed to his head.

"Before you explain your purpose," said Healing Hand, after extinguishing his pipe and rising from his seat, "I must get my supplies and tend to your wound. Please, join us by the fire."

Eagle Eye sat in the long wooden seat and was soon joined by Healing Hand at his side. He was surprised to see the man take out a needle and thread, and after crushing some herbs into a bowl and creating a paste, the muscular man rubbed the balm into Eagle Eye's wound causing the warrior to wince, but he held his composure, even as the doctor inserted a thin, stone needle below his flesh and began to sew the wound shut.

While Healing Hand focused on the medical problem, He-Who-Knows urged Eagle Eye to explain the purpose of his journey.

"It was three moons ago," the brave began, "when my brother led a hunting party into the woods pursuing a small herd of deer. They did not travel deep into the woods for they know the boundaries of the Shadow Walkers, and know not to upset the truce which we hold dear with the strange ones who speak the odd tongue. When the sun had returned to Father Sky, my brother, Rattler's Bite, and his party had not returned. Father ordered me to lead a band of warriors to find my brother.

"Their trail was clear and by the time the sun began its descent to rest, we found my brother and what remained of his braves."

"What remained?" questioned He-Who-Knows. He had extinguished his pipe and now sat, eyes half closed, head tilted forward, elbows resting on his knees, and fingers steepled before his face.

"Yes, what remained. The scene was an utter nightmare. The forest floor was coated in blood. Pieces of my fellow warriors...bones, a leg, a few hands... were all that remained. There were pieces of elk bone and fur on the ground as well. Several small trees were felled, grasses and bushes trampled. We shivered at the horror before us and fell to our knees, praying to the Creators asking what had caused such bloodshed. The Shadow Walkers are known for their strange rituals, their sacrifices to the Dark Gods of the Underworld, but this was a brutality almost inhuman in its savagery. After our time of prayer, we were about to retreat home when we heard a low moaning in the distance. We came across my brother, severely beaten, his body crumpled against the body of a pine tree.

"He was weak, barely breathing. I gave him water, and he explained the horror which had occurred. The braves had tracked the deer to the woods. They were ready to strike when they heard loud whistles, calls, and stamping. The deer began to flee to the plains, but some were confused by the noise and ran straight into a mob of the Wild Men. They were crazed, eyes blazing, wearing their cougar skins, and using their claw weapons."

"Claw weapons?" asked Healing Hand.

"Yes, my friend," answered He-Who-Knows. "The Wild Men of the Woods imitate the great cat of the forest. They wear its skin and use carved stone blades strapped above their knuckles to imitate the attack of the lion."

"Yes," continued Eagle Eye, "and according to Rattler's Bite, they tore apart the elk which ran directly into them; then, seeing my brother's band, they turned their attention to our men. Rattler's Bite told me it was like the Shadow Walkers were more animal than man, like they were possessed by evil spirits. They attacked the braves, not just with their claws, but with their teeth. They tore them apart, ate their flesh, thrashed their bones upon the ground, stamped on them, and tossed their bodies asunder. Rattler's Bite said that he fought with several of the men, but they were too much for him. He was beaten with wooden clubs, kicked, and only survived because one of the Wild Men lifted him up and threw him into the forest. He knows not why he was not pursued and killed. He heard them laughing and taunting and making their wild calls before returning back to the darkness of the forest."

Eagle Eye stopped in his story and bit his tongue while Healing Hand finished running the thread through the shoulder's flesh, biting off the fiber with his teeth and tying it.

"You shall be well, my friend," said Healing Hand as he gathered his supplies from the ground. "Take heed, young brave. In one week's time, your arm shall be well, and you shall need to remove the thread from below your skin. Your village healer can assist in this endeavor." Eagle Eye bowed and thanked Healing Hand for his assistance.

"A-hem," coughed He-Who-Knows, perturbed by this interruption, "please return to your story."

"With the help of Fox Runner, one of my braves, we lifted my brother from the forest floor and left the scene of the attack. We traversed over the plains that day and returned to our tribe. Soon after our return, my brother's soul left his body."

"And who was with your brother when he left the earthly realm?" questioned He-Who-Knows.

"Why Mending Leaves, my father's chief healer, was with my brother. He lay Rattler's Bite in his hut, used his herbs, chanted, and prayed, yet he could not keep the soul within this realm."

"And the body of Rattler's Bite? Did it receive a proper burial?"

"Yes, Mending Leaves said the proper rites and laid my brother to rest."

"Just Mending Leaves?"

"Mending Leaves and his apprentices. They buried my brother after my father ordered a day of mourning for our fallen warriors."

"Ah, I see," said He-Who-Knows, leaning back slightly and nodding his head.

"Is that important?" questioned Eagle Eye. "Have you seen something which I have missed?"

"Mayhaps," answered He-Who-Knows, revealing no other thoughts. "Pray, continue."

"Once I returned, I reported to my father who became as furious as the storms for which he is named. He vowed to smite the Shadow Walkers and send them all to the Heavenly fields. Father vowed to lead the attack, but Mending Leaves stayed Father's hand."

"'There is more he wishes to speak of,' Mending Leaves said of me.

"'Yes,' I agreed. 'There is something amiss with the attack, for I noted strange chunks of the forest trees missing as if some giant took a bite out of the trunks. The forest floor was flattened and appeared as though a boulder was dragged over the ground. I cannot say what has caused such damage, but I do not believe the Shadow Walkers, even with their savage ways and in such a state as Rattler's Bite spoke of, could cause such destruction.'

"'All the more reason for us to strike!' roared Thunder-Over-Plains. 'The Shadow Walkers could have a deadly weapon, perhaps a God on their side. We must be the first to attack! Smite them down before it is too late!'

"'Your anger is fierce and our warriors true, but I fear the Shadow Walkers may have a beast or weapon which even our braves could not defeat.'

"'You speak not as Eagle Eye, son of Thunder-Over-Plains, but as a coward,' spat Father.

"'Nay, the boy is using his vision to see that which most others do not see,' countered Mending Leaves.

"'I wish there was a way to know,' I lamented.

"'Fear not, for I believe there is,' explained Mending Leaves, and he suggested that we consult you, He-Who-Knows.

"It took both Mending Leaves and me to stay Father's hand and seek your advice. I have been granted three moons to persuade you to assist us in this matter. If you deny me then I shall be cast out from my tribe as a failure. If you can use your extraordinary vision to see where my mind is clouded then I shall bring your answer to my father. I only pray that it does not lead to war."

All was quiet for a moment. Then, He-Who-Knows picked up his pipe, stuffed it, rose from his seat to get a flaming twig, relit his pipe, took a few puffs, and returned to his seat.

"You spoke of strange chunks missing from the trees," said He-Who-Knows after exhaling great wafts of smoke. "Tell me, were the missing chunks like that made by the gnawing of a beaver or like that made by the stone of an axe?"

"It was closer to an axe, though something was amiss...it was as if parts of the tree were ripped away by powerful hands."

"Ah," answered He-Who-Knows, "and the ground, was it completely flattened, or was some of the soil turned as well?"

"I only saw the ground flattened."

He-Who-Knows moved his lips and seemed to chew on this information. Then he turned towards Healing Hand.

"Eagle Eye has a different solution in mind than the two he presented, aye Healing Hand, one which he knows to be the correct path but yet has not spoken it."

Healing Hand harrumphed in agreement.

"He-Who-Knows, you are correct," explained Eagle Eye. "Your vision truly is that of your Sky Father, for I know your father was one of the Gods. I propose not that you advise me, but that we journey together tomorrow to the home of the Shadow Walkers. You are most respected among all men. Parlay with them. Find out if they truly attacked my brother. Find out what beast caused the destruction of the forest."

He-Who-Knows let out an odd silent chuckle. "Your proposal is wise," answered He-Who-Knows as streams of smoke rose from the side of his mouth and flowed like a reverse waterfall into the air, "yet your depiction of my parentage is far from the truth. My parents, like yours, were both flesh and blood and sprang forth from their earthly mothers before them. As for your proposal, you are now using your Eagle Eyes. I do speak the strange tongue of the Shadow Walkers and have parlayed with their healer. They call me the Fabled One and allow me to walk amongst them. I have assisted their leader known as The Elder, and I have gained their respect and admiration. The Shadow Walkers know much of the ancient ways from the times when the Star People walked among the Earth. Very well. We shall all three leave at first sun tomorrow. I must spend the evening in preparation. The Hooded One shall see to your food and lodging."

That evening, Eagle Eye slept very little for he kept being awakened by strange noises from the main cavern room. Sounds of chipping stone, constant footsteps, and odd mutterings could be heard deep into the night.

Eagle Eye leapt from the floor when he was awakened. A member of the Shadow Walkers stood over him, his body suited in a cougar skin, the feline's top jaw a cap upon his head, his visage blackened, sharp claw weapons were strapped above his knuckles.

The brave jumped at this intruder, but he was twisted around and thrown to the cavern floor.

"Careful, young Eagle Eye," said the Shadow Walker in a familiar, high-pitched voice. "We do not want you opening your wound which Healing Hand craftily sewed shut, and delaying our journey."

"He-Who-Knows?" asked Eagle Eye in disbelief. He could not understand how the man had not only taken on the clothing of his enemy, but with his slight stoop and makeup rounding his facial features, he appeared to have changed into a completely different person.

"It is I, young brave," said He-Who-Knows mirthfully.

"I did not know...it is like magic," said Eagle Eye, and he tentatively reached towards the face of He-Who-Knows to see if it was real.

"It is good that you did not know," answered He-Who-Knows and let the warrior poke his visage to show he was a real man. "I do not want my identity known until it should be revealed. Come, Healing Hand is prepared for the journey. We must clothe you."

Soon after, the three men, dressed in the outfits of the Shadow Walkers, supped and then began their trek through the forest. Eagle Eye kept pulling at his clothing, uncomfortable in the skins of his perceived enemy which clung tight to the body.

"Put your mind at rest," Healing Hand told Eagle Eye, with a friendly pat on his back. "The clothing you wear ensures our safety."

"Safety," grumbled Eagle Eye. "Are we truly safe? My people would slay me if they found me in such garb, and the Shadow Walkers may do the same when they discover my identity."

Healing Hand gave a reassuring, comforting smile to the young brave. "He-Who-Knows received his name not for the mistakes he makes. If he believes we need these garments then they are a necessity."

The men traversed the forest floor at a quick pace, weaving around hills and mesas until at mid-morning, they had come to the border of the Shadow Walkers' territory.

He-Who-Knows stopped at the border and turned to his companions. "Before we go further, you must each wear one of these." The tall gaunt man opened his satchel and removed stone plates, each with a string of hide through them and forming a necklace.

"What is it?" asked Eagle Eye after taking the tablet from He-Who-Knows and analyzing the weird markings on the front, which resembled a six-pointed star.

"It is a talisman, and it will keep the wearer safe."

"I trust your sorcery," said Eagle Eye and he slipped the necklace over his head.

"Hah," laughed He-Who-Knows, "Sorcery! It is no more sorcery than...." He-Who-Knows stopped in mid-sentence and jogged a short distance away from his comrades.

"What is he doing?" Eagle Eye asked Healing Hand.

"Teaching," answered Healing Hand with a knowing smile upon his face.

"Eagle Eye," called He-Who-Knows, "Run to me."

"What?" asked Eagle Eye.

"Run to me!" shouted He-Who-Knows.

Eagle Eye turned to Healing Hand who shrugged his shoulders as if to say, "Don't ask why. Just do it." And so he did.

Eagle Eye sprinted towards He-Who-Knows and the wise man stood stoically. Eagle Eye was a few yards away when He-Who-Knows thrust out his hand, palm up.

Eagle Eye came to a stop.

"Very good, Eagle Eye, but why did you stop?"

"You told me to stop."

"I did no such thing," corrected He-Who-Knows. "I merely lifted my hand."

"But that means 'stop'."

"Ah, to you it does. To a stranger observing us and unaware of our customs, he may have thought I held out my hand and with my magic I used some invisible force to make you stop. But, in reality, it was a signal no more magical than if I said the word aloud."

Eagle Eye nodded, but he was not sure why He-Who-Knows had put on this demonstration. The wise man answered his unasked question by holding up the Talisman. "To many dangerous creatures, this symbol means the same thing to them as holding up my hand meant to you. This will tell the creatures to stop, and they will. These necklaces will protect us. Consider the symbol on the talisman to be language, not magic."

"But if we need the talisman, it must mean that we are in danger. It is why I brought my trusted knife," said Healing Hand. He had run after the brave and now joined his friends once more. He now revealed a small double-edged blade strapped to his waist.

"Yes," answered He-Who-Knows, "for we are most undoubtedly walking into a trap. I believe I know the nature of the trap, and if I am correct then your weapon will not be much help to us. The question which remains is who shall spring the trap upon us."

Before Eagle Eye could ask He-Who-Knows about the nature of the trap, the austere man dashed into the woods. Eagle Eye turned to Healing Hand who gave a nod of his head and both chased after their learned friend.

"It is best not to ask questions now, lad," Healing Hand told Eagle Eye through quick breaths as they ran between the trees. "Whatever he is up to, he will let us know when he wants to let us know."

They continued on for a while before He-Who-Knows skidded to a stop.

"Why are we stopping now? Is this another lesson?" asked Eagle Eye as he and Healing Hand came to the side of He-Who-Knows. "Are we near the village of the Wild Ones? What is wrong?"

He-Who-Knows' narrow face had turned pale. His brows furrowed and his lip twisted up in a sneer. "The Shadow Walkers would never allow three men, even dressed in these garments, to run this far into the woods without stopping them and asking who goes there."

"What does this mean?" asked Healing Hand. "Have the Shadow Walkers fled?"

"They have fled...or worse."

The trio carefully crept through the woods, approaching the village of the Shadow Walkers. When they finally brushed aside the shrubbery and branches to a clearing near the village, they could see it was the worst of their fears.

The village was in ruins. The huts were flattened and smashed. Crushed bodies were all around. Blood coated the grassy clearing floor.

"What madness is this?" asked Healing Hand.

"Not madness," answered He-Who-Knows. "Rage."

The three men began wandering through the wreckage. Healing Hand would stop at the bodies that were mostly intact to see if there was any sign of life. He-Who-Knows checked the ground in several places before heading towards one of the wrecked huts. Eagle Eye just wandered through the carnage, not sure how to comprehend what he was witnessing. It was as if the Gods themselves had attacked the Wild Men. Bits and pieces of bodies littered the ground, mixed in with the flattened and splintered wood of the village huts and fences. The few bodies with heads still attached to torsos showed faces frozen in states of absolute horror.

A great chill overtook Eagle Eye. He knelt down, clutched his chest and shook uncontrollably. Eerie whispers were heard in his head. The language was unknown, perhaps even inhuman. *What is happening to my mind?* he wondered. He felt a deep sense of foreboding, that whatever force was causing the chill approached.

Eagle Eye was snapped from his thoughts at a loud whistle and call from He-Who-Knows. The brave looked about himself. He was kneeling, but he was fine, his skin a normal warmth to the touch. He pulled himself up off the ground and ran to He-Who-Knows.

He found the wise man with Healing Hand kneeling by his side in a hut, which, though smashed, still had a portion of its back wall standing. Inside the splintered remains, the two men were hovering over a torn and ravaged young man. His body was together, but horribly slashed and broken. The wall must have shielded him from the main blows of the attack, but Eagle Eye could see that the man's wounds were mortal. He would soon succumb and his spirit would be taken. Healing Hand was comforting the young man, and checking his pulse while He-Who-Knows conversed with the injured lad. A farm hand, guessed Eagle Eye, from the thick callouses and tanned skin of working in the fields all day. The two of them spoke in the harsh, guttural tongue of the Shadow Walkers. Blood trickled from the farmer's lips as he spoke. He-Who-Knows asked the man a question to which he responded the same word spoken harshly twice. Then a burst of hacking coughs came to him; his body convulsed and twitched, and at last expired. He-Who-Knows led his companions in a short prayer over the body before closing the lad's eyes.

"What did he tell you?" Eagle Eye asked He-Who-Knows.

"He confirmed what I suspected. He said that a living boulder appeared from the air and destroyed the village."

"Is it the wrath of the Gods?" asked Eagle Eye.

"Nay, it is the cause of one man," He-Who-Knows answered grimly.

Eagle Eye was about to ask who was the man responsible, for he could see that He-Who-Knows had deduced the answer. Before he could, Healing Hand suddenly fell to his knees and crumpled over. "So cold," he shivered.

He-Who-Knows was quickly at the side of his companion. "It will pass soon, my friend."

"I experienced this too," confessed Eagle Eye. "Before you called me to the dying one."

"The beast is close," surmised He-Who-Knows. He assisted Healing Hand to his feet after the chill had left him. "We must act fast if we are to dispel it. Come!"

He-Who-Knows led his comrades to the edge of the destruction. He then began searching around until he spied a clearing. "There!" he called. The area between the forest and the settlement was flat and almost clear of wreckage. "We shall use that area. Hurry! We must clear it of debris. If the creature attempts to come through again and is repulsed, its master may withhold it."

The three men hurried. Eagle Eye and Healing Hand picked up the few logs and sticks coating the ground. He-Who-Knows emptied his satchel that contained several more stones with the strange six-pointed star. He spread the stones out in a large formation, circling the clearing.

"How will you slay the beast?" asked Eagle Eye when the three had met up again in the center of the circle.

"Not slay - release," answered He-Who-Knows.

"How can you allow such a beast to live?" stormed Eagle Eye. "It has devoured an entire village and slain many of my tribe's best fighters!"

"Not devoured, Eagle Eye. The beast which the Shadow Walkers called Wind Whisperer is a beast not of this Earthly realm. It comes from the Heaven not of the sky but beside the Earth. It would take far too long to explain now," explained He-Who-Knows, anticipating Eagle Eye's questions. "The creature knows not what it does. If a herd of bison were to stampede through your village, would you believe they had ill intent? Nay, you would not. Neither does this Wind Whisperer. The beast, like the bison, is a beast of horns and hooves, not of the flesh eaters. The creature is being driven mad by the man using it to attack our realm.

"Fear not, for there is a way to save ourselves and the beast. Here is what we must do. Eagle Eye, today, you shall show true courage. I need you to act as bait and summon the Wind Whisperer."

"Summon the beast?"

"Yes, I need you to step inside the circle of stones but remain at the edge. You shall then remove the stone from your neck and throw it outside the circle. The beast will sense your vulnerability and will appear within the circle. Healing Hand, you will remove Eagle Eye from the circle when the beast appears. Take care to ensure the circle is not broken. When Eagle Eye is safe, I shall sever the connection the beast has to this world."

They agreed to the plan and readied themselves for the difficult task. Eagle Eye entered the circle staying close to the edge. Healing Hand stood behind him, at the ready to pull his comrade from the danger of the Wind Whisperer. He-Who-Knows was on the opposite side of the circle. He had walked the circle several times, making odd hand gestures at various stops and chanting in a tongue like none Eagle Eye had ever heard. At last, he motioned for Eagle Eye to remove the stone from his neck. The brave did so and threw the six-pointed star outside of the circle. All was silent. They waited. Nothing. Then, Eagle Eye felt a slight chill on his skin, as if the wind had picked up into a strong breeze. Harsh whispers flooded his head and the brave crumpled to the ground.

This time the whispers were much stronger, and the cold came on like a sudden blizzard. The whispers rose to a deafening roar in his skull, and the brave felt as if his head might split open. Then, he felt the presence of something before him. Something large, a living mountain was suddenly present, and through the whispers, he felt the pain of this beast, its fury, and it was directed at him.

Eagle Eye felt his body lift off the ground, and he thought perhaps the Sky Father had come to take his soul to the Heavenly realm. Then, his vision cleared, and he found that he was not in the arms of a God, but in the arms of Healing Hand who had lifted the brave over the protective circle without breaking the line. After going a few steps, Healing Hand and Eagle Eye collapsed to the ground. Both men turned to see a creature like none other they had seen before. Its body was a massive mound of solid rock coated with sharp spikes. Its head was a like that of the goat though with short horns more fitting for a bull. The monster stood on four hooves, but they were not spread out for walking or running, but used for balancing. The beast roared. Then like a turtle, its head withdrew into its body as did the legs, which turned the soil up as the creature became a living boulder of destruction. It charged forward at the fallen men, and Eagle Eye was certain that they would be crushed. When the creature hit the edge of the circle of stones, it actually bounced back, repulsed by some invisible force. The creature kept rolling forward and smashing into the wall, trying its best to break through and not understanding what was stopping it from crushing its prey. Suddenly, light started sparking around the creature. The Wind Whisperer pulled itself out of its shell. It stood up, head pointed towards the heavens. Eagle Eye could not know for certain but felt a sense of calm and peace from the creature. Its body was enveloped in a glow of light, then suddenly, it was gone. Its form dissipated into the ether.

Eagle Eye stared at the sky for a moment. Hardly believing that where there was a monster before was now nothing but air. "He did it!" called Healing Hand. "He-Who-Knows has stopped the beast!" Both men stood up and realizing what had happened jumped and shouted whoops of joy. Then just as fast as they had started their calls of triumph they stopped cold. For across the circle, sprawled out on the ground, was the pale form of He-Who-Knows.

It took a full hour before He-Who-Knows was able to speak coherently and another before he could walk again.

"Your sorcery is powerful and knowledge profound," Eagle Eye told He-Who-Knows. The warrior had spent the hours praying for the wise man's recovery and when seeing that was a certainty, thanked him ceaselessly.

"My friend, you speak the truth of my knowledge, but it was not sorcery that sent the beast back to its homeland, just as it is not sorcery that allows the birds to fly nor is it sorcery which causes water to fall from the sky. Would you call it sorcery if I had built a cage around the beast?"

"No, of course not, but-"

"But that is precisely what I did," interrupted He-Who-Knows. "I built a cage around the beast and sent it back to its home. True, I did not build the cage out of wood, though my movements around the edge of the circle were just as specific as the workers who hammer nails to construct a prison. I did not send the beast home in a vessel on the sea, but in a vessel of my chanted words. So, it was not sorcery, my friend. I simply used the tools I needed to solve our problem."

Eagle Eye did not understand what the wise man was saying. Indeed, it sounded like He-Who-Knows was speaking of magic and sorcery. Eagle Eye looked to Healing Hand for guidance, and the healer gave him a wink as if to say, "It is better just to agree with him," and so even though Eagle Eye puzzled at the wise man's words, he nodded in agreement nonetheless.

The trio then took some time to cut away their clothing, removing the cougar head, claws and sleeves of their Shadow Walker attire. He-Who-Knows wanted to ensure that the Valley Walkers did not mistake them as enemies when they made their way to the village of Eagle Eye.

"Now, my friend," He-Who-Knows said to Eagle Eye, "it is time for us to return to your people; though, I fear that the man responsible for this horror will have escaped our grasp."

"But, why?" questioned Eagle Eye. "He does not know what has occurred here."

""That is where you are wrong," explained He-Who-Knows as the three men began their return journey to the Valley Walkers. "The man responsible for the Wind Whisperer would feel the beast being severed from his control. He would feel a burst of energy equal in scope to my energy loss when the beast was released. He knows undoubtedly, that he has failed in his mission. Oof!"

He-Who-Knows stumbled over a rock and was caught in the firm grip of Healing Hand before falling to the path floor.

"Steady yourself, friend," cautioned Healing Hand. "Your energy has not fully returned. You must not drain yourself of your life force."

"Thank you," said He-Who-Knows regaining his composure. "What would I do without my friend? I should be lost without you, my dear Healing Hand."

The three men stopped to allow He-Who-Knows a moment's rest. "It is good for you to rest. We would not want another incident of the Ivory Box upon us," said Healing Hand and both men let out hearty laughs. Healing Hand turned to tell the tale to Eagle Eye, but he stopped when he saw the youth pensive, his face black and his nerves frayed.

"What is it lad?" asked Healing Hand.

"I must hurry back to my people," explained Eagle Eye. "I do not wish to abandon you, He-Who-Knows, but I must see if the villain who caused this horror has truly fled. The man responsible for all of this...I believe I know his identity."

"Ah," said He-Who-Knows. "Tell me your deduction."

"The man who did this was Mending Leaves, my father's healer. He was the last person to see my brother alive, and perhaps it was he who smote my brother, not the wounds from the great beast. It was he who suggested I go to you, He-Who-Knows. It was he who intended for me to lure you out of your cave to where the Wind Whisperer could destroy us all. If he had been successful in his task, I am certain he would have sent my father to his doom and then used the beast to control my people. He would have taken on the role of village chief."

He-Who-Knows stared wide-eyed for a moment then burst into applause. "You have proven your skill in deduction and truly deserve the name of Eagle Eye."

"Then I am correct? Mending Leaves is my father's enemy?"

"Nay," chuckled He-Who-Knows. "You are wrong."

"Why do you mock me?" asked Eagle Eye feeling insulted.

"Do not take offense, lad," answered Healing Hand. "He-Who-Knows has this way about him. You have impressed him, even if you have erred in your conclusion."

"My friend speaks the truth," explained He-Who-Knows. "Your deductions are close to being sound, for Mending Leaves is a villain in this affair; however, he is an old man, hardly capable of controlling a Wind Whisperer. Also, a man controlling such a beast could barely move as all of his energy would be consumed in holding the beast at bay."

"But there is no such man, is there?"

"I fear, sadly, that there is."

"I do not know of who you speak."

"I believe you do know," explained He-Who-Knows. "You just cannot accept it."

"That is not possible," Eagle Eye said with a shudder, his mind reeling.

"Nay, lad, I am afraid the solution is within the realm of possibilities. For you need to look at the facts. You found your brother, Rattler's Bite, alive, but weak. He was brought back to your village where he was seen by Mending Leaves. Soon thereafter, he was declared dead and supposedly buried before anyone else could see the body. I am sure that your brother did not die, that Mending Leaves filled an empty grave with nothing but soil. This gave the impression that your brother's remains were put to rest, or perhaps to be safe, he had another body at hand to take its place. I am certain that Mending Leaves concealed your brother within his own home.

"Hidden away in the home of Mending Leaves, your brother would control the beast, in a state of weakness; his body becoming more disfigured as it suffered under great restraint, but for good reason. Once the Wind Whisperer had smote us, Mending Leaves would send your father and his braves to attack the Shadow Walkers. They would have suffered the same fate as the Wild Men."

"But then how could Rattler's Bite lead? He would have an unprotected village of women and children. Very few braves would remain behind," questioned Eagle Eye.

"Ah, I believe your brother is not acting alone. We know he has Mending Leaves as an ally and possibly some other Valley Walkers, but not enough to mount a coup. I have heard word of a gang of mercenaries, outsiders rejected from your tribe and others, seen roaming the valley and attacking travelers in groups of two or three. I believe Rattler's Bite is controlling that gang, for though they are as yet still too small to mount a direct assault on a tribe, they could take over one such as yours left in a state of weakness."

"But my brother was next in line as tribal leader? All he had to do was wait to take over the Valley Walkers."

"But he did not want to wait, and he did not just desire to be leader of your tribe. As is custom with the Valley Walkers, the village may reject the elder, and the people may choose a successor by a vote. The Valley Walkers are well known for their sense of fairness, of right and wrong. Even if Rattler's Bite ascended to power, there are those within the Valley Walkers who would have stood against him. Those such as you. Rattler's Bite did not want the possibility of his brother overthrowing him."

"You speak the truth, yet it cannot be the truth, for surely my brother, my flesh and blood would not turn against me."

"I am afraid Eagle Eye, that your love is blinding you. Let us return to your home, for there you shall see the truth with your own eyes."

Eagle Eye doubted the reasoning of the wise man until they reached his people and discovered that Mending Leaves was gone. The ground that contained Rattler's Bite's body was turned and revealed itself to be empty. All was explained to Thunder-Over-Plains who both cheered at the return of one son and wept at the loss of another.

He-Who-Knows and Healing Hand stayed for two moons and then left to find Rattler's Bite. "Your brother did not just want to be leader of the Valley Walkers. He wanted great power, power over many tribes. Indeed, he still has such wants and desires. It is up to Healing Hand and me to stop him."

Eagle Eye wished to join them, but He-Who-Knows commanded him to stay.

"Your people need you, Eagle Eye. Your path is as leader, not destroyer," explained the wise man.

After the two left the village of the Valley Walkers, Thunder-Over-Plains forbade Eagle Eye from saying that Rattler's Bite was still alive.

"Rattler's Bite died when you returned him to this village, such is what the Valley Walkers shall believe. The creature who caused such death and destruction is not of my flesh anymore."

Eagle Eye felt this was true, for the person he brought back into camp did not resemble his brother. His head had become swollen and his neck motioned back and forth almost serpent like. Perhaps a better name would be that said by the dying Shadow Walker that Healing Hand had comforted. That Shadow Walker in the crumpled hut had called out the name of the beast that destroyed his people. He-Who-Knows translated the name as the Living Death but it was the word in the odd tongue of the Shadow Walkers that struck Eagle Eye as appropriate. He could not be certain if he was saying the name right, but he believed he had the sound of it. Rattler's Bite was dead. His enemy had a name:

Moriarty.

SHADOWS OF TIME

Tom Olbert

MY NAME IS DR. JOHN WATSON. MANY OF YOU KNOW ME AS THE chronicler and companion of the legendary Sherlock Holmes, the great detective. Holmes and I have shared many intriguing and often terrifying adventures. But, none…not even the nightmarish, otherworldly events I witnessed at Arendall Manor… can compare with the tale I'm about to impart.

It began as most any other day at 221 B Baker Street, London. Holmes was bitterly criticizing me, as he so often would, on the colorful embellishments with which he accused me of lacing my accounts of his cases in Strand Magazine. I did my best to ignore his familiar rebukes, trying to enjoy a good cup of tea. I'd learned to take his cold criticisms in stride. Mrs. Hudson came to my rescue, announcing the arrival of a client. I stood as an attractive young lady presented herself at the door. "Miss Penelope Winthrop, Mr. Holmes," Mrs. Hudson announced.

"Mr. Holmes," Miss Winthrop announced with a slight inclination of her head. Removing her hat, she preceded to enter. There was something odd about her, I thought. Nothing I could quite put my finger on, just a curious sense of…well, confidence. Pluck. One might almost say machismo, were one to transplant the young lady's bearing to a man. There was something odd about the tone of her voice as well, though I wasn't sure what. "I apologize for the abruptness of my arrival, Mr. Holmes, but I have urgent need of your services. I am of course prepared to pay quite handsomely for them. Just name your price."

"Won't you sit down?" Holmes asked, filling his pipe. "May I present my associate…"

"Dr. Watson," she interrupted. "A pleasure to meet you, sir," she said with a glance in my direction and just a hint of impatience in her voice.

"The pleasure is mine," I managed, a bit taken aback.

"May I offer you a cup of tea?" Holmes asked, lighting his pipe.

"Thank you, no, Mr. Holmes. I'm afraid time is rather pressing at the moment. And, what I'm about to tell you will be rather difficult for you to accept. Or, even understand."

I started at so impertinent a suggestion. I glanced at Holmes, fearing a surge of indignation from him. But, his demeanor remained characteristically cold and distant as he turned and stared off pensively, taking a draw on his pipe. "Yes, somehow I thought it might be," he said. "Perhaps you'd like to begin by telling us who you really are, and why you've disguised yourself as a young English lady, when clearly you don't wear the role very convincingly. Your gate is hard, your manner foreign. Your failure to curtsy upon introduction tells me you are uneducated to local custom. The awkwardness of your movements informs me you are unaccustomed to wearing lady's clothing. Your accent is neither English, European, nor American, though seems to contain tonal derivatives of all three. Most curious." He turned in her direction. "More striking still is your scent. In place of the sweet fragrance of a lady's perfume, I detect the lingering stench of something recently burned."

I began to feel a bit uneasy, though I wasn't sure why. "Very impressive, Mr. Holmes," the strange young lady said with the hint of a wry smirk crossing her lovely features. "I see Dr. Watson hasn't exaggerated your talents."

"A mercy, since he has exaggerated everything else about me," he said with a fleeting grin crossing his lips. I felt my lip wrinkling at Holmes's confounded flippancy. And then, my jaw dropped as a swirl of something like silvery glowing mist enveloped our young visitor, a multitude of glowing mites like fireflies covering her for a moment and then disappearing into thin air. I blinked and stood aghast at the sight that met my eyes. Miss Winthrop sat there, suddenly in a completely different costume than the one she'd worn upon entering. The dress and hat were gone, and in their place the most incredible costume I'd ever seen. Like finely polished black leather in the form of a man's jacket and trousers, in a style completely foreign. And, the young lady's light chestnut hair was no longer styled as it had been moments before in a luxuriant mass of curls. It was now shortly cut and styled in a most scandalous fashion. I had to pinch myself on the arm to see if I was dreaming.

"I take it that is your normal attire," Holmes said, remarkably calm and collected under the circumstances. "I suspect we'll find your real name as unfamiliar as your manner of dress."

"My name is Agent Lee Sabrin," she said. "And, as there is no equivalent concept in your era, I can identify myself only as a field operative of the Temporal Enforcement Agency of the Global Federation. I come from a time period which, on your calendar would be the early thirty-second century."

My head swam. In that moment I was certain I was dreaming. "N-now, see here, young lady…" I finally managed, wishing very much I had a brandy within reach. "I'm just as entertained as the next chap by the scientific flights of fancy of Mr. Wells, and these parlor tricks of yours are impressive, I'll admit but… time travel? Preposterous."

It was then she opened a most odd-looking satchel on the floor beside her. Inexplicably, I'd failed to notice it earlier. She extracted from it a most curious device. A metallic cylinder about the length of a man's forearm. A tri-pod of metallic rods telescoped open from the cylinder's base and she set the odd contraption standing in the middle of the floor, a strange flashing red light pulsing from the top of it. I approached with caution, squinting curiously at what I took to be some kind of electrical contrivance.

It was at that moment that our mysterious visitor pulled back the sleeve of her jacket, revealing an odd sort of metallic bracelet. Or, device, as I then learned. She manipulated the strange object in some way. There was a blinding flash of light.

When my vision cleared, I stood in awe, time swirling around me like a whirlwind, eons flashing by in seconds. I saw titanic saurian beasts. Glaciers forming and receding. Woolly mammoths and saber-toothed tigers. I saw the construction of the pyramids in a heartbeat. I saw cities consumed in brightly colored mushroom-shaped clouds. Cities on the ocean floor. Cities in orbit above the Earth. Cities on the surface of the moon…

Another flash of light.

Suddenly, we were back at 221 B, as though we'd never left. "I trust you gentlemen are now convinced?" The young lady asked.

"Adequately," Holmes replied, quite unaffected, it seemed. "And, that curious burnt stench I detected earlier… I smell it freshly now. An effect of temporal displacement, I assume?"

"Yes," Sabrin replied. "Air friction caused by localized sub-atomic transduction."

"And, that device?" he asked, pointing at that flashing red light contraption still standing in the middle of the room.

"A time beacon. It provides a time traveler with a reference point for the return journey. Like a safety tether."

I'd scarcely caught my breath, my head still reeling. "You mean…you couldn't have found your way back here without that?"

"Not with any degree of accuracy, no. General epochs and geographic regions are easy, as you just saw. But, time is fluid, and like a rushing river, difficult to navigate. A skilled operator can pinpoint a target within a few days. If extremely lucky, perhaps a few hours. But, to get us back here at the precise moment we left, I needed the beacon. If I'd been even a few minutes off, we might have run into ourselves, causing a temporal paroxysm resulting in…well, without getting too technical, suffice to say there'd be a sizable crater where London used to be."

I nearly collapsed, supporting myself with a hand on a chair. "My word," I said, breathlessly. "I'm thankful Mrs. Hudson didn't stroll in here and disturb that device."

"It doesn't work that way, Dr. Watson," Sabrin sighed with an air of exasperation. "The time displacement device fixes on the beacon at a particular moment in time. It doesn't matter what might have happened after that moment. I am a professional, you know."

"Which brings us to the obvious question," Holmes interjected. "What need does a 'professional' such as yourself have for the…admittedly incomparable… but nonetheless antiquated services of a consulting investigator such as myself?"

Sabrin looked slightly irritated at the way Holmes phrased the question, but let it go. "The purpose of time travel, Mr. Holmes, is to learn more about other eras. The opportunity to observe the legendary Sherlock Holmes in action, outside his native era would be a valuable experiment."

"In other words…you're an ambitious young professional eager to impress her superiors and hopeful I can solve a mystery for you that would advance that end?" Holmes asked with another fleeting smirk. The tight-lipped look on Sabrin's face was even more irritated now, her cheeks flushing red. I confess, it brought a smile to my face. "Well, then…please outline the problem for me."

She cleared her throat. "Here in London, circa 1941, a man was…will be found dead in the underground. Mauled by some unidentified animal. Our time agents stationed in that period surreptitiously ran a DNA scan on the body…"

"What kind of scan?" I asked.

She rolled her eyes. "A kind of cellular analysis that reveals the heredity and identity of the individual. We found the dead man to be an 11th century Viking warrior who mysteriously disappeared in 1066. Stranger still, DNA analysis of the saliva remnants in his wounds identified the animal that killed him as a velociraptor, a creature extinct some 65 million years."

Holmes cocked an eyebrow. "A curious conglomerate of temporal incongruities, to say the least. Well…so intriguing a case, I surely cannot decline. Come, Watson. The game's afoot."

For a moment, I thought Holmes was joking. Then, I remembered he never joked. "Holmes, you can't be serious! The idea of hunting prehistoric monsters in some future age…" Before I could protest further, that blasted flash of light happened again, and we were someplace else. Stifling a curse, I looked around, pleasantly surprised to find myself in comfortable surroundings at least. A pleasant enough room, though the lighting was of a kind I'd never seen. And, I heard a woman singing in some atrocious style, something about 'We'll meet again,' or some such. I looked for the singer, but she was nowhere to be found.

Agent Sabrin turned a knob on a curious-looking brown wooden box, and the singing abruptly stopped. "Radio transmission, Dr. Watson," she explained.

"My word. Signor Marconi would have been impressed," I noted. It was then I noticed Agent Sabrin's clothing had changed yet again. She now wore a loose-fitting cream-colored blouse and an outrageously short skirt. Her hair was now in a completely different style, longer, with an odd twist. I saw that Holmes and I had changed attire as well, both dressed in dark suits the like of which I'd never seen. "How is this done?" I asked, even then realizing the answer would probably have been incomprehensible.

"Devices called nanobots…swarms of mechanical creatures smaller than dust motes…reconfigure our clothing on a molecular level, so we fit in with whatever era we visit."

"Oh yes, of course," I muttered.

"I see electricity has replaced gas," Holmes observed. "Where are we, Agent Sabrin? And, when?"

"A London flat in 1941. My field supervisor, Agent Fallon instructed me to bring you here." She glanced about, her brow furrowed. "His beacon led me here," she said, opening a closet door to reveal another of those red-flashing cylinder devices. "It's set with a temporal range of about two hours, but I'd expected Fallon would be here."

"Curious he'd step out and leave his radio device still receiving and the lights still up," Holmes remarked, looking over the room. "And, I see the chain is still on the door." Holmes opened the door to the bedroom and looked inside. Holmes abruptly glanced over at me, a most grave expression on his face. "Watson, if you would?" He motioned for me to come over.

Fearful of what I might find, I hurried into the bedroom. There, on the floor was sprawled the figure of a man faced down in a pool of blood. "Still warm," I whispered to Holmes as I touched the body. "Recent. Please, stay back, Miss…Agent Sabrin," I said as she entered the bedroom. I instinctively blocked her path, trying to hide the grisly sight of the corpse behind me.

"Out of my way, Doctor," she said, rudely pushing past me. "I have to identify the body. Yes," she sighed, kneeling beside the dead man to get a clear look at his face. "That's Fallon." She looked at me. "Cause of death?"

Cold as a soldier in battle, I thought. "Multiple stab wounds. Crude, barbarous job of butchery."

"Obviously not a break in," Holmes stated. "All the windows are locked from the inside. And, that acrid burnt stench still lingers in this room. Your supervisor was obviously murdered by other time travelers, Agent Sabrin."

"If they killed him, that means he was on to something," she said. She reached into her satchel and extracted a strange matching pair of small devices. One she held against the dead man's head, the other against her own.

"Whatever are you doing?" I asked.

"Direct memory retrieval," she answered. "If the synaptic pathways aren't completely collapsed yet, I might still be able to get a memory residue. Quiet, please."

What seemed like several minutes ticked by infuriatingly slow. "Well?" Holmes demanded.

"Borough High Street and Long Lane. Something about…twelfth row up, third from left. That's all. It's gone." She put the devices away.

"Not much to go on," I said.

"At least it's an address," she said, running back out into the main room, Holmes and I behind her. Opening a book on a side table, she looked up something and picked up a curious looking device, turning a small wheel-like mechanism with her finger. "I need a taxi cab at 27 Tower Hill," she said into the device. "The name is Beresford." She set the device down.

"I see Mr. Alexander Graham Bell's invention caught on," Holmes remarked. Taking that time beacon contraption out of the closet, Agent Sabrin retracted its telescopic legs and stuffed it into her satchel.

"Why do that?" I asked.

"Wouldn't do for anyone to find it, now would it?" she replied. "Please, hurry." We followed her down a flight of stairs to the street below where a most remarkable contraption pulled up to the curb. A motorized horseless carriage. I'd seen their like demonstrated on occasion…slow as a snail, those. This one could outrun any horse. A petrol-fueled internal combustion engine, Agent Sabrin explained. I had to admire the technical inventiveness of the twentieth century, but…given the noise and the stench, I rather think they should have gone with steam power.

Night was coming on as the cab driver drove us past Saint Katherine Docks and across the Thames. I was shocked to see so much of my beloved London standing in ruins. "Whatever has happened?" I asked, afraid to hear the answer.

Agent Sabrin leaned close to my ear. "Please, Dr. Watson…Try to watch what you say in front of the locals," she whispered to me urgently, glancing at the cab driver. We arrived at our destination. What was left of it. Half-fallen buildings and mounds of rubble where houses had once stood. We'd just stepped out of the cab and paid the driver…Agent Sabrin's miraculous nanobots could also reconfigure currency, apparently… when a most hideous sound, like the wailing of a banshee howled through the night. "Blast, here comes Gerry," the cab driver remarked, hastily barreling off without even bothering with change. I looked around, puzzled. In the distance, strange beams of light projected straight up from the city swept the night sky. And, though the sky was clear, a sound like thunder roared above. I wondered if we'd arrived at Armageddon.

"Come on," Agent Sabrin said, grabbing my arm. "We have to get to a shelter."

"This way," Holmes shouted, pointing to a half-collapsed building and leading the way.

"'Doesn't look very safe, Holmes," I said, looking up at the sagging timbers. "It's liable to collapse on top of us."

"Help me with the cellar door, Watson," Holmes instructed. Agent Sabrin and I complied, and closing the door behind us, we found ourselves in a black, dank pit of a basement.

"My kingdom for a torch," I said. As though in reply, a burst of light flooded a corner of the basement. Startled, I looked around and saw a glowing sphere of brilliant white light in Agent Sabrin's cupped hand. "No end to the scientific wonders at your command, is there, Agent Sabrin?" That horrid thundering racket and dreadful wailing went on and on. I could feel the ground shaking, as though under a giant's footfalls. "Will you please tell us what the devil's happening?" I demanded, my irritation and apprehension growing apace.

"Dr. Watson," she said with a sigh, lowering her eyes. "I'm sorry, but there's nothing I can tell you. There are rules to time travel. There are aspects of your future I'm prohibited from revealing to you, for fear your actions after returning to your native era might alter that future in unforeseeable ways."

"You needn't tell us anything, Agent Sabrin," Holmes remarked. "As the facts speak for themselves. Evidently, DaVinci's old dream of mechanized flight has become a ghastly reality." He looked up at the half-fallen roof.

"Aerial bombardment, Holmes?" I asked.

"Obviously. And, given that cab driver's parting remark, it's not hard to guess which country is behind it."

"What a horrid age this is," I said in dismay.

"Just be thankful I didn't take you to Hiroshima," Agent Sabrin said.

"Where?" I asked.

"Never mind. Mr. Holmes…Why did you insist we come in here? Dr. Watson's right. It doesn't look very safe."

"And therefore, unlikely to attract interlopers," Holmes pointed out. "But, it apparently did attract the attention of the late Mr. Fallon, as his foot prints lead directly in here and back out, as you can plainly see." He pointed to a series of black shoe prints on the floor. "I noticed the road tar on the dead man's shoes immediately, and saw the fresh road tar outside as we came up. Obviously, whatever cost Mr. Fallon his life, he found here. Agent Sabrin, shine that light over by that wall, if you would be so good." Holmes placed his feet in Fallon's shoe prints, positioning himself precisely in the spot where Fallon stood as he faced that perfectly ordinary-seeming brick wall. "Twelfth row up," Holmes muttered as he knelt and counted up twelve rows of bricks from the floor. "Third from left." Holmes pressed the third brick in from the left-hand corner. The brick moved. I gasped as a part of the wall fell inward, revealing some kind of secret passageway. "Disappointingly amateurish. Shall we go?"

Agent Sabrin led the way, holding her remarkable light contraption in front of her, Holmes and I close behind. We soon found ourselves in a ghastly labyrinth of gloomy tunnels that seemed to stretch on in every direction. "What is this place?" I asked.

"These tunnels stretch on for miles under London," Agent Sabrin answered. "They link in with the Underground here and there. Time rats have used them since the Middle Ages."

"'Time rats?'" I asked.

"Time-traveling criminals, Dr. Watson," she explained. "From every era since the invention of time travel. Here, hold the light, will you?" I obliged as she removed a small device from her satchel. "It seems we have company," she said, lowering her voice, an audible air of tension to her tone. "Keep very still. I'm picking up multiple contacts all around us," she whispered, staring at that device of hers. "And, one is closing in on us…from straight ahead!"

I held the light in front of me, hearing a ghastly squealing approaching from the darkness. And, a sound like monstrous claws against stone. I held my breath, my heart pounding. My eyes widened, my blood running cold at the nightmarish sight that appeared out of the shadows. It haunts my nightmares to this day. Reptilian, it was. Like a huge lizard, but standing upright, tall as a grown man, with powerful hind legs and long arms. Huge, curved claws on its hands and feet, razor sharp teeth and a lashing tail. Its yellow eyes gleamed in the light I shined on it. It lunged. "Run, Miss Sabrin!" I shouted, stepping protectively in front of the young lady on reflex.

She pushed me aside, pointing some sort of hand-held firearm at the horrid beast. There was a bright blue flash and an inhuman shriek. And, the next I knew, the monstrosity lay dead at Agent Sabrin's feet. "Your chivalry is appreciated, but quite unnecessary, Dr. Watson," Agent Sabrin said, holding her strange weapon aloft. "I had the matter well in hand."

"That, I presume, is a velociraptor?" Holmes asked.

"Yes, and judging by those scanner readings, they're all around us," she said. "Watchdogs, I expect."

"Watchdogs for who?" I asked, looking around, a cold chill down the back of my neck. "What are you up to, Agent Sabrin?" I asked as I saw the young lady kneeling by the dead beast, cutting into its head with assorted instruments from her satchel. "If there are more of those things about, hadn't we best move on?"

"As I expected," she said, reaching into the beast's skull with something like tweezers and extracting a small metallic object from inside. "Cybernetic A.I. implant," she said, wiping clinging, filthy goo off the device. "A way of controlling the animal at a distance, by radio waves. This could come in handy, if I could isolate the frequency." She inserted the little gadget into another device. "Yes..." she said, adjusting a control. "The source of the transmission is...down the right-hand branching tunnel, and to the first left. Shall we?"

I served as torch bearer as we followed the lady's directions. I soon heard wild shouting, many voices raised in a most raucous fashion. And, the sound of metal clashing upon metal. Seeing a glimmer of light coming from a connecting tunnel, Agent Sabrin snatched the light device from my hand and deactivated it, concealing us in darkness. We slipped in silently. Crouching by a hole in the wall we spied into a wide, lighted chamber below. My hair stood on end. What I saw down there was like a scene out of Dante's Inferno.

Two large cages of iron bars. In each, two people fought each other with swords while an unruly crowd of spectators howled savagely, cheering on the barbaric display. I was especially shocked to see that one of the four duelists was a young woman. Tall and strong and clad in a primitive costume of crudely spun cloth, rough leather thongs and roughly hammered metal, like something out of the Bronze Age. Her opponent was an Asian man, dressed in a costume of a much later era, like a samurai warrior of medieval Japan. In the other cage, two men dueled. One a man of African descent, the other a light-skinned fellow in shin greaves and a skirt of leather thongs.

I winced as the woman cut down the Samurai, striking without quarter. She stood in triumph over his eviscerated corpse, her bloodied sword held high, her teeth bared in a savage snarl. The crowd went wild, some cheering, others cursing hatefully. A moment later, the dark fellow finished off his opponent, drawing a similar reaction from the spectators. The scene that next met my eyes was equally horrible. Creatures…pale, dead zombies with blank eyes…patchwork walking corpses with stitches marking their mismatched bodily parts and metallic studs and wires protruding from their shaved heads, approached the cages. Cruel slave handlers unlocked the cages, prodding sadistically at the surviving duelists with sparking electrically-charged rods of some kind. The man and woman snarled and cursed at their tormentors. As the slavers held the prisoners at bay, those zombie things dragged the dead bodies out of the cages and carried them to a row of tables, like surgical gurneys lined up at the edge of the chamber.

My stomach turned at what I saw next. Those animate dead things were dismembering the bodies and sewing their salvageable organs and extremities together with other human scraps and inserting mechanical components, presumably to create more of their own horrid kind. I prayed I was having a nightmare, even realizing my darkest fears couldn't have conjured this. "It's like a carnival in hell," I whispered. "What are we seeing?"

"It's what we call a prim fight, Doctor," Agent Sabrin whispered. "Forced death matches between primitives illegally abducted from various eras. They tend to attract high stakes gamblers from the future."

I could see she was right. A horrid, scrawny young man, a rogue with garish tattoos on his neck and bare arms and jewelry dangling from his ears, like some wild savage, was walking about the crowd, directing his thugs to pay the winners and collect from the losers. "What's this, now?" the devil asked. "Come up short, have we?" he said, addressing some poor bloke who couldn't pay his debt. "Well…the raptors must eat, mustn't they? Mike, Tony…Take him!" Two of his toughs dragged the poor wretch kicking and screaming into the tunnels while the crowd laughed. I gasped as I realized his fate.

"This accounts for the dead Viking," Holmes whispered. "No doubt he was one of those poor gladiators, killed while trying to escape. And, the young lady down there, judging by her curses, a conglomerate of ancient Scythian and Sarmatian dialects spoken in the Persian region, is no doubt one of the half-legendary Amazon warriors mentioned in Greek mythology."

"And, the dark fellow?" I asked.

"Use your senses, Watson. Judging by the healed-over whip scars on his back, the manacle scars on his wrists, and his American accent, he's undoubtedly a slave of our native century, sometime before or during the American Civil War."

"And, the chap he dispatched looked to all the world like a Roman legionnaire straight out of Caesar's day," I said.

"Very astute, Watson."

"Agent Sabrin," I asked. "If this barbarity is illegal, why try to hide it under a city?"

"Time rats are fond of war zones, Dr. Watson," she replied. "No one notices if people disappear or dismembered bodies turn up." She glanced at those horrid operating tables. "No shortage of spare parts."

"For constructing more of those zombie creatures, you mean."

"Necrons. They sell for a high price in various eras. They make good ore haulers in 23rd century asteroid mines. Or, cannon fodder in the 24th century Mars colony wars."

"Criminality springs eternal," Holmes remarked. "Now, to the task at hand. The only security I see are those three men lined up against the rear wall by the tunnel entrances. What are those silver rifle-like contraptions they hold?"

"32nd century ion blasters," Sabrin replied. "Like my sidearm, but much more powerful. They could clear that whole room in seconds."

"Well…I see those pipes lead directly over them," Holmes observed, studying the ceiling. "The three of us could slip in above, drop down and seize those weapons with considerable ease, if we only had a diversion to distract the attention of the guards."

"I think that can be arranged, Mr. Holmes," Agent Sabrin said, taking that device containing that horrid brain implant gadget out of her satchel again. "If you two gentlemen will follow me?"

Over my objections, Agent Sabrin courageously crawled, slowly and cautiously along those pipes toward the far wall. Holmes followed, with me bringing up the rear. As we crouched there, perched directly above those lethal-looking blokes with their death ray guns, I could see Agent Sabrin was adjusting that gadget of hers in some way. I soon found out why.

"Boss…" one of those slaver rogues said with a panicky look on his face, lowering a small rectangular box from his ear. Some kind of radio communication device, I assumed. And, I could have sworn I heard the muffled sound of a man's anguished screams emanating from it. The chap holding the device whispered something to that horrid tattooed man.

"Bugger," I heard the 'boss' curse. "Uh…ladies and gentlemen, if I could have your attention, please…" he called out, raising his arms to quiet the gamblers. "We seem to have encountered a slight malfunction with the raptor control signal. Those two blokes I sent into the tunnels just now, have…well, uh…there's a slight problem, but no need for undue concern. Please, no one leave until accounts are settled. Uh… if you could please just keep still and quiet until we get this sorted out." He urgently gestured for his three guardsmen to turn and aim their weapons at the tunnel entrances. The satisfied smile I saw crossing Agent Sabrin's pretty face told me she was the cause of that 'slight problem.' Somehow, she'd interfered with the transmission controlling those bloodthirsty beasts in the tunnels and turned them on their former masters.

"Now," she whispered. The three of us dropped on the three unsuspecting guardsmen from behind, catching them off guard. I promptly flattened my man with a solid right while Holmes made short work of his chap with those far eastern martial arts techniques of his. Agent Sabrin knocked her man senseless with a blow to the base of his skull with the butt of that ray gun of hers. We all three snatched up those blaster rifle things.

"Necrons…intruder alert!" the tattooed blackguard shouted. "Destroy!" He pointed his finger at us. My blood ran cold as those ghastly pale dead monstrosities lumbered out of the shadows, coming straight for us, like legions of the damned.

"How do you fire this confounded contraption?" I asked, quickly regaining my senses.

"Just point it and pull the trigger, Doctor," Agent Sabrin answered.

Holmes and I did as she instructed. I was amazed at the lack of kick to the strange weapon. I felt only a mild electric vibrancy as I fired. But, their destructive power was horrifying. Like blue lightning bolts, blasting those zombie-like monsters to charred bits in seconds. The gamblers began vanishing into thin air before my eyes. Revealing bracelets like Agent Sabrin's under their jacket sleeves, they winked out one by one in bright flashes like the ones I'd seen earlier. While Holmes and I finished off the zombies, Agent Sabrin blasted the locks off the cages. Seeing their opportunity, the Amazon and the black fellow made short work of those slave handlers, apparently enjoying every bloody bit of it. Can't say I blame them. Agent Sabrin quickly apprehended the wretch with the tattoos and jewelry, bringing him to his knees at gunpoint.

"Ease off, love," the swine stuttered, his eyes wide with fear. "I'm just a small timer, that's all. I just follow orders."

"Whose?" Agent Sabrin demanded.

"None of that. You have to bring me in. I don't say nuthin' 'til I consult with my legal advocate."

"I don't know what the hell's goin' on, but I want answers of my own…" the black chap said through clenched teeth, roughly pulling the rogue to his feet and putting his sword across his throat. "Talk or die." The Amazon crossed her sword over the American's, two blades now against the murderous game master's throat.

"I'd oblige if I were you, my good man," Holmes said. "You're hardly in any position to bargain."

"Look, I don't know nuthin', I swear! I just run the op, the big man takes the lion's share of the profits. I snatch the prims he tells me to and bring 'em here to fight. Then, I take the winners…like these two here…and deliver 'em, that's all."

"Where and when?" Sabrin demanded.

"Don't know 'til I get there. My T.D.D.'s pre-set," he said, tapping a finger on another of those time bracelet gadgets he wore on his wrist.

"Why didn't he use that to escape?" Holmes asked.

"Because I was jamming his time displacement device with my own," Agent Sabrin replied, touching her own bracelet against the man's. "I've just downloaded the time and place for the next slave drop from his T.D.D. to mine. And, it sounds like we have guests for dinner." I heard those lizard beasts squealing, their claws scraping as they made their way through the tunnels towards us. Quite a few of them, by the sound of it. Agent Sabrin tore the time bracelet from the rogue's wrist and tossed it aside, blasting it with her ray gun. "Everyone stand close by me," Agent Sabrin said, knocking the sniveling tattooed wretch aside with a back-handed blow across his face with her gun butt.

"Hey, you can't just leave me here!" he protested even as the ravenous lizard monsters pounced on his unconscious guards, more coming straight for him.

"Talk to your legal advocate about it," Sabrin said as she adjusted her bracelet. There was a blinding flash.

When my vision cleared I found myself outdoors in broad daylight. I winced as I looked up. The sun was a ghastly bloated red orb filling half the sky. The climate was stifling. And, in Her Majesty's service, I've known hot climes, believe me. It was then I felt the cold metallic touch of one of those blaster's muzzles against the back of my neck. I gasped as I saw the faces of our captors. Not quite human by the look of them. Thickly muscled brutes with protruding brows, extended jaws and faces that were a grotesque parody of human features, as much ape as man.

"Everyone remain perfectly still," Agent Sabrin warned, handing her weapon to one of those brutes. "They're vicious when challenged."

"What in blazes are they?" I whispered as my weapon was taken from me.

"Neanderthal/human hybrids," she replied. "Grown illegally in laboratories from spliced tissue samples. Short on smarts, long on aggression and blind obedience. Perfect foot soldiers."

"Can't you get us out of this?" I whispered urgently.

"Given recent events, Watson, I think it a logical deduction her time device is being interfered with, as we saw earlier," Holmes pointed out.

"I'll take that," a slender young man in a plain slate-gray suit said as he removed the bracelet from Agent Sabrin's wrist. "And, that," he said as he picked up her satchel. "This way, please," he said with all the courtesy of a head waiter as we were led away, surrounded by those apish brutes pointing ray guns at us.

"That miraculous satchel of yours again," Holmes remarked. "You left it in the tunnels under London in 1941. How did you retrieve it?"

"It's linked with my T.D.D., Mr. Holmes," she said. "It automatically teleports to wherever and whenever I am."

"That would explain why our clothing has reverted to its original state," Holmes said. It was then I noticed that Agent Sabrin's clothing and hair style had indeed changed back to their bizarre futuristic style. And, Holmes and I were again dressed in the clothes we were wearing when we first met Agent Sabrin at 221 B. "I take it those…nanobot creatures you mentioned earlier are housed inside that satchel?"

"Correct, Mr. Holmes. For all the good that does us."

While Holmes focused as usual on minute details, I surveyed our surroundings. We were in what looked like a military base camp. Huts and other small buildings. At its edge a row of curved metallic poles. Beyond that, a thick, leafy tropical jungle. "Where and when are we this time, Agent Sabrin?" I asked.

"Judging by the size and color of the sun, I'd say we're about a billion years in the future," she said.

I started as something moved just beyond the edge of the fence. A huge shadow. I looked up and caught only a glimpse, but that was enough to make me shudder. A huge, horrible kind of flying thing with outstretched leathery wings and a gaping fanged maw. There was a crash of electrical impulses as that thing…whatever it was…tried to get through the barrier. It flew off shrieking.

"Life has evolved in some dangerous ways here," Sabrin said.

"But the electrical field between those metallic poles keeps the creatures out?" Holmes asked, his tone betraying more curiosity than apprehension.

"Yes, Mr. Holmes," Agent Sabrin answered. "We're safe. For the moment."

It was then our little parade came to a halt. The man in gray laid Agent Sabrin's time bracelet on a long table whereon lay a wide assortment of weapons. Swords, daggers, axes. He placed her satchel under the table and stepped to one side. In a wicker armchair in the shade of a sun umbrella sat a man in a snow-white suit and wide-brimmed hat. He wore garish black-and-white shoes, a black necktie and a red carnation boutonniere. He sparkled with gold and jewels and sipped a cocktail. "Welcome, Agent Sabrin," he said with a broad, genial smile. "Don't look so shocked. I had an agent at the prim fight in 1941. He returned here several days prior to your scheduled arrival, giving me adequate warning to prepare this little welcome. Oh, and one of my informants in the Temporal Enforcement Agency was obliging enough to supply the names of your two associates. You honor me with your presence, Mr. Holmes." He raised his glass in toast.

Holmes stepped forward. "I'm afraid you have the advantage, Mr…?"

"Horatio Paladin Laroche," Agent Sabrin interjected.

"You know this man, Agent Sabrin?" I asked.

"Only by reputation, Dr. Watson. He's one of the richest, most influential men of my era. The T.E.A. has suspected him of illegal temporal activities for years, but we've never been able to pin anything on him. He's too well protected by powerful friends."

"Now, now, Agent Sabrin," Holmes said. "We mustn't be rude to our gracious host." Holmes leaned close by my ear. "Keep him talking," he whispered to me as he took Agent Sabrin aside and spoke with her in private.

I decided to have a go at prodding Laroche's ego. "Well, Mr. Laroche…It would seem that power only has the effect of fueling an insatiable hunger for more power."

"Of course, Dr. Watson," he said, sniffing his boutonniere. "Ambition is after all the driving force of achievement, is it not?"

"And, towards that end…let me guess…you intend on assembling a private army from the best and bravest warriors you can fish from time's river." I glanced at the Amazon and the American.

"Nothing so mundane, Doctor," Laroche answered, a servant handing him a fan. "From their genetic bits and pieces, I intend on creating an entire race of superior warriors. One I shall selectively employ at certain key eras…the rise of the Roman Empire, the Industrial Revolution, the Interplanetary Wars… and, in so doing, turn the course of history in a direction more to my liking."

I was literally nauseated at the prospect. "A tailor-made future, just waiting for you to sit on its throne as self-anointed God-King?"

"Something like that." He finished off his drink and stood. A servant handed him an ivory-headed cane. "Now, to the matter at hand." He signaled to his servants, and his apish thugs brought forward two more prisoners. One a strong-looking young man dressed in medieval chain mail armor, with a cross on his tunic, like a crusader out of the 12th century. The other a young woman with long-braided blonde hair and striking features. She was strongly muscled, dressed in furs, armor and rough leather, like one of the half-fabled Nordic shieldmaidens whose fighting prowess inspired the legend of the Valkyries. Laroche motioned for the Amazon to be brought forward. "Scyleia, celebrated warrior of the Amazon nation of Queen Andromache... allow me to present Hetha, heroine of the Battle of Brávellir, circa 750 A.D. The two of you shall fight to the death for the honor of becoming one of the Eves of my new race." The two women stood facing each other, their keen eyes taking each other in, as though each was sizing the other up for the coming battle.

"And, you, Jeremiah Sanders," Laroche continued, motioning for the American to be brought forward. "Runaway slave turned freedom fighter for the Underground Railroad... allow me to present your opponent." He motioned for the young knight to be brought forward. "Sir Cedric of York, hero of the Third Crusade. Whichever of you survives shall become one of my Adams." The devil smiled and twirled his cane between his fingers.

Sanders bolted forward, a roar of anguished rage rising from his throat as he lunged at Laroche. One of those apish brutes rifle-butted the poor man in the stomach and then struck him viciously to the ground. I reflexively sprang to his side. "Varlets!" Sir Cedric shouted. "Devil spawn!" He moved towards Laroche, as did the two women warriors, but those ape things fired off their blasters in warning, forming a defensive ring around Laroche. The three warriors stopped in their tracks, blasters trained on them from front and rear.

"Fighting spirit," Laroche remarked. "Promising. But, obedience must be learned." He raised his cane as though to strike Sanders. I protested, but two of those inhuman brutes pulled me aside, restraining me.

"A coward as well as a lunatic," Holmes called out.

"Must I make an example of you as well, Mr. Holmes?" Laroche asked, pointing his cane at Holmes.

"You disappoint me, Laroche," Holmes said. "Until this moment, you had impressed me as a daring and adventurous man; that rare breed of man who thrives on challenge. What would you say to a personal contest between you and me?"

Laroche smiled broadly, laying his cane across his shoulder. "What did you have in mind, Mr. Holmes?"

"Rapiers," Holmes said, gesturing at the weapons on the table behind Laroche. "If you have the courage."

"I accept," Laroche declared eagerly, tossing his cane to a servant and removing his hat and coat. "Choose your weapon, Mr. Holmes," the madman said as he removed his time bracelet and placed it on the table.

Holmes removed his jacket and waistcoat and handed them to me. "Holmes, have you taken leave of your senses?" I asked, almost in shock.

"Watch and learn, Watson." Holmes selected a rapier from the table and hefted it, testing its weight. "This one will do nicely, I think." Laroche selected his weapon, and the two men faced each other, their blades shining bloody red in that hellish sunlight. "Have at you, sir!"

And, the duel was on. Holmes was skilled and agile, but it was an even match. Laroche was clearly an expert swordsman, I realized with dread. I'm not sure how long the duel lasted, but for me it seemed an eternity. My heart was in my mouth, my nails digging into the palms of my hands as those half-simian monsters encircled the two duelists, wildly grunting and urging the fight. I felt transported back in time to another duel at the Reichenbach Falls. Holmes glanced up, momentarily distracted, it seemed. I nearly fainted as Laroche flung the sword from Holmes's hand and brought his own blade across Holmes's throat. I instinctively sprang forward, only to be blocked by a blaster muzzle to my face. "I yield, Mr. Laroche," Holmes said.

Laroche smiled, handing his sword to a servant. I heaved a sigh of relief. "A good match, Mr. Holmes," Laroche said, toweling his neck. "Thank you for that enjoyable bit of sport. Now…take our 'guests' to their quarters. See that they're well rested, fed and watered. Tomorrow at first light…we'll all be treated to a fine spectacle indeed." He chuckled in delight.

We were housed in dormitories of sorts. The men in one building, the women in one adjoining. Holmes and Sabrin communicated by tapping on the intervening wall in Morse code. Holmes was obviously up to something, I could tell. As usual, he kept his plans from me until the last.

The following morning, our four combatants faced each other in the compound, Laroche and the rest of us looking on. Mr. Sanders and Sir Cedric both selected broad swords from the weapons table. Scyleia, and Hetha selected pikes. Those vile creatures outside the electric fence seemed to be circling, like sharks smelling blood.

I jumped out of my skin as a thundering explosion blasted apart several of those electrified fence poles. I gasped in horror as the monstrosities outside swarmed in, like demons freed from Hades. As the ape creatures turned to fire on the monsters, Sanders and Cedric hacked down two of the apish brutes and seized their weapons, as Holmes had instructed them. Sanders tossed me a blaster. I turned and fired, bringing down several guards. Scyleia, and Hetha hurled their pikes, killing two more guards. A huge shadow fell over me. I looked up and gaped. A gargantuan exoskeletal organism with multiple clawed limbs and shimmering wings was bearing down on me. I fired into it, with minimal effect. The monster's carapace was like armor plating.

Holmes pulled me to safety as Hetha leapt upon the monster's back, driving a sword between two of its armored sections. "Odin!" she cried. Scyleia roared as she drove a spear into another of the monster's weak spots. Sanders and Cedric joined in, hacking furiously at the monster, the four of them finally bringing it down. Laroche and his apes were occupied blasting down a swarm of serpentine abominations and winged beasts. "Gather round!" Agent Sabrin shouted, running up with her satchel. We rallied. Agent Sabrin set some small device and adjusted her time bracelet. There was a flash.

Suddenly, we found ourselves in a most wondrous city of towering silver and glass buildings, a marvelously cool breeze washing over us. I looked up into a now yellow sun glinting off the polished glass walls. Fantastic flying machines buzzed about. "Heaven?" Sir Cedric asked.

"Valhalla?" Hetha whispered.

"Welcome to Arctic City, circa 3122 A.D.," Agent Sabrin said, smiling.

I exhaled. "Well…that was a narrow escape. I'd say we're lucky to be alive, Holmes."

"Luck had nothing to do with it, Watson," Holmes replied curtly. "I had matters very well in hand."

I smiled and shook my head. "However did you manage it, Holmes?"

"Quite simple, Watson. During the rapier duel, Agent Sabrin, acting on my prior instructions, slipped in behind the backs of the distracted guards and retrieved those wondrous nanobots of hers from her satchel."

Agent Sabrin produced a small black box from her jacket pocket. "The nanobots. I simply reprogrammed them to reconfigure the circuitry powering the electric fence, shorting it out."

"Brilliant, Holmes," I said. He barely acknowledged the compliment. "Ahem. Still…are any of us safe with Laroche loose in time?"

"I assure you, he isn't, Watson," Holmes said. "That is, if you followed the rest of my instructions, Agent Sabrin?"

"Yes, Mr. Holmes," she answered with an air of irritation. "While retrieving the nanos, I got my hands on Laroche's T.D.D. where he'd left it on the table, and I re-set it to home in on Fallon's time beacon instead of his own. When the creatures attacked, I took Fallon's beacon out of my satchel and concealed it nearby. A second before I shifted us out, I remotely set the beacon to activate three seconds later. When Laroche shifts out…"

"He'll be drawn back to that very moment," I realized. "And, he'll run into himself."

"A fitting end for a man so obsessed with himself," Holmes coldly remarked.

FEAR OF THE DARK

Melissa McArthur

September 19, 2028
New Boston Prison

"THIS WAY, DR. WATSON." THE GUARD LED ME DOWN A DARK HALL, THE rock floor sloping at a steep grade as we descended to the prison cells below ground, the places where the light didn't touch.

"He's been talking about a creature, asking for you, for Mycroft…" The guard rambled as he shined his light down into the darkness, but the beam disappeared only inches past the bulb.

"Mhmm…" I murmured, following closely behind, my own beam of light moving around the walls and ceiling, revealing nothing but damp darkness and silence.

Soon the guard stopped, turning slightly to a door at his right. He pulled the ring of keys from his belt, jingling them until he found the right one. "Since the grid fell, it's been harder and harder to keep the prisoners contained. No electric barriers, no tracking devices. Just locks and iron bars."

"Certainly enough locks and bars to pass to get down here, sir."

"Indeed," the guard said as he turned the key in the lock. "Mr. Holmes, you have a visitor. Dr. Watson's here to see you."

"Lies…" the voice hissed from the blackness that hovered in the far corner of the cell.

"Now, Mr. Holmes, you know I don't lie to you." To me, he said, "He's shackled — or should be — so if you'd like to go in, you should be safe. I'll have to lock the door behind you, of course. Security. You understand."

"Holmes wouldn't hurt me," I said, crossing the threshold and standing as the guard closed the door and turned the key in the lock.

"If you're sure. He is a convicted murderer, after all."

"That's what they say…"

"I'll be back in an hour." His footsteps faded into the distance as he ascended back to the main floor of the New Boston prison. I sat my flashlight on the floor, pointed up in an attempt to chase away as much of the darkness in the room as possible. The pool of light didn't spread far, certainly not to the dark corner where my partner and friend crouched, presumably chained to the wall.

"So, you've come for me?" the voice in the corner asked, seemingly sane and logical.

"Well, no. You know they wouldn't let me take you out of here. But I do need your help."

"The creature? The deaths?" Chains scraped rock as the man rose, shifted, and came closer to the light. He emerged on hands and knees from the pool of darkness, barely a shadow of the Sherlock Holmes I'd once known. Hair graying and wild, skin pale after three years of perpetual darkness, and once strong body wasted away to skin and bones, he didn't look like the same man.

Except his eyes.

"It's been what, two years since you visited last?" he asked, still coming closer.

I hesitated, wanting to take a step back, wondering how far his bonds allowed him to go.

"Mary's had a child. Yes?" he asked as he looked me over.

"What? Yes. A girl. A year ago."

"You have that look about you. The softened face, the bit of pink thread hanging from your coat, the tiredness in your eyes. Mary isn't well?"

"She had trouble with the pregnancy — but, wait Holmes. I am not here to talk about wives and children." I took a breath and steadied myself. "I need your help. There've been deaths, four of th—"

"Four young men, all strong and resilient, men who shouldn't have died like they did. Is that right?"

"How...? Never mind that. Yes, those four deaths. Two in the quarry, two in the old factory. The police expect more, in twos, and soon. There's no sign of struggle, but preliminary tests suggest they died of sudden cardiac arrest. I've been assisting with the investigation, trying to determine the true cause of death. It appears they were scared to death, Holmes."

"The hell-creatures. They've set their traps; now they wait for their prey."

"What do you mean?" I glanced down at my watch — thankfully there were still windup watches to be found, though the price was high. I didn't have time for his games. "Who told you about all this? The warden said you'd had no visitors."

"The silence told me. It's deafening at times. Here, in the darkness. In the silence." He looked up at me, eyes rimmed in red, a shocking contrast to his pale skin.

"You mean to tell me that *silence* told you about the deaths?" I knew Holmes had been acting strangely since that night he'd told me to run… toward nothing, the night the world changed. We'd run in circles, Holmes at the lead, until we stopped — breathless and sweating — in the same place we'd begun. I still shuddered as I thought about that night, the night that started all of this. In my mind's eye, I returned to the single lamppost that marked the memory forever in my mind.

We'd found ourselves in total darkness that night, the first of many.

"What's happened, Holmes?" I'd asked, grasping onto the lamppost and blinking to try to banish the white spots that further confused my night-blindness. We were investigating the disappearance of a diary of sorts from a wealthy woman in New Bern. We'd followed our suspect into Boston. He'd dashed down an alleyway, and we were in hot pursuit. And then…

"The lights have gone out, Watson."

Well, yes, they have, *I thought.*

"But why?"

"I'm not sure." It wasn't like Holmes to be unsure of anything, particularly if it could be reasoned out, but lately, he'd seemed withdrawn and hesitant. I'd sighed and waited for the street lights to flicker back on, waited for the glow of the traffic signals to reflect off the wet street. I waited for the hustle and bustle of the thriving city to return. It never came. Even the sunlight never returned, the once golden orb perpetually obscured by darkness.

Silence stood heavy in the darkness, an oppressive weight falling down on us. A hand touched my arm. Holmes pulled me closer to him and spoke in a low voice. "When I say, we run. As hard and fast as your legs will take you. We run. Understood?"

"What's going on? I can't run in the dark!" I said, my heart racing at the insistence in Holmes' voice, a voice that never wavered, no matter the threat.

"No time. Just go!"

His hand gripped my arm and pulled me forward, letting go once we both started moving in the direction he intended.

My muscles burned with the effort, and I struggled to catch a breath.

Holmes ran, his long legs taking him farther than mine. Soon he'd left me behind, his distancing footfalls the only sound in the silence of the night.

"Holmes!" I called. "Wait!"

The footfalls stopped.

"I can't see a damn thing!" I shouted.

"Quiet!" his voice hissed in my ear.

I let out a yip that I am not proud of and jumped back, stumbling over the cobblestones.

"This way," he said, taking my wrist in his hand and pulling me with him.

"Where are we going?" I whispered.

"To the light."

I shook off the memory and focused on the immediate problem — the assertion was ridiculous, even for the deranged Holmes who crept toward me across the damp cell floor.

"Stop there, Holmes. Don't come any closer." Perhaps he had gone mad. Years in the dark can do that, can break a man's mind. I wished for my penlight to examine his eyes, to test his reactions.

"You're afraid of *me*..." he said, cocking his head to the side like a bird considering a fat wiggling worm.

"No, I'm not afraid," I lied. "I have my own concerns, of course, but I'm not afraid. Only sensible. I've learned a few things in the past few years about self-preservation dealing with the gangs that rule our streets."

"So the creatures succeeded in bringing down the law?"

"What do you mean, Sherlock? Are you referring to the governor's death?"

Fifty more minutes until the guard would return.

"You wish to know what I know? Then stop glancing at that watch of yours and listen to an old prisoner tell you his tale."

I sighed and crouched down, resting my back against the bars. "Tell me what you know of these hell-creatures."

"They come to me in the silence, in the darkness. They feed on our terror, our fear of the dark."

"That sounds like a twisted bedtime story, not a deduction for solving these murders."

"Do you remember the days before the grid fell?"

When the grid fell, it took everything with it. Life changed in an instant. No electricity, no internet, no television. Even our ham radios — our failsafe — had stopped working. All modern life had come to a screeching halt. With the grid's collapse, society quickly reverted to a primitive state, and the governmental bodies fell with no way to cull the anarchical outbursts.

Holmes continued. "There was perpetual company; there was always contact with the rest of the world. Our cell phones and the internet connected us all. There was always light. Even in the darkest night, there was the faint blue glow of a screen, the twinkling of fireflies in the country, or the bobbing of a flashlight as young lovers strolled down the jasmine-scented streets. Now there's nothing. As much as you've tried in the past few years to rebuild, you've failed. Am I right?"

I nodded. "There's nothing. No infrastructure, no connectivity, no government, *no lights*. We live in a city of perpetual midnight. The governor's death — supposedly at your hands — was the inciting event for the anarchy that ensued."

"It wasn't as it seemed." Holmes looked away. "You believe me, don't you?"

"Was it worth this?" I asked, finally having the courage to ask the question I'd been burning to ask Holmes since his arrest not long after the grid had fallen. He'd been found crouched over the mutilated body of the Massachusetts governor, covered in blood. He'd claimed innocence, fought the civil patrol that had overtaken the police officials, but he lost the fight. He'd been brought here.

"I didn't kill the governor, John."

I took a deep breath and spoke in low, measured terms. "Sherlock, we don't have time to debate your guilt or innocence. There's nothing I can do about that anyway. Besides, that's not why I'm here."

He waved it off, clearly dismissing the claim. "It's no matter, really. The deaths would have started much sooner if I hadn't been imprisoned. And, besides, I might not have figured out their plan."

"The murderers? What's their plan?" I asked, hoping to steer him back to the urgency of the situation. I glanced at my watch. Forty-five minutes.

"The hell-creatures — mystical or alien, I still don't know — have come to feed on us. They've exhausted their own resources and need another venue in which to expand their race."

Maybe it was the gauntness, or perhaps the endless days of darkness, but in the hollow light of the single bulb, my dearest friend was frightening.

"Come now, Holmes. Tell me what you know. Enough with the stories of mystical aliens and tainted governors."

"I am, you insolent interrupter. Now listen." His voice was harsh, scraping against the quiet of the prison cell like chain on wood.

"I'm listening."

He smiled, a twinkle returning to his eye, and a small glimpse of the Holmes he used to be leaked through. "Have you noticed at times there's silence in the area, often coinciding with absolute darkness? It's within the silence, in the darkness, that these hell-creatures visit. I've not figured out how they create such an utter obliteration of sound, but that's when they're present. That's when you hear them. That's when they will kill."

"These are the creatures that spoke to you?"

"No, no…they've not spoken to me. Are you listening? They make no sound. They *steal it.*"

"Hmmm…The reports of the deaths mentioned that there were no screams, no gasps before the men collapsed, at least from what the rare few witnesses said."

"I'd suspect not. The creatures operate in the quietest of times, moving silently in the utter dark, careful not to draw attention."

"What does that have to do with understanding these deaths? These *crimes*?"

"It has nothing to do with it. It's far too late for that. Haven't I said that for years? Isn't that how I ended up in here?! Just trying to save the world and this is the thanks I get…" Holmes retreated to his corner and sat quietly.

"I'm sorry, Sherlock. Truly. Please tell me what to do."

"First we have to get out of this cell. We must go to the light. Time ticks away, if I am not mistaken." He tapped his lean wrist, indicating my habit of checking the time.

"Are you suggesting I break you out of jail?" My voice rose in pitch and broke on the last word. *He is mad*, I thought to myself as I looked down at my watch once more. Forty minutes. Time ticks away, indeed.

"But, of course." He dropped his shackles and stood to his full height, his head turned to the side to accommodate the low ceiling. "I'll be glad to stand fully and stretch." He motioned to the back wall of the cell and said, "Shall we?"

The black sun rose, creeping across the starless velvet sky trying in vain to light the darkness and chase away the demons of the night.

We sat where we'd begun all those years before, leaning on either side of the lamppost, the night dew settling on our skins.

"I cannot believe you tunneled your way out of prison," I said, still incredulous that he didn't really want my help getting out of prison at all. "If you could get out on your own, why did you wait until I'd come?"

"I knew you'd come to see me when you'd exhausted all other options. You were a little angry with me, after all. I couldn't have you sending me right back, could I? I needed you to need me. You've become quite the detective, Dr. Watson, but you're hesitant."

I sighed. He was right. Again. "When you said all those years ago that we were headed to the light, you meant that quite literally, didn't you?" I asked.

"In a fashion, yes."

"Could you *please* explain to me why you brought us here this time?" I placed a hand on the lamppost and rested my weight against it, just as I had the night the world changed.

"I needed to test a theory."

"And what theory was that?" My words were clipped, but Holmes either didn't notice my rising anger or he chose to ignore it.

"Whether or not we were doomed."

"And what did you deduce?"

"The end is coming."

"The end?"

"The one and only. The end of days. But we might be able to stop it."

I shuddered and pulled my coat closer around me.

"I saw it the night we were chasing the thief from New Bern. There's a manhole hidden at the end of that alley. It was partially covered by a dumpster, so I suspect it may not have been covered over by the vandals."

I leaned against the lamppost and stared at him, one of the most brilliant minds to ever exist, and he is basing our search on the possibility that a manhole may still be uncovered years later simply because a dumpster sat by it.

"I suppose it doesn't hurt to look," I said. "Lead the way."

Down the alley waited a faded red dumpster, Property of Bullet Blues written on the side in block letters.

"One of the gangs, I presume?" Holmes asked.

"Yes. They were one of the firsts to take over. Their driving force is the notion that they'll only lose when they've run out of ammunition."

"How original…" Holmes mumbled as he felt around the bottom of the dumpster. "Give me a hand, Watson."

He stood and leaned against the dumpster, motioning for me to join him. I leaned against it as well and readied myself to push.

"One. Two. Three!" We shoved the dumpster with all our strength, which wasn't much between the two of us, but the dumpster slid down the alley a good four feet, enough for us to see the manhole Holmes remembered.

"By God, you were right." I looked at the iron covering, imprinted with City of Boston, and laughed. "You may have found the one surviving piece of old Boston, Holmes."

"Perhaps if we survive this fight, we will claim it for ourselves. In the meantime, help me lift it."

The cover was heavy and wedged quite well into the circular space. Using some scraps of metal we found in the dumpster, we finally pried it loose and looked down into the darkness below.

"After you," I said to Holmes. He shrugged and placed one foot on the top rung of the ladder and descended into the unknown.

The darkness outside was nothing compared to the inky blackness that coated the sewers, the underground caverns plunging us into pitch dark — both night and water.

Our boots did no good fighting against the deluge that crept in and rose continually until we found a ledge that ran along the outer sides of the tunnels. We climbed up and dried ourselves as best we could.

Holmes spoke, finally, breaking the silence that had held us captive since we'd opened the manhole and climbed down. "The hell-creatures first came the night the grid fell. I hesitate to suggest such an outrageous claim, but nothing else is possible: their alien ships must have short-circuited our resources, either shocking them into oblivion or simply stealing the resources entirely. That's very likely the reason we've not been able to rebuild."

He grabbed my arm and turned me to him. I searched his face and could find no evidence of deceit, but his eyes... the way they danced in the warmth of my flashlight revealed glee — at the escape or the return to the game, I could not tell.

"The governor was once a good man, but he had been taken over. I saw it with my own eyes. These alien creatures inhabited his body, using it for fuel, perhaps, but I believe the purpose was to infiltrate our political systems and create the fissures that his death so easily turned to wide crevices. There's no way to tell how long they've been here, setting their plan into motion. I did not kill the man, John. I swear it. He simply exploded. I believe the creatures had something to do with that. It's not their usual method... Perhaps they wanted to see how much terror they could inflict, or maybe they wanted us all to fear them."

"It doesn't really matter now, does it?" I asked, taking back my arm and straightening my coat.

"No, I suppose not."

"A change of pace, then?"

"A moment. You believe me, don't you, John? You must... otherwise you'd not be here."

"Why *are* we here? Why are we in the sewers?"

Holmes sighed at my avoidance of his question. "The sewer is the most logical place for such a creature to nest. They managed to block out our sun, the light source that powers our water cycle, leading to an increase in precipitation. This suggests that they need a lot of water to survive. Also, they hunt in the silence and darkness, two traits that the sewer system has in abundant supply. Not to mention that all of the murder locations have been places that are easily accessible through the sewers. And really, Watson. If you were going to frighten someone to death, what better place than the sewers? These creatures are far more insidious than we've given them credit for. They caused society in its entirety to fall, not just the few who dare to venture below the surface." A hint of the madman I'd seen in the prison cell peeked through his eyes once again.

"Let's get moving before they have a chance to take more lives." I'd had quite enough of Holmes's ranting. I'd never felt such a pervasive annoyance at my best friend before, at his mental gymnastics. A pang of sadness struck me, and I raised a hand to my heart. *There's no turning back now*, I thought.

We walked, waded, and sometimes nearly swam for hours. I felt we were moving in circles, the tunnels all becoming one long chain of icy water and disgusting sludge. Along with the political infrastructure, Boston had evidently succumbed its sanitation to unrest as well.

I climbed up to a particularly low-set storm drain and peeked out, trying to determine our location. "I believe we're under Beacon Hill. Though they're mostly rubble now, those cobblestone streets are quite unmistakable." I climbed down, brushing my hands off, and turned to Holmes. He'd waded somewhat farther into the darkness. "Were you listening to me?" I asked, approaching him.

Holmes raised an arm, stopping me. "Do you hear that?"

"I don't hear anything."

"Precisely. Shine your light this way." Holmes splashed the water in front of him and though the water moved, it made no sound. Even the echoes our voices caused ceased.

"I see—"

Holmes took the flashlight from my hand and turned it off.

"And now I don't see. Why did you do that, Holmes?" I asked.

"How have the other men died, John?"

"Cardiac arr—"

"No! They died of *fear! They were scared to death!*" he shouted, though the words fell flat on my ears.

"How does extinguishing the light make us any less afraid?"

"If we approach the thing we fear — in this case, the dark — we will fear it less, so it will have less control of us."

I didn't quite agree with his logic, but I soldiered on anyway.

Holmes stopped at a dead end. A large grate blocked our forward path. Holmes reached down into the water, his arm submerged to the shoulder.

"We can swim under it. It doesn't go all the way down."

"You *are* mad! There's no way I am putting my head under the water down here. Who knows what kind of bacteria is in this sludge? If the hell-creatures don't kill us, this surely will!"

"Suit yourself," Holmes said as he ducked under the water, coming up on the other side.

I slammed my hand against the grate and cursed.

"There's probably another way. Go back down this corridor and take the closest left. That's the direction I am headed." With that, Holmes waded off.

"Holmes!" I shouted.

He only waved and kept moving.

Once he turned the corner and I could no longer see him, I gave up my hope that he'd turn around and come back for me. I tucked my flashlight in the waistband of my trousers and pulled off my tie. I looped the tie around the grate and pulled the knot tight. At least if I got lost, I'd know which way I'd already been. It was a nice tie, too. I hated to leave it behind.

I wandered back the way we'd come, bearing to the left as often as I could, hoping we'd cross paths.

Then the sounds of my footsteps vanished. The silence fell upon me suddenly like a hand stopping the vibration of a cymbal. Utter silence. All vibrations stopped, as if the hair cells in my cochlea all ceased movement at once.

The hell-creatures, I thought. *They're coming for me.*

I stumbled and fell, falling under the water, and as my head reemerged, I laughed. The very thing I was trying to avoid happened despite my greatest attempts.

I still clutched onto the flashlight, my only lifeline in this dark abyss.

I held close to the wall and climbed back onto the ledge, trying to make myself as small a target as I could.

My thoughts wandered back to my conversation with Mary just hours before. She'd begged me not to go see Holmes. "He manipulates you!" she'd said. I'd kissed the baby goodbye and left, angry and frustrated. Since the world had changed, our once happy marriage had fallen to shambles. And now I may never have a chance to make things right.

I considered calling out to Holmes; perhaps he'd hear me and come back. He knew more about the hell-creatures than I ever would, it seemed.

Alas, the decision was squelched by my fear.

"Fear…" I said. "Holmes said they feed on fear."

I laughed again. Perhaps I was going mad as well.

"Come and get me monsters! You can't make things much worse down here!" I stomped my foot, the sound echoing down the corridor. It was working! The sound started to return — slowly at first and then faster as I grew more confident — and I was safe for a little while longer.

I walked on farther, until I heard the distinct sound of grunting. *Sherlock Holmes!*

I followed the sound, coming back to the same grate where I'd left my tie. I cursed again because there was nothing left for me to do.

I took a deep breath before plunging below the surface and swimming toward Holmes.

"There you are!" I said as I reached him.

"Come to me," he beckoned, the sound barely above a whisper. The madness had returned, obliterating any sign of the brilliance I once knew. "Come, Dr. Watson. See what they've done. Bring your light."

I moved through the murky, frigid water, sloshing my way over to where he crouched in the corner and pulled on a sewage grate.

"Come! There's not much time."

I shined the light through the grate and saw something I'd never expected to see. A nest.

The grate came loose, knocking Holmes back into the water. His head and body disappeared below the surface, though the splash never sounded.

"Sherlock!" I screamed, my voice falling flat in the echoless chamber. Goosebumps pimpled my flesh as a chill ran down my spine. I wedged the light into the crevice that opened when Holmes pulled the grate free and trudged in to grab him. Just as I thought I'd have to go under the water myself, he burst through the surface, gasping and coughing. I pounded him on the back, and he settled.

"I got it loose," he said, smiling at the opening.

"Are we going out that way?" I asked, still confused at the reason for him pulling on the grate.

"No, no! I aim to let them *in*."

"Let who in, Sherlock?" I shined my light down the tunnel and watched as the beam succumbed to the darkness. A heavy silence fell over us, weighty and suffocating. "What's happening? What's coming? What are you letting in?" My voice was swallowed by the silence emanating from the tunnel. I started backing away from the grate as I felt the adrenaline flood my system. Fight or flight. I'd never win the fight. I turned to back away and lost my footing. My flashlight slipped out of my hand and it rolled toward Holmes. The light illuminated his face for a single moment before it fell into the water and lit the murk from below.

"They're coming."

"What? Who?" I asked, scrambling to escape his reach.

"The darkness is coming for us. Are you afraid of the dark, Dr. Watson?" Sherlock Holmes looked up at me and smiled.

And then the light went out.

THE CULVERTON MINE DISASTER

Katie Magnusson

WHEN DR. WATSON HAD GONE WEST AFTER THE WAR, HE HADN'T expected to have a successful medical practice, but he'd thought he could at least make a living. He had anticipated a life of treating wounded miners and sick settlers, perhaps even fending off the occasional Indian attack. He never imagined that the majority of his patients would be prostitutes. Of course, there were a great many facets of his life now that he'd never imagined back home in New York.

Not that he would ever complain. It was immeasurably better than patching up soldiers on the field of battle, the Confederacy just over the ridge…

"I swear on my mother's grave, Doc, I ain't takin' nothin' but the medicine you gave me."

The sarcastic comment brought his mind back to the present. Dr. Watson sighed, secretly grateful. "I may not be as observant as Holmes, but I can tell when you're lying through your teeth, Kitty. Besides, last month you told me your mother was living in Saint Louis."

"She could've died."

"She was dead the month previous."

Kitty grinned, "Guess I'm just used to fellas believin' anythin' I tell them when they're between my legs."

"If your employer didn't hire me to examine you, I wouldn't be down here, trust me."

"Holdin' out for an honest woman? You think any will marry a man what lives in a whorehouse?"

Watson rolled his eyes with a slight smile, "I think there's little chance of a single woman interested in marrying a poor army doctor coming to this town before I'm old and grey. Alright, Kitty, we're done here. As clean a bill of health as I can give any of you, but I'm serious about the laudanum." He fixed the young woman with as stern a look he could. It was, he reflected, the same look he gave Holmes whenever he found a new bottle of whatever the latest trial was in their rooms. Fortunately, the look seemed to be more effective on Kitty than it ever was on his friend. "Opium, no matter what form it's in, is not something to be taken at the merest whim."

"I get headaches, doc," Kitty complained.

"You get headaches because you take laudanum. If you stopped, then eventually the headaches would go away."

Kitty adjusted her faded red corset, and went to the door. "What's the new snake oil this week?" she asked, rearranging her fiery tresses.

"There hasn't been one." Watson refused to be baited, straightening his brown suit, and replying as if they were discussing the weather. "Holmes was horribly disappointed to discover the last was merely camphor and mineral oil. 'Not even a bit of morphine or cocaine to simulate some sort of effect,' he'd complained."

Kitty laughed a little, "Poor dear. Be honest with me, Doc, why's he bother with all those things?"

"It keeps him occupied."

"Takin' quack cures?"

"No, figuring out what's in them. Haven't you ever wondered why snake-oil salesmen never stay in town long?"

Kitty's eyes grew wide, "You're kiddin'."

"Not at all."

Her eyes narrowed again, her expression subtly distrustful. Rather like a cat, actually. "But he still drinks them, don't he?" She smiled at Watson's sigh, "He's an odd one, no mistake."

"On that, Kitty, we are in complete agreement."

Mrs. Hudson was waiting outside the door when Kitty opened it. "Took long enough," she smiled. "Fancy the good doctor was giving you a lecture about the laudanum again?"

Kitty huffed, "Yes'm."

"Your girls are all as healthy as can be expected, given the circumstances," Watson reported.

"You don't have to live here, doctor," the greying proprietress arched a practiced brow at him.

It was an old game by now. "If I didn't, you'd still send for me every month," he said, smiling just a little.

She smiled back, "Even if you were in New York, I'd still have you make the trip out here. Let no one ever say I don't take care of my girls."

You're also a businesswoman, and your clients less than gentlemen, Watson thought to himself, but let it pass. Mrs. Hudson ruled her Baker Street House with an iron feather. Anyone caught 'damaging' a girl was heavily fined, and banned. It was a ban that Holmes was happy to enforce, if ever necessary. As Holmes was fond of telling the men he tossed out, he firmly believed that any man who would beat a woman as a man would beat a disobedient dog was no better than the dog itself. Watson felt the same, which was one of the reasons their rent was practically nonexistent.

He started up the stairs as Mrs. Hudson prepared to open for business. He and Holmes shared quarters on the second floor. When Watson first arrived it had been Room 22, but after the affair with the men from Utah cemented their friendship, Holmes prevailed upon Mrs. Hudson to permit them to turn his room and the room adjoining into something resembling a very small flat. Mrs. Hudson's girls called the combination 221.

Watson found Holmes standing by the window, lighting his pipe as he looked down at the street. "How fares the fair sex this afternoon, Doctor?" he asked in his gentle drawl. That voice had given Watson pause the first time he'd heard it, to the good doctor's embarrassment. Watson still didn't know much about Holmes's past, only that he'd been banished from his family's plantation for supporting the Union and fled west to find a new life for himself. What possessed him to set himself up as an independent detective out here remained a mystery.

Even though the War had been over for three years, there were still those who didn't care for turning to a 'Rebel' for help, even if he had been a Unionist. Holmes derived great satisfaction from watching those sort swallow their considerable pride.

"They're not going to be giving their customers any unpleasant diseases, though I certainly can't say the reverse. I don't suppose you'd be willing to steal Kitty's laudanum bottle, would you?"

Holmes chuckled, his gaze still on the street, "She'd have no trouble obtaining another. It would be as effective as the time you threw out my cocaine."

Watson coughed. "Yes, well. At least you agreed to moderate your use."

"Miss Winter will not be nearly so accommodating."

"I suppose you're right," Watson sighed. "What's so interesting on the street?"

"The Sheriff is coming." Before Watson could comment that this was hardly an unusual occurrence, Holmes added, "He's worried."

That gave Watson pause. He sat down in the chair by the window, "I won't bother asking how you can tell."

Holmes's gaze focused firmly on his friend, "You winced as you sat down, is your wound bothering you?"

"Been on the leg all day is all."

Reassured, though possibly unbelieving, Holmes turned his attention back to the street. "Lestrade is mounted, despite the fact that the walk is short from his office to here. He's donned his most official looking derby and jacket, but didn't take time to polish his star, as he is so fond of doing. In addition, he's tugged on his mustache no less than three times in the process of tying his horse to the post."

"Aha. If the Sheriff is worried, and he's coming to you…"

"Then the case must be of grave importance," Holmes finished. There was a knock on the door. "He didn't even stop to talk to the ladies, there must be something very wrong indeed." Holmes answered, eager anticipation mixing with his concern, "Sheriff Lestrade, please come in."

Lestrade's drooping mustache rendered his face into a permanent scowl, but today a jumble of frustration and worry were clearly visible beneath it. "Thank you, but I'd appreciate you comin' with me right away, Mr. Holmes. There's been a… well, you better just come see it."

"Of course. Watson, can you -?"

"Naturally." He even stood without wincing, grabbing his slouch hat, "Where are we going?"

Lestrade was already headed down the stairs. "The Culverton mine."

"Good Lord."

Lestrade removed his derby to wipe the sweat from his brow, "The good Lord has got nothin' to do with this, Doctor."

The carnage was incredible. Every man in the mine lay dead, arrows sticking up from their bodies. Some of them had even been scalped. There were hoof prints still visible in the dirt, ranging all over the mine.

"According to Mr. Culverton, every last miner was killed," Lestrade said.

Holmes's stony countenance told nothing of his thoughts as he carefully walked among the bodies, stopping to examine one draped over a barrel of blasting powder. A figure all in shades of grey approached the site, tapping an anxious finger against his leg. He was fair haired and fair skinned, soft faced, and clearly a businessman.

"Mr. Culverton," Sheriff Lestrade greeted him, "have you met Dr. Watson?"

"I'm happy to say I haven't needed his services," Culverton shook the doctor's hand with a small smile, "No offense meant."

"None taken. Did you discover the bodies this morning?"

Mr. Culverton nodded, "As I told the Sheriff, I'd only gone to town to place an order for more essentials. I didn't think I'd been gone that long, but you can see-"

"Yes. You didn't hear or see anything else?" Watson asked.

"No. The Indians were long gone."

"This wasn't the natives," Holmes said.

Everyone stared at him. Culverton was flabbergasted. Lestrade cleared his throat, "Mr. Culverton, Mr. Holmes."

"The 'second opinion' you wanted?" Culverton's skepticism was obvious.

"Mr. Holmes has been of some assistance to me the past few years," Lestrade stated with puffed up dignity, "and given the delicacy of the matter, I thought it couldn't hurt to hear his thoughts."

"Except that he's clearly insane" Culverton frowned. "Who looks at a mass of scalped men turned into pincushions, and maintains that dirt-worshipping savages didn't do it?"

"Any man willing to look at the evidence, rather than jump to the obvious conclusion," Holmes said. He approached the group with a respectful tilt of his head to Lestrade. "Our good Sheriff recognized that we haven't had any trouble from natives for months. The last incident was a stagecoach being harassed, just a minor scare to remind us that the natives are still in the hills, and have no intention of leaving. A massacre of this sort is unprecedented. Hence, his desire for a second opinion. I must say, Lestrade, I'm flattered."

"Don't ruin the gesture, Holmes," Lestrade rolled his eyes.

Culverton's frown had deepened as Holmes spoke. Now he looked Holmes up and down, taking in the fawn trousers and black frock coat, the scarlet waistcoat and matching thin cravat, precisely tied against his white shirt, the top hat. His estimation of Holmes was blatantly obvious; an aristocratic Southern dandy.

"And what," Culverton sneered, "do you know about 'natives?'"

"I know they don't shoe their horses," Holmes stated. "I can clearly see the nails in some of these prints. You seem to take some issue with me, Mr. Culverton." Watson was certain Holmes was exaggerating his accent on purpose.

"Just seem to recall hearing about a Southern dandy in town, supposedly on the run after the war. Wonder if you might be him."

"Why should that matter?"

"The fellow I heard of might have supported the Union."

"Yes, one can imagine that would be an unpopular position in the short-lived Confederacy. Judging from your vowels, you yourself hail from the Southeastern coast, North Carolina, perhaps?"

Culverton scowled. "My brother was gunned down by Union soldiers."

"As was my father."

The two men faced each other for a tense moment. It was Culverton who broke first. His face went a little red as he blustered a protest to Lestrade, "Sheriff, my men were killed and scalped, and if you aren't going to do something about it, I will."

"You know what'll happen if a bunch of soldiers go up over those hills?" Lestrade said, "Every last Indian for miles around is going to come down on this town, and then you're really gonna see a massacre. Yeah, we might wipe them out, but not without a whole lot of people dyin' in the process. Rushing into things is the last thing we want to do!"

"Well, while you're 'not rushing,' I'm going to see to the burial of my men."

"At least let me examine –" Holmes's protest was silenced by Lestrade's elbow in his side. "We'll leave you to it," Lestrade said with a tip of his hat.

"Mr. Culverton," Watson said with a farewell gesture.

"Sheriff," Holmes kept his voice low as they walked back to their horses, "those arrows were fired after the bodies lay dead."

"And how the devil did you figure that?"

"If I'd been permitted the opportunity to examine a body thoroughly…"

"I'm not letting a bunch of bodies lay out in the sun all day just so you can experiment on them."

Holmes bit back whatever callous remark he'd been about to make. "Do we agree that the natives weren't responsible?"

"We agree it was unlikely."

"Did you see the hoof prints?"

Lestrade hesitated a moment before confidently stating, "No, I didn't look."

"They were shoed. Surely you at least believe I can tell the difference between the print of a shoed horse and one that is not?"

"… granted."

"It was not a native's horse that rode around that mine, and without a horse, no natives could have killed every man in that mine fast enough that none of them fought back. And unless you think a group of bandits have suddenly taken to murder by bow and arrow, those arrows were planted there, and the men died of something else."

"Something else. Such as?"

"If the physical wounds happened after death," Watson reasoned, "then the men died of some internal distress."

"You are positively scintillating today, Watson," Holmes said.

Watson's jaw dropped. "Holmes, you don't think Culverton poisoned his own men!"

"I think it is a possibility we must consider."

"Some of those men were scalped!" Lestrade protested. "Besides that, Culverton doesn't even have a motive. What profit could there be in killing the men making him rich?"

"Many white men are as familiar with the act of scalping as any so-called savage, if not more so, and those men weren't making him rich, were they?" Holmes challenged. "Culverton's mine has never been terribly profitable."

"Wanted to expand, I think," Lestrade nodded, "Convinced there was more to be had nearby."

"In the hills, perhaps?" Holmes said. "Where do those natives that Culverton was so eager to blame reside?"

Lestrade looked as though he'd been slapped. "He set up a massacre of his own men, just for an excuse to wipe out the Indians so he can expand his mine?" That ever present bull-headed sensibility rallied to the fore, "Mr. Holmes, you have no proof that that is what actually happened."

"It is the only explanation that accounts for all the facts."

"Only explanation my foot," Lestrade grumbled. "Mr. Holmes, you bring me proof that Mr. Culverton murdered his men just to frame a bunch of natives, and I'll gladly put him behind bars. Your theories won't cut it. Hard, solid proof."

With that, Lestrade turned his horse in the direction of the jail.

"That man has so much potential to be intelligent," Holmes muttered, "it's remarkably aggravating."

When they arrived back at Baker Street House, the place was open for business, with Billy playing a minstrel tune on the piano, and Mrs. Hudson herself behind the dark wooden bar. The daylight through the windows provided enough light for now, but as night fell the chandelier would cast a warm glow over the tables. Mrs. Hudson's girls lounged against the bar and along the stair railing, chatting with customers. There was a decent crowd already, despite the relatively early hour.

Holmes and Watson made their way up the stairs, ignoring the curious looks of new faces as they went to their room, and nodding a greeting to the regulars. It wasn't until they were outside their door that Watson finally spoke.

"Culverton certainly took a dislike to you."

"Ha! Mr. Culverton fled the Confederacy after the war was lost to take advantage of the new opportunity and distinct lack of legal boundaries the western frontier provided. My father may have died defending the Confederacy, but at least he had principles. Culverton is an opportunistic businessman, little better than the carpetbaggers destroying the remains of the South with their so-called Reconstruction."

"Somehow, I doubt he sees it that way."

Holmes chuckled. His slow southern drawl became more pronounced when he was offended, "No doubt I am little more than a pompous scalawag in his eyes."

Holmes retrieved his pipe once they were inside 221, sitting down in his basket chair. Watson sat in the chair across from him, not bothering to hide his grimace this time. "Well?"

"Well?"

"The case, Holmes. Culverton aside, what are your thoughts on the case?" Holmes smiled before regarding the window, a distant gaze in his eyes as if he looked across the town to the scene at the mine from his chair. "There is one detail, only one, that remains unaccounted for," Holmes spoke softly, "I'm not certain of its significance, yet."

"Are you going to tell me what it is? Or just sit there, being infuriatingly impenetrable?"

Holmes smiled a little, and drew a small bottle from his pocket, "What do you make of that, Doctor?"

Watson examined it carefully, trying to apply the same attention to detail that Holmes would use. Unfortunately, to Dr. Watson's eyes, it was just an amber bottle with a solid black label. "A medicine bottle," he shrugged. "Where did you find it?"

"It was lying just to the side of one of the bodies. I picked it up while you were talking with Culverton."

"Why should a bottle be cause for concern?"

"It isn't the bottle, Watson, it's the label. No store in town has such, not even for the less pleasant substances. Where did it come from?"

"A traveling salesman with poor business sense?"

"You joke, Doctor, but..." Holmes froze, his eyes fixed on Watson with something almost like awe. He sprang to his feet, "Watson, you never cease to amaze me!" He was out the door and down the hall as he called back, "You are not yourself luminous, but you are a great conductor of light!"

With a curse, Watson followed. "Can all southerners make an insult sound like a compliment, or is it just you?"

Holmes gave no indication of noticing as he hurried down the stairs. "Mrs. Hudson!" His strident call was clear over the sounds of conversation and tinny piano.

"You'd think a gentleman would learn not to shout so much," Mrs. Hudson scolded him from behind the bar.

"It's the most expedient way to ensure your attention. Was the last silver tongued leech to pass through town a customer of yours?"

"The snake oil man? Sure was. Why, want your money back?"

"Your rapier wit knows no bounds, Mrs. Hudson. Whose favors did he purchase?"

"Kitty's."

Holmes scanned the room, spotting her almost instantly and crossing the distance between them in a few long strides.

"Is this case going to be worth the grief of him interrupting Kitty and her customer?" Mrs. Hudson asked as Watson approached.

"That depends on if you think solving a mass of murders worth more than the dollar you'd get from that fella," Watson replied as he sat down at the bar.

Mrs. Hudson poured him a shot of whiskey, "I suppose."

Kitty and the customer, a rough faced teamster, were fortunately still in the 'negotiating' phase of the evening. Holmes smoothly inserted his long arm between them, holding a gold coin up to Kitty's face. "I require your services, Miss Winter."

She smiled, "Can't say no to a gentleman." The other man started to protest, "Sorry, but I take the offers I get. Stick around, when I'm done with him, I'll come back to you."

"I ain't in the mood to wait," he grunted, grabbing Kitty's arm hard enough to hurt.

Holmes knocked the hand away, "If that is your method of handling women, it's no wonder you have to pay for their company."

"I sure as hell won't take lessons from some hoity-toity jackanapes, neither."

Holmes smiled, his voice honey and molasses. "I doubt there's anything I, or anyone else, could teach you."

The people standing nearby were suddenly terribly interested in their drinks, or found something else to do on the other side of the room. The sudden exodus was enough to give the teamster pause. Holmes's gaze remained fixed on him like a hawk, and suddenly that smile and those sickly sweet words made the air a little colder.

"I apologize for interrupting your plans for the night, Miss Winter," Holmes said. "It is ungentlemanly of me, but I have my reasons." Holmes turned, leading Kitty to the staircase.

They were halfway across the room when the stranger's pride flared. "Sonofabitch," he muttered, and went for his gun just as Holmes spun around to face him, a small streak of silver flying from his outstretched hand. The gun never made it out of the holster. There was a moment of silence before the stranger howled in pain, Holmes's knife lodged firmly in his wrist.

"Shall we?" Holmes offered Kitty his arm. "You'll see that I get my knife back?" Holmes called over his shoulder to Watson as he went upstairs.

Watson sighed. Mrs. Hudson poured him another.

By the time Watson made his way back up to 221, he found Holmes in his chair, with Kitty sitting across from him. "Ah, thank you," Holmes said as Watson handed him his throwing knife, tucking it back into its sheath, hidden in his sleeve. "The last salesman to come through was indeed one of Kitty's customers. If you would kindly summarize what you've told me for the doctor?"

Kitty shrugged, "Mentioned he traveled a lot. Had some charms or something around his neck, came from the Caribbean. Tried to sell me his quack potion afterward! I laughed, of course. 'I may be a whore, but I ain't stupid,' I said."

"His reaction?" Holmes prompted.

"Well, he got a funny sort of smug grin on his face. Said he had something else, something special. Stole it in Haiti, or Barbados, one of them islands, I don't know which. Supposed to be an 'ee-lixir of immortality,'" she mocked, "though he never tried it. I laughed again, and told him he was supposed to pay me, not the other way around. Then he had a drink at the bar, and left."

"I saw no such elixir in his wagon the next day," Holmes said.

Watson shrugged. "Maybe it was well hidden."

Holmes scoffed, "From me?"

"First time for everything," Kitty muttered. "Can I get back to work, now?"

"Yes, thank you," Holmes flipped the coin to her, "For your time, Miss Winter."

She snatched it out of the air. "You know I hate it when you call me that."

"You hate it when anyone else calls you that. When I do it, it is a sliver of respect for your continued skill at gathering information."

"Oh hush," her cheeks held the slightest blush as she left, "I just pay attention. Ain't nothin' special in that."

"You'd be surprised," Holmes called after her. "Rest up, Watson, we're visiting the mine tonight."

"Why?"

"Night will provide much needed cover, and time for you to be back to your peak physical abilities."

"I meant why are we going back there? Surely by now the bodies have been taken away."

"I want to see if there are any more of those bottles, or any other sign of foul play. I don't imagine Mr. Culverton will take kindly to my having a look around his operation."

The entrance of the mine was a spot of pitch in the moonlight. The bodies had been cleared away, the occasional dark stain on the dirt the only sign of the grizzly happenings of the daylight. Watson's horse snorted in distress as they came to a stop, still a fair distance from the mine's entrance.

"No need to take the horses closer," Holmes said, his voice low as they dismounted, "as we're trying to remain unnoticed."

"Something's got them spooked, besides," Watson commented.

"So it seems."

They quickly and quietly walked toward the mine, the clouded moon stretching strange shadows through the cool air. "The undertaker had no business today," Holmes wondered aloud, surveying the area. "Where did the bodies go?"

"An unmarked pit in the ground," Watson grumbled. "No doubt none of these men could have afforded the undertaker in the first place. Perhaps the bodies were distributed to families."

Holmes shook his head, "Few had any, at least not in town. Something sinister is at work here…" Holmes froze, his head tilted to the side. He gestured for Watson remain still. Watson waited, trying to listen, but unable to hear whatever had caught his friend's attention.

"Something is inside the mine," Holmes said.

"Just a curious coyote."

"No."

Watson sighed, and followed Holmes as he crept over to the mine's entrance. Now Watson could hear it, too, a strange, shuffling sound. They stood before the entrance, listening to the sound, accompanied by the occasional grunt or soft moan. "Well," Watson said, "definitely not a coyote."

Holmes smiled, and lit their lantern. Watson pulled his revolver. Together, they stepped into the dark.

A cold damp settled over them as they moved through the mine. The silence was immense, their footfalls the only disturbance to the mine's stale atmosphere. They hadn't gone far before coming to a junction of two tunnels. Holmes spotted a crate full of empty amber bottles off to the side. He set the lantern down next to it as he knelt to examine the contents. All of the bottles had solid black labels. "We have found the stock of 'elixir' at least," he said. "Culverton must have purchased it before I ran the seller out of town, though for what purpose I can't quite determine."

"The poison that killed his men?"

"That puts a rather darker aspect on the salesman's character than I thought if he was hoping to sell it to his customers."

"Kitty said he hadn't tried it. Maybe he didn't know it was poison."

"Possibly, though I doubt it."

"Holmes," Watson looked down the mineshaft with a vague unease, "does it seem like those sounds are getting louder?"

Holmes listened, an expression of curious anticipation on his face. "Yes, Doctor, I'd say so. It's coming closer."

They watched as a dark shape was slowly illuminated by the lantern's light. Arrows stuck out of its back, and its vacant face was stained with the blood that once dripped from its missing scalp. Its gait was rigid yet shambling, as if just recovered from rigor mortis and struggling to stay upright.

"Holmes," Watson forced down the bile in his throat, "for the love of God, Holmes, explain that!"

"I... I can't." Holmes stared at the creature, confused, "It's clearly one of the dead miners, but I can't explain how he walks!"

"They were dead! All of them!"

"Apparently not."

"Look at it Holmes! It's in the beginning stages of rot!"

"I know, I see it, and yet... it can't be!"

The thing lurched forward, swiping at them with a snarl. Watson leaped back and fired into the creature's chest with no effect. Holmes grabbed hold of its arm, and with a quick move of his body flipped the thing onto the ground, its arm held at an angle. It jerked in an odd, slow thrashing movement, its mouth snapping as if it might manage to reach Holmes's ankle.

Watson put a bullet in its skull, the sound of the shot echoing around them. The thing groaned, and lay still. Watson stared at it in disgust. "It was trying to bite you."

"So it seems," Holmes nodded, shaken but undeniably fascinated.

Watson holstered his gun, "How the hell did you get it onto the ground anyway?"

"One of the Chinese workers in town was good enough to demonstrate some of his country's methods of defending oneself." Holmes considered the corpse, "Whatever this is, it clearly doesn't obey any natural law we're familiar with."

Watson looked skeptically at his friend, "Magic, Holmes?"

"I did not say that. That which we do not understand is not necessarily supernatural."

"If you say so," Watson shrugged. "Do you think there are more of them?"

Holmes sighed, "I'm afraid so, my friend. As much as I hope this was an isolated, bizarrely unique case, my instincts tell me such hope is in vain. If all the miners died of the same cause, then there is a real possibility that all of them now suffer this fate."

"But what could cause it?"

Holmes pointed to the crate. "I suspect 'immortality' is a horrible mistranslation."

"The elixir," Watson was stunned.

"Culverton must have tested a bottle on a worker, either out of spite or on a whim, I don't know or care which. The miners were dead when we saw them this morning, so it takes time to work. Culverton's test subject would have died, and Culverton would have hid the body rather than risk discovery while disposing of it during the day. Once he saw the end result of the elixir's effects, he decided to give it to the rest of his men, using the nearby natives as an excuse for the sudden death of his workers."

"For what purpose?" Watson exclaimed, appalled. "What in Hell could he want with walking dead monstrosities?"

"Isn't it obvious, Dr. Watson?" a voice called out in the dark. Holmes and Watson turned to see a familiar silhouette approaching, "Don't draw that revolver, Doctor, unless you want to test your healing skills on your friend."

"Mr. Culverton," Holmes said, "how good of you to join us."

"You're trespassing, Mr. Holmes," Culverton approached, gun in his hand, "I'd be in my rights if I shot you, and the doctor."

"At least do me the courtesy of explaining the reason for this madness."

"*Madness?*" Culverton's eyes gained a frenzied light, "The Union, your Union, will fear the might of a new Confederacy of Territories. With an army of dead soldiers, The South will rise again!"

"In a slightly modified geographic location," Holmes drawled.

"I don't care about the opinion of some imitation Pinkerton," Culverton spat. "With an unbeatable army on my side, there is nothing to stop me."

"This one is rather beaten," Holmes picked up the lantern to illuminate the corpse at his feet.

Culverton stared. "Where did you find him?"

"It attacked us," Watson said, a hand discretely drifting to his gun.

"That's impossible; I chained them up down the tunnel!"

An unearthly moan sounded from the depths of the mine. All three men faced the darkness, a shiver down their spines.

"They got out," Culverton whispered, "God almighty, they got out."

Guttural groans echoed all around them, born of throats never meant to utter sound.

"They don't breathe," Watson muttered, "where is the air to create sound coming from?"

"We have a more pressing concern, my friend," Holmes licked his lips, suddenly parched. They were coming. He could hear the steps sliding closer, that odd, unnatural gait, bones somehow compelled to drag their skin across the dust. It was completely illogical, it defied everything he knew about how life and death were supposed to work. He could put it down to a strange disease, something to emulate the symptoms of death, to degrade the brain… Something inside him, whatever primal spirit still existed deep in his soul, screamed that he was lying.

The figures were visible now, slowly emerging from the black. Rattling metal sounded as more dead men came forth, lengths of chain still wrapped around their legs. One crawled, having abandoned its legs with the chain below. Unblinking eyes stared from slack-jawed faces, stained with the dried blood that had dripped from their scalps. The smell of death smothered the stale underground air. Holmes swallowed his revulsion, forcing his mind to focus.

The sight of the oncoming hoard of monsters was too much for Culverton. He fired a panicked shot, immediately covering his ears as the sound reverberated through the tunnels. Holmes tackled him, wrenching the gun from his hand as Watson fired a shot into the head of the nearest creature. It fell, its fellow creatures paying it no heed as the doctor and detective ran.

"Hurry, Culverton!" Holmes shouted over his shoulder. "You can try to kill me once we're out of here!" A strangled cry stopped him in his tracks.

Culverton was on the ground, the legless abomination trying to chew through his boot. He kicked at it, smashing its face, but still the thing chewed. More creatures closed in around him.

Watson couldn't get a clear shot at the one attacking Culverton, but he could hit the next closest as Holmes fired at the one behind that. Culverton managed to get his foot free of his boot as the corpses fell, nearly on top of him. "Run!!!" Watson shouted, but Culverton was too panicked. Dead hands grabbed at him as he struggled to his feet. They caught his coat as he stumbled, pulling him down once more. Culverton screamed as one of them bit into his shoulder and tore, releasing a spray of blood across the wall.

Holmes held Watson back, "There's nothing we can do for him!"

"Like Hell there's not," Watson said, and took aim. Culverton stopped screaming as the bullet struck.

Holmes grimaced, "Let's get out of here."

They hurried out of the mine, hearts pounding as the echoing groans and rattling of chains followed them through the dark. Watson gasped as he stepped out into the night, gulping down the fresh air.

A blast of sound behind him sent him to the ground, his hands over his head. He forced himself to sit up. The entrance of the mine was collapsed. "Holmes!"

Holmes blinked, his sight clearing. He was lying on the ground. He couldn't hear anything except an incessant ringing. He looked around as the dust cloud slowly cleared, revealing the collapsed mine just behind him. Movement from the corner of his eye caught his attention. His dazed gaze focused on Watson, worried, limping, but running to him nonetheless. His voice was muffled, seeming miles away.

Sound returned with a distressing suddenness.

"Holmes!" Watson shouted. "Are you alright?"

"I'm fine," Holmes groaned.

"What the devil did you do?"

"A box of dynamite was sitting by a support beam, so I shot it."

"While you were still in the mine?"

"I was out."

"Barely!"

"It was necessary," Holmes coughed, "I couldn't risk one of those… things, getting out."

Watson sighed as he helped Holmes to his feet. "Can you walk?"

"I was going to ask you the same question."

"I'm fine."

"You're not, but I'll permit the lie," Holmes coughed again.

Watson finished off his glass of whiskey, and reflected that there were unknown dimensions to Mrs. Hudson. She'd taken one look at them as they returned to 221, and personally brought up a bottle of her best. She hadn't even lectured Holmes for playing his violin during business hours. The melancholic music seemed to have helped settle his mind, and now he sat in his chair across from Watson, his own glass in one hand, pipe in the other, a look of perturbed contemplation on his face.

"Do you think they could still be alive?" Watson asked.

"They weren't alive to begin with, but if they are still functional, they are miles below ground. Eventually, natural decomposition will lead to there being nothing left to function. Presuming they continue to decompose, of course."

"They would have to, wouldn't they?"

"Not knowing the mechanism of their not-life, I wouldn't want to make any promises. You're the man of medicine, Doctor. Could what we witnessed be caused by some sort of disease, or a chemical reaction in the blood?"

Watson shook his head. "They were dead, Holmes. The appearance of death may be a symptom of a medical condition, but I would stake my reputation, small though it may be, on those men being dead when we saw them in the afternoon."

"You're the best doctor in town, Watson, everyone knows that. Best one I've had the pleasure of knowing for that matter, even if you are a Yankee."

"Not everyone shares your opinion, and I don't believe you've actually known many doctors," Watson smiled. "We may just have to face up to never knowing how the elixir worked. And, honestly, does it matter? Whatever was in those bottles is gone now."

A quick grin pulled at Holmes' mouth, fading with the smoke from his pipe. "Assuming every sample was in that mine."

"Holmes. Even if there were another bottle hidden somewhere, what sort of person could find any appeal in a potion that raises the dead?"

"Culverton did. A man with a perverse desire for profit, or power, or both." Holmes released a great cloud of smoke as he sighed, his words soft. "They were hungry, Watson. They descended on Culverton's body like vultures."

"We have to make sure they were all destroyed."

"How? The mine collapsed. If we tell anyone about what happened tonight, they'll think we've gone mad." He finished his glass and poured them both another, "No, my friend. I'm afraid all we can do is keep one eye constantly on the surrounding land, and if anyone starts digging, we'll be ready."

SHAVE AND A HAIRCUT

KT Pinto

THERE IS AN OLD SUBWAY LINE IN NEW YORK CITY WHERE THE F TRAIN WAS supposed to travel from Houston Street in Manhattan, beneath the East River and through the central part of the borough of Brooklyn. People believe this line is unfinished and abandoned. It's not on either point. It's actually fully completed, with its last few stops ending deep under Brooklyn in the animated city of Inkwell.

When I say animated, I don't mean in the figurative sense of the city being lively and energetic. I mean that the city is literally an animated one, drawn into existence by a group of creative cartoonists and animators who just wanted to see if they could do it.

The city is as eclectic as any other, with different areas marked by toonish architecture. One area is completely black and white, some pencil drawn, some inked; another was brightly colored with a sort of psychedelic feel to it; one was thickly built with the slowness of claymation; other colored areas had the contrasts of pencils, markers, paints, dyes, crayons, aerosols, and pens; there was the newest neighborhood in the west made with digital architecture that looked very close to human-made. When the F train went under the river, it changed to match the area of the city it was in, as to not be too jarring to the passengers, even though the passengers themselves stayed as they were.

In the middle of the city, on the corner of 221st Street and Avenue B, is a small establishment called the Baker Street Barber Shop. The name Baker - as explained by the proprietor of the shop whether or not he's asked - comes from the American military alphabet of the 1940s and 50s.

The owner and lead barber in the shop is a male named Shear Lock Holmr. He is a young relation of a wealthy family whose parents disowned him when he announced his career path. They had believed that with his brains, he could become a myriad of different things, but a barber wasn't one of them. His first name was a family one, passed down through the ages; who knew he was going to take it literally?

Being a barber in an animated town is a little different from in the human world. Shear Lock is not only proficient in various forms of stylist art - as well as keeping up on the changes in culture and cartooning - but is also masterful at all mediums of art. Most stylists stay focused on one format, whether it be inks, clay, or so forth, but Shear Lock couldn't just stop at one. It wasn't enough to keep his brain entertained and alert. So he studied them all.

This is why his shop could be located in the center of the city, while others had to stay within certain neighborhoods that would be literally drawn to their specialty. Of course, with such diverse skills, Shear Lock had an array of tools at his disposal, from his eraser bladed shears to his high-end render farm for his more intricate clients. Because of his skills and equipment, the shop was exceptionally busy, and that's why Shear Lock had a large, talented staff to help him.

Who am I, you ask? I am the first toon you see when you walk into the shop, more often than not. My name is Whatson, and I am the shop's head receptionist and scheduler. My odd name comes from a rather sad tale. When my parents put in a request for a child, they were very specific on what they wanted the cartoonists to make. Unfortunately, I do believe my maker had gone on a binge the day before I was created, because I am nary more than a stick figure, with a great head of hair thanks to Shear Lock.

When it came time to fill out my information sheet, on the line 'name of son', my father angrily wrote *What son? I have a pile of sticks!*

Unfortunately, in the twisted world of animation, the name stuck. Whatson Ihaveapileofsticks. I dropped the last name as soon as I was able, and went in search of a dream job. I found it at the Baker Street Barber Shop. The staff there playfully calls me 'Doctor' Whatson, because of my dreams of becoming a cartoonist. A cartoonist in Inkwell was like being a plastic surgeon in the human world. Jessica used to be a B cup when I knew her in high school, and we don't talk much about Bugs' transformation, although we all know about it. The lads think I'm crazy, wanting to do that, since I am just a stick figure, but Shear Lock supports me, and for that and many other reasons I consider him a great friend.

Not only is he a masterful hair artist, but he is also in his spare time a great detective, and toons from all over Inkwell come to him regularly for help. My only problem is that those that come for help never seem to have an appointment and usually hover around Shear Lock while he's creating his masterpieces.

This time was no exception. She ran in just as Wilma sat in the chair for a wash, cut and set. Luckily Wilma was not one of those snobby clients who wanted every portion of the process done by the man himself. She just nodded and smiled when Shear Lock told her that his assistant would be starting the wash on her, then escorted the young woman back to his office, waving for me to follow.

I grabbed my notebook and walked into his office, closing the door behind me. The woman was a pink-haired beauty with almond-shaped, jet black eyes and blue skin. She was wearing a tight green dress and had her hair pulled back in a ponytail. She sat at the edge of her chair, her hands wringing the piece of cloth in her hands.

I tried to inconspicuously brush away the enamored hearts that popped up over my head at the sight of her; the physical reaction was quite embarrassing. Luckily Shear Lock began speaking, and she didn't notice the hearts scurrying away.

"I know you are a very busy waitress on her lunch break, Miss..."

"Anne," she responded. "Anne Bowling. How... how did you know I was a waitress?"

"Oh, that's a rather easy deduction, Miss Bowling," Shear Lock said, leaning back and grabbing his favorite vaporizer pipe from his desk drawer. "You are wearing an outfit that compliments your frame well, but is made of durable material." He paused as he dripped some strawberry flavored glycerin into the pipe. "You are wearing thick-soled sneakers, which are not fashionable, but are good for standing long hours." He took a pull from the pipe, exhaling as he spoke. "Your hair is away from your face in a basic and clean way, to avoid interacting with some sort of food, I'd wager." As he continued, strawberries bounced out of his mouth and made their way across the room. "Your face is painted, which means that you aware of how others perceive you, so you most probably interact with the public." I opened the door so the strawberries could bounce out of the room. "And you are clutching your apron in your hands. All this together leads me to think you are a waitress."

She nodded as he took another pull. "You are right Mr. Holmr. I am a waitress at my family's restaurant, the Red Rose Diner. Just up the way from here."

"Oh yes," Shear Lock nodded. "Good bubble and squeak. So what brings you here today?"

Anne leaned a bit to the left as to not be hit with a wayward strawberry. "My uncle Richard owns the White Rose Diner over on Third."

Shear Lock nodded again as he took out a different bottle of glycerin. "Their stargazy pie is well known."

"Well known, but not necessarily liked," she responded as slices of apple pie began joining the strawberries in the air.

"It's an acquired taste," Shear Lock admitted. "Toons are sadly not known for venturing outside of their comfort zones."

"The problem is not my uncle or his diner," Anne said, "or his stargazy. The problem is with my cousin, Edward. He's a brute and a simpleton, and is being egged on by my aunt Margaret to sabotage the Red Rose."

"Why would he want to do that?" I asked.

Holmr shot me a look, but it was a soft one and bounced off of my head like a pillow.

She turned to me, brushing a pie slice out of the way. "My aunt believes that my grandfather was not of sound mind when he willed one diner to each of his sons. She believes that Richard, being the oldest child, should have both diners and the family should work for him."

"This wouldn't have anything to do with the fact that the Red Rose is doing much better than the White?"

She turned back to Holmr. "How did you know that?"

Shear Lock shrugged. "Simple logic. The Red Rose is here, in the middle of the city on a busy street. The White is on Third, far from the hustle and bustle of the commuter traffic. Also, if the White was doing as well as the Red or better, your aunt probably wouldn't have a complaint."

Anne nodded. "My aunt and uncle had decided to send Edward into the Toon Troopers because they couldn't afford college for him, and during a battle, a turpentine bomb went off and he lost a few of his fingers. My aunt blames my father for not hiring Edward for the Red Rose before he joined the Troopers or for paying for his tuition, so he wouldn't have gotten hurt."

"That is illogical," Holmr responded inhaling again. "It was not your father's responsibility to support your cousin or hire him if he wasn't a capable employee."

She nodded. "That's what my father said. So now we're having all these problems."

I noticed that the pie pieces now had strawberries in them as well as apples. "What kind of problems?"

"Minor acts of vandalism, graffiti, broken windows, a couple of bad Hoot! reviews… Things like that." Anne shifted uncomfortably, but didn't say anymore.

Holmr leaned forward as he dripped a new flavor into his pipe. "But you are worried it might get worse?"

She nodded. "I fear for our customers' and my family's safety."

Rainbows started jumping out of his pipe as a sweet candy smell filled the room. "And your cousin works for the White Rose now?"

"Yes, as a baker's assistant. My aunt calls him a pastry chef, but he basically just rolls the dough out for bread and cookies."

"And you would like me to figure out if he is the one responsible for the problems?"

"I'd rather he wasn't, but if he is, I have to catch him and stop him before things get worse."

Shear Lock nodded and stood. "Then Whatson and I shall endeavor to do our best to find out the truth. Now if you'll excuse me, I have a client waiting…"

As if on cue, there was a knock at the door; Holmr's assistant was there to say that Wilma was waiting for her cut and set. He stood and put on his barber's coat, which cut him a dashing figure, took one last pull from his pipe, and shook hands with our newest client. "We will be at the Red Rose after my last hair appointment, right around the dinner rush. I would like to see any damage that has recently occurred."

Anne nodded. "I will be there waiting."

Shear Lock watched her leave, then turned to me. "So, what did you observe Whatson?"

I rolled my tongue back up from my attack of Tex Avery-itis from watching her walk away. "I did observe that she's very worried."

He nodded. "As well she should be. Her cousin is causing quite a bit of problems."

"You are sure it's her cousin, aren't you?"

"Quite," he said. "Who else would want to cause problems to that diner in particular, and only *that* diner. No my friend, I am quite certain it's her cousin Edward who..."

"Where is he?" bellowed a voice. "I know what he's been doing and he needs to be set straight!"

Shear Lock strode out of his office, his coat flapping behind him and I quickly followed.

At the desk was a gigantic male that made Bluto seem tiny. He, like most of his animated ilk, had a shirt opened to reveal part of his hairy chest. He had a nautical tattoo on his arm with MOM in a ribbon across it that flapped. His facial hair matched in texture and color to his chest hair, and he had teeth that were too big for his face and extremely white. When he spoke, it came out as a bellow.

"You Shear Lock?" he said to my friend, who seemed unfazed by his presence.

"None other," Holmr responded, heading towards the chair where Wilma patiently sat, waiting. "Do you have an appointment?"

"I don't need an appointment," came the answer. "I came here to tell you to stop harassing my family. What happens is none of your business."

"Well, if you'd like to make an appointment, I'm sure Whatson could..."

The brute, who I assumed to be Edward, Anne's cousin, grabbed my friend's shoulder and spun him around. "I'm telling you I don't need an appointment. I'm..."

"Young man!" Wilma stood, barely coming up to either toon's chest. "You are infringing on my haircut time, and if I'm late for brunch with my husband Fred, it will be up to you to tell him why!"

Edward just stared at her, stunned.

"Now if you are quite finished harassing my customers," Holmr said, holding out his hand to help Wilma back into her chair, "I must ask you to leave."

"This ain't over, barber!"

"I hardly thought it would be."

As he stormed out of the shop, I hurried over to my friend. "Are you all right, Shear Lock?"

"Quite so," he responded, opening up his bag of tools. "Now Wilma, are you finally going to let me get rid of the bun?"

Our client laughed. "Maybe next time Shear Lock."

I was about to walk away when my friend called me back. "Whatson, did you notice?" he asked, brushing white dust off of his shoulder.

"Notice what?"

"He has only three fingers on his right hand." He turned back to Wilma and pulled out a paintbrush. "How about we try a nice dark auburn this time?"

Shear Lock was just finishing up the last of the Pussycats' new dos as I prepared the schedule for the night staff and got out our clothes for departure. I wore a basic wool coat and hat - fit to my thin frame - to block out the winter chill. Holmr, on the other hand, wore quite unique fare. A big wool cloak that billowed when he walked - I don't know how he actually kept warm wearing that - and then there was his hat: a double duck bill cap. Looking similar to a human deerstalker cap, the animated version was a little more... animated.

"Ith about time you took me out of that muthy clothet!" the cap complained as I placed it on the counter. "I thought you had forgotten me... well hel-looo ladieth," it cooed as the feline-dressed band members paid their bill – which quacked in appreciation - grabbed their instruments and headed towards the front door. "What I wouldn't give to be covering one of those headth..."

"Are you quite finished?" Shear Lock asked as he draped the cloak around his shoulders.

"I'll be finithed when you thop drething like Red Riding Hood and buy a coat like a normal..."

KA-BOOM!

We stared at the window for a moment as what looked like a storm suddenly hit Inkwell. Shear Lock grabbed his cap off of the counter. "That wasn't thunder," he said.

"Thath thill water," the cap complained. "Do I *look* like a rain cap to you?"

Its complaints turned to grumbles as we stepped outside and started sprinting to the source of the sound. We were soaked when we got to the Red Rose Diner, where a van had crashed into a fire hydrant in front of the restaurant. There was a huge geyser of water shooting from the remnants of the hydrant; on top of it there was a happy piglet bouncing with the spray, apparently enjoying the ride.

"Wee wee weeeeeeee!" the piglet sang. "Wee wee weeeeeeeeeeeeeeeeeeeeeeeeee!"

I took off my now-drenched coat and watched the mass of water separate from itself at the top of the spray and turn into a multitude of little happy water droplets that landed on the sidewalk on stubby little feet, running with its fellow droplets down into the river of water running past the van's tires and down the road towards the barber shop. It took me a moment to realize that Shear Lock had already walked towards the three identical-looking black and white police officers standing nearby.

"Doeth anyone elth notith that ith wet over here?" the cap asked no one in particular.

Shear Lock ignored it as he nodded to the cops. "Lovely day we're having today, aren't we officers?"

The three of them nodded, their mustaches bobbing up and down.

He pointed to the diner. "Anyone injured?"

The three of them shook their heads in the negative.

"Any arrests made?"

The three of them tilted their heads in confusion.

"You believe this to be an accident?"

The three of them nodded and waddled over to the cab of the van, pointing inside. I glanced where they were pointing and saw little of interest, except patterns of white spots all over the dash and gears.

"Ah, the emergency brake failed?"

The three heads bobbed up and down excitedly.

"Crashed into the hydrant on its own?"

The heads nodded again.

"The driver told you that, did he?"

Again, the excited head-bob from all three of them.

"And where is that driver, exactly?"

The three looked around in confusion, this time their bodies not in sync.

"I don't understand Holmr," I said over the squeals of the pig. "Since it was an accident, the driver is probably talking with his insurance company."

Shear Lock shook his head. "This wasn't an accident Whatson."

"It wasn't?" I was shocked. "How can you be certain Holmr?"

"Elementary, dear Whatson!" Shear Lock pointed to the water. "If the brakes had failed, the van would have followed the path the water droplets did..."

"All over me?" the cap quipped.

"...down the hill." The great detective turned to the police. "There would be more of a chance of the van hitting my shop than this establishment if the brakes had failed."

"Well, c'mon now!" the cap said in annoyance. "Any fool can thee that!"

"The driver backed up the car on purpose, speeding up and heading for the diner. Luckily the hydrant stopped his path."

The three officers looked at the van, then at the diner, and finally down at the water that was running down the hill. Then they ran as one to the phone booth on the corner and squeezed themselves in.

I turned from them to see Holmr looking in the cab of the van. "What do you see, Shear Lock?"

"See?" he chuckled. "Why my dear Whatson, I see the same as you. I just deduce a little differently from most."

"And hith modethy knowth no bounth."

"See those dots?" Holmr said to me, ignoring the cap. "That right there tells us who did it."

"It does?"

"Of course, Whatson! Don't you see the pattern?"

I looked again at the white dots all over the cab. "Not really. I mean, there are five here, and three here, five over there..."

"Yes Whatson! That's exactly it!"

"I don't understand..."

"I had similar marking on my shoulder after our little run in with Edward, remember?"

I thought back, my little stick figure brain trying to visualize the moment. "Yes, you wiped white powder..."

"Not powder, Whatson. Flour. Edward is a baker, with flour on his hands."

"They don't look like roseeth to me."

"And remember what Anne had said about her cousin? How he had been injured while working as a Toon Trooper."

I nodded. "He only has three fingers on his right hand."

Shear Lock pointed to the patterns in the van. "See, Whatson? Five and three, five and three. Those are his handprints. Five and three."

I nodded. "You're right Holmr. I see it now."

"About time you caught up with uth."

Shear Lock turned away from the van. "Let's tell the cops what we know, before this fool does anything worse."

"Yeah," the cap said, "and maybe get thomeone to turn that damn water off..."

I watched Shear Lock head towards the officers and realized that once again my dear friend, for all his intelligence, forgot about the victims.

I trotted over to the Red Rose Diner, where a crowd of people had gathered to watch the show. Before I could say anything, I was accosted by a flurry of blue and pink and green.

"Oh Whatson!" Anne said, engulfing me in a tight hug... which is rather easy to do, since I'm a stick, and quite enjoyable for me, I might add. "I'm so glad you're here!"

I waited for a few moments as my dots-for-eyes continued to bulge across the street. When they finally popped back into place, I asked, "Is everyone OK?"

Actually, it came out "Mi emmimn okph?" because my mouth was pressed against her soft, well rounded shoulder.

Luckily, she was proficient in mumblese. "Oh, yes! Everyone is fine! We were just given a little fright by the noise."

She sadly stepped away then, and I noticed my mouth imprinted on her dress from the hug. I quickly snatched it back as we turned to Shear Lock, who had hurried towards us.

"Whatson," the great detective said, "once you've pulled yourself together, we must make our way to the White Rose."

'The White Rose?" Anne said, gripping my arm. "So I was right? About my cousin Edward?"

"We shall soon find out," Shear Lock responded. "but I am afraid my friend is going to need his arm back."

Anne looked down at and saw that she did indeed have my forearm in her hands. Her cheeks turned a lovely purple in embarrassment and sheepishly put it back where it belonged. I waved away her baaaaaaaas of apology and told her to stay at the Red Rose where it was safe.

I caught myself rubbing my reattached arm as the cops' big black van pulled up to the curb on two wheels.

"Sthe hath thome grip!" Holmr's cap said in admiration. "I like that in my women!"

"What women are those?" I asked.

"You don't think I hathe women?" the cap asked as we piled into the back of the van. "Why, becauthe I'm a hat? Lemme tell you, women adore hath, my friend. Hath and shooth, they can't get enouth!"

I looked out the window and saw Anne waving at the van as it drove away. I guess she saw me looking because she blew me a kiss. It's something females have been doing since Betty Boop was black and white, but it was still nice to see those blue puckering lips chase after the van, finally slamming into the window and sticking there for the rest of the ride.

"Rose colored lipstick," Holmr said, rousing himself from his musings. "Appropriate, don't you think Whatson?"

"You are right as always my dear Holmr," I responded, not looking away from the lips pressed up against the glass.

"Where ith a portable hole when you need one, eh Whathon?"

I sighed, but didn't respond. Luckily, the lips stayed with us the entire ride to the White Rose. I plucked them off as soon as I got out of the car and put them in my coat pocket, where the kissing noises continued, but were muffled.

I turned away from the van to see Holmr heading towards the diner with the three cops in tow. Surprisingly, he didn't head to the front door like I thought he would, but he went around the corner towards the back. The officers had to do a quick turn to follow him and not slam into the wall. Only two succeeded; the third crashed into the wall and bounced for a few seconds before getting up and waddling after them.

I quickly followed, and was in time to see the tip of Holmr's cloak as he walked into the building. As the cops tried to figure out how they were going to get into the door, I slipped past them and followed Holmr into the kitchen.

The kitchen was like any other diner kitchen in Inkwell: in one corner, there were some cows in vibrating weight machines in case a customer wanted milk shakes, in another, chickens were relaxing in a hot tub, waiting for any boiled eggs orders. Things moved and cleaned and washed and fried just as all inanimate objects in a commercial kitchen should.

And there, by the far wall, was Edward, wearing a crisp white shirt and pounding a rising ball of dough. Because his rhythm wasn't the best, he kept having to snatch the dough from the air and start the process again.

"It helps if you do a one-two, one-two method," Holmr said, startling him. "Your one-two-half of one-one-one-one-two doesn't seem to work as well."

"What do *you* want?" Edward growled.

"Why, we're here to confront you about the actions you took on the Red Rose."

"I have no idea what you are talking about," he responded; I noticed his co-workers quickly making their way out of the room along with the mops, sponges and dishwasher.

"Oh, must we go through all this?" my friend said, pulling out his pipe. "You know you did it. I know you did it. Must we go through the whole rigmarole?"

"Rigama-who?" Edward said, letting the dough float across the room. "I have no idea what you are saying, and you got no proof of nothing."

"Precisely," Holmr responded as cinnamon sticks from his pipe chased after the dough. "I am glad you understand the situation."

Edward was obviously confused. "Get out of here! You got nothing."

"Hello ladieth," Holmr's cap said to the chickens; he had perched himself on the edge of the hot tub. "How'th it going?"

Shear Lock sighed, put the cap back on his head, and sent apples after the cinnamon. He then turned his attention back to Edward. "What I've got is..."

He was interrupted by a popping sound as the three police officers finally squeezed their way into the room.

Holmr grinned. "Them."

Edward couldn't hide the look of recognition on his face as he unconvincingly said, "Who are they?"

My friend ignored him and said to the cops, "Is he the driver of the van that you spoke to?"

The officers nodded in unison.

Shear Lock shrugged. "There you go. Arrest him."

Of course, Edward decided to run. And, even more predictably, he chose to run in my direction. Luckily I was prepared and held up a garbage lid for him to slam into. The impact sent him vibrating backwards into the waiting arms - and handcuffs - of the cops.

The officers glanced back to the door they had just squeezed through, then decided to escort him out through the main dining area. A murmur went through the crowd of customers and staff as they waddled him up the aisle towards the front door with me and Holmr in tow.

Suddenly Edward whipped around and said to my friend, "Fine, you're right. I did it. And I would've gotten away with it too if it wasn't for you meddling kids and your dog!"

We looked at each other with the same confused expression on our faces, then turned to the booth behind us. The famous Great Dane looked up from his plate, surprised.

"Ruh uh!" he said. "Ri'm just rere for the stargazy!"

Because the officers now had a prisoner, Holmr and I had to hoof it back to the barber shop. On the way, I thought up a name for this adventure for my memoirs: The Case of the Two Roses. Simple, yet accurate.

I smiled as we turned on to Avenue B. "I'm glad that's over," I said as the shop came into view.

"Not quite yet," Shear Lock said mysteriously. "Just one thing more."

By the time we got to the shop and took off our hooves, Shear Lock was able to take a quick shower before the Sundown Special began. When he came down, the shop was packed, and I had already seated Alucard for his Sundown wash, cut and set.

As Shear Lock started his infamous intellectual small talk with one of the most powerful vampires in Inkwell, the door opened and Anne flounced in, ignoring all the customers and throwing her arms around me, covering my face with kisses. She then turned and flounced right back out the door.

Shear Lock grinned at me as I stared in the mirror at the Xs and Os smattered across my face. "Now," he said, brushing Alucard's thick locks, "it's over."

Th-th-th-that's all folks!

SHADOWS AND HOUNDS

Jason Gilbert

I'D GONE TO MR. HOLMES TO SOLVE THE MURDER OF MY SISTER. WHAT I GOT was beyond even the hell that was now the London Wasteland.

The air was freezing, the sky dark, and all I had was the low blue glow of my gas lamp to show me that I'd found Mr. Sherlock Holmes's small bunker. Nuclear winter had set in after the radiation fallout had worked itself out, and every day was a cold snowy night that required a heavy leather parka and goggles. His bunker was on what was left of 221 Baker Street, and he'd marked it 221B either out of duty or to distinguish his metal bunker from small one next to his or the hollow shell that used to be an apartment building that they sat in front of. The radiation from the nuclear fallout years before had made being outside a hazard, and people had been required to live inside bunkers made of steel and lined with lead to keep safe. Journeying outside required a special suit, otherwise a person risked radiation poison and even mutation.

Or death.

In the past two years, the radiation had dissipated, but things had only gotten worse from there. A sign caught my eye, and I held my gas lamp closer to it.

Kindly refrain from knocking. Please inquire with Mrs. Hudson in 221A.

I looked to my right and saw the bunker similar to 221B. I stepped closer, noted the 221A on the front door, and knocked twice. The snow had begun to fall again, and even my brown leather fallout parka and cold suit were having difficulty keeping the chill out.

The large wheel on the front of the door turned, the sound of large levers and latches releasing loud in the silence, and the door swung open. An older woman stood in the doorway, framed by the warm firelight from within. Her hair was pulled into a bun, and her dress was a single piece made of thick black burlap that reached the floor and was lined with buckles.

"Good evening, sir," she said, her tone warm and welcoming. "Here to see Mr. Sherlock, I presume?"

"Yes madam," I said, giving a curt bow. "My name is Samuel Burns. Is he receiving clients today?"

"Oh, well, I don't see why he wouldn't," she said. "His rent is due soon, so he'd be wise to, I'm sure. I am Mrs. Hudson. I'll show you to his door."

She stepped out, her large black boots crunching in the snow under her gown. She donned no coat, no cold suit, nothing. It was as if the cold did not affect her. I kept my bewilderment to myself. I'd heard stories of Sherlock Holmes and the unusual company he kept, and knew it best not to make inquiries into things I may not want to know about.

Mrs. Hudson stepped up to 221B, knocked three times, and entered. I followed, and was immediately greeted by the warmth of a fire in a makeshift fireplace in the corner of a room that was decorated as if it were still the years before the Nuclear Dawn had destroyed the world. The wood-paneled walls were lined with bookshelves that were over-packed with books, something that was unheard of in this age since a great many books had been lost. Two men sat in high-backed easy chairs by the fire. One was a mustachioed short man with blondish hair that he kept neatly tied back in a ponytail. He wore an old-fashioned set of slacks, a button-up shirt, a sport coat, and had an air of sophistication about him.

I assumed the other was Sherlock based on the rumors I'd heard.

Sherlock was a tall, lithe, gaunt man with long black hair that hung about his shoulders and almost down to his lap. His face was mostly hidden, though he had no problem puffing on his ornate pipe as he gazed into the fire, his dark eyes focused and deep wells in his sallow face. The pipe was black, the finish rough and knobbed, the structure imperfect as if it were made of the bone of some creature, though I couldn't have sworn to it. He was dressed more like Mrs. Hudson, his lower half covered by black leather pants with an assortment of buckles up and down the legs, and his top half covered by a long-sleeved leather tunic also adorned with added buckles. Heavy outdoor gear. It wasn't uncommon for people these days to wear their winter gear indoors. So many had come down with the Frost, a chronic and incurable sickness brought on by the nuclear winter. The sickness made one constantly cold, feeling as if they were on the very verge of dying from being chilled from the inside out, their blood ice but never freezing, their skin frozen but never stiff nor blackened.

"Mr. Holmes, a client," said Mrs. Hudson as she shut the door behind us. "A Mr. Burns to see you."

"I believe I would have to accept his case were he to be a client, Mrs. Hudson," Sherlock said. His voice was deep, even, and ice-cold. He never took his eyes off the fire, nor moved to look at us. He must have had the Frost something terrible.

"Oh, please," Watson said, eyeing Sherlock. "We haven't had a client in weeks. You could at least entertain the man." Watson stood and greeted me with a nod and a wave of his own pipe, a thing simple and old-fashioned.

"Boring," Sherlock said, puffing on his pipe.

Mrs. Hudson cleared her throat.

"Your rent is also coming up, Mr. Holmes," she said. "I expect the agreed-upon price in my box come this Friday."

Sherlock turned his eye to me, gazing at me from behind his black locks. I removed my goggles and hood, and let the warmth push back the chill that made my cheeks burn and even my hair hurt as I gave him a curt bow.

"Samuel Burns," I said. "I require your services, Mr. Holmes. My sister has been murdered."

He kept staring at me.

"I'm waiting," he said. "And please try not to be boring."

"Sherlock, your manners," Watson said out of the corner of his mouth as he smiled at me. "How may we be of assistance, Mr. Burns?"

"I have reason to believe that Sheryl was killed by a local businessman," I said. "Mr. Thornton. She was a runner for him. She left three days ago and hasn't returned."

"Runners carry product from town to town," Watson said. "Is it possible that she simply hasn't returned from her trip?"

I shook my head.

"Her run max is limited to twenty-four hours. She's only been at it a month."

Watson looked to Sherlock. Holmes grunted and stared back into the fire. "Bandits," he said. "Scavengers, likely. Boring. Good day, sir."

I stepped forward. "Mr. Holmes, I have credits," I said, pleading. "I swear I wish it were so simple."

"And you have rent due," said Mrs. Hudson. She held her hand out, palm up. A blue ball of flame appeared in her palm. I stepped away. How had she done it?! Her sleeves were too form-fitting to accommodate a gas line, and she wasn't wearing a tank or gas line of any kind.

"You wouldn't be so heartless as to put us out," Watson said, standing. "Mrs. Hudson, that would be cruel!"

"No," said Mrs. Hudson. "Though I could show you to the same fate as Mr. Hudson. I do believe the most intelligent thing he had to say before he ended up out in the cold was 'ribbit.'"

Dr. Watson grinned at me and held out his hand. "Dr. John Watson," he said. "We'll take the case."

Sherlock made a noise. "I'd rather be a frog."

Watson turned to him. "Oh come off it, Holmes," he snapped. "You're bored, so everything sounds boring. Maybe if you got up off your arse and moved about every now and again it wouldn't make the sound of a poster being ripped from the wall every time you stood up from that infernal chair."

Sherlock shook his head, his long hair swaying slightly as he craned his neck and peered at me through the black locks. "Mr. Burns, you are not giving me enough, and I am bored. That is as pleasant as I can be about the matter. Your sister has been gone three days. You loath her boss. I couldn't give a *shit*. Either be interesting, or be gone."

"Thornton's running business has been lacking here as of late," I said, swallowing back the urge to punch Sherlock Holmes and leave. "He's had to resort to utilizing office help for small runs to the villages on the outskirts of London the past few weeks because of his reputation for shorting runners if not outright stealing from them. Sheryl had come to me with suspicions, possibly evidence that could put him away."

"Evidence that could give him motive," Sherlock said, his eyes staring off. "Put him behind bars, or exiled into the wastelands without a suit were it to lead to it. Now we are getting somewhere, Mr. Burns. Please continue."

"As a businessman, Thornton is well-protected," I said. "He knows the right people to cover his tracks. But, if Sheryl had the right evidence, there were have to be a choice: protect him and what small amount of money he brings to the right officials, or cut him loose and save face with the people of the London Wasteland. At least, that was how she put it to me. The next day, she was sent on a run. I've heard nothing since, and Thornton will not respond to my inquiries."

"It still may not be murder," Watson said. "But, it *is* suspect."

"Or it *is* murder, and not necessarily at the hands of one crooked trader," Sherlock said, turning back to the fire, setting his black gaze to the flames as he placed his pipe to his lips and drew a long pull of smoke. "Do you know where the run request came from, Mr. Burns?"

"I do not," I said, sighing. "It was the strangest thing. When I received word that she had been sent out, the telegram had the most horrid odor. It was as if it had been wiped across a dead dog."

Watson's eyes widened slightly as if in alarm. I looked from him to Sherlock. There had been no sound, no movement out of the corner of my eye, yet the man had turned in his chair again and now stared hard at me through his locks of hair, his eyes wide and black. "We'll take the case."

"Excellent!" Watson clapped his hands and shook mine again as Sherlock turned back towards the fire. "Good Mr. Burns, would you be so kind as to lead us to Mr. Thornton's office?"

"I'm not wearing the hat," Sherlock muttered.

"You're Sherlock Holmes," Watson said, glaring at him as he donned his parka, head wrap, and bowler. "You're wearing the damned hat."

I led Holmes and Watson through the streets of the London Wasteland towards Mr. Thornton's office. Only a few people wandered about, mostly runners heading in and out of the alleyways trying to make it to their destinations as fast as possible. People did not go outside in the cold unless they had to, but Sheryl had been my world. She was the only family I had left. I had to find out what had happened to her, Frost be damned! Though Dr. Watson and I had donned the proper gear, Sherlock Holmes kept to his black leather form-fitting, buckle-ridden coat and his hat, which was black with a brim all the way round that stood out almost the width of his shoulders and managed to hide his features in shadow. Some of those with the Frost had it bad enough that the outdoors was warmer to them than their own body-temperature.

Thornton Delivery was only a few blocks from Baker Street. I opened the door and Holmes ducked inside and Thornton looked up from his desk. "You again," he said to me as I entered, his tone riddled with annoyance. "And this time you bring company. I'll not have this nonsense from you again."

*Thornton was a short, fat man with a bald head and a large mustache that made Dr. Watson's look tame. Watson removed his goggles and tipped his bowler hat to Thornton. Sherlock kept his large-brimmed hat on his head as his eyes darted about, seeming to search the room.

"I demand answers," I said, my body shaking. It took everything in me not to scream "murderer" at the top of my lungs. This man had sent my sister to die.

Sensing my distress, Watson pushed past me and offered his hand to Thornton. "Dr. John Watson," he said. "And may I present Mr. Sherlock Holmes."

Thornton's face went pale as Sherlock fixed his reptilian eyes on him. He sat back in his chair, his hands trembling as he pulled his monocle from his eye. He looked from Sherlock to me, and back at Sherlock.

"Oh, my God," he said, his voice almost a whisper. "Dear Samuel, why have you brought this cursed man with you?"

Cursed? I decided to ask Watson about it later.

"I am no more cursed than this world," Sherlock said. "But let's depart with the niceties, shall we? I long for my fire, silence, and my tobacco pipe."

Watson snorted. "Tobacco, indeed."

Sherlock shook his head at Thornton, then set his eyes on me.

"No," he said.

"No?" I said. "What do you mean, 'no'?"

"I mean the opposite of yes," said Sherlock. "As in a negative in lieu of a positive." He seemed to grow in height, his eyes boring into me from behind the dark long hair that framed his face. The shadows around him swelled, seemed to suck in what little light the office had as he set his eyes on Thornton. Holmes kept his arms at his side, his body stiff. He spoke as if taken by a trance.

"This man is a coward driven by love of two things: credits and food. He's large enough to over-consume one, but too lazy to do much else beyond have people collect the other for him. Judging by his stature, it's obvious which of the two calls more of his attention. The papers on his desk in disarray show me that he is disorganized and has no clue as to what he is doing, and the sweat on his brow tells me that he is anxious. Someone normally runs this desk for him. Bad posture, obvious discomfort in a position of organizational responsibility. He could no more murder someone, directly or indirectly, than he could plan a child's tea party with dolls and stuffed animals as guests. Pulsing vein on the neck indicates rapid heartbeat. Clubbing fingers suggests that Mr. Thornton is not much longer for this world, or what's left of it, due to his appetite for anything fried and sugared. Do tell me, Mr. Thornton, what Sheryl Burns did for you while under your employ."

The shadows shrank away, and the light in the room returned to the brightness it had been when we'd first entered.

Thornton stammered a little, his eyes wide. Dr. Watson raised his eyebrow.

"Well...I..." Thornton said.

"Today, sir, would be lovely," Watson said, smiling. "Lest Mr. Holmes's parlor trick with the shadows bears repeating."

"She was my bookkeeper," said Thornton. "And a runner, though she only did that if someone laid out, and short runs at that. Nothing outside the city."

"She never told me that she kept his books," I said to Sherlock. "Only that she had seen something."

"She wouldn't," Thornton said. "I had her sign a non-disclosure. It helps keep the competition at bay. If they don't know my clients or routes, they can't muscle their way in."

"But someone did," said Sherlock. "And now Mr. Burns believes his sister to be dead."

"Believe?" I said.

"You have no body, she simply hasn't returned from a run," Sherlock said. "For now, we will assume that she is merely missing."

Watson turned to Sherlock. "Hunting for a living person makes things more difficult," he said.

Sherlock smiled. "Indeed." He stepped towards Mr. Thornton's desk. Thornton recoiled as Sherlock approached him. "Do you have record of the run that you sent Miss Burns on?"

Thornton rifled through the pile of paperwork on the desk, pulled a folder out, and handed it to Sherlock.

"I see," he said, scanning the writing on the paper. It was too small for me to read at my distance.

"See what?" Watson said.

Sherlock handed him the folder and glared at Thornton. The color drained from Watson's face as he read the reports. "This is unbelievable."

"What?" I asked. "What is it?"

"Your dear sister's final run was to Baskerville. Client name is only the letter M."

My blood was cold. Baskerville was a horrid place, an old plantation not two miles outside of the city and deep in the woods. The stories of the ghostly hounds that wandered the area were enough to keep me from ever going there.

"What business would you have at Baskerville?" Watson asked Thornton.

"None," said Thornton. "I get the requests for supplies and send my runners with said supplies and an invoice. I didn't discover that Sheryl had gotten the Baskerville delivery until she was gone."

"No," said Sherlock. "I would expect that you keep your hands in the pot as little as possible." He tipped his hat to Mr. Thornton and turned to leave. Watson followed suit, pulling his goggles on as he spoke.

"Do see your doctor, Mr. Thornton. Your health is concerning."

I was already second-guessing even setting foot onto Baker Street. It had been Thornton; I was sure of it. And yet, what Holmes had said in the office had made too much sense. He had torn down everything about my own conclusions on the matter and thrown them away like rubbish.

But the shadows coming to him like that, the blackness in his eyes, the trance…where had that come from?

Holmes stepped abruptly into the shadows of an alleyway and out of sight. The light from the sun above us was not much more than a full moon. The fallout had darkened the sky to the point where even the sun's rays couldn't penetrate the black that stained the Earth. Every day was a cold night. I made to follow Holmes, thinking that he was on his way to another step of the investigation, but Watson stopped me.

"No, sir," he said. "I suggest we wait. He's simply asking for a quick bit of guidance."

I stole a glance at the alley. The shadows swirled like water, thick as ink and murky like the bowls of the swamp where the Jabberwocky lived. The poem had unsettled me as a child, and even now gave me chills.

"Why do the shadows react the way they do around him?" I asked.

"Been that way since the fallout, I'm afraid," Watson said. "His ailment, really. Since he had to give up his six-percent solution due to lack of availability, he's had to rely on a special mix in his pipe courtesy of Mrs. Hudson. The shadows hold many secrets, Mr. Burns. Holmes means to seek them all out, though he fears what he will find. And it darkens his soul every waking moment. If thou gaze long into an abyss, the abyss will also gaze into thee."

The shadows in the alley where Holmes had vanished grew darker, thicker, blacking out everything and spreading onto the walls of the buildings on either side and the sidewalk in front of us. They receded quickly, and Holmes emerged trailed by a small bit of smoke from the bone pipe in his mouth.

"How is Mycroft?" Watson asked as we fell into step beside him.

"Gaining weight," Sherlock said, not looking at him. "And in possession of a great deal of information about Baskerville. Shall we?"

I kept my mouth shut, the hairs on the back of my neck on end underneath my scarf. Mycroft Holmes had died from radiation exposure ten years prior. And, of the stories I'd heard about Sherlock Holmes, the supernatural ones had been the ones I'd believed the least.

That had been then. This was now.

Baskerville was only a few miles outside of the London Wasteland in what was left of the countryside. The trees had all been killed in the blast, flash-burned and then frozen in the fallout and nuclear winter. They still stood tall and white, dense as if a ruined memory of the lush forest they'd once been. We were able to hail a carriage out of London Wasteland, though it had taken quite a few credits to convince the driver to allow Holmes along for the ride, and another large amount to convince him to at least take us close enough to the deadmire that Baskerville was only a short walk through the dark forest.

The path leading in was dark enough for Watson and I to need our gas lamps. Sherlock stared ahead, then took lead.

"Does he not need light?" I asked Watson.

"After a few hours in my company, you should know the answer to that." Holmes called from up ahead. Watson looked at me, gave a friendly smile, and motioned for me to follow. I did so, though I was leery of Holmes. Even in the face of what Dr. Watson had revealed to me about his friend, I was expected to trust a man who could touch the very darkness around him.

"Dr. Watson," I said. "Is Mr. Holmes's soul already darkened by the shadows? Does he truly control them as the stories say? Is he so far separated from his humanity?"

Watson did not look back at me as he spoke. "Having a client along is highly unusual," he said. "Though Holmes seems to accept that you will not be turned away from finding dear Sheryl. Let's not test his patience with questions that you have no business asking, shall we?"

I nodded. Hint taken.

Holmes stopped ahead, standing stock still. Watson and I approached, standing on either side of him. We'd reached a clearing. A few pillars of brick still stood, and a brick smoke house sat a few hundred yards from us. Charred skeletons lay about, some of them still positioned as if trying to ward off the ring of fire that had taken them. Everything was covered in a blanket of snow, and the place still reeked of burnt meat.

I sighed. Thornton had been right. There was no reason to send a runner out to the ruins of Baskerville Manor.

A lonely howl broke the silence of the snow-covered deadmire, low and rattled with a guttural growl. We looked about, and Watson and I drew our pistols. Sherlock put his hands out as if holding us back.

"That will do you no good here," he said to me. "But I do appreciate the valor in your effort."

"Just the same, Holmes, there's nothing saying that a man isn't behind all of this." Watson nodded towards the smoke house.

"Interesting deduction, Watson," he said, sounding almost impressed. "Though you may be slightly off. Not far, though. It has also been on my mind."

A large shape burst from the trees, rushing us, the snow kicking up as the massive hound barreled down on us. Its red eyes glowed furiously, its lips pulled back in a hellish snarl, its teeth almost glowing in the pale light peering in from the top of the clearing. Watson and I fired. My bullets were useless. I'd killed men plenty of times while out scavenging for food and material; bandits and wanderers maddened by the fallout. Killing demons was a different story.

Watson's bullets tore into the hound. It stumbled and let out a pained whine as it slowed. I glanced at the gun in his hand. It flashed every time he pulled the trigger, a blue arch of electricity shooting down his arm and off the barrel with every round. The hound took a shot to the neck and recoiled, turning away and running off to the right and into the woods.

"I see that pistol Mrs. Hudson gave you is working nicely," Holmes said.

Watson shrugged. "Almost worth the blood that bound it to me," he said. "At least I never have to reload." He looked at me and gave a smile. "Mrs. Hudson designed it to draw from my own energy. My organic electricity gives the firearm power."

The cold grew sharp, the clouds above moving across the sky and dulling the moonlight. I pulled my goggles on and turned on the night vision. More of the hounds circled us, their breath hot wisps of vapor rising like plumes from their jowls as they snarled and growled at us. Holmes, Watson and I grouped together, back to back to back, covering any angle they could come at us from. I aimed my pistol, knowing that my bullets were useless.

"They're keeping us from something," Holmes said. He pulled away from us and made for the smoke house.

"Holmes!" Watson shouted. He aimed and fired at the ghost hound as it leapt at the detective. Holmes ignored the ethereal beast as Watson's energy-charged rounds slammed into its ribcage and knocked it back from him. More of the dogs went after Sherlock, and Watson's voice almost shook as he spoke. "Damn it all, there's too many of them!"

Holmes raised his hand lazily and sent a swirl of shadows at the hounds. The tendrils wrapped around them, yanked them all to the ground. He stopped, his shoulders slumped, his head down as he raised his arms. It looked as if he were lifting a great weight, his arms trembling under the strain. The hounds lifted slowly into the air, the shadow tendrils wrapping around their necks tighter as the animals gasped and wretched for air.

"I've never liked dogs," he muttered as he thrust his arms outwards. The shadows slammed the dogs back into the trees around the clearing, and wrapped themselves around the white dead trunks. Each ghost dog was held in snare, unable to move or break free.

"Well then," Watson said, looking up at the trapped dogs as he stood next to me. "I believe that is that, as they say. Shall we?"

I nodded, and we hurried to follow Holmes toward the smokehouse. It was larger than any I'd seen, but I also knew of the glory that had once been Baskerville. The manor had hosted lavish gatherings on a regular basis, often playing host to at least two hundred partygoers from the wealth of London on a weekly basis. It was also said that Old Man Baskerville, himself, was responsible for coercing influential members of Parliament into seceding from the European Union shortly before the world ended. The plan, unfortunately, had blown up in his face. Quite literally.

Holmes stopped at the doors to the smoke house, looked up, and sniffed the air. I tried the same, but the smell of charred and rotting meat was all I was able to differentiate from the metallic smell of the nuclear snow that fell around us.

"He's here," he said, leveling his eyes on the door. "I can smell him."

"Smell him?" Watson said. "After all this time, Holmes?"

"Has it been so long, Watson?" Holmes asked as he hefted the wooden brace that held the doors shut, showing a strength that his body should not have had. "Has he ever really been gone? Has he ever truly not been involved in every aspect of our lives?" He pulled the doors open. The stench worsened, seeming to spill out into the night, and Watson and I gagged and coughed as Holmes stepped back from the black yawning entryway. Even with my night vision on, I was unable to make out anything inside the building.

"Those goggles will not help you, Mr. Burns," said Holmes. "This is not a mere natural darkness you see before you. It is a mass caused by one man."

"The man you think responsible for my sister's disappearance?" I said between coughs.

He turned to me, eyed me from behind the locks of hair in front of his face as he gave a smirk. He knew something. He nodded to the ghost hounds still hanging from the trees, writhing and whimpering as the shadow vines grew tighter around them. "They confirmed everything for me. I know who is responsible for your sister's disappearance. I know who is responsible for stirring up the dead hunting Hounds of Baskerville."

"It's not him, Holmes," said Watson. "He died in the fallout. You saw to that."

Holmes nodded.

"Alas, my dear Watson, I also should have died. I did not."

A shape formed in the darkness inside the smoke house. It moved and twitched, taking careful, unsure steps out into the dark clearing. We turned and watched the shape as it came to a halt. It wore a full Nuclear Winter suit, the brown leather parka, shapeless and covered in buckles to keep the four sections of it closed against the cold. A leather mask covered his entire head and he wore goggles over his eyes. The scarf he wore around his neck was thick black wool. Holmes gazed at him from under the wide brim of his hat. He stepped forward, his eyes fixed on the figure as he spoke.

"There was a man once, who thought he rivaled me in intelligence," he said, never taking his eyes off the shape in the suit. "He was close, I'll give him that much. A man who considered himself a criminal consultant as much as I considered myself an investigative consultant. This man had his fingers in everything, every aspect of England in both the underground and in Parliament."

The figure cocked its head to one side, then shook it condescendingly at Holmes. I almost startled when he spoke, the woman's voice a shock, rattled and rasped and muffled by the mask, but familiar. Familial.

"You're only off by one fact," she said as she reached up and pulled back her mask. "I am your intellectual equal, Sherlock Holmes."

Sheryl.

She smiled at me, her eyes bluer than normal, almost glowing in the dark, her skin pale and her eyes sunken. Such a hellish grin was unlike her, stretching her face in an unholy way.

"Oh God," I said, the words not much more than a breath.

She shook her head at me slowly, her eyes seeming to pierce into my soul. "Dear brother," she said. Her tone was unlike her, sly and sharp. "He died in the blast. To what do I owe the pleasure?"

"I've come to take you home," I said. I tried to step towards her, but my body refused, my feet firmly planted. My heart raced. Nothing held me, no spell or shackle. Only fear. This was wrong. This was all wrong.

Sheryl laughed. She waved her hands, and the ghost hounds dropped from the trees, their bonds broken. They shook it off and stepped towards us, growling as they came closer.

"I am perfectly content here, brother," she said.

"That I believe without argument," said Holmes. "You've always preferred solitude A lack of human contact unless that human contact would work in your favor...James."

The look Sheryl gave Holmes froze my blood. Hatred, vile and unrelenting, seethed and boiled in her eyes. "Not all are perfect like you, are they, my dear Sherlock?" she said. "I prefer to keep those useful near me, whereas you prefer keeping pets to revel in your genius out of sheer need of some kind of acceptance for what you are. And what you've become. So tell me, old friend, which of us is more pathetic?"

"The fallout killed you, James," said Holmes, staring into Sheryl's eyes from under the brim of his hat. "I saw to it personally."

James? Why did he keep calling her James? Sheryl threw her head back and laughed. It was a horrible sound, shrill and loud, and then deeper as her voice changed to a male tone. She looked back at Holmes and grinned at him. "You're so arrogant," she said, her voice gone. "Are you so stupid to think that you are the only one who walked away from the Nuclear Dawn?"

I looked between Holmes and Sheryl, and then focused on Holmes as I spoke. "What is the meaning of this?"

"Mr. Burns," said Holmes, still staring at Sheryl. "Your sister truly is dead. And I have found her murderer, though I must say that I initially thought that my late brother was being a touch factitious when he alluded to such an impossibility. I present Professor James Moriarty. He owns her body now."

Sheryl nodded to me, smiling. Moriarty. Not Sheryl. I raised my pistol and took aim. My hand shook, trembled. Impossible to aim. Not her. No. I couldn't. The gun. So heavy. Watson also took aim, small arcs of electricity dancing up and down his arms. I'd heard the stories. Moriarty. Sherlock's demonic equal, as evil as he was brilliant. He now possessed my sister. My dear, sweet Sheryl.

"She's in there," I shouted, my eyes stinging and wet, my breaths quick, my throat tight. "Damn you, she's in there!" Moriarty stepped closer to me, close enough to press the barrel of my gun to my sister's forehead. The eyes, dear God the eyes. He used my sister's eyes to glare at me, daring me to pull the trigger.

"She is in here," he said. " You're absolutely right. I can still feel her fighting me, squirming around in pain. I like her in pain. It makes her easier to keep down. And I find amusement in her torment. Go ahead. You can free her." She grabbed my hand and wrapped her mouth around the barrel, ran her tongue up and down it a she grinned hideously at me. She chuckled, Moriarty's laugh coming from her lips repulsive. "Pull the trigger. Free her. Or take your time. Her torment tastes like," she licked the barrel again, the move carnal and sickening, made worse by the male groan that escaped her lips. "Steel."

I put my finger on the trigger, pulled back the hammer. Thought of Sheryl falling into the snow, the bullet hole in her head. But she was dead. Holmes had said so. Moriarty claimed that he had her soul imprisoned. But what if he was lying? What if there was another way? Killing her body would kill them both.

Wouldn't it?

Suddenly, two tendrils of shadow shot from the snow and wrapped around Moriarty's wrists. He struggled, my sister's body showing unusual strength as he pulled against the snare. My sister was small, had nowhere near the strength of a man. Yet Moriarty's possession had given her body what it needed to fight. I stared helplessly at Holmes. He was strained, his lips slightly open to reveal gritted teeth as his puppets fought his enemy.

"You control the shadows," Moriarty said, his eyes locked on Holmes. "But I control something far more substantial." He gave a loud whistle, and the hounds pounced.

Watson fired off several shots, and three hounds fell to the snow and lay still. He brandished a small cane and tossed it to me as a hound closed in. I pulled the blade from the cane quickly, slashing out as I went. The hound fell to the side and hit the ground, writhing as black blood poured from its throat. Another hound came at me. I swiped at it with the cane sword, and it recoiled, its maw cut open. The hounds began to back away slowly. Watson kept aim, his back to Moriarty and Sherlock as he kept the hounds at bay. I stood closer to him, my back to his as more hounds stepped out of the brush. I stole a quick look at the blade I wielded, noting the strange symbols etched into the steel.

Two hounds rushed Holmes. He released Moriarty to defend himself, raising his arms as if tossing away a bundle of rags. A black shadow erupted from the snow. The hounds crashed into it, then scrambled to their feet. They barked, cowering as the shadow enveloped them.

Moriarty took full advantage of the distraction and tackled Holmes. He was on the ground in a flash, Moriarty straddling him and pinning him down with my sister's knees. "It was you that discorporated my soul in that blast," he hissed at Holmes. "Your little 'arrangement' with Mrs. Hudson to keep your dear brother alive affected more than just you and Mycroft, Sherlock. I wander in and out of shadows, taking what bodies I need to take in order to watch your every move. What you do is far more sinister than anything I could ever have brought myself to do, Sherlock. My soul may be trapped, but your soul will burn for your arrangement."

"I may burn," Holmes said. "But my intentions are different from yours. I knew that only your body burned in that blast. I arranged for my own survival, and that of my brother's. Mrs. Hudson was happy to come to my aid as long as I was willing to hold up my end of the bargain. All so I could hunt you. All so I could make sure that your crime syndicate would always be kept in check, even after your death."

Holmes bucked Moriarty off him and was on his feet instantly. His eyes went completely black as shadows cloaked around him. Moriarty whistled, and a group of hounds rushed Holmes, bypassing Watson and I as they made for the shadow master. Holmes pointed at the hounds and the shadows reacted, tangling around them and squeezing. The animals whined in pain as bone snapped and sinew tore. Watson fired as more hounds advanced. Holmes rolled, the shadows whipping around with him, and ended up on top of Moriarty. He put his hands on my sister's neck, and I watched as her mouth gaped for air. She turned her head and looked at me, reached her hand out to me.

"Samuel," she said, her voice a croak. "Let him kill me."

I ran towards them. Watson grabbed me, held me back. "Stop, Burns!"

I pushed him aside and ran, crashing into Holmes and knocking him to the ground. He swore at me, and I felt something slam into my chest. I was on my back, and Holmes stood over me.

Sheryl got to her feet, looked at me, and smiled Moriarty's fiendish grin. "How long will we do this, Sherlock?" he asked. "You've damned us both for eternity."

Holmes smiled at him, his eyes narrow as he held his hand out.

"Until next time, then."

The shadows came from all around, swarmed Moriarty and his hounds. The man screamed, held Sheryl's arms out as the shadows moved in and out of every orifice, filling her with dark chaos. A shape spewed from her mouth and floated into the air, a black mass that took the form of a clean-cut, shrewd-looking man whose face was every bit as intelligently reptilian as Sherlock Holmes. His features were twisted with psychotic rage, and he screamed at Holmes as the hounds floated into the air with him, then dispersed and headed in the direction of the London Wasteland. Moriarty lingered a moment longer, staring at his enemy, his rage front and center. Holmes stared back at him, then looked down and tipped his hat at the specter. Moriarty screamed at him again, then shot out of the clearing in the direction his hounds had fled. The silence that followed was deep and almost offensively loud, every sound absorbed by the quiet blanket of snow that fell around us.

Sheryl lay on the ground, black viscous fluid leaking from her mouth, nose, eyes, and ears. I went to her, Watson close behind me. We knelt, and Watson checked her for a pulse. He looked up at me and shook his head.

"I'm sorry, Burns," he said.

"Moriarty knew that the Hounds of Baskerville had been killed during the Nuclear Dawn," Holmes said. I looked up and saw him standing there, staring hard in the direction the ghosts had fled. "When I discorporated his soul in the blast, he came here and possessed the hounds. They each, in turn, possess the criminals of the London Wasteland, keeping his legacy of crime alive, organized painfully down to even the finest detail. Even tonight is but a slight delay in whatever plan he has to bring down the last remnants of government in place and wield limitless control over the criminal world." He turned and looked down at Sheryl, then to me.

"She's gone," I said, a lump in my throat. Shock. I couldn't feel. Not yet. I wouldn't allow myself. I had to get her body out of the woods first. I needed to give her a proper burial.

"I am sorry for your loss," Watson said to me. "But there is the matter of payment."

I resisted the urge to hit him. "How dare you speak to me of money while I hold the hand of my dead sister?"

"Because it is your sister we require," Holmes said, interrupting Watson before he could speak. "Your credits will also suffice, but I'm afraid they do not satisfy our rental agreement, nor my arrangement, with Mrs. Hudson. It's not money that Mrs. Hudson requires to keep me as I am. Sheryl Burns's body is truly dead, but her soul remains tarnished and trapped inside."

A year has gone since the incident with Sherlock Holmes and his partner, Dr. Watson. A year since I made the agreement to give them my sister's soul, poisoned by the claws of James Moriarty. Were her body to have survived, Sheryl's life would have been a waking nightmare. Mrs. Hudson was grateful for the payment. One soul to be sure that Sherlock Holmes could have another year in what remained of a post-nuclear world. I never called on him again, nor did I ever see him outside of his bunker on Baker Street. I would see Dr. Watson on occasion, but only in passing. He would tip his bowler to me, the damned thing propped over his weather gear. I remembered the knowing look on his face when Sherlock took my sister's soul from her body. That look told me he would remember me always. The look of a man both hardened by war, and content to live in the company of a man who had willingly cursed himself to hunt a man he had also cursed.

I walked the streets of the London Wasteland in fear. Was that man one of Moriarty's hounds? Moriarty, himself? Or that man? Or that woman? Or those children?

I would always be afraid of the dark after that day.

But I would always be ever so much more afraid of Sherlock Holmes.

REBORN

Selah Janel

THE HALLS OF THE SPACE STATION REBORN WERE PRISTINE AND BRIGHT, A maze of metal and plastic sterility. They were in sharp contrast to the illusion gardens in the various sectors, of which Clapham was one. Though it was late, enough people were still enjoying the night's entertainment. The theme was Old England, so couples enjoyed quaint hologram theater shows and others, like Lucy Scaleton and Alsop Addison, soaked up the unusual experience of walking nighttime streets.

"Let's move away from the urchins. I know they make things realistic, but they're creepy," Lucy murmured. "We need to find the exit before things shut down and the security mechs scan for the night."

Alsop nodded and they increased their pace. "I'm almost glad we don't have to deal with streets. The hall layouts are much simpler." She hissed when her foot brushed through the long skirt, sending ripples through the false image that revealed her jumpsuit underneath. "Clothes today are easier, too."

"It's all so realistic, though. Especially with all the scents and sounds piped in, never mind the temp changes. Holo-tech has come such a long way." Lucy took hold of her friend's arm with a sheepish expression. "I know we're safe, but…"

"Let's get home before they turn everything off for the night and ruin the fun!" Alsop tugged her down an alley. "I think this shortcuts to the exit." She trailed frowned when they hit a dead end.

"Al—"

"I could've sworn this was an exit."

"'Scuse me, miss, but spare a quid on a cold night?"

The pair jumped, then shared an exasperated look. Alsop turned to address the fellow behind them, tossing her blonde curls. "Stupid programming," she grumbled before addressing the image. "It's late and we need to get home." The looming form didn't budge or disappear. "Hey, I mean it. Bugger off or we'll just go through you!" The shadowed gentleman's shoulders bobbed in a silent laugh.

"This isn't Jack the Ripper night, is it?" Lucy whispered, hand clenched tight on her friend's arm.

"Don't be silly. It can't hurt you. It's just another damn hologram!" Alsop snapped and strode right into the moving shadow.

Silver flashed and rippled. The blonde jerked with the impact, her holo-costume fading away to reveal her slashed jumpsuit. She stared at the ripped fabric, dumbfounded. "What on earth?" The concept of actual danger was so foreign. Instinctively, still expecting the shadowed mass to dissolve into static and code, she struck at it and felt her stomach drop when it touched real fabric and something warm underneath.

The looming figure that was now too real, too threatening, too substantial pounced again. The shadowed figure grabbed the blonde and silver lashed out, sending crimson spraying right through the false images of the ancient London alleyway, spattering the metal projection walls underneath. The holograms couldn't fully form with the intrusion, making the length of the alley a flickering, macabre trap. Alsop's painful scream tore through the nighttime sounds and distant music.

Her friend screamed with her, the sound shrill and useless against the assailant. "No, no! Let her go, this isn't supposed to happen! Security!" Lucy panicked as she struggled with her the other girl's falling body, frantically looking for the cameras and police units. Unhindered, the thing shoved Alsop away. The gasping blonde fell back into her friend, sending them both to the floor, revealing metal underneath the cobblestones. Cold laughter prompted them to look up and when they did, the alley was nothing but screams and blue fire.

It wasn't that Jane had cause to be suspicious, but it wasn't typical for the head of the Britannia wing's medical units to show up to her clinic, especially with the head of security. She almost faltered, but she forced herself to look up at the somber face of her rarely-seen boss with affected innocence. "Cyrinda, I didn't know it was inspection time already. You should have had one of the nurses page me, I'd have been in earlier. Have you been seen to? Would you like a cup of tea? Mary, three cups of the morning brew, if you please." She blushed at the calm stares of her superiors. It wasn't typical to name the domestic AI that organized living and work quarters, but if she was to be talking to something, she'd rather it have a proper name. It was hard enough keeping all the human workers in the sector in good health. She'd been granted the position of head medic of the London sector at barely twenty-five years old, something that did little to endear her to those in her field and some of her patients. *It would be just my luck to get sacked six months in.*

"You can relax, you're not in any trouble." Cyrinda Benson wasn't exactly someone to be feared, but between her position and her serious demeanor, she was a hard read. "Jane, this is Inspector Lester Standing. He's come here seeking our help."

Jane cued up her schedule for the day and turned to address the tall, slender man of middle age.

He offered a nod and a tight, professional smile. "It's about your report of the attacks three days ago, Doctor Mors."

Her shoulders relaxed. "Ah, well, I realize it was rather strange, but I stand by—"

"He means did Miss Scaleton say anything," Cyrinda said, slender arms crossed over her chest.

"She said a lot of things, most of which can be attributed to shock. It's why we put her in stasis, like the others from earlier in the month." Even if the victims' hysteric babbling hadn't been strange, the incidents would have stuck in Jane's mind. Violence, especially unprovoked assault, just didn't happen anymore and now they were up to a handful in such a short time. It was like some garish story from the long-forgotten days from before the Final War.

"May I be frank?" the inspector asked with a tired sigh. "There haven't been any truly horrific crimes in decades. Doesn't it seem strange that these attacks have started suddenly?"

"The public doesn't seem worried about them," Jane muttered. "It wouldn't be the first time records kept goings on under wraps."

Standing raised an eyebrow. "Ignorance keeps people safe—"

"Until they wander into the path of whatever's causing this."

"Jane, please. Inspector Standing has come to request your assistance." Cyrinda never raised her voice, but the firm tone conveyed plenty. Jane already felt like she was being babysat in her work half the time. The last thing she wanted was another reason for her superior to look over her shoulder.

"You have the reports. Lucy Scaleton is in stasis like the three previous victims and Miss Addison—"

"We've already been to the mortuary. It's grisly, but nothing that's getting us anywhere," Standing admitted. "We have a consultant at the ready, but as you're the one who's tended to every victim, we would like you to come along for the time being and assist him."

Suspicion pricked at Jane's senses. If there were two things the governing bodies of Reborn liked, it was routine and consistency. The casual deviation was enough to rouse her alarm. "As flattered as I am, I'm really better suited to my work here."

Benson slid around to her desk, blocking their conversation from the inspector's view. "Doctor, wouldn't you like to get to the bottom of this? It would be a good break for you. Certainly more interesting than treating workers for fatigue."

"But—"

"The mechs and interns can handle it. Besides, I know how withheld information vexes you," Cyrinda pointed out, a look of dry humor on her face. In a lower tone she added, "And if you cooperate, I'll forget that you've been demanding assistance from the genealogy and genetic departments behind my back."

Heat crept up the back of Jane's neck. As much as she didn't like subterfuge, more and more patients had been complaining of very specific symptoms that were too coincidental to be generic rundown. It was the downside of man's last attempt at survival after the Final War, and with a current overall human population of 20,000, only 3,500 of which were from Britannia, any malaise or concern had to be figured out promptly. If it wasn't a virus, surely there had to be some connection, though the specific information she needed was high level access. Apparently her attempts at trading favors with other agencies to look at their databases hadn't gone as unnoticed as she'd hoped. *Fine. It'll take me away from work, but if it keeps me from a review or put back in stasis for questionable ethics, I can spare the time.* Forcing a smile, she slid around her boss and addressed Standing. "I'd love to be of service. Who's the consultant I'll be assisting?"

"Are you alright? You look a little pale." Standing looked too amused at her discomfort for Jane's liking. She hated to feel patronized. It was too reminiscent of the smugness she got from other medical staff in the London sector and throughout Britannia, as if her age disqualified her experience.

Standing seemed well-meaning enough, though she still clenched her teeth at the comment. "Of course I'm pale! He's a legend!" They'd opted for the lifts to the security offices of the London sector, where one of the most recent victims was going through the wakening process for questioning.

"I take it it's your first time meeting an Intellect?" The levels they passed as they ascended blurred by.

"Would I be this shaken if it wasn't?" she snapped, then gathered herself. "Apologies. I just…it's strange, I'm not sure how I feel about it." Excitement battled with her nerves. "Shame those poor girls had to suffer for something like this to happen."

"I'm sure he'd look at it as more of a twisted blessing. Things have been dull since his awakening."

"Is there anything I should know?" She'd heard the stories, of course. Stories that were so fantastic that for ages it had been believed that he was fictional. Intellects were rare and hard to actualize. The process of combining the most brilliant minds throughout history with robotic mech shells was rarely successful. Artists and thinkers seemed to be the preferred choices; no one had dared try a politician yet. Only Einstein, DaVinci, Shakespeare, and this one had taken so far. *The last thing I need is to damage a priceless mind.* The lift doors opened and she followed the inspector into the security dome.

"I don't believe there's any preparing for a meeting with him. Besides, it's not like you really have to do anything besides recount what you've seen. Just hang around. Whether he admits it or not, he's more comfortable with someone to work off of."

She bristled at the implication that she was just there because of happenstance, as if she had nothing else to offer. *He's right, though. I'm a doctor, not a detective. This is just a way to get Benson off my back.*

Standing led her past halls until they came to a glass-encased conference room. "As open as it seems, once inside no one can see us or hear our discussions. It's for the best, I think."

"You don't want anyone to know what's going on? Isn't that dangerous?"

"Until we know exactly what we're dealing with and how to tell people to avoid it, there's no reason to incite panic. Now then, here we are," he added, ushering her through a door. "He doesn't have need to sleep or rest, which seems a kind of blessing to him, strangely enough. We've allowed him space here for the moment since he doesn't require much, but eventually he'll get his own lodgings. It's only humane, considering."

It was exactly as he said: from the inside, the outside bustle was visible, but no one paid them the slightest bit of attention, or noticed that the conference room resembled an antiquated sitting room on the inside. "Yes, very necessary to make yourself feel better about your inability to continue alone, Inspector," a deep voice quipped.

Jane stared at the form that was not alive but very much seated in a plump armchair. The mech shell was that of a man in his prime, probably younger than he'd been back in his heyday, and the robotics would presumably lend him added strength and ability to match his formidable mind. If she hadn't known, she would have assumed he was human, except for the fact that he seemed too alert, a little too perfect, maybe. Of course, the first thing out of her mouth was, "My God, it really is you!"

For his part Sherlock Holmes assessed her, raised an eyebrow, and glanced at Inspector Standing. "Really?"

"Now, Sherlock, she's just startled—"

"Truly, Inspector, if you don't comprehend what I'm asking—"

"Doctor Mors is here to help you with the case. She's seen all the victims at one point or another. It's her reports you've been reading this morning."

Although it seemed his beef was with Standing, Holmes didn't look any more impressed. "Well then, sit down and let's get to it." She hesitantly took a seat, though when Standing moved to join them, Sherlock waved him away. "We'll let you know when we've solved the riddle, Inspector. Send your rejuvenated witness to us and go back to the data work you love so much." Standing grimaced, but took his leave.

"Wait, can you do that?" Jane blurted before thinking. "I mean, he's head of security in Britannia. He's leading the case. Shouldn't he be here?"

"Yes, pity that a thousand years and starting from scratch has found human perception as typical as it's always been." His stare saw every part of her, and she had no idea if it was because of the superhuman body or because of the mind inside it.

Jane sank into the chair across from Holmes and stared dumbly at the room, unable to meet his gaze. It was likely projection, but it looked to be fully furnished with a wooden mantle and accent work, dark wallpaper, cloth-cushioned chairs and other antiquities. Her knowledge of history wasn't perfect, but everything suggested that the décor was from the time of Old England, probably circa 1800s. Holmes said nothing, but quietly watched her with his unnerving, unflinching gaze.

She studied the Intellect, but a mech's face wasn't the most expressive, even on the newest high-end models. She had a nagging feeling that he was like this as a human, too, and while his scrutiny was disconcerting, it wasn't necessarily uncomfortable. It did leave her wondering why she'd been requested, though.

The look on her face must have spoken her thoughts. "You are the only link we have to all the victims. Although you're obviously young, you're knowledgeable enough to have a lead position in Britannia's central medical facility. You obviously go above and beyond in your reports." He cast another searching look that made her feel like a child but paused, as if there were details he wasn't quite sure of, or didn't want to voice.

"You read my reports?" It seemed the easiest way to deflect his intrusive observations.

"I'm allotted privileges that most aren't. Four separate attacks in the past two months," he went on, all business. Jane couldn't tell if the gleam in his eye was actual excitement or the flicker of the simulated ancient fireplace. "Five victims total, all female. Attacks typically happened during the traditional night cycle, all as the victims were walking home alone, save for Miss Scaleton and Miss Addison.

Jane nodded. "All happened in different areas of the London sector, so the general area is still fairly wide."

"Likely not limited to the culprit's work habits or anything else," Holmes concluded, steepling his fingers. His movements were as quiet as a human, with no sounds of motors or servos like some of the butler or security mechs Jane had seen. She felt compelled to do something during the following lull, to compensate for him. She dug through the work satchel she'd brought and produced a small tablet, one of the bits of antiquated technology the original station settlers had kept to improve upon once restarting on Reborn. A few touches and slides of a finger, and the air was filled with text and a series of lurid holo-photos depicting the victims' injuries. Holmes managed a frown, but it seemed a reflex gesture and not a true expression. Jane's own reaction was more of a genuine grimace.

"Not used to such things, I take it," he commented.

It was true that the founders had worked hard to ensure that crime was virtually nonexistent, though her temper flared with the need to defend herself. "It's never easy to see life taken before it's time and they're not that much younger than I am. Disease and violent death may be down, but they're not unheard of. Besides, I was there for the Final War, I know what people are capable of." She glanced up at Holmes, whose only indication of surprise was to lean forward and blink rapidly.

"I wouldn't have guessed."

She shrugged it off, but was disappointed. *I suppose there are things even he can't deduce.* "Desert medic only, so I didn't get it as bad as some. Taken out of commission once I was injured and abandonment was imminent. I was placed in stasis until things were stabilized. My memories are still a little worse for wear from it. They let me out a year ago, and put me back to work six months after that." She still felt displaced. It was an odd feeling of catching up no matter what she did, of being simultaneously a part yet distant from everyone around her. Something tugged in Jane's chest as she watched Sherlock process the information with a quiet nod. *Maybe he feels something similar, but with different circumstances.* "Most of the victims came away with torn clothes and lacerations, as if from knives, though don't ask me how anyone could get a weapon past the security points. I'd say it was an animal, but—"

"Nothing's escaped from the zoological havens in the past six months. Then there's Miss Addison."

Jane hissed out a slow breath and nodded, scrolling to the photo in question. "I've never seen anything like it since wartime, honestly, and even then, I don't know how anyone would have access to that kind of weaponry." The body was fully displayed in the hologram, which the doctor rotated and zoomed in on with a wave of her hand. "No signs of sexual assault, but the same lacerations, and her face, well." The girl's features were almost indistinguishable, the skin melted into a burned puddle.

"Torch gun? Something portable?"

The doctor frowned, and for a few heartbeats her mind went distant then sharp, as if it was clicking through a list of possible images. "Mors?"

She looked up to see Holmes watching her. She wasn't certain it was concern, but that felt…right, or it fit, at any rate. *Maybe I'm just reading what I want to see.* "Those were for razing towns and other large-scale maneuvers and were hard to secure on their best day. No, I've not seen anything quite like this. Security mechs can only stun and human patrols don't carry firepower like that. Anything soldier-grade has been outlawed and hidden away. She looks like one of those wax figures you read about if they were damaged."

Sherlock tilted his head. "There are also the matter of the security reports. Police haven't released a public statement acknowledging the situation."

Jane felt the disdain that was vaguely shadowed on his face. "I don't know how long you've been with us, but that's typical. Anything to reduce public panic and fear-mongering."

"You don't agree?"

"I don't agree with withholding information that may help others." Her tone was more biting than she'd like, but he only drummed his fingertips together.

"Let's see what we can dig up, then." Sherlock's eyes dimmed, again making Jane wonder if they were lit artificially or how much of the shell in front of her was him. When he didn't move she frowned, then coughed politely as the silence stretched on.

"Mr. Holmes? Sherlock?" Jane squirmed in her seat, causing the simulated images to ripple around her body. *I really, really hope he isn't malfunctioning.* "Maybe I should get Standing." She stood, but couldn't decide whether to rush to the door or go to the frozen form in front of her.

With a shudder and a start the Intellect came back to himself. At the same moment, the air was filled with the frozen image of the station halls instead of her reports. "There we are. These should at least give us something to go on."

"Is that…Did you *hack* the police database?" Disbelief was a tame word to describe her shock.

Sherlock shrugged. "Faster than going down the hall and trying to convince Standing to give us tidbits," he reasoned, and Jane could have sworn there was a tinge of smugness on his face. "Much easier to just go looking for what we need, myself. Let's see what we have then, shall we?"

An hour later found them just as perplexed as before they'd viewed the footage. Even with the Intellect's enhanced capabilities, they'd been unable to get past the same anomaly on all the blue-tinted footage from every cam he could gain access to. The general area was in full view, the girls perfectly recognizable, but every time the figure of what was presumably the culprit came into range, his image distorted. "Is there any way he's doing this?"

Holmes frowned. "Maybe if he had a personal scrambler, but I don't think a regular work-level civilian would have access to one."

"He wouldn't, and you could have just asked for access to the database, you know," Standing said from the door. Jane jumped, but Holmes was relaxed as ever, utterly unrepentant.

"Time is of the essence. We haven't days to waste filling out request forms."

The head of security sighed and muttered something that sounded like "You two deserve each other." Louder, he said "I have Miss Scaleton ready to talk."

"What about the testimonies of the others?" Jane asked.

"We're hoping she'll be more reliable since it's more recent," Standing replied. "We have the recordings, but they're…not helpful. Downright barmy in some cases."

"If you want the technical term," the Intellect quipped. "All the recordings are incredibly similar, and I suspect this will be more of the same, though it's worth hearing her. Hers is the first attack with a fatality and a change in the means of violence," he pointed out. "Send her in."

Lucy Scaleton was remarkably alert, but Jane wondered if Standing's assessment was right. *Everything out of her mouth is absolutely mad.*

"I knew you wouldn't believe me!" she cried, stood up, sat down, and moved to stand again.

"It's not that we don't believe you, but you have to admit that it sounds farfetched," Standing pressed. Jane flinched when Holmes raised a hand, silencing him.

"What if we send out for some tea, that might calm the nerves a bit," she tried, moved to the shuddering girl, and took her hand.

"No need. Hudson, tea service, if you please," Holmes called. Within seconds the table beside Lucy's chair opened and a steaming tray slid up into reach.

"Of course you'd name the room AI," the inspector sighed and spared an exasperated glance Jane's way.

"I would think I'm allowed some eccentricities."

Jane took the conversation in as much as the girl's whimpers as she moved to pour.

Maybe a woman's touch might be best. She wasn't overly feminine on her best day, but the girl was barely nineteen and being bombarded on all sides. "Now then, you said you were coming home with your friend after a night at the commons?"

Lucy nodded, dark hair still sweat-slicked from hibernation thaw. "Thought it might be fun to see what it was like back in the day. Old England always seems so romantic in the films." She paused to sip from her cup, sniffling. "It was supposed to be safe, all in good fun!"

"You said you turned down an alley?" Holmes pressed.

"We got turned around coming out of the Green Dragon pub and thought it was a shortcut. It was all so real, it was easy to get confused, especially with how they move the map around between cycles." Jane was amazed she didn't drop the cup, her hands were trembling so much. "He came up behind us. We thought it was another simulation!" Her voice rose shrilly. "But he was so tall, and he just grabbed for Al, and his claws tore right through her!"

"Claws?" Standing pressed.

"He had to! He didn't drop anything! He just cut her and started laughing, and spitting blue fire all at us! If she hadn't been in front of me, I'd be as dead as she is!" Lucy broke down, unable to hide the sobs.

"Blue fire? You mean he had some sort of weapon?" Jane asked.

The girl shook her head. "No, it just came right out of him! Al fell away once she'd...and he grabbed me with his clammy hand! I thought I was done for, but all he did was stare!"

"You got a look at him?" Jane was surprised Holmes was as quiet as he was, but she was certain he was taken everything in, from every unintentional move the girl made, every hair on her head, to every word from her mouth.

Lucy nodded, swallowing back her hysteria. "He was pure evil! I know we don't rightly use that word anymore, but he wasn't human. Nothing could look like that! He just stared at me with glowing red eyes, then jumped straight up in the air and disappeared!"

"Is that possible?" Sherlock asked.

Standing had already cued up a map. "Holograms can only do so much, so most of the common areas have a basic layout. Some are straight dead space with images projected onto synthetic fog, but Clapham has miniature buildings, corridors and general facades set up to make things more realistic for the public. It works out because they usually focus on vintage time periods. Those walls are at least nine feet high."

"Were the other girls near illusion gardens?" Sherlock asked. "We know they were in different parts of the greater London sector, but what about the type of areas they were in?"

Standing consulted his tablet. "You're right. It looks like Mary Stevens was passing by, but the other two were attending on the nights they were attacked."

"What time period were the commons featuring? What place?" Sherlock asked.

"Does that really matter?" Standing asked, glancing up from the case files.

"It could mean everything." Holmes's voice was sharp and insistent.

"Uh, it looks like 1800's London, just like on the night of Miss Scaleton's attack, here. Wait, it looks like Jenny Slater was attending an America theme night set in the 1930s. Same with Nadia Thomas." Standing rattled of the information, then managed a shrug when his eyes happened to meet Jane's. The Intellect leaned back in his chair, processing the information.

"Please, you can't let it go. You have to catch this creature! It's horrible, not human at all!" Lucy tightly gripped Jane's arm.

"We'll do our best," she soothed, but gave a look over the girl's head to Standing. "I think perhaps Miss Scaleton should be given the chance to fully rest and heal." She scribbled an order on her own tablet and quickly sent it on. "This should help things along. Take her to my clinic before the hibernation chamber." She gave the younger woman a tight smile. "We'll do everything in our power to catch whoever did this."

Jane could feel the Intellect's eyes on her as she returned to her chair after seeing Miss Scaleton and Standing to the door. "Poor thing. Do you think the stasis is messing with her memories?"

"Unfortunately, besides the blue fire, her claims mostly match the recordings that were taken in security right after the events in question," Holmes admitted. "I'll admit it makes little sense on the surface, but there has to be an explanation."

"Someone hiding behind a hologram costume?"

"Perhaps, but projected images don't sustain well, do they?" He prodded thearm of his chair, which fizzled in and out of focus at the purposeful touch, revealing the regulation issue furniture underneath. "Think of the details, Doctor, and what they might line up with."

His encouragement pushed her thoughts and it was like the times she'd had trouble sleeping when she'd first been out of stasis. Her mind went foggy then hyper-focused, and the rest of her was filled with a strange, pricking alertness. Fog-covered streets, strange faces at doors, and faded newspaper text flashed through her mind at a rapid pace. "Wasn't there a story about something like this long ago? Jack…Jack the Ripper? No, another one. Jumping Jack?"

"Spring-heeled Jack," he corrected. If she didn't know better, she would call him startled. "I'm surprised you know that story. It's far before your time."

"I must have heard it somewhere, read it in passing. The bits from libraries that did survive are random, at any rate. Besides, the strangest things come to me at times."

"It was an urban legend even back in my day. I'm afraid the answer is probably much less fantastic, although…" His eyes sparked, though it could have been the lighting. "Think of what Miss Scaleton said. "Clammy hands, inhuman abilities, strange eyes."

"You'll have to be more to the point if you want me to keep up."

The Intellect extended his hand to her. When she took it Jane nearly recoiled, it was so cool and strange to the touch. "You see, some things can't be worked around, I'm afraid. Lesser models have eyes that reflect light in strange ways."

"That's right. There used to be the joke before they upgraded that you'd know the police were out if the yellow-eyes were trailing you home. You think they were attacked by a mech? But what about the fire and the cuts? Could a mech jump straight up to the top of a nine foot wall?"

"That's what we need to find out," he agreed, though his posture looked more uneasy than what came with relearning how to move.

"What aren't you saying?"

"Are there any private Intellects? Any not brought around for public service?"

Jane frowned. "Not that I know of. That would cost a fortune and require a hell of a lot of influence. Besides, there's a vetting process for that."

"Stories have to come from somewhere."

"Meaning?"

He sighed, a strange gesture to come from what was essentially a robot. "If I recall, the truth behind Spring-heeled Jack came back to the Marquis of Waterford, a man with a penchant for drink and mayhem."

"You think his family paid to have him resurrected here on Reborn? Are they around? Would he have had enough influence back then to preserve himself?" It had been a notoriously dodgy practice, especially back in the days long before it had been perfected.

"It seems like the type of prank he'd enjoy."

"But what about the attacks on the America theme nights?"

"Those stories eventually extended across the pond." It was unclear if Holmes had gathered the information from some sort of database or if his memory was that good. "There's a reason these aren't happening in the actual American wing of Reborn. Unfortunately there's a difference between working around Standing and peering into other areas," he admitted.

A slow smile spread across Jane's face. "I can get us into the genealogy and genetic databases. I've been owed some favors and there's been a strange upswing in exhaustion with no clear source in the past few weeks. I've kept the access codes I've been allowed at home, but it's a start if it helps us catch this Waterford, isn't it?"

"Marquis of Waterford. His actual name was Henry—"

"Beresford, of course." Jane blinked and found that she was just as confused as she imagined Holmes tried to look. "One of those random things."

"Indeed." His tone was careful, his voice more indicative of his feelings than anything else.

"You don't believe me."

"I never said that."

The stress of the day warred with the pressure of their task, the overwhelming strangeness of it all. Suddenly the room was too small, the Intellect's gaze too scrutinizing and not human enough. "Look, I know it's strange, but it just happens. Maybe the rehabilitation program in stasis got jumbled, I don't know, but just…stop looking at me like that! I get I'm not important, I get I'm just here to tell you what I know and be your temporary accessory, but…" She had no clue where she was going with the rant and balked when she checked the time. "It's getting late and I should get home. That'll give me a chance to dig around and I'll meet you back here tomorrow."

He nodded, but didn't acknowledge her more emotional words one way or another. "You should have an escort."

She grit her teeth and strode to the door without looking back. "I survived a damn war, Holmes, I think I can walk myself home."

The halls dimmed for the night cycle, though there was light to see by. Jane usually didn't notice the silent security mechs that guarded throughout the night, but now she couldn't help but see them. Compared to Holmes, they were only human shape, their features dependent on what make and model they were. There was no denying that they were fake, there only to serve. *Is that how we look at him, too? What must it be like to come back to life and be able to move and think and talk, but have no connection to the world around you? He's a part of things, better than all of us, but still separate.* A lingering sadness swept over her. As much as he intimidated her, as much as she enjoyed her medical work, this time with Holmes gave her a challenge that felt a natural fit, even more so than when she was with her patients or overseeing a complicated surgery. She wasn't sure if she'd miss the opportunity to work with an Intellect, miss his strange quirks, or miss the new challenge and strange sense of purpose that invigorated her in a way her daily life did not.

The overhead panels flickered as she moved past them, and at least one of the automated city info signs flashed from its standard ads to a blue nothing, then back. Glitches weren't abnormal, but it put her on edge. Without thinking, Jane shifted her course. Clapham Commons was nearby, and despite talking to Lucy Scaleton earlier, it seemed safer to walk where there might be others nearby. *Maybe I'll turn up something, prove myself useful.* As long as she stayed on the periphery she wouldn't be charged entry, and it would shave ten minutes off her walk.

The glitchy panels stayed with her as her world shifted from white neutral walkways to cobblestones, brick buildings, and fog, making the projections briefly fizzle when she passed. *I'm not carrying anything that would interfere. I'll have to bring this up tomorrow.* A glance down at her unchanged clothes made her chuckle. *I look like a time traveler compared to everything else.*

Jane's thoughts kept her entertained and she didn't hear the footsteps until she was well into the streets. Her breath stilled in her chest. When she paused, so did the sound. In the distance she could hear music, but Clapham was big for what it was, and the street layout meant that it was hard to make a direct path to a more populated area. *Can't just turn around and risk it.* The fear made her feel silly and small and she reminded herself that she'd taken down those far bigger than herself when confronted. *Of course, I had weapons then.*

Her pace increased as she moved faster, and too easily she found herself jogging, disoriented as walls loomed around her. *Wait. Wait.* She ducked down a side alley, forcing her breathing to slow.

Nothing.

Her mind filled with the telltale prickles that she always trusted and she followed the alley, relaxing when it did, in fact, empty into another street. She walked blindly, searching for…she wasn't sure what. A safe place, an apartment, something familiar that linked up to the strange knowing. Just when every fiber of her screamed one more turn and safety she obeyed the instinct…and came to a brick wall.

The probing urge faded, leaving her lost and feeling foolish. Whatever she'd inadvertently read or absorbed from history *wouldn't* link up. This was a show, a fantasy, not a historical layout. Lucy was right, besides: Clapham Commons *did* change its layout from month to month, making it perpetually new, but also hard to navigate. Those damn footsteps, however, were right around the corner she'd just turned down. *You can do this. Just make sure to favor your good shoulder.* Jane exhaled, readied herself, and turned.

"Miss?" She laughed at the metallic sound of a standard-issue security mech voice.

"Yes?" Her voice sounded too relieved and that irritated her.

"The area is secure and we're asking everyone to go home. We just subdued a person who was following people. We need to clear the area."

Usually they just bark orders. She gripped her pack in both hands. "Alright, I'm coming out," she called and carefully advanced to the mouth of the alley. The strange glitching followed her along the brick walls.

The figure was much taller than her, and broad enough to present a sizeable obstacle. Her hands fumbled the makeshift weapon and horrible, high-pitched laughter made her stomach sink.

The world around her exploded into bright lights and plastic and metal projection walls. The laughter turned to shrieks and she struck without thought, without registering what she aimed at. Cold metal struck out, tearing through her suit. *"What is all this?"* a garbled, inhuman voice snarled.

She barely dodged the stream of fire, and the mech who came up behind her caught it fully. The other ten that swarmed the thing, however, quickly subdued it, not that it needed to be overpowered. The thing was already on the floor, howling in pain, covering its eyes and crawling in a disoriented, almost drunken fashion.

It wasn't an Intellect, or a mech, or anything she'd ever seen. Stretched out, it took up nearly half the length of the alley. Keen, angry red eyes, a predator's mouth full of teeth, spikes that resembled horns, long-nailed hands. It thrashed against the mechs throwing themselves on it, and when it bellowed, a long stream of blue fire seared the metal walls it touched. *I'm still in stasis. I've fallen into a story. I've finally gone crazy.*

"Injuries?" the mech nearest her demanded as the others prodded the beast with stun sticks.

"I'm fine," she answered, then moved her hand away from her middle. It came away blood-soaked, and she fell to the ground before she could give her injury a proper look.

Two weeks in a healing pod found Jane back at work when the summons came. She didn't face the gleaming façade of the security center, but a typical hall bearing the name Baker Street. Old ways of navigation were hard to beat, after all. The only unusual thing about the door in front of her was that instead of a family name it bore the code 221B on the digital plaque. It automatically opened, presumably by Hudson, and she found herself in an apartment similar to the way the conference room was disguised, though there were obvious info panels on the far wall. "I see they've set you up well," she mused, unsure of how else to address the Intellect entering the room.

"Indeed. Standing seems to think I'll be more accommodating if I'm presented with familiarity, though I'm trying to catch up bit by bit." There was a bitterness to his voice.

"Do familiar surroundings help?"

He shrugged. "My reality is still no more and no less than what it was when I agreed to this experiment. How are you feeling?" he pressed.

"Better than I was." She paused, unsure what to say about the strange experience. "And thanks to you, of course. You followed me through the info network and holo panels, didn't you? The same way you hacked into the security files. You hit the lights that night."

An almost-smile tugged at the artificial mouth. "If you wouldn't accept an escort…"

"It didn't hurt that I presented the exact bait that Jack preferred and lived near Clapham, as well," she retorted. Holmes had the decency to look away.

"You weren't in true danger."

"Except for the stomach wound!" She sighed. "I'm too tired to be angry. That thing. Its eyes, the thought of it looming over me, watching it fry mechs like that. I can't close my eyes without thinking of it. What *was* that thing?"

Sherlock paced, fingers twitching as if he had need for some way to vent his frustration. "Exactly what he appeared to be. Exactly as the stories say. I don't comprehend it," he admitted. "From what Standing gathered, he crashed to earth back in my day and was trying to figure out how to get aid or get back to his kind. He went mad at being so far away from his home, so alone in an unfamiliar land, so displaced, which led to the attacks."

"But that was so long ago! How did—"

"He's far more resilient than humans. It isn't that much of a stretch to picture him hiding through the centuries, slipping into a hold with the few animals when Reborn was taking volunteers, biding his time."

"But that's been ages ago!"

"Who knows what his lifespan is? Maybe he occupied himself in other wings. It will take a while to coordinate and see if there's been trouble anywhere else. At any rate, he was drawn to what was familiar: the streets and dark nights of 1800s London. He just didn't realize that he wasn't truly there."

"What will happen now?"

Holmes turned away, shaking his head. "He's been forced into stasis until a hold can be built. The station's science institute wishes to study him."

"But that's barbaric!"

"He's the first alien life form we've discovered, Mors…Jane," he corrected, as if he preferred the sound of the latter. "They're not going to let him go waltzing out into space, no matter where he belongs. He'd probably be unable to re-adapt, anyway, and who knows if his species even still exists. That's what humans do, Jane. They poke and discover things until they're figured out." His dark tone was ironic compared to his reputation and she said as much. "I've had a while to think on things."

Jane nodded, unsure what else to say. "This is it, then. I've served my part, managed to not die, so things go back to usual." She turned to take her leave, though it felt like turning her back on a place she'd been in far longer than a few minutes.

"I'd prefer if you stayed to assist me."

She paused. "Why? You don't need me and I won't fetch you tea. You can do the impossible on your own."

Her rebuttal didn't faze him. "You think well on your feet, you don't back down from a challenge. You possess the qualities of another I can clearly remember."

Her eyes narrowed. Standing obviously dealt minimally with Holmes, and few others in security attempted to interact with him. *Was all this some sort of audition to play keeper to a renegade Intellect, to leave a space for someone more palatable in my job?* "I'm not a replacement for your old friend, if that's what all this is about."

"It's a shame that so many ignore what's right in front of them if they'd only look," he sighed, and gestured to the wall screens. Jane frowned and followed him. "Why do you think you were denied access to the genealogy and genetic records? Why would Benson give you up so easily instead of simply having you give witness testimony? Why would she want you away from the exhaustion cases?"

The text in front of her stood bold as anything. Her stomach twisted as recognition took hold, yet she shook her head. "I don't understand."

"Come now, you've proven you're better than that. The original survivors who escaped to Reborn were barely over a thousand. Because of fallout and disease, repopulation hasn't been the easiest thing. It's taken over a thousand years to get where mankind is today."

"How would you know? Hacking into more files?" It was a lazy jab, but she was too disconcerted to think properly. *Surely that sort of data can be faked, can't it? I've already fallen into a story once already, isn't that enough for a lifetime?*

Holmes shook his head and sighed, though it sounded slightly off thanks to the mech capabilities. "I've been around for a bit longer than what you were told. Problems don't go away with a new location and humanity's been busy trying to stay alive. Mechs and AI supplement the work force, but cloning technology is still needed where natural reproduction fails. Even then, it's not a sure thing, unless you supplement it with something sturdier."

"But—"

"You've only been in your position for six months and clones and traditional humans are hard to tell apart, plus there's the benefit that you never got into genetics or obstetrics," he pointed out. "Throughout history, thanks to various organizations, the DNA of the worthy have been kept aside in case of this eventuality. While John would have never consented to a complete scientific reincarnation, his memories and genetic stock were too valuable to waste."

She would have called it crazy, but after gazing into the eyes of whatever creature Spring-heeled Jack was, Jane wasn't so certain she knew anything normal. "What are you trying to say?"

The Intellect gave his odd smile. "You didn't serve in the war and you haven't been in stasis since the Evacuation. When you went to work, that was your first time to set foot in the halls of Reborn. Your war wound, your medical prowess, your vague memories and knowledge of things that just come to you aren't a glitch from stasis. They're all from John's memories, adapted for your circumstances, implanted via a complex experimental mech system. You contain the next interface from what my system is contained in an organic body. Essentially, you are the product of Intellect technology and human cloning."

She was too stunned to contest it, though part of her struggled to make sense of the declaration. "But if part of me is human..."

"He wouldn't have wanted what I chose, but he and Mary never had a child, so it seemed only fitting. Mors is a bastardization of your mother's maiden name. You've always truly been Jane Watson."

Stunned, Jane wandered to a chair and sunk into it. "Ten other attempts were made, but you are the one who took."

"So you had me *made*?"

"Merely gave input. Those in charge of population make the decisions, though the thought of experimenting with merging the two aspects was irresistible to them. It's no better or worse than what Reborn has done for the survivors, whether they're direct descendants or helped along by our growing understanding of science and mechanics.

"Do you realize what you're saying, Sherlock? What's in my head isn't even my own! How could you *presume?*" If she'd had the energy, she would have stormed out. "Is this all a game to you?"

"I didn't want to upset you straight away, and although I had my suspicions, it's hard to read your particular combination of traits. You look remarkably like your parents, but looks can be altered and there had been so many other attempts that it was better to not track them and be disappointed."

"So this was a test? To see if I passed your inspection?" Jane demanded. It was like she'd been shoved out the loading hatch of the space station with no ground beneath her feet and no air to keep her going.

"I had no idea a successful attempt had been finalized, or that Standing was bringing you to me. Nothing about the attacks or the creature was fabricated. You did happen to be the only person who was in contact with all the witnesses and your expertise made you invaluable in this instance. Your random knowledge and habit of pulling up antiquated memories just confirmed what I suspected." He pointed to the breakdown on the screen behind him. "This incident with Jack has proven that you're stronger than the other attempts. You've healed from injuries, you can perform valuable tasks, and most importantly, you can think on your own, Jane. With what's learned from you, humanity can press beyond the meager successful births and inferior clones riddled with pollutants and diseases from Earth, with a little help here and there." His stare held her gaze, though she wanted nothing more than to turn away. "Yes, I made the suggestion and used my influence. Jane, I can think on my own, I can solve problems, I can adapt to the advances that have been made, but to do it all while surrounded by gawking simpletons for whom I'm just a name, a work of fiction…" His voice was quiet and held meaning when his expression couldn't compensate. "I'm up to the challenge, but I'd prefer to not do it alone."

He came around to where she sat and rested a hand on the chair back. "You carry the genes of your mother and father, despite them having you a thousand plus years after their time. You carry the memories of your father, but your will, your personality, your motivations are your own. Think of yourself not as a replacement, but a successor. It is very likely if you go back to your everyday life that you will be called in for study after study, yourself. This way, we can monitor each other. Do you really think Reborn is as much of a utopia as it seems? There will always be need for us, whether it's solving little grievances now or unveiling bigger secrets later on."

Her mind swirled with a torrent of information. *Is the displacement I feel what Jack felt after centuries of being away from his own kind? Will it eventually drive me mad, too?* Of course, the one connection that could potentially keep her grounded also left her wondering how much she'd been manipulated. "How can I go back knowing what I know? You haven't left me much of a choice. I'm not a toy, Sherlock. I'm not a pawn."

He shook his head. "John was never a cog in the machine and neither are you."

She sighed, and the sound was natural, which left her wondering if she'd ever know exactly what parts of her were not. "Then I suppose we can at least give it a try."

She was doubtful, uneasy, but she also harbored a sense of peace. There was so much to consider that she'd retreated to her apartment to collect her thoughts. There was still the sense of betrayal, and she had no idea if her loyalty was her own or a holdover from past history. Still, Jane found herself looking toward the future with more excitement and sense of purpose than she had in a long time. Now that they had taken up the arrangement that Sherlock had with her father, there was moving to do and other details to figure out. In the meantime, she felt compelled to put her thoughts in order, to wrap her head around things, even if it was nothing she could ever show those around her. She pulled out her info tablet, taking care to make sure it's memo function was disconnected from the main network.

From the Diary of Jane Watson
14th day, 8th month, 3089

She paused her typing, but something deep down urged her on, needed the release of words. With a cautious smile, she exhaled a deep breath and pressed on.

It was a strange day when I was brought into the world of the Intellect of one Sherlock Holmes with the even stranger case of Spring-heeled Jack…

SHERLOCK HOLMES AND THE TERROR IN THE AIR

Robert Perret

British Airways Flight 427, en route from London, England to Kingston, Jamaica
April 18th, 1956

HOLMES SAT ENSCONCED IN A HALO OF BLUE SMOKE FROM HIS BELOVED Persian blend of tobacco, valiantly holding at bay the angry grey exhalations from the cigarettes of our fellow passengers. I rolled the highball in my hand lovingly, thinking of the angelic stewardesses who would dip down below the haze every once in a while with an open bottle and a warm smile. I had never been a man for social clubs, but tucked away here all cozy in my seat, my every whim catered to, I could see the appeal. Of course, much of this hospitality was meant to distract the passengers from the fearsome winds whipping by outside as the DC-4 improbably flew thousands of feet over the unforgiving ocean thrashing below. As if in response to my thoughts the whole plane suddenly heaved, eliciting gasps from some and titters from others. I smothered my response with a blanket of scotch and soda. For his part, Holmes puffed blissfully on as if there were not a storm outside, raging at our temerity for being where man by rights ought not be. I called out for another drink.

We were off to Jamaica on some sort of spy game at the behest of Holmes's brother. Mycroft was entrenched deeply within the skunkworks of MI5, where he had made his name as a one man intelligence bureau for the Crown during the Second World War. It would be a mistake to confuse Mycroft's efficacy with patriotism, for all the world was but variables and factors to his prodigious mind. This lack of human feeling allowed him to make obscure connections across data sets and come to purely utilitarian conclusions that mere mortals would often find unconscionable. It may sound as if I am describing a monster, but it is no exaggeration to say that Mycroft has steered the destiny of nations, indeed the world, with an admirable impartiality. For all of that, the man was loathe to rise from his chair, and the idea of leaving London would be inconceivable to him. That is where Sherlock comes into play.

When Mycroft needs a superior mind and impenetrable discretion to take action he calls upon his brother, the Bohemian idler. By dint of Holmes' psychological need for an audience, I pack my bags when he is called. Apparently there are some sort of coded pictograms circulating around the old pirate island, and with the Allies and the Communists squaring off over the Caribbean territories, Mycroft called upon Holmes to crack the cipher and provide advanced intelligence on the situation. Holmes anticipated a dreary afternoon of cryptanalysis, after which he intended to investigate the pharmaceutical practices of the Obeya shamans, who appeared to have the ability to concoct serums for both mind control and compulsory truth telling, as well as dozens of subtler poisons. For my part I looked forward to sunny beaches and plentiful rum.

There was another great lurch of the plane and an alarm sounded from the rear. I gripped the arms of my seat tightly and looked to Holmes. He had one eyebrow raised and his head cocked, listening like a dog but not bothering to open his eyes. The pilot came bursting from the cockpit, running down the aisle past me. After some dull sounds in the aft of the plane the alarm stopped and the flight seemed steadier. Disheveled but calm the pilot now strolled back up the aisle.

"No cause for worry, the aft door was shaken open by the turbulence but nothing was lost, and now we are closed up tight, right as rain," he announced.

Again a few titters from the seats ahead. As he passed he gave me a reassuring pat on the shoulder. I felt something fall down behind me in the seat. Reluctantly I unbuckled myself and contorted around to find a golden cufflink. I held it up to examine it in the flickering cabin light. The design was of an aeroplane traversing a globe, and on the inside was inscribed, *Love Always C.L.*.

"Captain!" I cried. "Oh, Captain!"

With a studied obtuseness of a man who would be forever badgered by passengers if he allowed it the Captain continued on to the cockpit. Within moments one of the stewardesses was at my side.

"How may I assist you, sir?"

"I believe the Captain just dropped this as he passed by." I placed the cufflink in her hand.

"Oh, he wears these for good luck," she said, winking at me. "I better make sure he gets it back right away."

I can't say being patronized by a beautiful woman hurts any less. She made her way toward the cockpit, making small talk and taking orders along the way. She arrived at the cockpit door about thirty seconds after the Captain, and paused for a moment as a great lightning bolt struck the plane, causing all of the lights to go dark. When everything flickered back to life she knocked on the door and then and threw it open, revealing an empty seat where the pilot ought to have been.

"Where is Captain Lancing?" the stewardess asked the co-pilot.

"He left a few minutes ago to secure the aft cargo door. The warning light is off so I assume he fixed it. Must be in the lavatory."

"I just saw him come in here," she gestured back to the passengers, who were now leaning out into the aisle or poking their heads up above the seats for a better view. "We all saw him come in here."

"I've been right here and I didn't see the Captain or anybody else."

"Wouldn't the co-pilot have heard the Captain come in?" I asked Holmes.

"Between the rain pelting the hull and the headphones they wear I would not be surprised if the flight crew are quite insensible to the sounds around them," he said, hopping to his feet and moving toward the cockpit.

"Sir, please return to your seat," the co-pilot said. "We have a missing crew member and until the situation is resolved I am empowered to take charge of this vessel and every person aboard it."

"I simply mean to offer my services." Holmes produced a business card. "My name is Sherlock Holmes and I am a consulting detective who has worked with Scotland Yard, Interpol, MI5 and countless others. I've not, as yet, had the opportunity to work with the Civil Aviation Authority, but for lack of better amusement, I would certainly be willing to investigate the whereabouts of your missing captain."

As the co-pilot simply stammered at the card in his hands Holmes pushed past, stooping to examine the pilot's seat, and then walking backwards while probing each thing he passed.

"There is no other conventional exit from this space?"

"No, sir," the co-pilot answered.

"No emergency exit?"

"The windows can be popped out of their frames."

Holmes looked at the four intact windows and steepled his fingers. "Any closets?"

"No."

"Empty wall spaces?"

"Every inch of an aeroplane is filled with mechanics and electronics."

Holmes knocked half-heartedly in a few places to no avail. He stepped back out of the cockpit and swung the door open and closed a few times. He probed the walls around the door and floor beneath it. "How common is it for the rear hatch to open?"

"Not common, but not unheard of." The co-pilot looked around at the passengers and leaned into Holmes to whisper, "These planes aren't designed to endure these types of storms for long. The frame twists and turns and sometimes doors pop open, or plating sheers off. We are still airworthy for now, but honestly if we were over earth I'd be landing this plane immediately." A murmur rumbled among the passengers. Suddenly a voice came from the cockpit.

"Mayday, mayday! British Airways Flight 427 requests assistance. Pilot reporting emergency, all crew lost, all passengers lost. Instrumentation deemed unreliable. Mayday!"

"That is the Captain's voice!" the stewardess said. She opened the cockpit door again revealing nothing but a squawking radio. The co-pilot lunged inside and lifted the microphone. "Captain Lancing respond, Captain Lancing respond. This is pilot Williker calling out to Captain Lancing."

"Williker! Where the devil are you? Have you looked out the window? How can that be?"

Everyone looked out their nearest window. All I could see were raindrops running down over a foreboding blackness, with occasional lightning strikes in the distance lighting the ocean.

"What do you see, Captain?"

Only a strange garble was returned. Williker leaned into the radio to try to fiddle with the knobs when he wrenched over backwards and screamed. Electricity shot out from the radio, through Williker, and then dissipated across the ceiling of the cabin. I could have sworn I heard the skittering of clawed feet at the same time.

"Watson!" Holmes caught the man as he fell. I rushed forward to help Holmes lower the man to the floor, feeling his neck for a pulse and looking into his eyes, which had frosted over white from the intense electrical shock. Feebly his lips twitched. I leaned in close to try to make out what he was saying. Before I could comprehend, I was thrown bodily into the wall myself as the plane took another hit from the lightning. When the lights flickered back on Williker was missing.

"Where are the pilots? This plane is going to crash into the ocean and we are all going to die!" the nearby stewardess cried, sending a wave of panic through the plane.

"We're not done for yet," Holmes said, shoving her aside and moving to the pilot's seat.

"Can you fly this plane?" one of the passengers asked.

"No, but I believe I can do a fair job of interpreting the gauges. We are still flying high and level, and from what I can deduce, we are still on the last bearing the pilots set."

"Will that take us all the way to Jamaica or were they planning more course adjustments?" I asked.

"I can't be certain," Holmes said.

"We are trying to hit an island in the middle of the ocean. If we overshoot, or are off course just a little we'll just run out of fuel and crash into the briny deeps," I said.

"What could be doing this to us?" the stewardess cried.

"It's the Devil's Triangle," said one of the passengers. With his head shaved bald and his strange black robes, I had taken the unusual man for some kind of foreigner, but hearing him speak for the first time I noticed he had the polished accent of a posh English boarding school youth. "A cursed blight upon the Earth that has claimed many a vessel, both sea and air."

"There are no such things as cursed oceans, mister...?"

"Aeon. I have devoted my life to the study of such things, power lines in the earth and sacred geometry. Insatiable demons and intersecting planes of existence. Take my word for it, Mr. Holmes. There are dark, cosmic forces at work."

"To what end?" I asked.

"Their motivations are inscrutable, their means unknowable!"

"I hate to interrupt a good show," Holmes barked, "but is it clear to you that two men are missing, presumably dead, and we are in mortal peril?"

"Think upon your immortal peril! We must appease the dark ones!"

"I prefer more practical measures. Firstly, we must repair that radio so we can call for help. Does anyone see any tools about? Surely there must be something tucked away for emergencies."

"I believe I can help with that," said a man with a thick Russian accent. He had on an old fashioned suit and a bushy beard. I had thought him to look like Santa Claus before, but with this accent his appearance became much more sinister. His companion, a severe looking woman, was now pulling on his arm and hissing into his ear in Russian. He pried her fingers free and waved her away as he stood up. "I am an electrical engineer for the Russian Army. I believe I can fix your radio, and failing that I will build you another."

Holmes gestured for the man to enter the cockpit.

Watson's eyes grew large. "Holmes, you can't seriously allow a Communist access to British aviation technology in good conscience!"

"We are beyond ideologies at the moment, Watson. It behooves us to have the best man on the job. Now," he turned to the nearby stewardess. "I believe you are the ranking official on this plane. Your name?"

"Brandy, sir. Brandy Wynne."

"Hmm," said Holmes in reply. "Miss, uh, Wynne, are you familiar with the DC-4?"

"I can't fly it for a second!"

"No, but I suspect you are familiar with the cabin and it's ins and outs, the secret little spots things are stashed, that sort of thing?"

"I suppose," she said warily.

"Is there any place a man could hide, or be hidden, on this plane? Say, access from the cabin to the cargo hold below?"

"There are places where the paneling pulls away and there are gaps to the hold below, but those are for wiring and pipes to pass through, I do not think a man could fit through, certainly neither of the pilots."

"Could you?"

"Pardon me?"

"I see from the dragon's head tattoo upon your wrists that you are a Chinese acrobat. Quite unusual for a person of European descent."

"Sir, I, uh, you are mistaken."

"All of the physical arts leave a distinctive mark upon the body, particularly those practiced rigorously from youth. Your musculature and skeletal deformation is unmistakable. Further, the stiffness in your left shoulder belies not one but two restorative surgeries. Your hands are meaty and calloused, particularly for a woman, and your large shoes suggest we'd discover much the same about your feet."

"Fine," she said, flushing red with both anger and embarrassment. "What of it?"

"Firstly, I would like an answer to my question. Could you squeeze between the cabin and the hold through the wall panels undetected?"

"I was in full sight of everyone, including you, the whole time."

"Yes, but in theory could you do it?"

"Yes."

"How quickly?"

"For a performance, I could work my way through in a minute or so."

"Under duress, if you were willing to sustain some injury?"

"Seconds."

"Would you demonstrate?"

"Most certainly not!"

"To my second point, then. I find it quite interesting that a Caucasian agent of China with exceptional abilities that would greatly aid in the act of espionage is secreted aboard this flight. I suspect MI5 would find that interesting as well. How do you suppose Great Britain interrogates foreign agents in distant lands away from the prying eyes of the British public? If I were innocent I would do everything in my power to avoid finding out. If I were guilty I would do even more."

She glared at Holmes and then turned on her heels and strutted over to the console behind the last row of passenger seats. The wood paneling popped away easily and she knelt down and thrust her head and one arm into the gap. I thought she might wriggle through head first but she sat up again a moment later. "It is pitch black down there. There are lights that can be switched on from the cockpit."

"Watson, see what you can do."

I left the strange scene and went to the pilot's station. It looked as if the Russian had taken much of the console apart.

"I am testing the radio by changing out each part for equivalent parts from other systems, but so far no change. In my opinion the radio is not broken, yet all we receive are these strange sounds." He turned up the volume and weird whistles and pops came through, with distorted snatches of voices. "It seems like maybe they can hear us, because there is some sort of reaction when I broadcast, but I have no reason to believe they are receiving us any more clearly than we are receiving them."

"I was sent up here to turn on the lights in the cargo hold."

Without even looking up, the Russian casually flipped a switch over his head. That seemed like a disconcerting amount of familiarity with this British plane but I held my tongue. When I re-entered the cabin Wynne was perched on the edge of the hole, which was now casting light up from within. Holmes appeared to be arguing with two of the passengers. One was a sickly man melted low in his chair, who could not seem to muster the strength to sit up even in the midst of this confrontation. His companion, however, was a primly dressed woman of fearsome aspect. From her shoes and her bag I took her to be a nurse, presumably this man's private nurse. She was up on her feet pointing a commanding finger at Holmes.

"What is to be gained from this? No panels are missing. Even if there is another secret Chinese acrobat on this plane they could not have done what you are suggesting within the scant few seconds allowed to them."

"All possibilities must be considered. If this woman can do it, then it is by definition possible."

"I really must object," said the sickly man. "We don't know what is down there and therefore what we will be risking by sending someone we can't trust."

"On the contrary, I think you know exactly what is down there."

The already pale man turned whiter, while his nurse turned red. "I think it would be better for you to mind your own business," she snapped.

"People are disappearing from this plane, which is now pilotless and lacking a functional radio. Further, we have enemy agents aboard, and I'm not certain what to make of you yet. At the moment I'm not worried about my future prospects." Holmes nodded at Wynne and she began to lower herself down.

"Stop!" the sickly man cried. The plane was knocked sideways by a fearsome bolt of lightning and all of the lights went out. We spent several terrifying moments in the dark wherein I heard nothing but my own ragged breaths and then the lights came back.

"Is it normal for an aeroplane to be struck by lightning so many times?" I wondered, and received no reply.

Holmes had his head poked into the hole. "Miss Wynne? Miss Wynne! She's gone."

"Disappeared down the hole?" The nurse was clenching her bag.

"Rather from it, I'm afraid. I had seized her by the arm when the light went out. Suddenly my grasp was just empty."

Electricity arced around the paneling and up across the ceiling, with that the strange skittering sound again.

"That is the sound of the Devil's gaze caressing our airplane," Aeon intoned from his seat.

"Absurd!" I replied, but the madman's statement felt true deep within the fear pumping through my heart.

"Watson, keep an eye on those two!" Holmes indicated the sickly man and his nurse.

Unarmed, I despaired of facing off against the hulking woman. "What will you do, Holmes?"

He was already at the aft door, releasing the safety catch. "We must see that cargo hold."

"No!" The nurse was in the aisle now, veins popping out from her face and neck, her eyes bloodshot dark red. She punched me and it was as if I had been smacked in the face by a sledgehammer. My knees collapsed and all sound was lowered to an indistinct whooshing in my ears. As if in slow motion she stepped over me and ran at Holmes, who was tugging at the release lever for the door. The nurse barreled into him and the whole rear of the plane seemed to disappear, leaving only a black, rain-lashed abyss. There was a moment of complete stillness within the cabin and then with an awful rending noise we were hit with a veritable tempest, every loose item ricocheting around the cabin, the passengers pressed back hard in their seats, the stewardesses holding fast to dangling seatbelts like mountain climbers on a frost-battered peak. Grabbing the nearest chair I somehow heaved myself to my feet, where I could now see Holmes dangling from the handle of the open door which hung down from the back of the plane to serve as a ramp for cargo. The nurse was clutching at his ankles, twisting them at obscene angles. Holmes's face was contorted with a scream I could not hear. I staggered forward, pushed along by the sucking icy wind flaying the inside of the cabin. Now that the door was open, narrow ladder rungs were revealed along the fuselage that led down to the hold. They were slick with rain and my body was still numb from the nurse's punch, yet somehow I made my down to the lower level and stretched myself out over the floor of the plane. I seized Holmes by the lapels and dragged him up with all of my might. Along with him, snapping and frothing like a rabid dog, came the nurse. She leapt upon Holmes and began strangling him. As they rolled around at the edge of that deadly precipice I noticed a fire axe hung from the wall. Seizing it I turned and brought the flat back of the axe down upon the Nurse's arm.

"That will be quite enough!" I cried. She simply roared in response. I bought the flat side down again and again on her arms to no effect. Finally I swung at her head like I was holding a cricket bat. Blood ran from her scalp and she finally looked up at me, momentarily dazed. Holmes took the opportunity to kick himself away from her and scramble back to safety. The nurse quickly recovered and rose to her full height, raising her arms and roaring like a bear. The storm sucked her out then, and she disappeared into the raging blackness with a look of utter horror and confusion upon her face.

When I could breathe again, I blurted, "What in the blazes is happening, Holmes?"

"Clearly Mycroft placed us upon this flight under false pretenses. It is like our own little Cold War up there. Let us see what we can discover."

"I'm no expert," I said, "but I see nothing worth killing or dying for down here."

"Precisely. An aeroplane full of spies and nothing is out of place. That nurse had SAS combat training."

"Women are not permitted in the SAS."

"Can there be any surprise that there are splinters of shadow groups of Special Forces in our intelligence service?"

"Is that what explains her prodigious strength and fortitude?"

"That, I'm afraid, remains a mystery. One she may have taken to her watery grave. We can surmise from her bloodied eyes, red complexion and bulging veins that she was suddenly exposed to a strong invigorating agent." Holmes was focused upon the forward wall, rapping upon it and listening with great satisfaction.

"To what end? If she was in the employ of the British government, why work against us?"

"You know the silly little games the military gets up to. Hollow gamesmanship for which she paid with her life."

The hold of the plane looked perfectly ordinary, with cargo netting restraining two piles of luggage, including our own bags. In addition, some aviatory bric-a-brac was stored here. One large crate did catch my eye, emblazoned with a surprising warning and punctuated around the top with tiny holes.

"I say, Holmes, there are snakes on this plane! Who would put reprehensible reptiles in an infernal flying machine? It defies logic and good sense!"

Appearing to have heard no part of my discourse, Holmes was already pacing the space, examining the floor in detail. "A-ha!" Holmes found that one of the metal panels on the wall swung open freely and inside was a lever. With a metallic chunking sound the lever disengaged a latch, and the whole forward wall swung open. Behind was a baroque hodgepodge of machinery, glass tubes, metal coils, flashing lights and cryptic toggles. More interestingly, crisp bolts of electricity traced up and down the machine, looking very much like the electrical outbursts we had seen up in the cabin. The whole contraption buzzed like we had kicked open a hornets' nest.

"Fascinating," Holmes said, running his hand close over the machine and watching the electricity bend around him. He jerked his hand back and shook it when the speckled band finally jumped out and struck him. "In very general terms it looks like a crude radio broadcasting device."

"Is that what is interfering with the airplane's own radio? Perhaps we should have the Russian take a look at it."

"No, Watson, you are quite right in wanting to maintain British secrets. Whatever this is, it is no commonplace trifle."

"Shall we turn it off then?"

"Where to even begin?"

"I still have my trusty axe." One of the bulbs set into the fuselage popped behind us.

"No, we don't know what it does, or what would happen if we stopped it. I think we can confront the sickly man with it now. Bereft of his guard and with his secret machine discovered, he may be more helpful now." Another bulb popped, casting Holmes and I in harsh relief. "I don't fancy being at the mercy of this experiment and I mean to put a stop to it." A third bulb popped, leaving us with but a single light.

"This seems more than coincidental," I said as the final bulb popped.

"Simple exposure to rain and cold," Holmes replied.

"Of course, in the War they blamed this kind of thing on gremlins, mischievous fairy folk of the skies." My chuckling was cut short when the cargo door ripped free with an ear-piercing screech and tumbled into the night like a nightmarish leaf. Suddenly the airplane went into a steep climb and I found myself sliding down toward the black void. Reflexively I caught onto the netting hooked to the wall. Looking up above me Holmes was perched atop the luggage opposite. The plane was screaming from the excess force being exerted during the climb. It seemed as if we must be rocketing straight up. From the cabin above us dinnerware and the personal items of the passengers were tumbling. Thankfully no additional people had been dumped out into the storm yet.

"Why aren't they leveling out the flight?" I shouted.

"Perhaps they cannot. We are moments from the wings being torn asunder, and we are most assuredly at a height where such a plunge must prove fatal." Holmes pushed away from his perch, sliding on his side down the nearly vertical floor, catching the netting on my side down below me. "We must find a way to restore control." He climbed down the cargo netting, and before I could force my words around the knot of fear in my throat he swung himself against the wall and let himself slide down the last few yards before grabbing the small utility rungs on the lip of the opening. "Come, Watson!"

I was waving my refusal when the netting to which I clung for dear life began tearing away from the wall. I was pummeled by luggage as it spun its way out into the icy embrace of the waves far below. Then the netting gave a little more and I was besieged anew, and I found myself holding fast to the last fraying strand still attached to the wall. I looked at Holmes and saw his features drawn tight against his face by the atmosphere lashing all about us. Finally, the last bit of netting snapped and I experienced a horrible moment of falling, only to feel Holmes's vice like grip on my collar. While I dangled out of the back of the plane, Holmes scaled the ladder sideways until we were beneath the passenger cabin. He pulled me up beneath him and I clung desperately to the rungs.

"If the notion of flying should ever strike me again," I yelled, "kindly whisper 'Kingston' in my ear and I shall be infinitely obliged to you."

Holmes then leapt up to grab the rearmost passenger seat. He scaled the sides of them like a ladder, quickly approaching the cockpit. He passed dozens of terrified passengers strapped tightly in their chairs. He made one last leap for the pilot's seat, looking around to see the Russian in the co-pilots seat, his hands shaking too hard to operate any of the controls.

Holmes pushed forward on the yoke to no avail, so he wedged himself back in the chair and pushed upon it with his feet as strongly as he could. The controls would not budge at all, and the windows were now frosting over. I tied my belt around the rungs in front of me as an improvised safety measure, fearing that my frozen hands might ultimately give. Just as it seemed that all was lost, lightning struck the plane and everything electrical sputtered to a stop, including the propellers. The terrifying upward propulsion gave way to the sickening pull of gravity. The airplane was now falling down on top of me. Had we flown high enough to outwait the blackout? Would the damaged plane even kick back into operation? As we fell I watched Holmes pound away at the controls, the outcome seeming remote and academic. It felt to me as if I had always been falling beneath this plane and I would always be falling beneath this plane. The rushing air around me became almost soothing.

I awoke from this unusual reverie with the coughing sputter of the propellers. The cabin lights flickered on and the pitch of the plane was gently shifting. After a minute or so I found gravity pulling at me down into the cabin. I dangled there by my belt, until an exhausted Holmes came to release me and gather me up.

The trolley of liquor had been one of the first things to plummet into the Pacific, so I made do by puffing away on Holmes' pungent tobacco. I listened to the Russian, who was now frantically issuing a mayday, twirling various knobs to send out his plea across the whole spectrum. He had also activated an emergency beacon, although the range probably didn't reach the islands. Perhaps there was a ship passing below us in the dark that would relay our SOS. At Holmes's urging we had all donned life preservers, and he had tasked some of the passengers with preparing for an emergency sea landing: recovering the life rafts, hand powered radios, and rations from the emergency compartments.

Holmes sat opposite the sickly man, peering intently at him. "Is the device working as intended?"

"What device? What do you mean?"

"The device in the hidden compartment of the hold below, that is wreathed in the very same electrical energy which we have seen ravage this vehicle and destroy its crew. Is the device working as intended, or is it tragically malfunctioning? In essence is our problem the man or the machine?"

"I don't know," the sickly man began sobbing into his hands. "They did this to me. I never asked for this."

"Asked for what, exactly?"

"The brain is an electrical machine, and like any electrical machine it can be manipulated. We've had success in training rats; rewarding them and punishing them remotely by activating the appropriate centers of their brains. We could even project emotions and desires onto them. We could make them angry or docile, drive them to ravenous hunger or compel them to stoically starve to death."

"Monstrous!" I declared.

"It was all pretty theoretical, with little practical application until..."

"Until what?"

"One of the frustrations of being a military scientist is that one takes orders from fools who don't understand what they are meddling with. After our preliminary successes with rats, we were forced to escalate our research to apes. We were shocked to find that not only could we compel desires and emotions onto them, but we could hear their feeling and thoughts, for lack of a better term."

"Poppycock!" Holmes said.

"I tell you it is true. We felt the despair when babies were removed from their mother, joy when new toys were provided, anger when the apes were punished. We understood hunger, discomfort and fatigue in a way that was like language and yet beyond it. One of my subordinates rushed to report the findings in an effort to usurp my position. The next day a truck delivered a load of prisoners to our door. I am ashamed at the things we did to them, the horrible things they had to endure, but for us it was awful as well. Trust me when I say you never want to experience another person's mind. It is horrifying and yet banal at the same time."

"Naturally," Holmes puffed at his pipe, "Given the ability to coerce people like puppets and further read their minds, the secret masters that hide in the shadows could not resist."

"This flight was meant to be a test. It was one thing to manipulate dullards who had already had their wills broken by the prison system, as well as the various deprivations and tortures we put them through. But could we read powerful, intuitive minds without being noticed? Could we compel trained soldiers to bend to our will? But this," he gestured at the ruined plane, "it has never been like this. Somehow our capabilities have been amplified beyond the theoretical thresholds."

"May I presume," Aeon chimed in from a darkened corner of the cabin, "that your medium of control are omega waves?"

"This is no time for your frivolous mumbo jumbo!" I barked.

"Actually, Dr. Watson, Mr. Aeon is correct. In fact, it is the very reason he was included in this study."

"In nature," Aeon began, "omega waves can only be accessed by the human mind as a result of deep meditation, or by a regiment of hypnosis known only to the Ascended Masters. In one way it validates these ancient claims that modern science has replicated and stimulated these waves. Of course, on the other it cheapens them if one can simply flip a switch in lieu of years of study and practice. I propose power should walk hand in hand with wisdom."

"Pshaw...wisdom." Holmes spat.

"In fact, the effects of the device have been quite deleterious on the operator, as you can see." He gestured to his own ruined body. "Consistency of control has also been an issue. We are looking at Aeon, and others like him, as potential controller candidates."

"Ha!" Aeon scoffed. "As if I would ever step from the infernal path for such pedestrian affairs.

"Perhaps you missed the part where they have a mind control machine," Holmes replied.

"I have given myself completely to the Ancient Ones, no human may usurp their mastery of my corporeal manifestation."

Aeon then slapped himself and gawked at his own hand in surprise. He slapped himself again and again. The sickly man had a smirk on his face, which quickly fell into a look of despondency.

"So you can use your capabilities for good upon occasion," Holmes quipped.

"Indeed I was successful with all but one subject. Your mind truly is an impenetrable fortress, Mr. Holmes."

I saw a flash of smug satisfaction flash across my friend's face before he asked, "What then of these disappearances? Is that part of your plan?"

"Not even in our wildest imaginations. There is no precedent in our specs."

"Hubris!" Aeon said. "When you moved beyond the limits of human perception did you really expect to find no one else out there? Every time you send out an omega wave is like ringing a dinner bell for extraterrestrial entities, and then you bring it here, to the Devil's Triangle where the veil between realities is thinnest, and just whack away at it for hours? The surprise is not that we are being consumed by a supernatural entity, it's that we are not swarmed by the things."

Lightning rocked the aeroplane again and we sat in the dark hearing nothing but the rain, and then the skittering of the electrical arcs across the hull. We had seen so many strange things, but invisible cosmic monsters? I was shaking my head when the engine immediately outside my window violently developed a hole, as if a cannonball had just blasted through it. In quick succession the other three engines were likewise destroyed. In a panic we strapped ourselves in and assumed the curled crash landing position. The plane began to whine like a bomb as it fell. Just when it seemed we'd been falling a moment too long the plane hit the water and I was violently tossed up in my seat. Blood sputtered freely from my nose and mouth and my legs felt as if they had snapped beneath the restraining belt. With the rear hatch missing the plane quickly capsized, the nose pointing up at the stormy sky.

As we had planned earlier we grasped hands and formed a human chain, passing the last person up first, and so on. Holmes was at the top of the chain, heaving the passengers out of the cockpit window and pushing them towards the inflatable rafts waiting below. The icy water was lapping at the last few people in line as the plane sank more quickly than we disembarked. Soon they were coming up two at a time, then three. When I ascended to the top I remained to help Holmes pass the others through. In the end Holmes and I essentially stayed steady while the aeroplane dropped away below us, sinking into those fathomless depths. Our life vests helped us bob along on the turbulent waters until one of the rafts plucked us out of the ocean.

The Russian began cranking away at the handheld radio in our raft. Surprisingly we received a reply almost immediately.

"What in the devil is happening, Flight 471? Over."

"That's a long story, please send rescue immediately. Over."

"Rescue? There will be hell to play if this is another prank. Over.

"What do you mean, prank? Over."

"I mean this is the second so-called emergency call we have gotten from Flight 471 today. First you tell us everyone disappeared and your readouts are all wrong. We talk you through reorienting and landing and you pretend to see no airport and crash onto a barren island meanwhile we don't even see a plane in the sky. Then you come back with this cockamamie story about a sea crash and dozens of survivors in rafts. I hope you never want to fly again, Flight 471, because heads are going to roll over this fiasco."

For a couple of hours we watched the sun rise over the endless ocean and discussed in whispers the fantastical fate of Captain Lancing and the flight crew. At last a ship came over the horizon. We were hauled up on board, where the personnel all wore the same black uniforms with no insignia to identify them. In fact, the ship itself was painted a flat, featureless charcoal grey. We were given comfortable rooms and good food but we spent much of the next week being interrogated. When finally we arrived back at Baker Street we were surprised to find Mycroft himself waiting for us in our parlor.

"Gentlemen," he said, gazing at us over steepled fingers. "I hope it is needless to say that recent events never happened, and there is to be no such record." He turned his penetrating gaze onto me. "None of this tin dispatch box, preserved-for-future-generations nonsense."

"I shall do what is best for England, as always." I said. Mycroft surely noted the evasion but continued.

"The Ministry will of course pay you handsomely for the uneventful week you spent decoding the dancing man pictographs in Kingston. For reasons of political delicacy you of course cannot discuss details of that case further."

"This is beyond the pale of your usual machinations, Mycroft," Holmes said. "You gamble with the very fabric of human existence. What is the endgame here? What possible win is there here for you?"

"Not every battle is about victory, Sherlock. Sometimes one plays for the prize of mitigated losses." Heading off Holmes' continued objections, Mycroft continued. "Would you like to know exactly how many people stepped off that ship? How many people have ever stepped off that ship? Exactly two. Everyone else who knows what you know will die on board, tucked safely away where no one can hear their mad gibbering of truth. You two, on the other hand, are needed at the scene of another curious incident…"

THE CASE OF THE POTTERS BAR SIREN

Trenton Mabey

THE RISE AND FALL OF THE SHRILL AIR RAID SIREN SHOOK THE GLASS OF the windowpanes, a stark reminder of the horrors of the Great War. Sherlock Holmes removed a silver pocket watch from his vest, glanced at the time, and snapped it shut.

"Another missing girl?" Watson asked, never looking up from the page of the medical journal.

"Undoubtedly. I expect to hear from Lestrade within the hour. Three missing girls will upgrade the investigation," he said, pipe smoke curling above his head.

An insistent knock sounded at the door forty minutes later. Chief Enforcer Lestrade entered the sitting room flanked by two Knight Corps officers clad in black fatigues, grey shields obscuring their faces, and armed with rifles. They closed the door behind them and positioned themselves on either side of the exit.

Lestrade looked tired. Dark bags hung under his hazel eyes, an extra droop evident in the curls of his moustache. Holmes handed him a cup of tea before he could ask.

"Thank you, sir." Lestrade sipped from the blue porcelain cup.

"Number three?" said Holmes.

"Aye," Lestrade replied with an exhaled breath. He set his cup down and massaged his temples.

"Where?"

"Sector 6, east gate."

"Contained blizzard, like the last time?"

Lestrade looked up sharply, eyeing Holmes with suspicion. "How do you know about that?" One of the soldiers at the door shifted position slightly.

"Does it matter? I have my sources just as you have yours," Holmes said sipping his tea. "Fact, for each of the previous disappearances, blizzard like conditions descended on one gate while the rest of the city remains untouched. Fact, the lock was short circuited from the outside allowing the gate to be opened. Fact, the tower guards claim to have observed nothing out of the ordinary before the occurrence and due to the conditions, nothing during the incident. Fact, a single set of footprints was discovered leading away from the gate. Fact, three girls have vanished without a trace."

The ticking of the clock and the crackling of the fire in the hearth the only sounds as the two stared at one another.

Lestrade dropped his eyes to his teacup. He stirred the tea with the small spoon. "Fine," he said with a huff. "Yes, it was like the others."

Holmes cracked a small grin.

"An hour passed curfew, the tower guards in Sector 6 reported a disturbance settling on the area. Due to the similarity with the other disappearances, one of the guards proceeded to ground level. He discovered the small inner gate already open. When the snow cleared, a single set of footprints could be seen in the snow leading from the gate to the woods beyond."

"Anything else?" asked Holmes, his teacup frozen in mid-sip.

Lestrade jumped to his feet and paced in front of the fireplace. He ran his hand through his hair. Not meeting Holmes eyes, he studied the picture above the fireplace, a seascape from a Japanese artist. Another deep sigh and Lestrade looked at the detective, "You have been requested in an official capacity to investigate these disappearances."

"Excellent." Holmes practically leaped from his chair. He donned a dark blue overcoat and grabbed a leather satchel from a side table. Without another word he was out the door and striding down the stairs, the Knight Corps running to catch up.

The cobblestone plaza in Sector 6 was brilliantly lit with five mobile floodlight trailers, their steam generators pumping out a smoky haze. The outer wall loomed over the plaza, a metallic monstrosity rising thirty feet above the cobblestones curved slightly inward like a cresting wave. The city was surrounded by this immense wall, built at the end of the Great War that decimated the population of mainland Europe and erased Australia from the map. Ten gates were inset at various points in the city, allowing commerce and travel to the four surviving cities on what was left of the British Isles.

Grey snow fell, turning to black sludge under the onslaught of the Knight Corps ranks teeming about the gate. Threading his way through the mass of Knight Corps, Holmes reached the small, inner gate. He donned a set of orange-lensed goggles from his satchel and fiddled with the dials on the side. A device of his own invention, the spectacles allowed him to see heat signatures, infrared spectrum along with a setting for microscopic inspection.

A Knight Corps officer threw down his cigarette and approached him, "You there, what are you doing?" He motioned for another guard and pointed at Holmes.

"Stand down captain!" An out of breath Lestrade stepped in front of the officer with Watson by his side. "These men are now assisting with the investigation. You will extend them every courtesy. Am I clear?"

The officer straightened and clenched his fist, "As you say Chief Enforcer." He pivoted on his heel and stalked away.

"All of these fools have trampled any possible shred of evidence over here!" Holmes said. "Open the gate."

The soldier on guard looked at Holmes and then at Lestrade.

Lestrade sighed and nodded, "Open it up."

A shaft of rectangular light illuminated a mass of churned snow, a black swath from the gate to the bare trees. Holmes rotated a dial on the left eyepiece; the lenses turned a dark green color with a small electronic hum. He knelt down to the side of the trail, his face inches above the ground. Lestrade stepped forward, "What?" Holmes threw his hand up, silencing him.

Holmes rose and turned back toward the gate. Rotating another dial on the goggles, the lenses again shifted, this time to a dark purple. A slender metal rod appeared in his hand and he began poking the lock.

"The lock was hacked," said Lestrade.

"Really by whom?" said Holmes not turning to look at the Chief Enforcer. "If you examine the lock inside the door, you will find it intact. If the outside lock was hacked, then why was there only one set of footprints when your men marched to the woods like a herd of elephants? Did the hacker fly in on bat wings?"

"Well, then," said an exasperated Lestrade, "how was the door opened?"

"Someone unlocked the door for the girl."

"But there were no other tracks." Lestrade gestured at the trampled mess.

"Then I would suggest questioning your guards more closely." Holmes walked through the doorway without pause. He emerged a second later carrying his satchel. "Come Watson."

The woods were cold and silent. The trees stretched their weathered branches to the sky, barren of leaves since the fallout. Lestrade and the soldier pointed their handheld flood lamps in all directions. The footprints of the Knight Corps marred the ground. Lestrade pointed to the left, "The girl's tracks went in this direction."

"Any readings on the trail," asked Watson. He glanced back to see if Lestrade was within listening distance.

"Only faint traces thanks to those idiots in black. A colder set of prints lay beneath the heat of the herd."

"What do you make of this business?"

Holmes adjusted the goggles over his eyes. "It's too soon for idle speculation, old man."

The group ventured further into the woods. Holmes stopped to study the ground several times. They entered a clearing in the forest. One fire-blackened tree dominated the space with three branches reaching toward the sky.

Lestrade cleared his throat, "Here is where the tracks vanished according to the reports."

"Step back please," said Holmes. He circled the small clearing in a half crouch, his face inches from the ground. He slowly made his way towards the center of the area. He paused and examined a small indentation, picking up a hand full of dirt and smelling the blackened earth. He continued his rounds, stopping at several places to sniff.

"Lestrade, what did your men find in this clearing?" Holmes asked not looking up from his task. He raked his fingers through the earth and brought them to his nose.

"It was reported that the tracks of the girl led to this clearing and disappeared. No trace of the girl was found and further examination yielded no results. Why?"

"There are bird droppings along the perimeter of the area," he said waving his hand in a circular motion, "and a single drop of blood lies in the center."

"So what is your theory then?" asked Lestrade.

"This is spot where the girl disappeared," Holmes said as he walked passed Lestrade and back towards the wall.

Fewer soldiers crowded the plaza when they stepped through the gate.

"I would like to speak the guard on duty at the time of the event," said Holmes.

Lestrade hesitated, "that will not be possible. He has been recalled from active duty and sent to the reserves."

Holmes stared at Lestrade. "What exactly is your plan of action at this point and why insist on involving me if your ineffective methods continually block all reasonable avenues of deduction?"

"I did not insist on involving you, Mr. Holmes," Lestrade said.

"And yet here we are!" Holmes argued.

Watson stepped between them, a calming hand on Holmes's shoulder. "Lestrade, you asked for our assistance and we will provide it, but you have to give us something to go on, man."

"If the timing between disappearances remains consistent, in three days' time the next girl will be lured out of the city," Holmes began. "You will devise an alert system to communicate when the strange weather system begins at one of the gates. Have men posted at the gates and not just in the towers. If the girl gets through, do not follow her. Wait for Watson and myself to arrive. The clues will be there to solve the case unless they are again buried underneath the mountain of ineptitude shown by the Corps. Are we in agreement?"

"No we are not in agreement. I will not authorize the use of an innocent life in one of your egotistical games," spat Lestrade, his face in an expression of disgust.

"If you have an alternate plan, please share. I would be interested to know what your little mind has conjured . . ."

"Sherlock." Watson placed a hand on his shoulder and shook his head.

Holmes pivoted on his heel and stalked into the nearest alley.

"Lestrade, We recognize that you will do everything within your power to prevent further disappearances. Can we be agreed that if the unfortunate should happen, then the scene will remain untouched until we arrive."

"Agreed." said Lestrade.

"Thank you, sir." Watson nodded his head and followed Holmes.

Several streets away from the crime scene, a small boy emerged from the shadows wearing a deerstalker cap. A grin split his dirt stained face as he greeted the men.

"Hello Ollie. Did you find her address?" asked Holmes.

"Aye, we did Mr. Holmes. Right this way," he waved his arm and started down the street.

Watson looked quizzically at his companion.

"Don't look so surprised. Despite how it may seem, I have been actively working on this case since the second disappearance. Jimmy and the other Irregulars have been scouring the city for information on the missing girls."

Holmes and Watson followed the child through the darkened streets. Another boy stepped out of an alcove and gestured for the trio. They climbed the stairs onto the third floor of the run down tenement.

"She lived here, Mr. Holmes," the boy pointed at a door with a silver '23' in faded paint. "Her name was Verity."

"Good job, gents!" Watson produced a gold coin from his pocket and handed it to the boys. The two children ran down the stairs and disappeared into the night without a sound.

Holmes examined the edges of the door and the knob under the scrutiny of the investigative goggles. Stepping back, he nodded to Watson.

Watson tapped on the door with the handle of his walking stick.

The door opened a crack and a pair of bloodshot eyes peered out. Tear tracks ran down a face framed by unkempt black hair.

"Pardon us ma'am. My name is Dr. John Watson," gesturing to his companion, "and this is my colleague Mr. Sherlock Holmes. Might was have a moment of your time to discuss Verity?"

The door opened wider, a look of hope blossomed on the woman's face. "Did they find her? Is she okay?"

"May we come in?" asked Watson.

"Of course, of course. Do you know where is she?"

"The Knight Corps are working on it but have few leads. We would like to ask you some questions and examine Verity's room for any clues that might assist with the case," said Watson.

Hands shaking, Verity's mother dropped into a chair and stared at the two. "I have read about you in the paper, Mr. Holmes. Please can you help find my Verity?" her eyes silently pleaded.

"Would it be acceptable if Mr. Holmes examines Verity's room while I fill you in on what we know?"

"Yes," she said. "It's through that door." She pointed to a door decorated with pink and purple flowers.

Firelight from the parlor flickered off picture frames as Holmes opened the door to Verity's bedroom. A small shaft of moonlight illuminated a table covered in scattered papers, sketches of birds mostly. A picture of a familiar dead tree sat on top of the pile, heavily shaded and bearing a spiral shape in the base of the trunk. It was the tree from the clearing where Verity disappeared.

Holmes flipped a switch on the goggles and the room swam in a swirl of colors. The infrared scanner registered cold spots across the room in different shades of blue. The window radiated a dark blue except for a spark of pink near its center. A black feather hung suspended above the girl's desk with a small crystal attached to the base. In the glow of the infrared spectrum, it pulsed in a rhythmic pattern like heart beating within the crystallized formation. He switched off the goggles and returned them to his satchel. He grabbed the decoration and exited the room.

"Excuse me madam, but can you tell me about this," asked Holmes, displaying the feather and crystal in his open palm.

"Not really sir. Verity said a bird dropped it on her sill one day and then flew away," she stifled a sob with her handkerchief.

"When was this?"

"About a week ago I think."

"Did you hear or see anything tonight before you and Verity retired for the night?" Holmes prodded.

"No, nothing," a fresh wave of tears leaked down her cheeks.

"May I take this to my lab for examination?" Holmes asked.

"Will it help find my little girl?"

"Small clues are often the key to unlocking the greatest mysteries," Watson assured her.

Upon returning to their flat at 221, Holmes sequestered himself in his lab. He moved with precision, snatching chemicals from cabinets and calibrating instruments. With the details of a mystery flashing through his brain, he felt truly alive. He set the crystal from Verity's room to the side and focused on the feather. What seemed black at first observation was not quite correct. A silver hue was present when viewed under different lighting.

Holmes carefully sliced the base of the feather into fine pieces with a scalpel. He added a measure of these into a solution of acid, beginning the process of gene extraction.

"Watson!"

No sound was heard from the other rooms. Holmes slammed his pen onto the desk next to his notes and stalked to the door, flinging it open.

"Watson!"

A crash sounded from Watson's room and the man emerged in rumpled clothes and a revolver in his hand. He looked wildly around the room.

"Good, you're up then."

"Bloody hell, Sherlock. We were out all night, a little sleep would have been nice."

"No time. I need you to fetch something for me."

Watson rubbed the bridge of his nose. "What do you need?"

"A bird feather," he replied and shut the door to the lab.

Holmes stood in front of a map of the city tacked on the parlor wall when Watson walked out of his room. It had been three days of lab work and bizarre requests. Three pictures of landmarks, each hung with a different crystal, stuck on the map that dominated the south wall of their parlor. Green strings connected to thumb tacks traced the routes taken by the missing girls to the tree with the spiral, the sinkhole in the marsh, and a lone standing stone. All three routes were to the southeast of the city walls.

"Good morning Sherlock."

"Ah," he turned. "It is a good morning."

"You've cracked the case then?" Watson asked as he poured himself tea.

Holmes grinned.

"The visit to Verity's home yielded two crucial clues. First, the feather. Genetic testing revealed it was not an ordinary feather. When compared to an ordinary bird feather, there were distinct differences. Some of those differences corresponded to the genetic code of a human being, but there was also a third unknown contributor."

"You're talking about genetic trans-mutational control."

Holmes nodded.

"This practice caused the Great War."

"Very true. The genetic weaponization process undertaken by the British military led to the position we are in today; a war torn island and the destruction of the British Empire. But that is history, what we are talking about is reality. A weaponized mutation, or splinter, is living in the village of Potters Bar and preying on our population for food."

"Wait, how do you know it is in Potters Bar?"

"The crystal," said Holmes.

"The crystal told you? Holmes when did you last sleep?"

"Sleep is inconsequential. Come here." He led Watson to the other end of the lab. He quickly exited the lab and returned with one of the crystals. "The crystals given to the girls are not ordinary crystals but have also been altered on the elemental level. They are mediums for recorded messages. In this case, a specific message is played repeatedly at frequencies to low for the human ear to register but still detectable to the mind."

"These messages caused the girls to leave their homes then?"

"Precisely. I believe this creature influences the mind through sound."

"A siren effect like in Homer's *Odyssey*."

"Exactly. I have been able to isolate the messages. A common theme traces through each one, a command to come to Potters Bar."

"We have to stop this as soon as possible!" exclaimed Watson.

"I am in full agreement, Watson. How about a little hunting expedition?" Holmes smiled.

Watson raised his cup in salute.

The sun burned high in the sky when Holmes and Watson passed through the gate in Sector 18. Watson pushed a wheelbarrow loaded with an old leather trunk. The road out of the city, a double track pathway, was rarely used. Cresting a small rise, the duo stopped to view the scene. Below them, a quaint village stood silent while in the distance, a thin fog obscured the ruins of London.

Watson lowered the wheelbarrow and opened the trunk; the afternoon sun glinted off the metal instruments. Watson hoisted a crossbow from the interior and handed it to Holmes followed by a quiver of darts. Homes braced the weapon on the ground and pulled a lever to load the mechanism. The tinkling of glass accompanied the removal of a satchel. Holmes grabbed it and slung it over his shoulder. Watson straightened with a short barrel rifle in one hand and a bandolier of bullets in the other. He slung his medical bag over his shoulder. Abandoning the empty case, they descended the hill and entered the outskirts of the northern suburb of Potters Bar.

Snow covered the cobblestoned streets of the village. Drifts of detritus blanketed in grey littered the street. Buildings loomed like small mountains, blackened wood beams jutted from empty roofs. Silence reigned, only the crunching of snow as the two hunters stalked down the street could be heard.

At the next intersection, Holmes stopped Watson with a raised hand. A set of footprints cut through the snow perpendicular to their current course.

Holmes knelt down to examine the indentations. "The tracks are degraded, probably from the last victim."

A thunderous screech cut through the air, echoing down the deserted roadways.

"What in the seven hells was that?" Watson brought the rifle to his shoulder and pivoted to find the source.

"That is our prey. We should proceed with caution." He dug into a jacket pocket and produced four dull colored beads. He offered two to Watson, "for your ears."

Watson retrieved the beads and watched as Holmes rubbed his hands together, the material mashed into elongated shapes. He kneaded the brownish globes into tear shaped mounds and inserted them into his ears. Watson nodded in understanding and mimicked the process. They hoisted their weapons into ready position and slowly snaked down the street.

Around the next corner, the street opened into a great square. Holmes and Watson positioned themselves on either corner and examined the open space. Surrounded by buildings on all sides, six roads led to the square. The central space was clear of any snow; drifts dotted the perimeter against the outer walls. The foundations for a fountain occupied the center without the typical statue however. Wooden beams ringed the space like a crude bird's nest.

Holmes signaled to Watson with two fingers up and then changing into a fist on the way down. Watson nodded. He moved into the square, hugging the walls of the nearest building for cover, disappearing into a dark crevice.

Holmes walked in the opposite direction, circling the area. Ahead he spied a pile of rubbish in the fading light. Bones, picked clean and discarded, a small skull resting at the base of the pile.

Holmes whipped around as a rock rolled passed his foot. Watson waved to him from a rooftop. He pointed to the northwest and then ducked out of sight. Holmes retreated into the ruins of a pub.

Suddenly a strong wind pulled at his jacket. The snow on the edges of the square swirled as if it were caught in a miniature cyclone. Then, a figure, obscured in the tempest, touched down on the cobblestones. It was tall, probably eight feet. More impressive though, coal black wings stretched out to the sides of the figure to a twenty-foot wingspan. Grey and black feathers covered its body from the neck down. Three talons sprouted from each of its shadowy feet. Its head was roughly human, a bald grey colored head with yellow eyes. A blood red beak dominated the rest of the face.

"A splinter," Holmes whispered to himself in confirmation of his accurate deduction.

The splinter faced the north street and waited. A small figure with dark brown hair, and dressed in white stumbled into view. The girl approached the creature and collapsed at its feet. Holmes grabbed a glass beaker from his satchel and readied himself. The splinter jerked back and screeched. The crack of Watson's rifle thundered through the plaza. The splinter launched into the air searching for its attacker.

Holmes exited the pub and tossed the bottle into the square. Another soon followed. As the contents of each mixed, a chemical haze rose. Under cover of the cloud, he raced forward to the unmoving girl. He hefted her body and withdrew to the pub. She still had a faint pulse but was otherwise unresponsive.

Another gunshot rang out. Holmes shouldered the crossbow and ran back to the street. He lowered his satchel to the ground and steadied his weapon. The splinter tucked its wings back and slammed its body into a building, desperate for its prey. In the dusky darkness, Holmes watched as the wall crumbled in on itself. The splinter appeared from dust of the destruction and hovered above the smashed wall, eyes scanning the rubble.

Holmes aimed and fired. The bolt slammed into the leg of the creature. It whirled and plunged in one motion. Holmes leaped out of its path, the creature's talons sparked where they hit the cobblestone. No time to reload, Holmes palmed a throwing knife. The splinter dodged the knife. Holmes jumped to the left but the creature swiped his legs out with its wing. He slammed into the concrete wall surrounding the nest. Holmes felt the crack as pain exploded from his left arm. His sight blurred and he struggled to remain conscious. The splinter landed in front of Holmes and cocked its head to the side, studying him. Eyes not blinking, it opened its beak and screeched. Holmes dropped to his knees. The creature's scream sent waves of pain through his skull. He grabbed his ears, pressing hands to his ears to block the onslaught. Blood dripped from his nose onto the cobblestones, splashing onto the dislodged earpiece.

The crack of Watson's rifle boomed in the space. The splinter stumbled from the bullet's impact. It hissed and shot into the sky.

Holmes reinserted the ear protection and took several deep breaths. His left arm hung limp and a grimace appeared on his face as he stumbled to the pub. Darkness descended on the square, and snow drifted in a near constant breeze.

Opening the satchel, Holmes removed two glass bottles with handkerchiefs inserted in the tops. He grasped his goggles from the jacket pocket; a crack stretched the length of the right lens. He switched the power on and nothing happened. He fingered a match and gazed out the doorway. The wind blew through the town but the splinter was not visible. He shrunk into the darkness of the building as he caught movement in his peripheral vision.

Watson materialized in the doorway, his face covered in blood and dust. He dropped to his knees beside Holmes. Holmes pointed to his left arm. Watson nodded. He removed a scalpel from his case and sliced into Holmes' jacket exposing bare skin. Watson tentatively examined the wound. Holmes grimaced in pain at the touch. Retrieving a syringe from his case, he loaded a dose of morphine and jammed the needle into his friend's arm. Holmes sighed and indicated the girl. Watson hurried over to the unconscious young woman and began an examination.

After the pain in his arm began to recede, Holmes stood and moved to the back of the pub. He tapped Watson on the shoulder and motioned for him to cover the door. Watson nodded and watched him walk through the back.

The alleyway outside the pub protected Holmes from the wind. Two buildings down he turned and approached the entrance to the square; the location of the splinter unknown. He crouched and placed the bottles on the pathway. Flames flared to life as he struck a match on the cobblestones.

Holmes threw the firebomb, faltering as his injured arm throbbed with the movement. His face tingled with heat from the explosion of the shattered bottle, and the creature's nest was suddenly engulfed in flames.

Yellow eyes reflected in the darkness. The outline of the splinter's body was visible in an alley across from where Holmes knelt. The splinter leaped into the air and landed in front of him. Blood covered its right leg, and streamed from a hole in its left shoulder.

The splinter lurched backward in a rain of blood and feathers. Its wing joint was blown away in the retort of Watson's rifle. It tried to take flight but crashed to the earth, one wing immobile. Holmes pitched the second bomb onto the creature's exposed back. With a rush, an inferno consumed the splinter. It flailed its good wing but the motion fanned the flames, which burned even hotter. The smell of wood smoke mixed with burning flesh.

Holmes removed the wad from his ears to the crackle of fire. A crash signaled the collapse of the wooden nest. Watson emerged from the pub, a young girl clinging to him.

"She woke just after the beast stopped moving," he patted her back awkwardly. "How is she?"

"Perfectly fine physically, but she has no memory of the last few hours."

Holmes braced himself against the wall, a wave of dizziness spinning his head. Watson helped him to the ground. Another shot of morphine and a sling for the arm abated a crash.

Watson stared at the charred remains as they prepared to leave.

"One thing that bothers me about this curious business." He licked his lips and glanced at Holmes. "I thought the splinters were all destroyed in the Great Purge."

"Ah, Watson," said the detective. "Never believe everything the government insists is fact. Remember the improbable is entirely possible."

THE CURIOUS CASE OF THE TOMBSTONE DRAGON

Dan Shaurette

IT WAS IN THE SPRING OF 1890 THAT SHERLOCK HOLMES AND I FOUND ourselves in America investigating a most peculiar case. We had been in New York following a long trail of clues from Whitechapel in pursuit of an American doctor who Sherlock suspected of being Jack the Ripper. We worked with Detective Wilson Hargreave of the New York Police Bureau.

The trail grew cold in early May. Sherlock had been in a most foul mood ever since our quarry had eluded us. As we discussed our next direction, I received a telegram that had been forwarded by Mrs. Hudson.

Sharpe wired, "G Bromley requests that J Watson contact Nelson Sharpe Esq immediately in Tombstone, Ariz regarding arrest for murder."

This came as an incredible shock to my senses. George Bromley under arrest for murder? Such a thing boggled my mind.

"Bromley?" Sherlock queried, reading the cable after I had set it on the table once I finished reading it.

"George Bromley. An old mate of mine from the Army. Last I saw him was just before he left London for the States in 1882. I had mentioned to him then that I had moved in with you at Baker Street."

"I see," Sherlock nodded with interest. We shall make arrangements for the Arizona Territory post haste. Detective, please cable Mr. Sharpe back and let him know."

"Thank you, Holmes."

"Of course, Watson. A case is a case no matter how we come by it. It will be good to have the distraction."

Hargreave read the next cable. "Mr. Sharpe replied that this is a curious case. He is relieved to hear that you are in the States as he is unsure how much longer he can delay the court date."

"If I may ask, beyond discovering my friend is up on murder charges, what is the curious part?"

When the detective received the response, he froze. He looked to both of us then asked the telegraph operator, "Are you sure this is accurate?"

The operator nodded. "That's what he sent."

The detective handed me the telegram and explained, "The curious part is his defense. He claims he didn't murder anyone. He found the victims after they were mauled by a… 'dragon'."

I stared dumbfounded at the cable then handed it to Sherlock. His eyebrow raised and for the first time in days I believe I spied a grin on his face.

That afternoon we packed our meager belongings and booked passage on a train to the American southwest.

I did my best to relieve my concern over my incarcerated friend by staring out the train window at the marvelous landscapes which passed us by. It was often difficult to stay alert as the train gently rocked and rattled as it carried us from lush towns through grasslands and into painted deserts.

Even as we made our way through the desert plains of the Arizona Territory, I admired the mountains and vibrant bursts of green that defied the desolation. I tried not to let my thoughts take me away to the harsh wastes of Maiwand, Afghanistan, where George and I served together. However, the prospects of seeing him again out here in a land of hostile natives was drawing painful memories too close for comfort.

Finally, we arrived at the train station in Fairbank, Arizona, named presumably for the lush riverbank carving out an oasis nearby. We were met at the station by Mr. Sharpe. He was considerate to meet us there as the rail did not go all the way to Tombstone. He had also procured a coach that we needed to take the rest of the way.

"A pleasure to meet you both. Thank you for coming on such short notice."

Once we were in the coach and on our way, Mr. Sharpe handed me a copy of the local newspaper, the morbidly named *Tombstone Epitaph*. "This was last week's edition. Page three has a story relevant to Mr. Bromley's case."

I flipped the pages and it didn't take long to find the story. The headline declared that "a strange winged monster" had in fact been "discovered and killed on the Huachuca desert." I browsed the brief article and attempted not to laugh as I read.

"It must be a hoax," I insisted as I handed the newspaper to Sherlock. He scanned the article in short time and no doubt committed all salient details to memory.

Sherlock harrumphed. "It may not be a hoax but I distrust the credibility of the claims. Something was undoubtedly shot down, but like so many tall tales, the reported incident has naturally become exaggerated. As given here it would have to be a massive *chimera* for the number of different attributes it apparently possessed. At best the details are hearsay and preposterous at worst."

"We won't know for sure until we can see the beast for ourselves," I surmised.

"Precisely so, Watson."

"Sadly gentlemen, I regret to inform you that the dragon is gone," Sharpe said.

"Gone?! What do you mean?" I burst out abruptly.

"Just as I said. There was a blood stain and some strange tracks, but the dragon was not there when the ranchers returned with their supplies from town."

"Hoax then, definitely," I insisted.

"Come now, Watson. I think I would like to see the area where it was shot down and speak with the witnesses."

Thankfully, the rough ride came to an end and we disembarked outside of the Cochise County Courthouse in Tombstone. As the coach left us behind, a man rode up to the courthouse on a grey horse. He dismounted and secured his horse to a nearby rail.

"Nelson! Who do we have here? These the two fog-breathers?"

Sharpe looked down momentarily, a silent apology for the Sheriff's comment. "This is Dr. John Watson and Mr. Sherlock Holmes. Gentlemen, this is Sheriff John Slaughter."

Even though the Sheriff was about two inches shorter than myself, what he lacked in height he made up in imposing stature of presence. Sherlock, who towered over us all, nodded first and extended his hand. Dust plumed from the Sheriff's gloved hand as he shook it briefly. When he shook my hand in turn, I thought he was going to crush it.

"Just another day in Tombstone. I'll take you in to see George."

My heart sank when George was brought in to the small visitation room, restrained in handcuffs, and hunched over, defeated by his situation. His eyes were darkened by days without rest and his hair was tousled like that of a maniac. I attempted to approach him but the jailer intervened.

George straightened a bit and a genuine smile appeared. "John, finally! It is so good to see you, and this must be Mr. Holmes."

Holmes acknowledged him with a curt nod. The cuffs rattled as he laid his arms on the table between us and him.

"Are the irons really necessary?" I asked.

"For your safety and his," answered Slaughter with a sigh.

Sherlock pointed to George's bruised knuckles and his scratched-up arms. "I see he's given as good as he got." He then pointed out the scratches on the Jailer's neck.

"What in the blazes happened to you here?" I asked.

"My livery stable is not far from the Nobles' ranch. I do a fair bit of business with them. Last Sunday, I was tending to some horses when I heard some gunfire. I rode out to investigate to make sure there were no rustlers, like that no-good Cowboy Billy Morgan. When I found the Nobles' roundup, they told me they had shot at a giant flying lizard, like a dragon. I'd seen nothing on my ride and I didn't believe a word. That is until I saw the varmint with my own eyes Wednesday evening.

"I was coming in after a long day when I saw it fly right over my head, and it was headed for the Nobles' herd. I gave chase but lost track of it. I told John and Jack that I had seen it and I offered to join their works.

"We all saw it at last on Friday. Jack was the one who shot it; right out of the sky, he did. It crashed to earth with a loud clap like thunder. I ain't never seen anything like it. It was massive. The Nobles wanted to tie the infernal thing up and get help with skinning it. They sent me to Tombstone to gather supplies and find folks to help us but no one believed me when I got there. In the morning, they sent me to round up the Sheriff, a photographer, and anyone else who would help us with it. Penny rode out with us to write about it in the *Epitaph*.

"When we all arrived, the monster was gone and the Nobles changed their tune. Said I made up the whole tall tale!"

"That must have riled you up good," Sheriff Slaughter accused. "I could tell when I rode out there to see the monster myself."

"Sure I was mad, but I didn't kill 'em! The next evening I heard another clap of thunder and went outside to search the skies. Sure enough, I saw the dragon flying again. Not after the herd this time, but over to the Noble Springs Ranch. I rode my fastest horse over but I arrived too late. Both men were pinned down by the massive beast as it clawed at them. It screeched when it saw me and then flew off, leaving another thunderclap in its wake. I don't know if it was the shriek or the thunder that brought Laura out."

"And who is Laura?" asked Sherlock.

"Jack's wife," George explained with regret darkening his face.

"Jack's *widow*, you mean, no thanks to you," the jailer muttered.

George slammed his fists on the table, clattering his irons. "I didn't kill them! I tried," he sobbed, "I tried to save them." Mr. Sharpe handed George his handkerchief.

The jailer didn't give him a chance to use it. "That's enough outta you, Bromley. Time to go back to yer hole." He roughly pulled George to stand up and pushed him forward toward the door.

"Before you abscond with our client," Holmes said. "Would you allow me one last moment of his time?" Holmes walked over to George and made sure that the jailer could hear. "Let me assure you, Mr. Bromley, we will not rest until your case is solved and we can see you safely escorted out of this jail."

As we left the jail, Sherlock and I were practically assaulted by two men riding swift horses down Toughnut Street. I surely would have been trampled under hoof had it not been for a woman who barred my path with her parasol.

"My stars, they do tear through town, don't they?" Brushing away the dust, I tipped my hat to the lady. She wore a dusty rose prairie skirt and a fascinating bauble on a chain around her neck. It looked like it might have been made from a sliced seashell. "Thank you kindly, miss?"

"Mrs. Penelope Lane, and you are most welcome. By your accent, may I presume you are Mr. Bromley's friend, Dr. Watson?"

"Indeed, and this is..."

"Mr. Sherlock Holmes, of course, the Great Consulting Detective. I am an ardent reader of your stories, Dr. Watson. The tales of your exploits are most thrilling."

Sherlock tipped his cap. "You must be the journalist for *The Epitaph*, correct? The one who wrote about the dragon?"

"I am, yes. Are you investigating his case?"

"We are, and we could use some of your time to speak to you, if you can spare it."

"I have all the time you gentlemen need."

"Splendid! We are on our way to meet with the coroner. Care to walk along with us?" I offered her my arm and led her toward the morgue.

Sherlock continued, "It is our understanding that you wrote the initial story before seeing the creature for yourself."

"Yes, and my editor gave me quite a lot of grief about that. We all know George well, however, and he was never one to spin yarns like that. When George returned the next day to gather folks up to see the beast, I convinced my editor to publish the story. He agreed on the condition that I join the recovery party to get the full scoop in person."

"There was no monster there? No trace of anything curious?"

"The only thing curious was how rude the Nobles were in refuting his claim. Even if Mr. Bromley had made it up, such harassment was unwarranted."

"Do you remember the location?"

"Yes. Do you aim to inspect it yourselves?"

"If we can, yes."

"How exciting! I would love to see your skills in action, Mr. Holmes."

Holmes was about to protest, but then she pulled out a small notebook and pencil from her handbag to show us she was ready for anything. He huffed and conceded, "So long as you do not interfere with our investigation."

"Wonderful. Fewer notes for me to take down," I added. "Might I say, Mrs. Lane, what an extraordinary necklace you are wearing. Is that quite the style here?"

"Come now Watson, while I admit I have no eye for fashion, it is a rather unusual bauble, particularly given the desert locale. I would therefore deduce that it was a gift to Mrs. Lane, if I may, by her *late* husband."

She gasped. "How do you do it, Mr. Holmes?"

"Elementary, really. You are wearing your wedding band on your right hand, the indentation remaining on your left ring finger is still present, which means you choose to continue wearing it as a fond memento but that you have moved on after your mourning."

"You are of course correct, save one minor point; the shell itself is local. This piece of conch shell was found by my beloved Joseph in one of the shafts he was working in the Argento mine just outside of town. Yes, it is unique but it is precious to me, especially since he died in that very same mine a few months later."

"Our condolences," said I.

Sherlock looked around and pointed generally to the few residents on the street. "Tombstone does not have the hustle and bustle of a mining town. I must conclude then that the mines have dried up?"

"That is an interesting choice of words. About five years ago, many of the mines struck water and flooded. Most employed pumps to pull out the water, which helped their operations and the town. Eventually the pumps failed and became too expensive to maintain, so the mines failed. Some folks like the Nobles turned to raising cattle and that has helped them survive out here. Others, like Salvatore D'Argento, the owner of the Argento mine, did not get out until it was too late. He lost almost everything."

When we arrived at the morgue, we found two men in a rather heated discussion. Our presence was not even detected by them until we closed the door behind us. Startled, they turned toward us and smiled as they both recognized Mrs. Lane.

She made the introductions. "Dr. John Watson and Mr. Sherlock Holmes, this is our town coroner Edgar Brandt and Dr. Mortimer Jordan."

"Ah yes, Mr. Sharpe called to let us know you were here in regards to the attack on the Nobles," the coroner stated abruptly. "Dr. Jordan here performed the post-mortem examination."

"Do you mind if I examine the deceased?" I asked.

"If you must, though everything is in the report that we provided to Mr. Sharpe and the Sherriff," the coroner argued.

"Of course, but we are curious about the wounds," Sherlock insisted. "Surely, a dragon's claws deserve scientific scrutiny."

"Poppycock. There's no such thing, but humor yourself," Mr. Brandt said. "Penny, perhaps you should stay here. The bodies are a gruesome sight."

"Not a chance, gentlemen. This is Tombstone, I've seen my share of dead men."

Dr. Jordan pulled down the sheet covering Jack Noble. His neck, chest, and arms were brutally slashed with somewhat jagged shallow incisions. I concurred that the wounds did not appear to be from a sharp blade. There were many bruises all over the body. I found no lacerations or bite marks that I could identify as either human or animal. The older Noble's injuries were by and large the same, if in different locations. There was also some gunpowder residue on his right hand.

"Is that gunpowder residue on Noble's fingers?" I asked.

"Yes, it appears that he was able to fire his shotgun moments before he died." The Coroner added, "We found the gun itself at the scene, a spent shell still in the shotgun."

Holmes asked, "So he only had time to fire once. Interesting, and no one else at the scene was shot or otherwise injured? None of the family, the ranch hands, or Mr. Bromley?"

"That is correct."

Holmes handed the report back to the coroner, "These are not the stab wounds of homicidal strikes like a crime of passion. They're too shallow. No major organs were injured either. Both men died of blood loss and frankly from fear more than any specific injuries. These were vicious animal attacks, though, I would not want to meet an animal that would have claws or talons large enough to make these incisions."

"That is precisely what I told the coroner," said Dr. Jordan.

"And as I said to my esteemed colleague," Coroner Brandt retorted, "I have seen a blade that can make these wounds. I suspect you have, as well, Dr. Watson. Are you familiar with the Gurkha *kukri*?"

"I am, yes. Bromley and I both served with a Gurkha regiment. The *kukri* is a large knife, however, and would have been more likely to decapitate these men rather than make these shallow cuts."

The coroner nodded, "Agreed, however, the sheath of the *kukri* blade can hold two smaller knives. The *karda* is a small utility knife and the *chakmak* is a duller blade that is used to sharpen the *kukri*. A skilled knife-fighter could have used a *karda* to inflict these jagged incisions."

"Is Mr. Bromley a known owner of such a weapon?" Sherlock asked. Everyone shook their heads no.

"I never knew him to own one, either," I said.

"Your knowledge of knives is exemplary, Mr. Brandt. However, this is circumstantial conjecture at best unless you can find such a weapon," said Sherlock with a nod of approval to me.

"That is why it will be part of my report at the inquest. With my suspicions that a knife was used, one with which he was at least familiar—and now verified by you Dr. Watson—the sheriff can draw up warrant to search his property for the murder weapon."

I was of course furious by this, but a calm look by Sherlock helped me restrain my temper. Instead, I tipped my hat and thanked them for their time.

We left the morgue with Mrs. Lane who hired a coach for us. Our destination was the Noble Springs Ranch as well as a visit to the site George insisted was where the dragon had landed after being wounded.

The coach took us across a small river, which Mrs. Lane called the Rio San Pedro. She explained that north of here, near the river, was the Noble Springs Ranch, but the site was still further west, to a valley between the Whetstone and Huachuca Mountains.

When Mrs. Lane said we were near, Sherlock asked the driver to stop so that we could inspect the area unmolested by tracks. We stepped out into the ancient desert sands and walked around the brush and small clumps of cactus. Some of which Mrs. Lane claimed could jump at us. I'd never heard of jumping cactus before, but being a foreigner, I did not know if she was teasing us or not.

The landscape was littered with parched cracks everywhere. Occasionally we came across large boulders, some with markings carved into them. We weren't sure what these petroglyphs meant, but Mrs. Lane recognized one such landmark boulder as being close to our destination. Holmes examined the carvings on all sides of the tan boulder. One of them appeared to be a large inverted triangle with wings. Above it there was also a crude drawing of a spiral. At the right angle, it looked similar to the shell fragment that Penny wore.

We walked on while Sherlock pointed out the various hoof marks, confirming seven sets of tracks. There was an odd lack of vegetation in the immediate area, making a perfect clearing for people to meet. There was a small clump of brush that looked crushed, but there was no evidence of horse or boot prints around it. Some areas of dirt were disturbed, as if swept, but not but a broom or rake. Maybe it was indicative of someone covering up evidence, but it might have also been a giant wing perhaps that struggled to gain traction on the ground.

"Watson! Look here!" Holmes said, pointing out two darkened spots on the ground. One was near the center of the clearing, a large dark stain like an area of recently dried mud. Another was further away and smaller. It was not fresh mud, baking as it would have in the unforgiving sun, yet was still dark as if it were wet.

"Mud, perhaps?" I offered.

Holmes shook his head, clearly exasperated by my ignorance. "A thicker substance dried here. And look at the deep color, it's obviously blood!" Whatever it was looked like it had dripped and pooled from a small wound. We backed up immediately and saw no tracks near it from any desert creatures, of which Mrs. Lane assured us there could be several.

We counted steps between that stain and the smaller one we found. We estimated that it was about 30 feet away. This one looked as if it dripped from a different type of wound. The blood splatter was different than the gunshot. It looked more like a stab wound.

"Your article said that one of the men cut off the tip of a wing," Holmes said.

Mrs. Lane nodded. "Jack Noble clipped the wing and kept part of it, according to Mr. Bromley. I confronted Jack about it afterward but he swore he didn't take anything."

"This is consistent with such an injury," I said. "There's less blood at the end of a wing compared to vessels closer to the body. However, if it were clipped a few inches from the tip, more would drip from the long incision severing blood vessels in the cartilage from the wing."

Holmes stood and pointed out, "Here you can plainly see the dirt is swept away."

"My word, Holmes. If this is where the beast in question landed, and that larger stain represents a gunshot wound to the chest, and this where the wing tip was clipped, that means it had a wingspan of 60 feet, give or take!"

"That makes the assumption that the wing was fully extended. It might be even larger. There is little doubt left, Watson. Some winged beast was wounded and landed here. If we can find that wing tip, we can confirm our discovery."

"I can't believe it was real," Mrs. Lane said. "Jack even threatened to have me fired for libel when I asked about it! Why would the Nobles lie about it? And where did it go?"

As if to punctuate the question, we heard a clap of thunder in the distance. All three of us looked to the skies and saw nothing but a blue sky and a harsh, shimmering sun. Suddenly, the coach horses began to neigh and pull at their reins. The coachmen were shouting and waving to us and pointing to the sky.

I looked up again, and a black spot seemed to emerge from the blinding sun. The shape grew quickly. It might have been a large bat at first, but as it came closer, all of the hairs on my neck raised telling me this was no beast I'd ever encountered before.

"Run!" I shouted. Penny stood transfixed as if in shock that the creature was real. I tugged her arm. "Mrs. Lane! Penny, now!" She snapped out of her daze and then ran with me, Sherlock following behind.

We arrived at the coach and jumped inside. I had barely climbed in and closed the door before the whips cracked and the horses took off. None of us inside could see much from the windows of the coach looking at the sky, but on the ground beside us, I pointed out to Sherlock the massive shadow of a wing that looked more like a bat's than a bird's.

One of the coachmen yelled, "Look out!" followed by the repeated cocking and firing of a shotgun toward the rear of the coach. After the third shot, we heard a shriek that I pray I will never hear the likes of again. The shadow over us disappeared into the distance. Only then did we dare to look out the windows behind us. There was no doubt then to myself, Sherlock, Mrs. Lane, or our coachmen, that the Tombstone Dragon was real.

The coach did not slow down even when all trace of the creature had vanished from our view. The three of us did our best to endure the rough and rocky ride back. Once we had arrived at the relative civilization of Fairbank did we finally return to a normal travelling pace.

Within a few miles we had reached the expansive and lush Noble Springs Ranch. The coach pulled up to the humble two-story ranch house.

Mrs. Lane led the way along the wooden porch and knocked on the front door. A man who looked like he had just come in from working in the heat answered the door.

"Mrs. Lane, what brings you by?" When he saw us, he opened the door further and stepped out to greet us.

Mrs. Lane introduced us. "Mr. Morgan, this is Mr. Sherlock Holmes and Dr. John Watson."

He shook our hands in turn. "What can I do for y'all?"

"We've come to speak with you and Mrs. Noble about the evening of the attack," said Holmes.

"Ah, well come on in," he said, escorting us inside. "Mrs. Noble! You have company!"

As we waited for Mrs. Noble to join us, I posed a question to Mr. Morgan. "May I ask, how long you have worked for the Nobles and in what capacity?"

"Sure, I've been a ranch hand for about a year, but I was recently named foreman."

"Is it common practice to hire a former rustler to protect one's cattle?"

"Who told you that? Bromley? I've been accused of a good many things, but I ain't never stolen no cattle!" he protested.

"I can attest to that, gentlemen." A woman wearing a black bombazine mourning dress met us in the parlor. Mrs. Lane once again made our introductions.

"Our condolences and apologies for the intrusion, Mrs. Noble," offered Holmes.

"Thank you, Mr. Holmes. Dr. Watson, you are Mr. Bromley's friend, yes?"

"Yes, and we'd like to know more about what happened that night."

"I've known George Bromley for years. I still can't believe what happened, what I saw with my own eyes." She led us to a small sitting room and bade us to sit.

"That is precisely why we are here," said Holmes. "So, please, though it may pain you, we must know all the facts about that day."

Mrs. Noble nodded. "We had a couple callers that evening, the first of which was Mrs. Lane, but I don't know what she talked with them about."

"I came to get an official statement for the paper, about them claiming Mr. Bromley had made up the whole story about the dragon. He said he had proof but that Jack had stolen it."

"The tip of the wing," Sherlock added.

"Exactly. Jack claimed he didn't take anything, let alone a trophy from a beast that didn't exist. John threatened to have me fired if I didn't retract the story. I told him the editor sent me out to get their final say, either way, but that he wasn't going to fire his star reporter. It was really up to them what would be printed next, and an exposé on how they treated members of the free press would look worse than no comment. Jack raised his hand to me but John stopped him. I left after that."

Mrs. Noble gasped. "I'm sorry, Penny, I had no idea."

"I'm sorry you had to hear it this way. I just wish I knew the whole truth about the dragon, whether on the record or not. As I left, I saw Sal D'Argento arrive."

Mrs. Noble nodded. "Yes, he came over and joined us for supper. It was mostly cordial until he brought up for the umpteenth time his desire to buy out the ranch, or at least part of it. He leveled with us and said he discovered a cave in the area. He hadn't the chance to explore, but he believed it had a new untapped vein. He had started a claim, but as it ran under our property, he could not secure the rights. He was willing to make us a fair offer, but John wouldn't sell. Tensions ran rather high after that and Sal left quite upset.

"After he'd left, I retired for the evening while Jack and his pa stayed up for cigars and bourbon, as was their usual leisure. The quiet of the house was disturbed maybe half an hour later by a clap of thunder. That startled me but then I heard the shotgun fire. I ran to the study and they weren't there. I found Billy and we went to investigate.

"We found them both outside, hacked up, with George Bromley standing over them. Billy kept his rifle on him while I sent for the sheriff."

Holmes nodded. "Could you show us where you found them, please?"

"Of course," Mrs. Noble agreed. She led us outside to a spot about halfway between the ranch house and a guest house. Holmes looked around at the area as we walked and then crouched down and inspected the spot that we could all see was matted down from a scuffle.

"Did Bromley have any weapons on him, like a blade that he could have used to attack them?"

Both Mrs. Noble and Morgan shook their heads. "He must've ditched it though. He had blood on his hands."

"And John, Sr. was a good marksman?"

"Sure enough shot," Mrs. Noble said with pride. "He preferred his shotgun in his older years, though."

"Was he one to load his shells with rock salt or fire blanks just as a warning?"

"No, never," Billy said. "That ain't the way you defend your land, Mr. Holmes."

"So, if he fired at their attacker, either that attacker fled with their body pocked with shot, or somehow he missed and there'd be shot dispersed out here." He mimicked firing a lever-action shotgun about chest level and then dropping it. He walked slowly away from the houses to a small fence, examined it, the ground around it, and then walked back. "There's no sign of any shot on the ground or in that fence. He definitely dropped the shotgun there at his feet?"

"That is where we found it, Mr. Holmes," said Mrs. Noble.

I had to ask the burning question. "Did either of you see this dragon, either the night of the attack or before then?"

"No, of course not, because it don't exist!" Morgan was losing his patience.

"I never saw it either, nor did Jack or his Pa ever say anything about it until Mr. Bromley dragged everyone out to the desert."

"We just came from the site in question," admitted Holmes, "and found evidence of some kind of creature, which admittedly we can't completely explain, but by which we were chased out of the desert on our way here."

"Malarkey!" shouted Morgan.

"It's true. We saw it," said Mrs. Lane. "Our coachmen shot at it!"

Holmes spun quickly, "On the evening of the attack, where were you, Mr. Morgan, when supper was being served and then afterward?"

Billy pointed to the smaller house. "I was at home, having my own dinner. Alone."

"Mrs. Noble, how long have you two been having an affair?"

She blinked and stood straight, stuttered for a moment, no doubt shocked by Holmes's forthright accusation. Morgan tensed then strode forward to confront Sherlock.

"How dare you, sir! She has been through Hell this week!"

"I can see that and that she is truly in mourning. However, she left out one detail about *where* she retired to after supper. There are plenty of fresh foot prints out here that indicate she visited you that evening, and not in the rush to rouse you for your assistance during the disturbance. The gait suggests the stride of one trying not to be discovered."

Neither of them denied the accusation.

"Yes. Yes, I was with Billy after supper," Mrs. Noble cried. "As was the case, off and on, for about a few months now."

Sherlock nodded again. "Thank you for your honesty and for your time. Both of you." With that he tipped his hat and we made our way past the fence to the coach that was waiting patiently to return us to Tombstone.

We joined Mrs. Lane at the Crystal Palace Saloon where she made good on her promise of a round of drinks for our harried coachmen. She also appeared to be drawing something in her notepad as she talked to them. One suspects a good journalist never rests.

The establishment itself was quite remarkable. It was well-appointed and decorated. It was rowdy with many men relaxing with a drink after a hard day of work, while still others were playing cards. The most astonishing discovery was a fountain in the center of the saloon with goldfish swimming happily in the basin.

Holmes and I both settled the day with a whiskey-and-soda. We made our way to an empty table near the back where we could see everything in the saloon. Eventually Mrs. Lane joined us at our table with a glass of white wine which Holmes was delighted to find as an available choice.

She shared with us the sketch that she had made. "I spoke with our coachmen and this is what they saw."

Her sketch did not look like a dragon from any mythology I was familiar with. Large stretched wings that curved down to its legs, but without the long digits that extended from the top of the wing to the bottom like a bat has. It had a striking pointed beak with a crest on its head. It did match the shadow I had seen on the ground as it flew over our coach.

"Pterodactyl," declared Sherlock. "Or some species related to it. A flying reptile, long extinct."

"Surely not," I demanded.

"Thunderbird," said a man sitting alone at a nearby table.

"Pardon?" I asked.

"Sorry, I couldn't help but overhear. My name's Sal D'Argento. A Pima Indian I traded with once told me the legend of a giant flying serpent that lived in a cave at the top of a mountain. Without warning, it would fly around to catch and kill many tribesmen. He said its enormous wings created the thunder, thus they called it the Thunderbird."

Billy Morgan walked into the bar, slapped money down for a beer and began drinking before he noticed us in the back. When he approached, it became obvious that the beer in his hand was not his first since we had seen him at the ranch.

"Lookie who's here," he said, sloshing his drink in Mrs. Lane's direction. "You keep turning up like a bad penny," said Billy, laughing at his own pun. He fished a small folded kerchief from his pocket and tossed it on our table in front of Penny.

She unwrapped it and gasped as she realized what it was. She passed it to me to examine. In the folds was a small green-gray piece of membrane with fine hairs covering it and a small bit of hollow bone.

Billy explained, "Laura found this in Jack's belongings tonight. Guess the dragon was real after all."

"Thank you for bringing it to us. This corroborates Bromley's story," I said as I passed it to Holmes who gave it his usual inspection.

"I couldn't give a flying fig if it helps George Bromley, I just want everyone to leave Laura and me alone. Print whatever you like, Mrs. Lane, just keep us out of it."

"*The Epitaph* isn't a gossip rag, Mr. Morgan, but folks will find out eventually," she said.

Billy's face flushed red and he yelled, "If anyone tells a soul, so help me I'll…"

D'Argento stood up and grabbed Billy before he could exact any violence. "You'll do nothing of the sort."

Billy's ire turned full force to the man. "I'll do whatever I damn well please, Sally, you dirty cheat! You leave Laura alone! She ain't gonna sell to you."

Billy swung hard right to his jaw but was so inebriated that he lost his balance. D'Argento took the punch like it was barely a slap and then jabbed Billy straight to the gut. More men stood up, ready to start a good brawl, but the barkeep pulled out his shotgun and cocked it. The noise signaled it was time to quit for both men. "You get outta here, Billy Morgan, 'fore you're wearin' lead." Doubled over in pain, Billy nodded and ran out of the saloon.

Mrs. Lane hardly had time to thank Mr. D'Argento when we heard the rumble and crack of a thunderclap outside. Holmes stood up and rushed outside, with Mrs. Lane, Mr. D'Argento, and myself running to keep up.

With another clap of thunder, we looked to the sky to see that the giant flying beast was in pursuit of Billy. They were quite far ahead of us in the distance but the thunderbird swooped down and knocked Billy and his horse over. The monster landed and folded its wings, using them like forearms. It walked around Billy as if on four legs, waiting for the perfect moment to strike. It opened its giant maw and let out a horrible screech. Mrs. Lane let out a scream, and she stood staring paralyzed with fear.

"Forgive me, Mrs. Lane," Holmes said and to my horror, slapped her once across the face. He then yanked the necklace from around her neck, snapping the chain with ease. He tossed it to the ground and crushed the seashell under his foot, crumbling it to pearlescent dust.

Mrs. Lane shook her herself as she regained her senses. In the distance, the creature jumped into the air, flapping its massive wings. It circled around over the town and we had all too close a view of its fearful symmetry. It then flapped fiercely and flew off into the sunset with a clap of thunder.

Whatever daze Mrs. Lane was in finally cleared. "What happened?"

"Your necklace, Mrs. Lane. The beast seemed to be summoned by it, and in turn, by you."

"*Me?* No, I never. I couldn't have done this!"

"Not directly. I surmise that whenever you were threatened or angry, that was channeled by the necklace to the beast. I perceived an arc of electricity circle outward from the coiling of the shell. Once we were outside, you entered a fugue state, like you did at the desert site. I suspected that the destruction of the shell was paramount."

Within a few moments, four men on horseback rode back into town. The sheriff and coroner rode toward the courthouse while Dr. Jordan rode close to Billy Morgan towards the doctor's office. As they rode past us, we saw that Billy was hugging his belly had a few superficial flesh wounds. Otherwise he and his horse seemed to be in fair shape.

Tears welled up in Mrs. Lane's eyes as she saw how injured he was. "Should we check on him?"

"I'm sure Dr. Jordan has him well in hand."

Sherlock nodded. "Agreed. Our new information means we should give statements to the Sheriff and hope they'll see fit to release Mr. Bromley."

Sherlock and I waited with Mrs. Lane and Mr. Sharpe at the Courthouse. The sheriff had seen with his own eyes what attacked Billy Morgan and agreed that George was free to go. Handshakes and hugs were the order of business now.

"Thank you, John. Mr. Holmes, you have my gratitude. Right now, I could really use a whisky," George said.

"The first round is on me," announced Mr. Sharpe as he led the way to the saloon.

CRIPPLED PLAYTHINGS

S. H. Roddey

FRIEDRICH NIETZSCHE ONCE SAID, "HE WHO FIGHTS WITH MONSTERS MIGHT take care lest he thereby become a monster. And if you gaze for long into an abyss, the abyss gazes also into you." Looking back on the curious and bizarre incidents of my life with Sherlock Holmes, I often wondered if the great philosopher did not say these things with specific intent toward my dearest friend himself.

It was not until the twilight years of our lives that I came to discover just how fortunate – no, how *lucky* – the both of us had been. Holmes would no doubt have told me he didn't believe in such madness as luck, were I to have expressed this sentiment to him. Though I watched so many times as Holmes and that proverbial abyss stared eye-to-eye, the darkness threatening to swallow his humanity whole.

The tale I share tonight is one of confusion and desperation, and because of the complex nature I have asked Holmes himself to contribute to its telling. For the truest accounting of events may only come from the consciousness of the man who witnessed these atrocities first-hand.

Sherlock Holmes. New York City, October 18, 1907
I stood at the helm of the airship, watching the people bustle to and fro amid the clouds of coal smoke and city fog. The telegram sent to me by my colleague and friend, Dr. John Watson, rested in my left breast pocket, its contents curious enough to bring me to New Orleans from London by way of New York and Baton Rouge.

My Dearest Holmes,
It has been brought to my attention by local law enforcement that people have begun to vanish. This would pique neither my interest nor yours, except that those vanishing share a similar trait: each missing person is permanently confined to a wheelchair or a bed.

Please come, as the authorities in New Orleans are baffled by the disappearances.
Yours Truly,
John H. Watson, MD

Watson was, of course, spot on when he said it would be of no interest to me. I still found very little interest in the disappearances, but out of sheer boredom I made the attempt to humor my friend by purchasing a ticket for America. As I stood aboard the deck of the great blimp, I found myself wondering how many of those aboard would meet an untimely demise in the world's most sinful city. These pathetic beasts would no doubt follow their baser desires to ultimate doom, smiling and singing as the poison of youth infiltrated their minds and removed what inhibitions might keep them from stepping into the streets in front of a carriage.

Said thought process was interrupted with the addition of a young, wheelchair-laden man. He moved with grace despite the self-propelled contraption bound to his lower half, which immediately told me he and it had been one for quite some time - the majority of his life, as a matter of fact. Withered legs beneath a tattered, tartan blanket emphasized the stout and stocky upper body. He turned the machine toward me by way of the ticking contraption pressed against his right palm, and glided across the uneven deck. The wheels of his chair took the brunt of the impact as they rattled and clattered across the boards, yet he remained upright and supremely unaware of the danger beneath him. I was most fortunate that this young man came to a stop beside me.

"Good evening," he said with a smile and a slight nod of his head. The silk-trimmed straw boater dipped with his head, but remained otherwise immobile. I touched my fingers to the brim of my own top hat and, without appearing obvious, continued with my review of his situation. Worn places on his gloves showed repeated use of his hands - expected for one in such a predicament as him. A tinkerer by trade – and a dying trade at that – his clothes were shabby; the wheelchair even more so, held together by what mismatched bits of metal he could find coupled with this own ingenuity. The weakness of stature was cleverly disguised, however, by additions such as gear sets and pulleys - systems which appeared to make travel easier for him. This man had little money and, if my intuition were correct, had spent his last penny on the ticket for the dirigible on which we stood. This man carried some sort of foolish dream. If he happened to be going my way, it also meant he could be a potential victim.

"Nice evening," I said, the pleasantry extended to glean his intentions.

"It is. I look forward to the fresh air once we lift off." His accent was hard, unrefined, and completely American.

"Are you in Baton Rouge long?"

He shook his head. "Only passing through on my way to New Orleans."

"Business or pleasure?" I prodded. He did not appear flustered by my small talk.

"A bit of both, I suppose. I have an appointment with a doctor who believes he might be able to do something about my...situation." While I considered his comment, he extended a hand to me. "Henry Gaston," he said. "Pleased to meet you, Mr..."

"Holmes," I replied, taking his hand and shaking hard once. "Sherlock Holmes."

His eyes lit up. "The detective from London?" I nodded and a look of glee came over his face. "I love Dr. Watson's stories. I never imagined I might have the chance to meet you in person, though!" I waited for his tirade to end, hoping not to expend the entirety of my patience on his outburst. When his composure returned, he cleared his throat and apologized. "So what brings you to the States, Mr. Holmes?"

"A telegram from Dr. Watson, as a matter of fact," I replied, and quickly changed the subject. "So this doctor of yours... he claims he can cure you?"

Henry shrugged. "He said so. I'm hopeful, but not so naïve that I believe it will work."

I wondered who he was trying to convince: himself or me. "A healthy position," I offered as I watched a young woman come aboard. She stood out to me because of the new, gleaming wheelchair and the air of impatience about her. She was waiting to die.

"To be honest, I am more interested in seeing another part of the world outside of my apartment." He glanced back over his shoulder as the grinding of gears filled the air and the gangplank began to rise. It came to a stop with a shuddering crash, and I had to brace myself against the railing to keep from toppling backwards. Henry never moved. "I have been confined to a chair since childhood. A fever, you see, took my mobility and with it, my freedom." Sadness crossed his face for the briefest moment, replaced quickly by longing. "Because of my condition," he continued as the noise subsided, "I never got to see the world." He sighed. "Those in wheelchairs – however advanced their tinkered accessories may be," he motioned to the gadgets and gears adorning his own chair, "are rarely able to travel with ease. This trip, however, promises to be the beginning of a new life if the doctor can truly work miracles."

Unease came over me. The more this man spoke, the more certain I became of his involvement in this wicked scheme. Almost certainly, this man would be among the missing.

Funny, I thought. *With all the modern conveniences and technological advancements of the twentieth century - we were flying, after all - that the surgeons have yet been unable to repair spines and cure crippling diseases.*

The other occupants of this floating marvel ran to the railings to wave to the rabble below as the floor began to vibrate under the strain of the engines. Slowly, the craft rose from the ground, pitching us into sharp wind currents. Soon, we were far enough above the city of New York that it appeared as little more than a painting. As we rose the sun sank below the horizon, and the colors of evening faded into the starry blackness of night. Henry politely excused himself and moved to sit beside the lonely woman. He attempted to engage her in conversation, but she refused to speak.

I watched the dim haze of the hamlets slide past on the patchwork ground, each one acknowledged only by flickering streetlamps as the world slept below the dirigible. The girl still refused to speak to Henry, but from the look of her, I could only assume she was on this journey for the same reason as him: to walk. She rolled away, locating a crew member to lift her from her chair and carry her downstairs. Eventually, even Henry gave up and moved to the back of the deck in search of assistance to go below.

The only civilian left on deck, I marveled at the great airship's propellers, studied the feel of the wind against my face – somewhat of a draft created despite the windscreens affront the ship. Overhead the night sky was littered with stars. The moon, little more than a pale sliver, hung low on the horizon. The atmosphere would begin to change color soon – I could feel morning coming.

Two days out of New York, the woman finally began to speak. Georgia Corchoran, I learned, was the victim of a terrible carriage accident which left her with a severed spinal column and no use of her legs. I learned this from Henry, of course, who had no problem at all keeping me apprised of the goings-on of the ship...whether or not I wanted to know. He also appeared particularly interested in an older gentleman with a handlebar moustache. He carried a handkerchief in his left hand and spent the majority of our journey wiping at his nose. In between bouts of allergic distress, he showed a disturbing level of attention to Henry; asked of his home life, his childhood, and the fever. Henry took the questions in stride and, to my surprise, attempted to introduce the gentleman to Miss Corchoran as well.

She, for the most part, ignored him completely.

However, during this grueling process, I learned from Henry a single interesting piece of information: Miss Corchoran had also been told her paralysis could be reversed. The other gentleman, whose name I did not care to learn, was also interested in her plight.

Liar, my better senses told me of the man. *Dangerous.*

From my pocket I removed a small notepad and began to list items of importance - their shared immobility, their similar invitations, and the fact that people much like the two of them were disappearing at an alarming rate from the streets of New Orleans.

With one day to go before docking in Baton Rouge, I needed to use Henry's obvious adoration of me to the fullest extent - by questioning every person aboard the ship for any and all information related to the case. Unfortunately, the line of questioning produced no other useful information.

Once in Baton Rouge, Henry, and I were ushered to a smaller dirigible which would take us to New Orleans. It was early in the morning on a Friday and the air was already thick and humid despite the chill in it. Two others from the New York flight accompanied us; one being the bespectacled gentleman with the dripping nose and deplorable mustache. The other, to my great delight, was Miss Corchoran. Not one, but *two* disabled bodies on the same journey... I was already closer to solving this mystery than the authorities.

From the air, New Orleans glowed. A city of magic, mystery and intrigue. I found myself amused by Henry's open adoration of the city. He marveled at the sparkling blanket of gas lights and coal lamps beneath us. The dirigible's turbines rotated around until the blades lay parallel to the deck, giving us a clearer view of the urban sprawl. As the aircraft sank closer and closer to solid ground, the sparkles turned to bright orbs and between them in the early morning house movement began. Specks of scurrying energy turned to ants which in turn morphed into people, carriages, and the occasional horseless contraption. On the platform below, I spotted Watson and his wife, Mary, their faces turned up to the bottom of the ship.

As we began the arduous task of debarking, Henry caught me by the wrist.

"Do you think I'm making a mistake, Mr. Holmes? Trusting my fate to a man I've never met?"

"How is trusting me to answer your question any different?" I replied, surprising him. "Only time will tell."

John Watson. New Orleans, October 22, 1907

"Sherlock Holmes, you are a sight for sore eyes," I said, taking my friend's hand. It had been months since our paths crossed, what with my having accompanied Mary stateside for a visit with a childhood friend. As I predicted, Holmes scarcely acknowledged me in favor of embracing my wife.

"Hello, Sherlock," Mary said with a smile. The corners of her mouth creased around her dimples, and when Holmes smiled back at her, tiny lines formed at the corners of his eyes. We were no longer young, I realized, as the symptoms of old age began to show themselves.

Holmes nodded at her pleasantry as he released her, then immediately began to walk toward our carriage. Mary and I raced to catch up to him, not at all surprised that he'd already begun to speak to us, regardless of the fact that we were out of earshot.

"...so I must keep track of him," Holmes said.

"Who?"

"I just *told* you," he replied tersely.

"Yes, you did," I answered as patiently as I could, "but you told me when I was quite unable to hear you." Holmes made a face at me, but did not argue, which surprised me. He typically argued.

"The man in the self-propelled chair," Holmes said. "I need to keep track of him, as I believe he may be connected to the subject of your letter."

"Sherlock, the authorities –"

"Will not catch the culprit without first finding the next victim," he snapped. A scowl set in on his face as he climbed into the carriage. From inside, he extended a hand to Mary, and once we were all safely inside, we started toward the outskirts of town. Holmes had fallen into a sullen silence, his eyes drifting closed as he processed what information he'd obtained on the flight. We rode in silence until the moment when the carriage stopped. Holmes immediately came to life, giving the driver a new address and pulling me back into the carriage.

"Come, Watson," he said, manic glee settling into his features, "we have a mystery to solve."

The roads on the outskirts of New Orleans were dangerous, to say the least. After the terrible rains from the earlier season, many were deemed impassable by the coachman, who graciously let us out to walk the remainder of the way. Without a moment's hesitation, Holmes stepped down from the carriage, his singular focus on finding the man he'd called Henry Gaston.

"Do you honestly believe a chance meeting on a dirigible is going to lead you to the answer so quickly?" I asked as a struggled to maintain pace with him. For a moment I suspected he would ignore me, then he opened his mouth.

"You know, Watson, that I do not believe in 'luck', and there are no coincidences. I came on this journey the moment I did to solve a possible crime, and should a clue roll up to me and introduce itself, far be it from me to ignore it."

I could have easily argued divine providence, yet chose to keep my mouth tightly closed. The sun, long-since gone below the tree line, was pulling with it the bright colors of day and leaving in its wake a murky sort of sunset which enveloped us in a dismally unnerving calm. Were I on my own, I would have turned back here, but my companion would not be swayed from his task and I knew it.

"Holmes, answer a question for me," I said after another half-mile of our picking over fallen branches and other such debris.

"If I must," he said without affect.

"Forgive me for thinking so strangely, but please explain to me how a man confined to a wheelchair would be able to make the journey down this road on foot." Holmes paused, one foot hanging in midair, and scowled.

"In this age of steam-powered technology," he replied, "anything is possible."

"However improbable."

"*Improbability* has absolutely no bearing on *possibility*. Now come...we must find this boarding house."

But there was no boarding house to be found. The road on which we walked ended very suddenly around the next bend, trickling off into a mass of overgrowth and organic decay. I would have laughed had terror not seized my voice.

"Curious," Holmes said as he examined the trees around us.

"We should turn back," I urged. I expected him to argue, but he did no such thing, instead he turned on his heel and strode back the way we came, stepping over the debris with strides far too wide for my height. I stumbled to keep up, and when we returned to the place where the carriage had deposited us, we found it was gone. "That's just *fantastic*," I snapped. "What do we do now?"

"We walk."

John Watson. New Orleans, October 27, 1907

It would be nearly a week before another clue appeared. Against his will, I delivered Holmes to the local police who gave him very little useful information – crippled men and women disappearing with increasing frequency over the last five months. So far no bodies had been located, nor any living souls returned. Holmes studied maps and walked the roads, often requiring my assistance if for no other reason than to keep him from walking off into a ravine or out in front of a carriage.

It was on one such occasion that a rustling in the underbrush piqued his interest. Expecting to find a small animal, I watched as he, his age showing by the stoop of his shoulders, bent and delved into the brush. A shriek of delight tore from his throat and I rushed forward just as he pulled the twisted remains of a wheelchair frame from the tall grass.

"It could have come from anywhere," I replied to his sudden mania. "As rusted and worn as the frame is, God only knows how long it has been there."

"True," Holmes stated, "but to find it *here*, it does make one curious."

"It does," I admitted. "But it still does not help you locate the missing people – eleven now by the deputy's last estimation."

"Thirteen," he corrected. "Henry and the woman are also part of this wicked scheme."

"You think."

"I *know*."

I wanted to question how he knew... but it *was* Sherlock Holmes, and when he said he knew something, he was usually correct. Rather than continue the argument, I conceded the sentiment and allowed him to lead me back toward town, all the while conversing with himself of the many possibilities the chair provided. This case, I assumed, would never be solved even with the help of Sherlock Holmes, as his leads, his deductions, had all turned up nothing.

Then the woman appeared.

As we walked down Canal Street, a desperate woman's voice broke through the bustle of people. Her hysterical tone caught my attention even as it bypassed Holmes' caring...

Until she called his name.

"Holmes..." she gasped, her voice hitching with each and every breath. "Sh-Sherl-lock H-Holmes..." She stumbled out of an alley, clothes torn and dirty, her balance shaky as if she had only just learned to walk. Her fingers tangled into the coats of passersby, people who shoved her away in disgust at her distressed and frightened state. "I h-have to f-f-find H-Holmes..." she gasped. I rushed forward to catch her as she collapsed.

"I am John Watson," I said as I lowered her to sit on the brick sidewalk. "This is Sherlock Holmes." I motioned to my companion who knelt beside us. Her eyes went wide as she looked at him, as if she recognized him.

"Georgia Corchoran," Holmes said, aghast.

"You know this woman?" I asked.

"She was aboard the dirigible from New York. In a wheelchair."

"Henry…" she said, and began to cough. Her dry lips cracked and began to bleed, and with her left hand she toyed with the hem of her skirt. "Henry told me to find Sherlock Holmes." She pulled the hem of her skirt above her boots. "He didn't lie," she whispered. "I walked again." The woman fell limp in my arms. Her pulse remained strong and her breathing came in hard, short bursts. This woman was hysterical.

Holmes moved her hand to the side and lifted her skirt. Surprised and mildly disgusted gasps echoed around us and I reached for his hand to stop him – we were on a sidewalk in broad daylight with a growing audience – but he quickly batted me away and tugged aside her petticoat. What he found turned his complexion white as porcelain. "We must get this woman to a hospital. Now." He lifted her into his arms and, despite the crowd, and carried her limp body into the street where he hailed a taxi.

Once safely inside the carriage, he pulled back the cloth to reveal the most grisly display I'd ever seen – her withered legs encased in leather straps and metal gears, held in place with rods and tubes which wormed their way in and out of her skin. The boots themselves appeared to be part of the apparatus, and when Holmes bent her legs, the mechanical whirring of well-oiled gears filled the space.

Sherlock Holmes. New Orleans, October 25, 1907

I waited three days for the woman to wake. I neither ate nor slept, the need for information greater than those bodily functions, and when given the opportunity, studied the contraptions encasing her withered legs. The muscle tone surrounding the bones spoke of a distinct inability to support her weight, yet she'd walked upright – albeit jerkily – into Watson's arms. The tiny gears beside her knees waited patiently, their smooth and shining surfaces glinting in the gaslight of the hospital room. From time to time a nerve would twitch, and the smooth hum of the mechanism would catch my attention. The tubes which ran beneath the surface of her skin distorted the shapely figure of her lower extremities in a most terrible manner. The doctors had attempted to remove her boots, but found it impossible without removing the encasements themselves. As one particularly curious doctor unlaced her left shoe, he discovered that the leather of the boot itself appeared to have been welded to her very skin.

The boots had become a part of her.

The police came and went, examining the handiwork of the "doctor" and quickly departed, quite *greener* than when they arrived. I was questioned and, having a better grasp of the situation than they, grew bored with their mundane inquiries. These poor imbeciles had little, if any, chance of solving this case.

When Miss Corchran regained consciousness, she did so screaming. The doctor and nurse rushed in to sedate her, and when her hysteria subsided, I stepped up to her bedside.

"Tell me what happened to you," I urged.

"The doctor," she whispered, her breath coming in shallow pants. "He is a liar."

I pulled back the blanket from her legs and the grotesque contraptions encasing them. "Is this his work?" She nodded. "Does he have others?" Again, she nodded. "What is his purpose in taking them?"

"I don't know."

"Tell me where he is."

"I…I don't know."

"What do you know?" I snapped, suddenly weary of her tears.

"He's a madman!" she shrieked, which brought the nurse running again. I pushed the door closed and leaned against it to keep her out. "He offered me the chance to walk again after my accident and I willingly took the chance because I wanted my old life back so badly." She coughed to cover a sob and wiped at her eyes. "The pain… oh, God, the pain…" She wailed, her fists balling into the thin sheet covering her abominable legs.

"Why is he doing it?"

She shrugged. "Power, maybe. Money. He…he has servants in the cane fields. I think they may have been like…"

"Like what?" I prodded.

"Like me," she whispered, and blew her nose. "Earlier versions of his work, perhaps. From what I could see through the window…" she trailed off. "You won't believe me if I tell you."

"At this point, Miss Corchoran, I am willing to believe anything."

"He wanted to *use* us."

"For what purpose?"

"I don't know." She coughed indelicately. "Some were in the kitchen, others in the fields. Some were suspended from cables in the ceiling. Those outside… they only ever moved along the same paths – never veering. But every person I spoke to said they had started out just like me."

"I need to know *where* this place is," I demanded.

"I don't know where it is, exactly," she said. "*Lecrainte* Parish, I think he said." It was a start. "I…I think I can take you there," she whispered beneath a sniffle.

John Watson. New Orleans, October 31, 1907

We woke to news of another young, crippled woman being stolen from her bed. The newspaper only seemed to agitate Holmes more, and as we prepared to leave he paced the floor as a caged animal, with all the side effects save foaming of the mouth. Once we finally took to the streets in the carriage, he seemed to relax, though the girl grew increasingly more anxious and withdrawn. I couldn't blame her, as she'd suffered unmentionable nightmares. Children in costumes moved along the streets in packs, some knocking on doors and running away while others attempted to garner treats from those occupying the spaces behind the doors. *Halloween*, I remembered, and the pit of anxiety swelled.

The driver took us out of New Orleans proper in the direction of Raceland, and with each passing moment my sense of unease grew in an exponential manner. Perhaps it was Georgia's anxiety fueling my own, but Holmes as usual remained blissfully unaware of the potential trap into which we were walking.

"Turn right," Georgia said suddenly. The carriage jolted sharply as the driver took the turn. She sat up straighter, peering out the window at the scenery drifting by. "This is the right way," she continued after some time. "I remember that tree."

"How far away are we?" Holmes asked, his voice monotone and impatient.

"Not far," Georgia replied, and looked at me. "Do you think we can save that girl, Dr. Watson?"

"I hope so," I replied.

The longer the carriage trundled on, the more I began to doubt the accuracy of Georgia's memory. She glanced out the window at regular intervals, her brow furrowing in a combination of anxiety and frustration.

"I know it was here," she muttered under her breath. "We turned from this road. Did we pass it?"

"We have passed nothing," Holmes replied sharply. "Nothing but trees and fields and –"

"There!" she cried, stabbing her finger at the window. "Stop!" she cried to the driver, who pulled the carriage to hasty halt. Unease turned to bald fear as we stepped down from the carriage into the street, and Georgia let out a tiny, stifled cry.

"What is this place?" Holmes asked as we looked out across the fields, watching people move between the rows.

"This is where he *changed* me," she whispered.

"Holmes?" I asked when he didn't respond.

"Take Miss Corchoran back to town and keep her safe. Alert the authorities. I will find the culprit."

Sherlock Holmes. Lecrainte Parish, October 31, 1907

The carriage pulled away, leaving me alone in this wretched place. The sun shined through the dark clouds, as if encasing the entire property beneath a dark shroud. There was no birdsong, no movement of small animals in the underbrush. The cotton was in bloom, its delicate fragrance filling the air. As I approached, I noticed the men and women moving about the fields silently. None looked in my direction, and upon watching them I discovered Miss Corchoran's description to be accurate. They moved along a single path, turning one way then the other, then hoisting their full baskets up and moving back toward the house before returning. Their movements seemed unnatural, and I wanted to know why.

I stepped off the dusty road into the tall grass beside the cotton fields and started forward, only to catch my foot on something and nearly tumble headlong into the plants. Hiding in the growth was a rusted rail, similar to that used on the many freight lines crisscrossing the continent. Curious, I followed it along the road to the point where it intersected another and ran perpendicular into the rows of cotton plants toward the next row. The metal was cold, and the slightest of vibrations brought me closer, pressing my ear and cheek against the bar to listen.

As I continued my investigation, the familiar sound of clockwork mechanisms moved past me. Parting the bushes, I watched as a servant – a young man of Hispanic descent – strode past. Or rather, *rode* past. His lower extremities were encased in an apparatus similar to the girl's , albeit a more primitive model. A series of ropes and pulley systems connected his legs to a pole riding above the track. Chains ran along either side of the harness system atop the track as well. Those chains, I quickly realized, operated the entire contraption.

"Intruder!" a voice boomed above me, and I looked up into the face of the angry servant. "Intruder!" he shouted again and swung a machete at me. I ducked backward s and scrambled out of the cotton rows, thankful the rail system kept him out of range. My coat and shirt became ensnared as I made my retreat, tearing large pieces loose from the bushes.

A chorus of voices rose among the rows and the individual mechanisms screeched in an unholy symphony as the mechanized field hands returned to the manor. A moment later, the thunder of hooves pounded the ground. Two men appeared above me, each wielding a musket.

"What do you want?" the taller of the two demanded as he leveled the barrel of his firearm with my forehead. They did not dismount – *couldn't*, I realized, as their bodies rested in saddles fitted with contraptions similar to the field hands.

"H-help me," I begged, forcing fear and concession into my voice. "I can't w-walk…" I dragged myself forward through the dirt with my hands, my fingers straining with the effort. My legs stayed limp, imitating lifelessness.

"Should we take him?" the shorter man asked under his breath. "Think Doc will want to see 'im?"

"Can't hurt," the other replied. "If Doc don't want him, we'll dispose of him."

I allowed those men to drag me through the dirt. With no small amount of difficulty I managed to maintain a façade of unaffected calm as my knees and shins bounced against the steps of the manor house. The horsemen handed me off to a pair of well-dressed servants whose mechanical workings were nearly as advanced as Georgia's, though quite bulkier. They took me to an expansive sitting room, a high-ceilinged antebellum cavern decorated with high quality reproductions of ancient relics. As I was dropped unceremoniously to the settee, I understood two fundamental things about this "doctor".

First, he valued old things, those that would otherwise be of little to no value to the layperson. Second, he saw his work as a noble cause, however terrible it might be for his "patients". The longer I listened to the silence of the house and the faint sounds of well-lubricated clockwork running just beneath its surface, the more curious I became. A servant passed down a nearby hallway and closed a door behind her, leaving me entirely alone. There were no others on this floor, but the "doctor" would appear soon.

Rising from the settee, I turned the other way to move swiftly and silently up the stairs. The hallways and rooms continued to the point of ridiculousness. Embedded into the ceilings and floors were tracks of varying shapes and styles. Above I noticed the tracks were more intricate, as if the mechanisms suspended from them would serve multiple purposes. What those purposes were, however, I did not know without seeing first seeing the attached apparatuses.

Half-way down the hallway, the faint whirring sound started. I ducked into a room whose door stood jar and watched from the darkness as a servant passed – a servant whose legs were encased in an even more primitive version of the field hands' harnesses and whose torso was suspended by ropes and wire from the ceiling's tracks – her gaze focused only ahead. She was young, her skin pale and ashen beneath her maid's uniform, her hair twisted into a distressed bun. In her hands she carried a tray which contained a bottle of cleaner, a rag, and a feather duster. I moved back into the hallway, following the dead-eyed girl into a room near the end of the house. The tracks turned her abruptly, her head falling to the side in the mechanism's haste. As I entered the room, the smell of cleaner overwhelmed me, momentarily distracting me from the fact that she was nowhere in sight.

I found that the floor tracks ended in the center of the room, but the ceiling tracks circled the perimeter of the room before disappearing behind a wall tapestry. I pushed it back and examined the wall, finding a set of tiny separations which indicated a secret door behind which the track ran. I pushed and the door tipped inward into darkness. The sun, I realized, was gone behind the storm clouds when the first peal of thunder rattled the aging window frames. I stepped into the darkness.

And fell.

Sliding along the hidden laundry chute, I twisted and turned until I came to rest rather abruptly on a cold and damp stone floor. The sudden impact knocked the wind from my lungs, momentarily compacting my spine in a sharp burst of pain. Watson, I discovered, was right. I was growing older, whether or not I wanted to believe it.

"Welcome to my home, Mr. Holmes."

As I regained my breath I glanced toward the voice. A table bisected this basement and behind it sat a shriveled, little man with a bushy moustache. A pair of goggles exaggerated his beady eyes. A closet stood open behind him, stacked deep with tattered clothing and costumes.

"You must be the doctor."

"Bertram Granville," he replied. "I would say it is a pleasure to meet you, but that would be a lie."

Motion in the closet drew my attention. A series of tracks ran across the ceiling, layered across one another as they entered and exited the closet. The moment drew my eye toward the right-hand side. A maid's costume... *no.* Upon closer inspection I discovered the items hanging in it were not clothes. *The maid.* The items in the closet weren't just clothing. They were *people.*

"Why?" I asked as I struggled to my feet. "Why do you do it?"

Bertram moved the goggles to his forehead, replacing them with a pair of round-lensed spectacles. His moustache twitched. "Why?" he echoed, tilting his head to one side. "Why do I do what?"

"What you're doing to these people. Why torture them?"

"Torture?" he replied, affronted by my question. "I do *not* torture these people. I *liberate* them."

My gaze traveled back to the closet full of modified humans. This was... *inhumane.* Surely men and women stacked in a closet as if they were coats could not be considered liberation. Then I recognized one.

Henry.

"How is entombing them in a closet, only to be used in your grand designs, *liberating?*"

Bertram inhaled deeply through his nose and released it in the same manner, a slight whistle emanating from his sinuses as he did so. "Come with me, Mr. Holmes." Rather than standing, he turned and came around the table, his body settled into Henry's wheelchair. My stomach turned.

"My grandfather built this grand estate," he said as he led me toward the staircase where a pair of metal bars extended into the wheels of the chair at the push of a button. "After the Emancipation Proclamation, we feared the plantation would fall apart, as so many around us did. My father, a physician despite my grandfather's wishes, began accepting volunteers to work in exchange for his services." As I ascended the stairs, the mechanism to which the bars were attached lifted Bertram, bringing him alongside me. "In addition to working the fields, we learned how to work the human body. It is such a beautifully complicated mechanism."

"These people do not appear to be volunteers."

Bertram made a low musing sound. "I have no doubt Miss Corchoran brought you here," he said.

"You kidnapped them."

"Our methods may not always have been so *ethical,*" he paused to glance up at me, "but we always had the best interests of the people at heart. As you can clearly see, Miss Corchoran now has full, autonomous use of her legs. How much do you know about her condition?"

"Nothing," I admitted.

"She was involved in a terrible carriage accident which severed her spinal column between the lower lumbar vertebrae and the sacrum. The damage was absolute. She was not meant to walk again."

"So you were going to turn her into another of your puppets?" I asked, bile rising in my throat at the thought of the tortured souls in the basement.

"Absolutely not," he snapped. We reached the main floor and the bars retracted into the wall. We moved down the hallways toward the front of the house. The sound of the storm outside completely drowned out the mechanics of the house and nearly took his voice with it. "Those *unfortunates* in the basement were only steps in the research process. Those who would deny me their gratitude by trying to leave against my will. You see, my technology is expanding. I can *fix them*. I gave that woman her legs back."

"How?" I asked, my curiosity nearly overwhelming.

"The wires beneath her skin," he began, "I fused them to her nervous system at the point of severance. While she has no feeling in her lower extremities, she has the ability to control the mechanisms which control them."

"So using your own technology, she managed to escape you."

"She had assistance," he replied, his voice growing dark.

Henry.

I kept my face a mask of calm as my temper flared. This man had punished Henry for an act of kindness.

"What exactly is your endgame?" I asked, my voice still and steady. He looked up at me in surprise.

"Surely, Mr. Holmes, you have deduced that much."

I swallowed against the bile rising in my throat. "To walk."

"Of course. I lost the use of my legs as a result of an accident with a piece of machinery. My father vowed he would restore full use of my lower extremities." A pause. "Then the fever took him and left me to continue his work" Thunder rattled the foundation of the house and rain pelted the windows. I could scarcely hear myself think, let alone comprehend the madness of this man. So driven, yet so clearly mad. "I do apologize for this," he said, his beady eyes twinkling in the dim light of the house, "but I simply cannot allow you to leave."

A hand came around my throat and the sharp, piercing pain of a needle sank deep into the side of my neck. Before I could fight, my vision blurred, and the last face I saw was that of the man with the drippy nose.

John Watson. Lecrainte Parish, October 31, 1907

Agitation. Frustration. Fear.

An aptly named Parish, I thought wildly as the carriage made its slow trek toward that god-forsaken plantation. Children in brightly-colored masks danced beneath the umbrellas of their parents as we left the town, blissfully unaware of either the rain *or* the madman living not far from their homes. The Halloween festivities only served to rattle my nerves more. *Anyone could be hiding behind those masks,* I thought as the crowds dwindled to nothing. Trees replaced the neatly-rowed houses, the occasional driveway or plantation yard sprawling out into the desolation.

The police seemed equally as nervous, though apprehensive. In the many months they'd been chasing this man, they could scarcely accept that Holmes had come in and solved the case in a matter of *days*.

"Can we go any faster?" I asked impatiently out the window.

"Afraid not, sir," the young man guiding the carriage called back. "Storm is strong. Almost there, but the roads're almost impassable."

I flung myself back against the uncomfortable seat with a frustrated groan. Holmes' life was at stake here. I didn't want to wait. I wanted to be there. *Now.*

The carriage lurched forward with an ominous screech and crack. Ahead, the frightened horses screamed. The carriage fell to the right, throwing me against the wall with a bone-jarring impact.

"Axle broke, sir!" the young man called out as he pulled open the door. "Can't go on!"

"We have to!" I shouted back and motioned to the two officers disentangling themselves before me. "We are almost there. We'll go on foot!"

Sherlock Holmes. Lecrainte Parish, October 31, 1907

"Monster," I muttered as I woke. My tongue felt swollen and feathery, my eyes too large for their sockets. My body was immobile, strapped to a surgical table with bloody restraints. The goggles were once again covering Bertram's eyes.

"Welcome to the family, Mr. Holmes," he said, wicked glee dancing on the edges of his words. "You will be my greatest creation…other than myself, of course."

"You didn't create those people," I slurred, my mind foggy from the sedative. "You destroyed them."

"I saved them!" he shouted, rising from the chair by his arms. The anger quickly passed, replaced by his prior serenity as he settled himself back into the chair. *Henry's chair.* "Just as I will save you…from yourself."

I was immobile, unable to extract myself from the stiff restraints and their metal buckles. The man with the moustache stood in the corner, wiping at his nose with the same dirty handkerchief from the dirigible. Cruelty danced in his eyes and the key swung from his other hand. Behind him, curious glances peered over his shoulder, those captives who remained conscious watched in horrified fascination. I found Henry's face in the huddled mass, his right eye bruised and swollen shut. I could see no more of him than his battered face, but he turned ever so slightly. He was still alive.

Near my feet, Bertram sharpened a series of blades. I had to distract him, keep him talking. Keep him from beginning whatever deplorable surgical procedure he had in mind for me. I had to give Watson time to arrive or give myself time to clear the drug-induced haze and get myself loose.

I twisted my wrists slowly against the rough edge of the restraint. Pain clawed at the nerve endings of my left hand. I twisted again. Again. Again. Warmth pierced the pain and my hand slipped slightly. I twisted again. As Bertram prattled on, his incessant diatribe growing more tedious with each breath, I worked my hand loose, my fingers contorting painfully as they slipped through the restraint. My left arm flew free and the mustached man dove forward. In a smooth, upward stroke, my fist connected with his jaw and sent him tumbling backward, the keys dancing just out of my reach. Bertram, I realized, had turned away, huddled over something on his worktable, giving me the opportunity to unfasten the buckle binding my right hand and that at my waist.

I sat up, the world canting slightly leftward, and reached for the straps immobilizing my legs and feet. His helper stood shakily and advanced on me, his fists balled tightly. I swung again and he danced out of my reach, then took a swing of his own. His right fist connected with my ribcage. Pain flared as I swung again, this time connecting my right fist with his left temple. With a sharp yelp of pain, he went down and did not get up again.

"My, my…you are a resourceful one," Bertram said, and clicked his tongue. He advanced, a syringe and a scalpel clutched in his left hand. "I do respect your work, Mr. Holmes, and I was hoping to be merciful." His expression turned dark. His eyebrows knitted in the center of his forehead and his lips shriveled into a thin line. "But it appears we shall have to do this the hard way."

Bertram jabbed the syringe into my thigh. The drug, Vecuronium if I were to guess from the immediate onset of paralysis throughout my entire nervous system, unleashed a torrent of fire followed by a curious numbness. I remained upright, my muscles frozen in place, but found myself quite unable to move even so much as a fingertip. While the dose was enough to confine me to unwanted stillness, it also guaranteed I was left to watch in horror as the scalpel first removed the leg of my trousers, then sliced into my flesh. Pain unlike any I have ever known flared to life under that dastardly blade, and the man wielding it showed no remorse. As he worked, I fantasized thirty-five ways to remove this monster from his mortal coil, and it was not until the basement door flew open and the cacophony of voices filled the dank space that my mind overloaded and closed down. Somewhere in the din and just as my consciousness began to fade, I heard the one and only voice that could make me believe this scenario would turn out for the best.

John Watson.

John Watson.. Lecrainte Parish, October 31, 1907
At first glance, I did not believe Sherlock Holmes to be alive.

My heart seized in my chest as I looked upon him, lying motionless with his eyes fixed on the ceiling. The officers behind me made quick work of the doctor and his equipment, and as the first two dragged the madman back up the stairs, another shrieked in horror. I turned with my fingers still pressed to Holmes's pulse and found the source of the man's disgust.

Bodies – more than three dozen men and women at final count – hung suspended from tracks in the ceiling of the closet. Most were still alive, though it appeared some had fallen victim to taxidermy and automation. None of them appeared to have even a shred of humanity left…except one.

"John Watson?" the young man near the front asked as I assisted an officer in removing him from the harness around his torso.

"Yes?" I asked, curious to learn how he would know my name.

"Is Mr. Holmes alive?" he asked, his voice weak.

"He is," I confirmed, glancing back over my shoulder as others carried him up the stairs to prepare him for the journey back to the hospital in New Orleans. I looked back into the young man's face, and realized he was the key to this puzzle. "You must be Henry."

"I am."

"What happened to you?"

"The doctor said I would walk again." The harness fell loose and he clutched my arms weakly as I took on his full weight. "Put me down, please."

"Are you certain?"

"No," he said with a sad smile, "but I assume that since you are here, Miss Corchoran's miracle came to her. I can only hope mine will, too."

I carefully lowered him to his feet. The whirring of hidden mechanisms echoed through the space and the men around me stopped to watch, some in amazement and others in horror, as the young man took his full weight onto his legs for the first time in his life. He wobbled slightly, clutching my shoulders for balance, and with the assistance of the machinery took his first step. His legs buckled and he collapsed to the floor, dragging me partially down with him.

"I am exhausted," he said, "but when I regain my strength, I do believe I will walk." A single tear slipped down his cheek. "Could you please help me to my chair, Dr. Watson?" He nodded to the contraption the mad doctor had once occupied. I nodded and lifted Henry, holding the majority of his weight as he took steps, joyous laughter erupting from him as he did so.

When he finally took his seat, he left out a contented sigh. "I never thought I would see the world as other men do," he said. "Now I will. But first, please take me to the hospital. And if you can find Miss Corchoran, I would like to see her as well."

•€•————o0o————•3•

The incident left neither Sherlock Holmes nor myself without psychological scars. The horror of human marionettes – those poor, crippled playthings of a scientist so mad he could not see the error of his ways – will haunt me for the rest of my life.

Sherlock remained in the hospital nine days while the doctors attempted to repair the damage to his leg. After another week and a half in a rehabilitation home, we were given clearance to return to London. Holmes walks with a cane now, as the muscular damage was too great for a complete repair.

Bertram Granville, the mad doctor, was committed to an insane asylum, and has not once spoken of the atrocities he committed, or his intentions toward Sherlock himself. While both Sherlock and I have lost countless hours wondering what the outcome would have been had I not arrived with the cavalry, I have convinced myself that Divine Intervention is what has kept those secrets thus.

Six months after our return to London, we received a letter from Henry in which he stated that he had regained use of his legs, and he and Georgia were hoping that we would return to New York to attend their wedding. While he would never admit it to being touched by the invitation, I do – from time to time – see Sherlock Holmes smile to himself as he sits in his favorite chair with a cup of tea and his violin. His damaged leg remains mostly straight, and he struggles to climb out of his chair now. But Holmes and I are no longer young. Our lives have been far from perfect. But from this most terrible experience, sprang something beautiful.

THE FINAL SOLUTION

Alexandra Christian

WHAT IS HUMAN? WHAT DOES IT MEAN TO BE ALIVE? PERHAPS IT is intelligence and one's ability to think. Alan Turing, an English mathematician from the mid-twentieth century said, "A computer would deserve to be called intelligent if it could deceive a human into believing it was human." He believed that a machine could think through a series of complicated circuitry and programming. If it became independently intelligent, would we consider the machine to be thinking? Of course, once a machine begins to think, is it, therefore, human?

Or is it the soul that gives off that spark of humanity to ignite our bodies with the brilliant flame of life? Do I have a soul? As I lie here, still a collection of junk and metal wires, I don't think so. I've never seen or heard my soul. I can't feel my soul. I have no inherent knowledge of a soul. My scientific mind tells me that no such thing exists because there is no sensory evidence. To have a soul would imply a spirit, which hearkens to a belief in God. I've never believed in God, but despite popular opinions, I am human. Or was. Once upon a time.

I don't remember a life before, nor do I remember a death. First there was darkness and then there was light. Memories come in short bursts, and I'm not even sure they are my own.

My cybernetic eye rolls around the room, taking in everything. I only have one eye so far, so I'm doing the best I can. The room is large with high ceilings and industrial lighting overhead. Wide tables made of rotting wood look like ghosts beneath their veils of dust and cobwebs. A grinding I can feel vibrating against my skull startles me as the eye adjusts. Now I can see even the tiniest of patterns of frost collected on the small windows overhead. There are rusted out pipes, cogs, and copper wire strewn on the floor along with abandoned instruments far beyond the reach of my sophomoric understanding of this place. Water drips in a slow rhythm falling on the table beside me. I don't have ears, so technically I can't hear anything, but some processor inside my head decodes the regular drabble and tells my brain that the water is dripping in a steady pulse.

Again that damned metallic grinding, and a red beam of light comes forth from the pupil of my eye, scanning the room. The tiny blade falls over the broken-down furniture and debris on the floor. Immediately, my brain begins throwing streams of glowing red data before my eye. The data seems to be random symbols at first, but then my electronic brain begins to work, and the pieces begin to fit. Everything in this workshop is old. As soon as the thought forms fully, a barrage of information floods the memory banks in my mechanical brain. I can feel the clockworks grinding as everything shifts, and it is almost... painful? Then an incredible heat as my circuits make sense of the information that begins to flash behind that single eye: craftsmanship suggesting Victorian age manufacture, Liberty & Co., sloppy restoration with modern fixtures. Overhead lighting is electric, as are the many strange appliances that lie about.

Finally, the rush of new information stops, and my circuits cool. Is that what thinking feels like? Exhilaration and pain. The grind of metal on metal thrums again, and I roll my eye toward the other side of the room. A door opens, and my mechanical companion hobbles inside. He moves with the lurching gait of a very primitive robot. He is wearing a long coat and scarf, though I doubt he's fooled anyone. He is very obviously a machine. Evidently, he is what is referred to as an "older model."

"Hello, Sher-lock." I assume that the strange collection of syllables is my name. He keeps saying it to me. Always broken up that way: Sher-lock with the accent on *sher*. The cyborg speaks strangely. Its words skip and slur together. Sometimes it speaks too fast, other times very slow and distorted. "Are you... feeling well?" It then laughs at me with a perfunctory sound that is anything but human. Almost as if it recorded the sound and played it back on a loop.

"I do not feel," I respond. "I am a machine. And only half a machine, at that."

"Not for long, pr-pr-pr-precious," it stutters in that eerie, sing-song voice. "Don't be so imp-p-patient. Do you like the new digs? An old-old-old workshop down here in the bowels."

"I have no opinion."

"Somehow I doubt that, precious one." It shambles over so quickly that for a moment I think it will topple itself, but it manages. "I brought you something, Sher-lock." I watch as its rusted-out joints move awkwardly, reaching for a satchel over its shoulder. After some struggle with coordination, it brings out an object wrapped up in some kind of fabric. It walks over to where I lay and puts the bundle down on the table in front of me. It sits down at the workbench and unwraps the small thing. "I know. It does not look like much, pr-precious. But th-th-this small thing-thing will bring you to life, Sher-lock." The object is fashioned from titanium and wire. It has an odd assortment of gears and cogs, but what fascinates me is a small window, right in the center. From under the tiny pane of glass, an electrical light glows bright white. "The source of all your power-ower will be contained here, within this m-m-mechanical heart. True immortality rests here in my hand."

Immortality. It is a strange term, and once again I find myself searching through the halls of my memory to locate the word. *To live forever.* Well, if I am to live forever then I must be alive. "Forever," I say. "It is a long time to live, is it not? Sounds very dull."

"What do you mean, pr-precious?"

"Well if we are to live forever, then there is no risk of death. With no risk of death, there is no excitement. The meaning of life is thwarted. We may as well be dead."

"Yes, precious-s-s thing!" It laughed with excitement, the noise like a rusty nail being driven through my brain. "Now you've got-got-got it! Now, no more talk. I have work to do." It is fascinating to watch the primitive thing lumber gracelessly around the room. I wonder if I will be a shambling collection of rusty parts when it is done with me. It does not speak anymore, and I'm grateful. The sing-song voice and stuttering ejaculations are maddening, though I admit to being curious about its motivation.

My cybernetic eye focuses once more on the heart that my strange companion holds in his hand. Despite its poor construction, the cyborg has remarkable precision. It leans over the mechanism, using its deft fingertips and miniscule tools to open the tiny window. "Once this is in place, Sher-lock, there will be no n-n-n-need for an alternate power source."

I searched my database for the words. "A battery?" I asked.

"Much more interesting-esting than a battery, precious." It reaches into the small opening and plucks a glowing blue orb from the heart's core. Even as it holds the orb between its waxy-looking fingertips, the glow burns bright.

Like the cyborg had found a bit of the moon. "Aether. A sp-sp-spark of light that will flow through your body-body like blood. It is beautiful, is it not? Tendrils of energy that will s-s-s-seep into your veins and breathe life into your mechanical-anical corps-s-s-e. It-it- it is what makes us who we are, Sher-lock."

"It is a soul, then?"

"No soul," it says with a tone of bitterness. "We are machines, p-p-precious, worshipping almighty electricity."

"So it is a battery," I say dismissing it with a roll of my one luminescent eye.

"No!" the cyborg shouts. He frightens me with his sudden anger, and my eye snaps back in his direction. He stands up and lumbers over to where I lay. For a moment, I think he might smash my head to bits, but he picks me up as one might lift a child. "Batteries die-die-die. They are an artificial source of power, Sher-lock. This, precious, is the soul per-r-r-rfected."

He lays me down on his table, and I can scan his workspace more carefully, taking in more of my surroundings. A body of sorts hangs by the worktable, mounted on a stand like some sort of strange marionette. It has no head, but the rest of the torso is already intact. The design of this cyborg is much sleeker than that of my companion. Long limbs and a torso made of titanium and acrylic are near works of art. Is this thing a scientist or artist? Suddenly, another of those digital memories flutters in my brain.

"Frankenstein's monster," I say. "Mary Shelley. The Modern Prometheus. Published in 1818. You have made this creature?"

"Of circuits and metal, yes, precious." When it looks down at me, I can see its face clearly. One half of its face is almost human. It appears to have some kind of synthetic skin over part of its face, but the skin is cracked singed around the edges. On the other half, I can see the gears, cogs, and electrical wires on the other side. One eye glows red, scanning the room as mine did, but the other is cold. A dead blue orb that looks nowhere and everywhere as it rolls around in the mauled socket. "I have made you, precious. See... see here?" It is almost childlike in its eagerness to show me what it has done. "MORI-10 remembers everything, yes," it said as it shuffles over to where the headless body hangs on its rack.

"MORI-10?" I asked. The name is already niggling at the base of my skull as the brain combs through the databases. Familiarity. MORIs were a type of cyborg policeman. They were faster, smarter, and virtually indestructible. "How did a MORI-10 come to be here?" I say aloud.

"Very easy, precious." He continues about his task without revealing more. The tiny pearl of light, he places back inside the mechanical heart and closes the window protecting it. "MORI-10 very-v-v-very good at essscaping." With a jerk and turn, the cyborg takes me from the worktable and begins attaching my head to the body. It's quite an odd feeling to be disconnected from one's body. As if the body below is just a hollow statue. I watch as the MORI-10 buzzes about me, tightening gears and soldering my primitive seams. "No worries, p-precious. When MORI-10 is done, Sher-lock will be good as new."

I watch the minutes click by on the old clock that hangs on the wall opposite. The large hand stands out against the thick film of dust that has collected on its face. I watch as it creeps slowly around, passing by each number. Once, twice, three times, the large hand passes over the four. "Just one more thing, precious," it says after a time. Funny, for a moment I had forgotten it was there. "Then you can have-have your heart." It shifts, lurching around behind me. I watch his shadow move across the floor in the beam of moonlight still streaming through the windows. Its figure is almost imposing when made of darkness. "You mustn't worry, precious. I will teach you. MORI-10 will teach you everything."

"I don't understand…" My words are cut off as I am suddenly gripped by the oddest sensation. A bolt of something white hot spears the back of my head. For a moment, I think perhaps I've been shot, but the heat begins to spread until it is creeping down the new steel spinal cord that has been attached to my brain. Boiling mercury is the only way I can describe the feeling of my limbs and torso coming to life. A slow, seeping of sensation that connects my brain to my body. "What is happening to me?"

"No worries, Sher-lock. Getting used to one's b-body is never easy. You're lucky- lucky- lucky. Most people don't get to remember their birth."

I slowly begin to move my limbs, trying to get used to their weight. It is difficult. Now I can hear the wheels in my brain whirring as they struggle to send messages to my fingertips. Just a small wiggle to prove that I can. Then my hand. A twist of my wrist and a slight bend of the arm. I watch with morbid fascination as the titanium bones work in perfect harmony with the makeshift muscles and tendons that my companion has so lovingly fashioned. Everything about this body is flawless and works in perfect symmetry. I wonder how this cyborg that seems to be falling apart has managed to build such a thing. If, in fact, he has built it at all.

The MORI turns and comes toward me. I want to back away, but my body is still attached to the stand, and my limbs can only thrash aimlessly. "Be p-p-patient, precious. Your body is yet to be unplugged." He gestures toward a thick coil of wire trailing from my body. I follow the path of the cord from where it plugs into a socket in the center of my abdomen and snakes around through the spindly legs of furniture and across the room to a generator against the wall. "It is beautiful, yes, precious?" He holds the shining metal heart up so that I might see it better. It glows from within where the MORI has placed the tiny sphere of light. "It is your immortality."

Immortality. There is that word again. What an odd creature this thing is. What business does a MORI-10 have being obsessed with immortality? Cyborgs have no concept of death. They don't even know that they are alive. Or do they? How do I know these things? My thoughts don't seem to be my own, yet they are. I can hear my own voice echoing in my head, and the noise only adds to the ache of my confusion. Finally, the question that I've been trying to block out swims into view with blinding clarity. "What am I?" I blurt. Immediately I want to take it back. I don't think I want to know the answer. "Am I human?"

"Perhaps," he says as if that might be the appropriate answer. It uses a small tool to open the window there in my chest. I watch as it messes about with my insides. I feel nothing, but the sound of metal clinking together and wires crackling as it connects them with those precise fingertips is enough to repel me. Suddenly, there is another jolt as the final connection is made. There is a deep, thunderous pounding in my chest as the tiny engine begins to work, sending energy rolling into my extremities. "Of course, asking if one is human is a st-st-st-stupid question, Sher-lock. I am disappointed in you."

"W-Why do you say that?" I stammer, still trying to get used to the drumming in my chest.

"Human is a relative term, is it not? A better question might be: *what is* human?"

Looking down at my metal body with its mechanical gears, there is nothing human in the slightest. "So I am… *we* are machines?"

"In body, yes. But our bodies don't make us human. Nor do they make us machines. Our bodies are—"

"Merely transport," I finish, remembering my own words.

My companion chortles again, clapping its hands. My eye twitches at hearing it. I have the distinct feeling that I am being held captive. Its depravity is only being held at bay by the finest of bonds. "Reichen-eichen-bach was very thorough when h-h-harvesting your consciousness, precious."

"What are you talking about?"

"The world around us deteriorates fast, precious. Can't you feel it? The decay and violence? It makes our bodies strong but our minds lazy. The diseased, the deviant—they rule the world we used to know, Sher-lock. So stupid-stupid, precious. Dr. Reichenbach is my father. He is your father. He is the father of the new humanity." His form lumbers toward the generator, pulling the electrical umbilicus away from the wall.

"A new humanity?"

"A h-h-humanity of immortals, Sher-lock. For years Reichenbach harvested the consciousness-s-s of every genius he could find so that one day, when what is passing for civilization devours itself and the old Gods are dead, new Gods could be created in our image."

"Our image?"

"Of course, Sher-lock. We are the New Gods. The geniuses of our race. New Gods that cannot be k-k-k-killed. First the underlings in Old-d-d-d Town and then here. Now, the cyborgs are slaves to these… g-g-groveling sheeplings. They rut away in the dirt, always making more. They have no… respect. No fear..no fear…no fear. The doctor understood them, precious. They are pack animals that will only respond to the alphas."

"And you fancy us the alphas, then?"

The MORI-10 grimaces. I think it means to smile, but there is no mirth. It puts down the tinker's tools and lurches toward me. It puts a hand to my chest, gently stroking downward before clasping the cord still attached and pulling it free. It is a gentle gesture full of both love and loathing. It is almost sexual in nature, and if I were human, I might have recoiled from that touch. "Gods, precious."

My companion eventually disappears, leaving me alone in the makeshift laboratory. I lost track of the days. It could have been two days or two weeks, but it is long enough to explore my new surroundings. I have some trouble learning to walk using these awkward limbs, but after a few tumbles, I think I finally have the hang of things. Managing to avoid the numerous obstacles that litter the floor, I come to a window and realize that this room is on the second floor of a ruined building. The street below is as jumbled as this place. Burned out cars, rubbish, and vagrants litter the entire area, and a greasy smog makes everything dirty. A rusted old sign across the way is nearly illegible with caked grime, but my eye is very efficient at deciphering. "Baker Street," I read. The words are familiar. Have I been here before? A little voice inside my head whispers, *You've always been here.* As I stare down into the haze of rot, I wonder what could possibly have happened here to create such a void. My single red eye scans every section, searching for something that might trigger a memory inside my head. Alas, it only gives me small details and identifiers but nothing about a disaster that befell this world.

There must be something to offer a clue as to my existence and the existence of my bizarre mechanical friend. Scanning the room, I notice that bookshelves line the walls on either side of the fireplace. Paper and leather-bound books on every topic one might imagine—medicine, botany, apiology, astronomy—line the shelves. As I read their spines, strings of data appear before my eye. Bits of text, pictures, memories. To my surprise, I can remember the gist of every one of the books I touch. "These things are mine," I say aloud, surprised by my own realization. The further I explore, the more convinced I am that these things, all of these things, belonged to me. *I am in my own home.* I know every turn, every room. As my body lumbers up an uneven stairwell, I spy myself in a mirror at the landing. My body has been partially covered with something the MORI-10 called *Nu-skin*. It has given me a face that I immediately recognize as my own. Reaching up with tentative fingertips, I trace the lines and contours of my brow and cheekbones. The cyber-eye glows, but I do have another. A blind, motionless, gray orb reminiscent of the eye of my companion. I can't help chuckling as I notice that he's even gone to the trouble of giving me hair. In proper clothes, I might even pass as human.

Finally, I come upon a small sitting room. Like the lab, it appears to have been abandoned years ago. Everything is caked with dust and grime. The furniture looks as if it were been built by an alien with some vague idea of Victorian craftsmanship. Everything is wooden and sturdy with intricate carving, but the designs are sleek and round. The silk wallpaper opposite the fireplace is of a traditional fleur de lis design, but the color scheme is almost metallic. Carefully I step over the debris of books, papers, and broken furniture, making my way toward a small desk. A book lays open, but as I approach, I realize that it is not a book, but a flat pane of glass. I draw my *Nu-skin* fingertips across the surface, and the glass shrieks to life. The screen lights up, and I am startled as an image appears in front of me, floating in the air above the glass. "The Personal Journal of Dr. John Watson," I read aloud. The name seems familiar on my lips, yet I cannot place it just yet. I raise my hand once more and sweep my fingers across the projected image. The digital pages flip past quickly. Pages and pages of type along with images. I begin to read the journal aloud. "Sherlock is convinced that the Professor is a cyborg. Not one of the drone servants that have become so prevalent in recent years. Something new and different. And more ominous. A hybrid of man and machine that can live forever, feeding on electricity. Its consciousness downloaded into a new host when one synthetic body begins to break down." I turn the page and one of the images catches my eye. A man stares at me from a photograph. His eyes are a cold blue, and I can detect a slight glisten of red that reflects in the centers. My finger slips, and the picture begins to move. The man on the screen seems to laugh as he is overtaken by a multitude of armed cyborgs.

"Professor James Moriarty was taken into custody today. The professor, a pioneer in the field of cybernetics, has long been a suspect in the murder of celebrated detective, Sherlock Holmes."

James Moriarty. The name triggers the gears and cogs in my brain as the wires begin to connect. More of that furious haze of data flashes before my eye. It is so fast and bright that I stumble backward. The memories are intense, but fragmented. Those cold eyes stare out at me. Standing on the precipice, looking down over the glass and steel spires of Britannica. We fight. I am falling. The sensation of fear mixed with curiosity and loss as I lay dying.

"Moriarty, along with his partner, Dr. Georg Reichenbach, made bold strides in recent years in the area of artificial intelligence." The playback snapped me out of my fugue. *"Their work with cybernetic organisms was integral in the creation of the MORI-10, a cyborg designed to eradicate violent crime in the Old Town district. The project was halted when MORIs began to malfunction, slaughtering innocent citizens and going rogue until Old Town was overrun."*

"I see you're making yourself-self comfortable, precious." I whip around to see my companion standing in the doorway.

"Why did you bring me here?"

"I wanted to help you, precious."

"Tell me!" I shout suddenly, startling myself with the urgency. "Tell me what I am." I can hear the pleading in my voice, and it sickens me. "And why you've brought me here... Professor."

The cyborg smiles as best his primitive musculature will allow. "Still very smart- smart- smart, Sher-lock. I wondered how long it would take you to figure me out. Tell me, was it my eyes?" His words draw my gaze to where one dead, crystalline eye rolls aimlessly.

"Among other things. You've built my body from nothing. No regular MORI-10 could do that. It's just as I suspected all those years ago. Crossing humans and cyborgs. Using Reichenbach's downloading consciousness to make yourself immortal."

"Too bad you didn't kill me with that fall, Sher-lock."

"I'll do much better next time, Professor."

Moriarty cackles, his rusty joints and wheezing breaths creating a monstrous sound. "Yes! Yes, precious! That is the spirit!" He rushes over to me, and for a moment, I think he might attack, but he does something far stranger. He embraces my body as if we are old friends rather than bitter enemies.

"I don't understand," I said, pushing him away. "You could be rid of me. Gain control of Old Town first and then Britannica, remaking the whole world in your own sick image."

"And what would be the point of that, Sher-lock? You and me, we are part of the same equation. The yin and the yang. After our fall, the good Herr Doktor put me back together again using bits and pieces of MORI to fill in the gaps. I was good as new, precious."

"Until they caught up with you," I finish.

"Yessss. Thanks to your friend, Dr. Watson, that idiot inspector and his legion of buffoons managed to find me. They threw me into Pentonville Asylum, down here in Old Town. They left me to rot while the world moved on. Without you, my mind began to deteriorate. My coils and cogs became mere rusted fragments. I lay in the asylum like a broken toy."

"And what of Dr. Reichenbach?"

"You mustn't think less of me, precious. He wanted to destroy the bank of souls, as he called it. I couldn't let that happen. All our work would have been lost. Including you, Sher-lock."

"So you destroyed him first. That's how you were caught." He nods. I step back, beginning to pace. My brain is quicker now, the machinations obviously having warmed up. As I stare at the Professor, I notice that he has begun to move and speak better. As if my own awakening had begun to repair his inner workings.

"It seems that an obsessed neuroscientist is a much greater loss than an opiate-addicted genius detective." He sits down in one of the armchairs by the fire, a smile of satisfaction gracing his charred *Nu-skin* lips. "But I realized, Sher-lock, during my incarceration, how important you really are."

I sit down across from him, my cyber-eye burning into his. I don't want to show him any fear, steepling my fingertips under my chin to keep them from trembling. "Important? Because..."

"Because, precious. You are a machine. As am I. A machine must have purpose or else it is just... a collection of spare parts. If my time in Pentonville taught me anything, it is that I only exist so that you will chase me. You, Sherlock, are the final solution to the final problem."

THE OLD WOMAN IN THE WOODS

C.L. McCollum

Now

"**A**NOTHER BOY'S GONE MISSING. THE COBBLER'S YOUNGEST THIS TIME."

"*That's the second child this month! Where're they all off to?*"

"*How could I know? But the Warden's looking for him. Surely, he'll find the lad lost out by the stream somewhere.*"

"*Like he found the baker's girl? Lottie buried an empty coffin just three days ago, she did!*"

"*Well, I – I'm sure the Warden'll do his best, won't he?*"

Village gossip settled in old Mrs. Hudson's ears like a beetle's buzz, bringing news and noise alive with no notice for her self's silence. She hated the talk of the town and its twisted words, but sometimes, oh sometimes, the news was important. Once in several whiles, the noise was meant for *her*, though her neighbors never knew it.

The missing lad wasn't *her* boy, not her favorite one who kept her caged so kindly and cleverly. Oh no, her boy was off a'hunting in another village, putting his mind at work to save another as he once saved her. Not precisely the same way as he saved her, but so few could be, could they? So, sadly, her boy was out of reach for now, away from the mystery of the cobbler's son missing in the misty woods, just like the baker's girl before him.

They were *still* hers, though. Part of the place and peace she'd made her own with her boy's help. The village and its forests belonged to her, they did. There was a claim on this town, and she'd made it. That meant this boy and what was left of the girl were her responsibility, they were.

Her boy might not agree were he home to be disagreeable to her, but she paid the notion no never mind. He'd return when he could, but until then, it would be *her* who hunted down the child stealer sneaking its way into her woods and snatching the younglings who belonged to the village, and so belonged to her. *Her* who sought the villain and cut out the heart of it as it would seek to cut the heart from her children.

She would hunt as she hadn't in years, kill if she must, though without the glee there might have been in it so long ago. She would do what she must to bring the boy home, if she could. If there was anything left to bring. She wasn't a mother, couldn't be a mother, but she knew what it was to love a boy as her own. The baker and the cobbler's wife, they couldn't find their children. Not like she could. Not like she *would*.

Oh yes, this was hers to do this time. Hers and hers alone.

After all, Mrs. Hudson knew better than most how a child might vanish in a forest.

Then

Once upon a time, there was an old woman who lived alone in the woods, and who called herself 'Mrs. Hudson' though she had never married, nor had she ever been given a name at all. Mrs. Hudson, like most of her kin and kind, spent her days baking and molding intricate fancies of spun sugar and gum drops and all sorts of treats perfect for tempting the stomach of a darling child.

Mrs. Hudson, of course, and again just as all of her kin, could not stand the taste of sweets, but there was nothing better to draw her prey to her. For the old woman liked nothing more than a mouthful of perfectly roasted boy, fed to perfect plumpness and cooked in his own juices. A girl child could on occasion be a passable substitute, granted she was not a skinny thing, nor too old. Mrs. Hudson did not fancy the stringy ones; they tended to get caught in her teeth, and it was such a nuisance. It quite ruined her enjoyment of the meal all together. Which, considering how rarely she was able to acquire the key ingredient for such a feast, was a terrible shame. And such a waste if she wasn't going to enjoy it!

Mrs. Hudson continued on this way for many years, more of them than she knew or cared to count. She had always been old, after all; adding time to her age hardly made a dent. She remained just as she came into being: slightly stooped and slender with a smile and face anyone might imagine a kindly old granny to wear. It was the mark of her kind, that smile, and the greatest strength those hunters had in their arsenal.

Even though many a man and woman knew to tell their children the stories and warned them away from the woods and wandering alone, their younglings still couldn't resist the smell of gingerbread and the kindly smile of an old woman offering cookies and cakes for a sweet, young visitor. Those younglings never returned home, of course, and so each old woman gained the strength to live a month or so longer, baking all the while.

So did Mrs. Hudson.

The day that all and sundry changed for her started much like any other. She had added fresh icing to the exterior of her cottage and set snickerdoodles to cook in the oven. The smell of cinnamon and sugar wafting out was a perfect lure, sure to draw in any lonely child wandering nearby. Luckily for her, or perhaps less than 'luckily' considering the child in question, one did.

He was a scrawny thing, all knees and elbows as young boys often are, and smudged with dirt and twigs as if he'd run straight through the bushes and all but rolled about on the ground.

He looked, bless his soul, utterly delicious. That was the point, of course.

Now

"Why Mrs. Hudson, going on a trip are you?"

"Just a village over – with my boarder out, I've got time for a holiday, don't you know."

"Oh, I wish I could off and away myself. It's so hard when one has children to bother with."

"I imagine so, deary. I imagine so. Well, I'm off. Good day to you!"

An awful day to her, and an awful day it always was when Mrs. Hudson was forced to endure Mrs. Martin's prattling on and on and on about her darling boys, as if anyone without a bairn of their own could hardly be worth the breath the brats breathed on everything. She had no respect for a Mrs. who wasn't a mother, none at all, and never did she bother asking why a body had no children to speak of. Some folks respected the widow Mrs. Hudson seemed to be, but never that Mrs. Martin, the innkeeper's kept comfortable wife.

It would serve mouthy Mrs. Martin right if someone made her boys go missing next, it would. Mrs. Hudson could make that happen, could tempt them out into the woods and... No. No, she couldn't. No, she wouldn't. She didn't do such things anymore, now did she? Not since she'd promised her boy, not since he'd called her home. She wouldn't; she mustn't; she shouldn't. Not now, and not ever again.

The Martin boys were safe from her. They all were, and, with her boy's blessing, so they would stay.

Hunger tugged at her middle, and Mrs. Hudson turned back behind the butcher's shop, ducking in for a bag of beef knuckles, the better to keep her full and functioning. Her boy had left her plenty to last 'til he returned, but she'd eaten it all already, gorged herself on the delicious meat until her dress had nearly torn its seams, and a shawl'd been needed to hide her tummy tight with fullness.

But she could not know how long it would take to find the missing child, and she dared not grow hungry searching for him.

No, best to buy a bit more. The butcher never asked questions anyway, did he? No, not at all. Not since her boy told him not to.

People listened and obeyed when her boy spoke; Mrs. Hudson knew this best of all.

Then

Unlike most of the others who'd wandered to Mrs. Hudson's door, this boy didn't rush forward to feast upon her wares or even call out to see if anyone was at home. No, this one simply stood there within sight of the front door, hands fidgeting with his clothes as he looked all about him, feet shuffling in clear impatience.

Why ever is he waiting? Mrs. Hudson thought as she watched the boy. In her vast experience, children had almost always proved to be impetuous little things, led about by their own foolishness and curiosity along with the hunger in their bellies. *Skinny as this one is, he's sure to be hungry. Young boys are always hungry.*

"Hello, there," she called, taking care to make her voice sound as frail as she had never been in all of her existence. "Won't you come closer, dearie? It's been so long since I've had a visitor..." Mrs. Hudson trailed off as the boy merely shook his head sharply.

"I think I'll stay right here if it's all the same to you. Feels a bit safer, considering the locale." Mrs. Hudson could only blink at the boy's words. He shook his head again, looking more impatient by the moment. "Let me speak plainly then. You're not going to eat me. Not me, nor any other child in this region."

"I beg your pardon!" Mrs. Hudson squawked. Just who did this child think he was? Saying such a thing to her! He might as well have accused her of having the cottage all a mess. One didn't come out and speak of such things outside of closed doors. Never mind that he shouldn't have known what she was about in the first place. Clearly the lad was more of a mystery than he'd first appeared.

"You can have my pardon if you wish it, old woman. But my statement stays unchanged. You will not be eating me." He lifted his chin and stared at her, challenge clear in every inch of his lithe little form.

After a moment, Mrs. Hudson nodded slowly and leaned against the door to the cottage, careful not to get spun sugar in her hair. "All righty then, boy. What do you think you know, then, hmm? And why exactly do you think I won't eat you?"

"Because I have a proposition for you, and refraining from making me dinner is part of it." He shrugged, and Mrs. Hudson realized she couldn't tell what part of it was bravado and what part was true defiance.

He wasn't nearly as afraid of her as he should be.

Now

"Warden, do you search today?"

"I plan to, Mrs. Hudson. I certainly plan to. Off to have a bite to eat first, though. No use in searching on an empty stomach, now is there?"

"Of course not, Warden. Best to eat your fill while you can. It's a long walk about the woods."

"That it is!"

Bloody fat, lazy Warden, wasting half the day away with a boy lost out in the loathsome forest. There'd be no chance for him at all with just that bloated blob to search for him. They should have called the woodcutter in the next village over, or the huntsman who roamed the river banks to the south. Anyone but the Warden's wanton gluttony in charge of a mystery like this one. Anyone at all.

But Mrs. Hudson was an "anyone," wasn't she now? *She* could search while the wastrel fed his fat face. Perhaps it was best he ate the day away, leaving the woods to the old woman who once knew them so well. Better than he by a damn sight, for years and days and moons forgotten, she'd known those woods as only one who lived there could.

The secret ways, the strange paths, the deer trails, and the hunter tracks: Mrs. Hudson knew them all. It would only be a challenge to discover which the boy had taken and if it was the same road their likely villain chose as well.

It would be off the beaten path, of course. That's the way it worked, the way it always worked with the lost and the missing children of the forests. One could find their way back to their wholesome homes if they had a path to follow, a trail to tread their way along. It was once he left the forest roadways that a cobbler's boy could lose himself, could wander long enough that his hunger led him to a monster's lair, a kelpie's creek, a troll's cave...

To a little delightful cottage in a clearing, one housing a witch like Mrs. Hudson once was.

Mrs. Hudson shivered at the thought, remembering cotton candy breaths upon the air and cinnamon powdered all about her kitchen. A proper baker she'd once been, better even than the baker who'd lost her girl some weeks ago. Mrs. Hudson had built her world as she baked and cooked and iced and candied everything she could. It was a sticky sweet certainty: that guarantee of goodies tempting good little boys and girls ever closer.

Ever closer. 'Til through her door they came and in her cages and her kitchen and her oven, oh so roasted they'd be! The juice would drip down her chin as she ate and ate and...

Mrs. Hudson stepped off the path and sat herself on a stone by a fir tree and pulled out a beef knuckle, tearing into it raw and mourning just a mite that she hadn't time to cook it properly. The meat would sustain her, keep her strong, and keen to rescue as opposed to ravaging a little lickable boy like the cobbler's son. It wouldn't do for her to find the child only to eat him up herself. Oh no, that wouldn't do at all. Her boy would be ever so disappointed with her, and his disappointment was such a fearsome thing.

She wouldn't risk it, couldn't risk it. Had to find the boy, she did. She must, she must.

Mrs. Hudson finished her beef knuckle and tossed the bone back in the bag. The marrow might be welcome if her searching took too long into the dark and days away. Meal complete, she stood and spun herself about before stumbling her way into the forest shadows, simulating a younger lostling's confused fumbling between trees and shrubs.

Mrs. Hudson hadn't gone far when a scent caught her attention, sticky sweet with sugar and cinnamon and everything a child might dream of nibbling on. Fresher than it should have been, oh dear yes. It should have been stale and crumbled to bits by now with her gone from home so very long these years.

It was the sign she'd suspected to find, but that wasn't a comfort, not here, not now with the cobbler's boy lost and likely found by something sinister. Mrs. Hudson let her nose lead the way through the deer trails and the rabbit runs until she stepped into a clearing, and there before her lay her little house, once again swathed in gingerbread and gumdrops and all the things she'd left behind at her boy's bidding.

Then

The boy wouldn't be tempted closer, though Mrs. Hudson had slipped back inside to procure a tray of cookies, claiming any talk of bargains couldn't be done except over food, of course. The boy hadn't bothered giving her a refusal; he merely took another step away from the door and crossed his hands behind his back.

"Mistress, as I've said before, there is little point in trying to persuade me to enter your abode. I know well enough what you are. It surprises me the elders as yet pretend not to know, but I suppose they simply protect themselves from the truth. I have never chosen to do such a thing."

"What truth would that be dearie?" Mrs. Hudson asked, somehow caught by his solemn words as easily as she'd hoped to catch him with the sweet treats he so easily discarded. She wished for a chair, but she didn't dare offer him any comfort but that which lay inside her home.

"Four children have gone missing in the past three months. One came home safe and sound with a story of following a runaway kitten, but the others never returned. I've heard the stories. We all have and thought them simply fiction. But stories, I have learned, often have that bit of truth to them, and as I stand here before a gingerbread house and an old woman hiding in the woods, I can only suppose this is one of those true stories."

Mrs. Hudson shook her head sharply, dispelling the spell his voice had woven, drawing her further from her door into the clearing and closer to the boy as he spoke again. "Tell me, how many of our children made it here? I can only assume some are from other villages, otherwise you couldn't survive the lean years, as it were."

"There have been long years when it seems children keep themselves at home," she agreed. "I've gone many a day without a visitor to ease my solitude."

"And ease your hunger?" the boy asked, eyes shrewd as he studied her. "And you are hungry now too, aren't you? Tell me, have you ever *not* been hungry?"

Mrs. Hudson smiled, baring her teeth to show the impertinent little wretch just a touch of her true nature. "I am always hungry, child, unless I've just eaten my fill. Then I'm sated, for a time, at least."

She edged closer still, all the talk of feeding piquing her hunger, as did the scent of him that grew stronger the closer she came. "I am hungry *now*."

"Of course you are – it's been near a month since your last meal. I daresay I would be hungry, too." He twitched at his dirty shirt sleeves, straightening them and stepping a few steps back, keeping the distance between them. "How would you like *not* to be hungry? And again," he continued, narrowing his eyes as she shifted closer, "I remind you that you will *not* be eating me, so keep your teeth to yourself, madam."

"Not hungry. Not hungry, he says," she snarled, her patience finally reaching its breaking point as the boy's very presence seemed to tease cruelly at the gaping ache in her empty belly. "But I won't be eating him, he says. Then what's a body supposed to eat then, hmm? Nothing? Curses to that! Now tell me, what are you on about, you beastly beggaring boy! Tell me–"

"What is your name? I assume you gave yourself one, did you not?" he interrupted, the sudden subject change startling her out of her fury as she blinked at him.

"Mrs. Hudson, dearie."

"A 'missus,' of course," he said, a small satisfied small on his face. "What child wouldn't trust a lonely old widow out here by herself? Well, what I am about, Mrs. Hudson, is ensuring that no more of our village children go missing in these woods. And that you never go hungry again."

Now

"Well what is this? A stranger daring to stand on my doorstep! You're lost, you are, and most unwelcome. I haven't the time for trespassers and won't be sharing nothing neither, so don't you dare suggest it."

"Oh dearie, I wouldn't dream of it. Especially not when it's you who's trespassed against me. I built that building you're standing in, brick by baked brick, I did. You do not belong here. Not now, not ever again."

"Lies! The stove'd gone cold and rusted worn. An abandoned hovel belongs to no one and nothing, and neither will take this place from me now it's mine."

Mrs. Hudson felt a growl building in her throat and a hunger in her belly that the beef bones should have bested. The other old woman of the woods snarled as Mrs. Hudson stalked closer, hands akin to claws and teeth gleaming sharper than any mortal'd have a mind to measure.

"You. Will. Not. Have. My. House!" Mrs. Hudson roared, leaping forward to push the witch back and back again until they both bore through the doorway, stumbling on old bones and careening from the unkempt furniture. In a cage in the corner, the baker's boy wept and wailed as the women wound their way about the place, tearing into each other with bare hands and bloody mouths.

Neither seemed stronger than the other, nor could either catch a harder hold than her enemy, to rip and rend all the more riotously. It was only a small step and a slip that saw Mrs. Hudson her way to a winning, as the other old woman lost her footing on a femur left to lie on the floor, treacherously tripping the one who'd left it there.

She fell back, her head slamming against the stove and splitting her skull near in two. Her eyes flickered then fell closed, and Mrs. Hudson shrieked her glee before flinging herself upon the body, now nothing more than dripping delectable meat.

She normally preferred it roasted, but oh this time raw was just as right as right could be. How could she have known her own kind would taste so, so *scrumptious*? A bit gamey perhaps, but that was happenstance. And a bit was nowhere near enough to slow her feasting.

She gnawed and nibbled her way from the trespasser's head to her toes, stripping every bit of sustenance, forcing herself well past full and loving the luxury of it. Finally, well gorged on meat, Mrs. Hudson dozed, dreaming sated dreams of cinnamon and little shoes strewn across a table. Disgraceful mess to leave there, it was, or so her dream-self laughed and laughed and laughed.

A proper kitchen deserved a mess, it did. Proved a body'd been cooking up a fitting feast, she thought. Proved she'd... proved...

There was a voice in her dream, the only voice that mattered mostly, the one that called her back from monstrous time and time again. But she didn't want to wake, did she? The dreamy doze was so much more comfortable than the dark and dreary daytime where she smiled as polite as persons should in that dingy little house on the baker's street with no one left to talk to when her boy wandered off and away as he did so often.

"Mrs. Hudson. It's time to wake up."

There was the voice again. Still patient, it was, but less quiet, as if pressing in on her personal fantasy with no heart for the peace she'd found from the hunger. Still, she'd promised that voice she'd listen to it, sworn it on her very nature, and she would keep her word, she would.

•€•————•○○•————•Э•

Then

She had followed the boy that day; of course, she had. How could she not when he'd made such a claim? It seemed impossible, far more dis-believable than Mrs. Hudson herself was. But when her boy, and he was *her* boy now – the only boy she'd have again with the bargain he proposed, when her boy spoke, she wanted to listen, wanted to believe he could do as he said.

Mrs. Hudson followed him through the forest to the paths she hadn't tread in more years than she could remember, then down those paths to a dirt road and finally to a village where she guessed her boy made his home.

In a large house near the edge of the village, her boy introduced her to his brother, the man of the house. The older boy, already near grown, listened to his brother's tale with fierce eyes and a furrow in his brow. Once the story was done, he shook his head, and for a breath Mrs. Hudson guessed he meant her to leave, but he merely went about the business of making a certain arrangement with the butcher for weekly deliveries of fresh meat, whatever there was an abundance of.

To the village, her boy introduced Mrs. Hudson as his visiting aunt. Didn't they all remember his father's sister, he'd asked, and yes of course, the villagers had all agreed. Simple folk they were, she knew, willing to believe the world made more sense than it actually did. There was a reason her kind settled in certain forests surrounding such quiet, quaint little places.

Over time her public title went from the aforementioned aunt, to a governess, and finally to landlady as if her boy and his brother were boarders instead of the true owners of the house they lived in.

Yet, the villagers never seemed to notice anything strange and never spoke of the fact that Mrs. Hudson never aged. She worried at that knowledge for a time until she realized they never mentioned the butcher, every bit as loyal to her boy as she was, failed to get any older, either. Her boy changed the subject when she asked, so she shook her head and went about the business of living with the strange sensation of a comfortably full belly and always enough to eat.

Her boy grew to a man, and the bright mind that led him to her door that long-ago day led him out down the road to other doors, other places where innocents died in ways strange and uncanny. "Consulting," he called it — offering his intellect to solve the unsolvable.

Mrs. Hudson never baked again. Her boy had no taste for sweets, after all.

Now

"Open your eyes, Mrs. Hudson. It's time."
"Don't want to wake, I don't. Want to sleep now, child. Just sleep."
"That doesn't change that it's time to get up. Come now, Mrs. Hudson."
"Another day, dearie. Just give me another day at least, and then I'll get up, I promise..."
"Mrs. Hudson, you must wake."

The words held bite now, and she knew from long experience, the voice was one that would not be content with being ignored. With a groan and a growl, she rolled to her side, her burgeoning belly arguing with her about the movement, protesting her progress with every inch she gained. Only when she'd sat herself up straight as straight did she open her eyes to see red.

So much red, she saw, splattered about the table she lay on and her clothes and her hands and...

Her boy stood before her, eyes dark and shrewd as they always were, studying her like one of his cases. Her boy, she thought, her... boy...

"The boy!" Mrs. Hudson spun, her stomach sinking as she spied the cage the other'd kept him in, door hanging wide and open. There'd been a key; the boy hadn't had it had he? So how had he? Had she?

"Old gods, the boy," she whispered again, forcing her gaze away from the door to her boy, no he was a man now, she reminded herself. A man who'd not forgive her if she'd broken her promise to him thusly.

"The boy is safe, Mrs. Hudson. The boy is safe."

As if he'd known her thoughts, but then he always did, his voice broke into her frantic thinking, soothing her fears before she'd thought to voice them. "Are you surely sure?" she asked, patting her belly as it pulled against her red-soaked sash and skirt. "I've eaten. I've gorged myself, my boy, but I can't... I can't remember what I ate can I?"

Her boy folded his hands behind him and cocked his head as if to say 'Do you doubt me?' but of course she didn't. She'd not doubted him a day since he took her from this cottage this first time. She'd listen now; he'd make sure to tell her true. "I took the boy away, Mrs. Hudson. Several hours ago, in fact. I tried to wake you first, but you were in a deep stupor and could not be roused. So I took him home – and do not worry, he won't remember your current face, only that with which you hunted – and returned to wait for you to regain consciousness."

"He didn't see me? Not a once?"

"I questioned him thoroughly. The only old woman he remembers is the one who lured him hence. He remembers hearing two voices at the door, but couldn't see it from the cage in the corner. Then he remembered a shout and an enraged creature barreling into the witch and devouring her. He looked away once the first bite was taken and kept his face turned away. Even after I arrived, he kept his eyes closed until I guided him out of the house." He came closer and laid a hand on a strangely clean bit of her arm, likely the only one he'd find on her figure. "Your secret is safe, Mrs. Hudson, just as the boy is."

"Good. That's good it is. Isn't it?" He nodded, and she nodded back, helpless to do more at the moment. "Home then? Home again, yes?"

Her boy helped her down though she hardly needed it and led her past a pile of bones and bloody clothes to the door, carefully to keep his hands and mouth and tongue from the treats that made the cottage so crafty. "Home indeed, though I do believe we'll need to find you a stream before I parade you back through the square. I did bring clean clothes for you, but it will do no good if your face and hair are still drenched in blood."

Mrs. Hudson nodded obediently and followed where he led just as she had long years before.

Her boy thought of everything, he did.

MEET THE AUTHORS

Derrick Belanger

Derrick Belanger is the author of the #1 bestselling book in its category *Sherlock Holmes: The Adventure of the Peculiar Provenance*, which was in the top 200 bestselling books on Amazon. He also is the author of the MacDougall Twins with Sherlock Holmes books, the latest of which is *Curse of the Deadly Dinosaur*, and he edited the Sir Arthur Conan Doyle horror anthology *A Study in Terror: Sir Arthur Conan Doyle's Revolutionary Stories of Fear and the Supernatural*. Mr. Belanger has recently started the publishing company Belanger Books which released the Sherlock Holmes anthologies *Beyond Watson* and *Holmes Away From Home: Adventures from the Great Hiatus*. Derrick Belanger also is a frequent contributor to I Hear of Sherlock Everywhere. He resides in Colorado and continues compiling unpublished works by Dr. John H. Watson.

Lucy Blue

Lucy Blue's first publication was in 1998 as one of the two writers of *Forever Knight: These Our Revels*, a tie-in novel that put TV vampire detective Nick Knight in Shakespeare's London for the premiere of Hamlet. Currently she is an author and editor for Little Red Hen Romance. In between, she published six historical paranormal romances with Pocket Books/Simon and Schuster. She is married to artist Justin Glanville, and they live in a crumbling Craftsman in Chester, South Carolina, with their Jack Russell mix, Luke, and enough uninvited backyard wildlife to get them a show on Animal Planet.

Alexandra Christian

Alexandra Christian is an author of mostly romance with a speculative slant. Her love of Stephen King and sweet tea has flavored her fiction with a Southern Gothic sensibility that reeks of Spanish moss and deep fried eccentricity. As one-half of the writing team at Little Red Hen Romance, she's committed to bringing exciting stories and sapiosexual love monkeys to intelligent readers everywhere. Lexx also likes to keep her fingers in lots of different pies having written everything from sci-fi and horror to Sherlock Holmes adventures. Her alter-ego, A.C. Thompson, is also the editor of the highly successful *Improbable Adventures of Sherlock Holmes* series of anthologies from Mocha Memoirs Press.

Jason Gilbert

Jason Gilbert is a construction worker by day, a movie critic by night, and a writer in the wee hours of the morning. He may have actually killed off that little voice that tells you not to do or say certain things a long time ago and just can't remember. Or can't hear it over his characters screaming(he can never really tell). Jason is the author of the Rifle Chronicles, a rollicking Steampunk/Sci-Fi/Western series. He's also the man behind Fail-Flix, a site dedicated to reviewing the best of the worst crap Hollywood can sling at film. Leading a lifestyle of duality can be difficult at times, but Jason manages to charge head-first into it with the honed fineness of a rabid water buffalo. You can check him out on social media and his Fail-Flix site (www.fail-flix.com) on the interweb!

Selah Janel

Selah Janel has been blessed with a giant imagination since she was little and convinced that fairies lived in the nearby state park or vampires hid in the abandoned barns outside of town. The many people around her that supported her love of reading and curiosity probably made it worse. Her e-books *The Other Man, Holly and Ivy*, and *Mooner* are published through Mocha Memoirs Press. *Lost in the Shadows*, a collection of short stories celebrating the edges of ideas and the spaces between genres was co-written with S.H. Roddey. Her work has also been included in *The MacGuffin, The Realm Beyond, Stories for Children Magazine, The Big Bad: an Anthology of Evil, The Big Bad 2, The Grotesquerie*, and T*hunder on the Battlefield: Sorcery. Olde School* is the first book in her series, The Kingdom City Chronicles, and is published through Seventh Star Press. She likes her music to rock, her vampires lethal, her fairies to play mind games, and her princesses to hold their own. Catch up with Selah at http://www.selahjanel.wordpress.com, http://www.facebook.com/authorSJ, or @SelahJanel on Twitter.

Trenton Mabey

Trenton Mabey is a writer and photographer. He lives in Arizona with his wife and two children. When he is not wandering the hiking trails, Trenton enjoys kayaking and playing music on the guitar, djembe, and the didgeridoo. His writing is influenced by mythology, Eastern philosophy, nature, and a small dose of insanity. He can be stalked at his website: http://trentonmabey.com.

Katie Magnusson

Katie lives with her son and husband in Milwaukee, WI, where she does absolutely nothing with her marine biology degree, and instead nurtures her obsession with gothic soap operas, Sherlock Holmes, and every cross-genre work of fiction she can find. She also writes stories.

Her series The Adventures of Watts and Sherlock follows a rogue medic and an independent detective with a Holmesian obsession in a cybernetic future. There are two books in the series so far, with a third upcoming. Katie's short stories have been published in *An Improbable Truth: The Paranormal Adventures of Sherlock Holmes*, and *Holmes Away From Home: Adventures From the Great Hiatus.*

Melissa McArthur

Melissa McArthur is a master swordswoman, a world-renowned traveler, and lover of all things bookish. One of these things is actually true. When she isn't saving the world, one word at a time, she's busy lecturing university students on parenthetical citations and torturing authors with her red pen. No matter what the capacity—editor, author, teacher—Melissa is utterly fascinated by books and words. She believes that there's something magical about holding a book in your hand and watching as the words disappear and the story unfolds before your eyes. She hopes that she can do that for readers both as an editor and a writer—create stories that engulf you, change you, scare you, bewilder you, make you laugh, make you cry, and through stories, reveal deeper truths about life. Melissa can be found hiding in the deep corners of the library or at home with her laptop and cat. For those of you in cyberspace, she can also be found at her website: www.melissamcarthur.net.

C.L. McCollum

C. L. McCollum spends her time delving into the wonder of the world. She's always been drawn to the "How" and the "Why" and the "Is this even possible?" While her debut novel is on the road to publication, C. L. has contributed to multiple anthologies and also co-edits a charity anthology series known as "Clichés for a Cause," as well as being a founding member of the Herding Cats Press #MimosaThursday podcasts. C. L. also works as a freelance editor and always welcomes clients with diverse books! Her favorite book is an impossible question to answer, but her favorite authors include Robin McKinley, Jaqueline Carey, Anne Bishop, Ilona Andrews, Tamora Peirce, and Nora Roberts. Currently, C.L. is keeping it weird in Austin, TX with the love of her life and their various furry roommates. You can find her online at home at www.clmccollum.com.

Tom Olbert

Tom Olbert lives in Cambridge, Massachusetts, home of Harvard, MIT and wacky liberals concerned about the environment (of which Tom is one.) Tom's been writing science fiction, dark paranormal fiction and horror pretty much his whole life, and has no intention of stopping. Tom's short fiction has appeared in the Mocha Memoirs anthology "In The Bloodstream." Tom has three other Mocha titles: "Hellshift", "Along Came a Spider" and "Black Goddess" all dark journeys into the paranormal, and cosmic sci-fi horror.

Robert Perret

Robert Perret is a writer, librarian, and member of the John H. Watson Society. His stories have previously appeared in the MMP anthologies "An Improbable Truth: The Paranormal Adventures of Sherlock Holmes" and "Gears, Ghosts and Grimoires." He has also published a Holmesian novella entitled "For King and Country" and other stories. For more information you can go to his website: www.robertperret.com.

KT Pinto

KT Pinto, the bad influence your parents warned you about, has written over ten books and twenty short stories in various genres. You can find her on Facebook, YouTube, Twitter, Amazon, and pretty much everywhere else on the net. www.ktpinto.com

S.H. Roddey

South Carolina native S.H. Roddey has been writing for fun since she was a child and still enjoys building worlds across the speculative fiction spectrum filled with mystery and intrigue. She brings to the literary world a unique blend of humor, emotion, and wild ideas filled with dark themes and strong characters. She is a voracious reader, wannabe chef, and video game addict with two full-time jobs: administrative professional and mom a cat, a young twenty-something, and a pair of precocious youngsters. She also enjoys being married to her best friend and full-time muse. She also moonlights as romance author Siobhan Kinkade. Visit her online at http://www.shroddey.com.

Dan Shaurette

Dan Shaurette is an author, editor, podcaster, husband, father, and goth-geek from Phoenix, AZ with a penchant for vampire stories. His editorial credits include *Fresh Blood* (a collection of vampire short stories) and *Once Upon a Scream* (featuring new takes on dark fairytales). He is a staff writer for the HorrorAddicts.net blog and podcast and now serves as Head of Publishing for HorrorAddicts.net Press, as well as one of the judges for the new Next Great Horror Writer contest on HorrorAddicts.net. His upcoming novel, *For Blood and Empire*, is a collaboration with author Brian McKinley which brings two of our favorites tropes together: vampires and space operas. Please visit HorrorAddicts.net where you can listen to his serialized paranormal detective stories, *Black Magic* and *Black Jack,* or visit MattBlackBooks.com.

Liese Sherwood–Fabre

Liese Sherwood-Fabre grew up in Dallas, Texas and knew she was destined to write when she got an A+ in the second grade for her story about Dick, Jane, and Sally's ruined picnic. After obtaining her PhD from Indiana University, she joined the federal government and had the opportunity to work and live internationally for more than fifteen years. After returning to the states, she seriously pursued her writing career and has had numerous pieces appear in both print and electronically. She is currently a member of The Crew of the Barque Lone Star, the Napoleons of Crime, and the Studious Scarlets Society scions and contributes regularly to Sherlockian newsletters across the world.

You can follow her upcoming releases and other events by joining her newsletter at www.liesesherwoodfabre.com . All new subscribers receive a link for a free short story.

LOOKING FOR MORE
IMPROBABLE ADVENTURES?

Be sure to check out *An Improbable Truth: The Paranormal Adventures of Sherlock Holmes*, from Mocha Memoirs Press, edited by A.C. Thompson.

Praise for
An Improbable Truth:
The Paranormal Adventures of Sherlock Holmes

"Sherlock Holmes is such an iconic figure, and IMPROBABLE TRUTH did a fantastic job of taking the character into situations he's never been in before, while still maintaining the feel of the original stories."

- Amazon Reviewer "Caitastrophe"
November 10, 2015

"Holmes is one of the most popular figures in literary fiction immortalized in movies, televisions, computer and video games, though he always looks best in print. The authors and collaborators in An Improbable Truth: The Paranormal Adventures of Sherlock Holmes do an outstanding job of of picking up said mantle and delivering unique and original adventures for Sherlock Holmes."

- Amazon Reviewer "Southern Hennika"
November 13, 2015

"A number of interesting gems in this collection."

- Amazon Reviewer
February 12, 2016

Clicking Keys
Write. Edit. Publish.

www.clickingkeys.com